POISONED EMPIRE

Elyse Thomson

TWO LAURELS PRESS

Content Warnings

For my readers who prefer not to read the content warnings, please feel free to skip this section and dive right in.

For my readers who would prefer a list of content warnings before proceeding, I've provided what I hope to be a fairly substantive list below.

Content Warnings: child death, death, blood and gore, maiming, torture, kidnapping, swearing, alcoholism, sexism, homophobia, classism, infertility, poisoning, consensual on-page sex.

GLOSSARY

<u>Royal Titles</u>

Emperor/Empress: Supreme ruler of the Empire of Lethe, often co-rules with the heir to the throne. Addressed as Your Majesty.

Crown Prince/Crown Princess: Heir to the imperial throne. Addressed as Your Royal Highness.

Prince/Princess: Child of the emperor and empress. Addressed as Your Highness.

Prince Consort/Princess Consort: Fiancé(e) or spouse of a prince/princess. Addressed as Your Radiance.

<u>Noble Titles in Descending order of Rank</u>

Magister: Male governor of an imperial province. Addressed as Your Grace. Plural = Magistri

Magistra: Wife of a magister. Addressed as Your Grace. Plural = Magistrae

Dominus: Son of a magister. Addressed as Your Resplendence. Plural = Domini

Domina: Daughter of a magister. Addressed as Your Resplendence. Plural = Dominae

Illustrus: Male landowning nobleman with a significant estate and/or distinguished military service. No stylized form of address. Plural = Illustri

Illustra: Usually, the wife of an illustrus. Rarely, a landowning noblewoman with a significant estate and/or distinguished military service. No stylized form of address. Plural = Illustrae

Nobilissimus: Son of an illustrus or a minor nobleman with a small estate. No stylized form of address. Plural = Nobilissimi

Nobilissima: Usually, the daughter of an illustrus or wife of a nobilissimus. Rarely, a minor noblewoman with a small estate. No stylized form of address. Plural = Nobilissimae

<u>Governmental Titles in Descending Order of Influence</u>

Praetor: The head of the imperial bureaucracy. Answers to the imperial family directly. Directs all administrative officials in the Empire of Lethe.

Logothete: High minister in charge of a large administrative department (Taxes, Public Works, etc.), answers to the praetor directly.

Asekretis: Middling minister assigned to tasks or specific projects by a logothete. Answers to a logothete directly.

Notarios: Lowest ranked bureaucrat, assigned humble tasks by an asekretis. Answers to an asekretis directly.

<u>Military Titles</u>

Strategos: Top general of the empire's military forces. Answers to the imperial family directly.

Knight: Soldier with specialized training who stands above common soldiers in rank.

Admiral: Top officer of the empire's naval forces. Answers to the strategos directly.

<u>Slang</u>

Elemental: A mage with an elemental magical gift (water, fire, earth, air, light or darkness). Elemental gifts comprise the vast majority of mage gifts within Lethe, and are expected in all those of noble birth.

Elementalist: Elemental magic elitists who discriminate against those without elemental magical gifts (control of fire, water, earth, wind, lightning, darkness or light). They believe theirs is the superior form of magic.

Menial: A derogatory term for a mage without an elemental magical gift.

Feral: A derogatory term for beast mages.

Ignoble: A noble born without the expected elemental gift of their family bloodline.

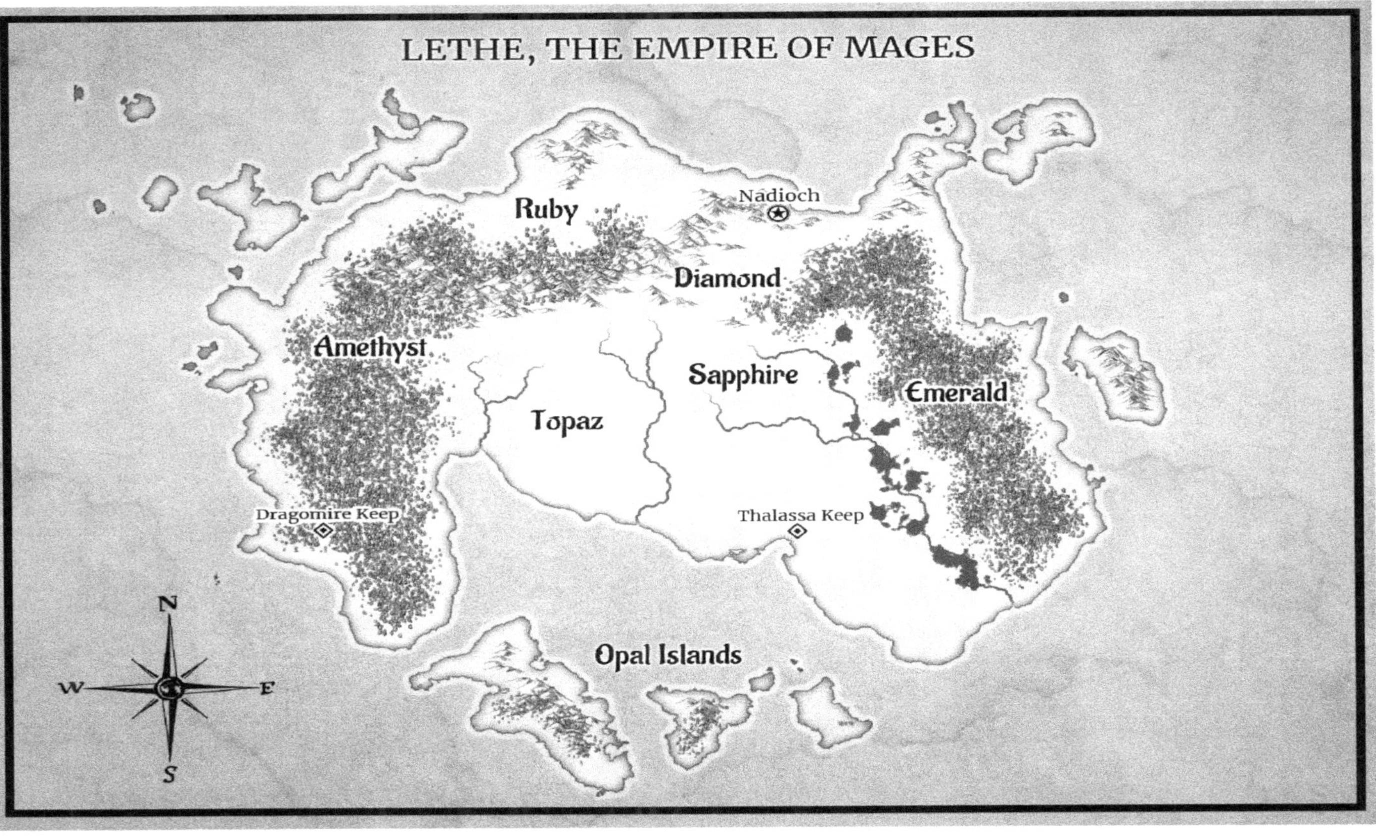

LETHE, THE EMPIRE OF MAGES
Ruby
Nadioch
Diamond
Amethyst
Sapphire
Emerald
Topaz
Dragomire Keep
Thalassa Keep
Opal Islands
N
W
E
S

To Paulina,

This one is for us.

PROLOGUE

I'm not fast enough.

Nadia's heart was sick at the thought. Babe cradled in one arm while the other hand gripped little Sylvester's, she ran through the marble halls of a palace in flames. Still the child-devouring beast pursued her. Her baby wailed, jostled by the pace, while the tortured cries of soldiers rang out through the halls. Ashes of a thousand smoking tapestries choked her. The stench of burning flesh announced the grim tally of the dead and wounded. Neither she nor her child would have the strength to run for much longer. Even now she pulled on reserves she didn't know she possessed, just to keep him from falling onto the blood-slick mosaic floors.

"Empress! Follow me!"

Nadia turned her head to see the young man she had recently selected to be her babe's guard. Marduk was no more than a boy himself. She immediately turned to follow him, his dark, leathery wings and sharp horns a welcome sight. But her relief had slowed her. Already the beast was upon her, the heat like a dragon's breath on her skin. Her palms were slick with sweat. This time when Sylvester tripped on the mosaic floors, his hand slid from hers. She was already steps away from him when she skidded to a stop. Before she could rush back to his side, Marduk grabbed her by the waist to drag her away.

A ring of flames trapped her boy. His screams tore the breath from her as his terrified hazel eyes vanished in a blaze of unbearable heat. Marduk pulled her resolutely, and she found she didn't have the strength to resist him. He towed her along by her hand, his claws piercing her flesh.

Eudocia had been found first, her flesh cold to the touch, her sweet girl only just reaching her teenage years this past spring. As if hunting her babies like a sick countdown, the beast had taken Cyril next, just before the alarm could be raised. The twins, Xanthippe and Viktor, had died despite a heavy guard. Still the beast's bloodlust had not been quenched. Even now, although it had torn Sylvester from her, it still coveted the very last of her children; her baby, Belisarius.

"In here, Empress!" Marduk pulled her through a heavy door to a storeroom, throwing it shut behind them.

She felt nearly outside herself as she watched the young, winged boy trying to fit himself through the opening of the small window. Thwarted, he ran towards the second exit to a set of servant's stairwells. He threw himself against the doorway, but it wouldn't budge.

"The escape is blocked. We must prevent him from entering." Marduk looked to her, calm but resolute. "Can you make something sturdy to keep the door in place? We only need to hold out a little longer before the knights arrive."

"I... Yes, I will try."

Nadia's hand shook as she placed it against the door. There was nothing living within the room but the three of them. She gave her crying baby to Marduk and used her bloodied hand to paint a line on the floor. Power flowed from her, and thick brambles rose up from her blood, engulfing the door as they grew. Vines had almost covered it when the plants stopped in their tracks.

"You cannot stop, Empress!"

"Something has happened! I cannot make it grow any further!"

Panic made her frenzied. She poured as much of her magic into the plants as she could, but they grew in fits and starts. All the while her baby wailed. Suddenly, an awful heat enveloped the room. Marduk pulled her from the door.

"Take him." He handed her the baby then unsheathed his short sword, positioning himself between her and the beast at the door.

For a moment the heat seemed to disappear. Then it returned tenfold. Marduk gasped before turning himself towards her and throwing his body over hers, his wings outstretched to envelop her and the baby. Nadia heard the explosion and felt the searing heat in tandem. Marduk's screams of agony rang in her ears. When she opened her eyes to the horror, she could see through the enormous, sizzling holes in his wings. His body slid from hers and fell to the floor, bloody and charred.

Nadia met the beast's eyes—eyes as red as rubies and as cold as a winter storm. Eyes she knew too well.

"Hello, Mother."

CHAPTER 1

People were scum.

It was the rule that only proved truer the longer Selene lived. It was a fact she exploited to pay her way in the world. It was the mantra she would chant to herself at night when the faces of her clients—battered, desperate, hopeless—haunted her.

Still, there was one person who was exempt from that rule—Iliana.

"What have you put in your porridge?" Iliana wrinkled her nose.

Selene smiled at her companion. The simple wooden stool scrapped across the warped boards of the floor as she pulled up a seat across from her.

"Never mind. I'm not sure I want to know." Iliana leaned away, grimacing.

"It's a very rare neurotoxin I ordered months ago from the Emerald Province. First, it—"

"No, we talked about this. No more gory descriptions at the dining table."

Selene shrugged her shoulders and downed her porridge. The benefits of being a poison mage were extensive. She could conjure any poison she'd ever touched, tasted, been stung by or otherwise introduced into her body. The best part was that it would never truly harm her. The worst was that the first time around she would suffer through a very mild version of the toxin for a short while. Well, that and social stigma, but she had long ago stopped caring for the opinions of anyone not named Iliana.

"Crap—paralytic!" was all she managed to say before her body tensed up, her spoon frozen in mid-air.

Iliana watched her with a bemused smile as she ate her toast and sipped her watered wine from a chipped earthenware cup, her finger tracing the deep grooves in the only table they owned.

"Remember when you ate the one that made you mute for a whole two minutes? Be nice if you could get more like that."

Selene gasped for air when the neurotoxin was done working its way through her system, her magic neutralising its effects as the poison added itself to her repertoire.

"Sadly, 'Silence is Golden' is a one-off as far as I can tell. Top seller though, that's for sure."

Iliana shook her head.

"So, what are you going to name this one?"

"Hmmm." Selene ruminated on it for a moment. It was very fast-acting. There were no unique sensations to the kind of death this one would deliver. It had sounded more interesting than it was. A pity. Best go for some whimsy if she wanted to earn back what it cost her. "'Duck, duck, dead.'"

A knock on their crooked door interrupted them from their repast. Selene was about to stand, but Iliana put her hand on her shoulder and smiled. She was already finished eating her meagre meal.

"I'll get it."

Selene nodded as she shovelled the rest of her porridge into her mouth. Who had come to disturb them in their humble cottage? Rent wasn't due for another few weeks, and Selene had already threatened the land-lord's son with a painful death if he tried to make eyes at her beautiful friend.

Selene leaned back on her rickety stool to see the face of the man in the doorway.

"Iliana?" he asked as she opened the door.

Iliana didn't answer. In fact, her posture stiffened.

"I've just come by to, uh, inquire about the state of the cottage. Does it require repairs?"

"N-not since the roof was patched," Iliana murmured.

"And I've had some complaints from the blacksmith that you've been using his forge."

"He must have been mistaken." Iliana gripped the door tighter.

Selene caught a glimpse of the man behind the door. Damn landlord's brat, dressed in a brand-new tunic and gleaming leather sandals. He caught Selene's narrowed gaze as he peered inside, swallowing nervously when she mimed slitting his throat.

"Very good! Just coming around to check on tenants. Rent is due in two weeks." He stumbled over his words in a panicked rush as he backed away.

"Good day," Iliana replied woodenly as she shut the door.

When Iliana returned to the table, she collapsed on her stool, an ashen cast to her usually tawny, bronze skin. She shakily pushed a few strands of platinum blonde hair from her face as her haunted sapphire eyes made contact with Selene's.

"What's wrong?" Selene asked.

"He called me Iliana."

"And?"

"I've never told him our real names."

"Shit!" Selene swore as she stumbled to her feet, nearly tripping on her threadbare skirt. "Get the goods and our coin. We'll lighten our load at the market and head directly for the docks."

If they didn't sell at least a few more wares, they wouldn't have enough coin to make it to the islands. Walking through the night to the docks would be gruelling, but if they waited around, it could get dire.

Iliana nodded, staring at the fire in the hearth, her hands trembling. The metals mage fingered the enchanted dagger she habitually kept at her hip and muttered a prayer to the forgotten gods.

Selene noticed the tick and hurried Iliana into the bedroom to pack.

Born a bastard as well as with a mage gift considered menial, Iliana, along with her mother, had been cast aside by her elementalist noble father for failing to breed true to his bloodline's water elemental mage gifts. Magister Sapphire had feared she would bring shame in his elitist circles, and so he'd ignored her very existence.

It was Iliana's loving stepfather who had taught her his blacksmithing trade, but the family's fate had been sealed when Iliana proved to be too good at what she did. Whispers about her magical talents, as well as her uncanny resemblance to the imperially appointed governor in charge of the Sapphire Province, began to swirl.

Only luck had allowed Iliana to survive the flood he had sent to engulf their small village, stealing the lives of her mother and stepfather. The magister wanted the shame of her existence erased from the world, and Iliana had known then that her sole option was to spend the rest of her life fleeing and staying hidden.

It seemed the time had come to flee again. The magister had ferreted them out once more.

Stubborn prick.

Selene grabbed her sack full of small, sealed containers and began plucking her favourite poisons from the cupboard. She wouldn't be able to carry them all.

A devious little thought came to mind, and she grabbed their precious ink and a few scraps of parchment.

Iliana soon returned from the bedroom, wrapped in a travelling robe and sturdy tunic dress with her case of enchanted wares slung over one shoulder. Built like some mythical heroine—curves like a goddess of love and the height of an average man—Iliana was striking no matter where she went or what she did to hide it. Selene, on the other hand, was a short, dark-haired, pale skinned waif who could blend and disappear into any crowd, so long as she kept her mouth shut. Only her purple eyes gave her away as anything other than ordinary.

"What are you doing?" Iliana asked.

"Leaving a few presents for whoever loots our cottage," Selene answered.

Iliana trudged over, depositing Selene's only robe atop her bulging sack of poisons. She squinted her eyes at the labels. Iliana, like Selene, was literate—a true feat for commoners—but her skills were rusty. Her true talents lay in enchanting metals, convincing them to be more than they were or to do the unexpected. Selene was better at conjuring poisons than enchanting them, but even she had a few tricks up her sleeve.

"Why are you re-labelling everything as sweet syrup?"

Selene gave her a winning smile.

"So that they'll swallow it, of course."

Iliana rolled her eyes and dragged Selene from her macabre prank.

"Come on. We don't know when the magister's men might get here."

Selene sighed, donned her robe, heaved her wares over her shoulder and followed Iliana out the door. Best not to tempt fate.

They kept to the less travelled footpaths and in no time at all they had reached their destination, the crumbling former summer home of a dead noble. The top half had been blasted off during the Great War, the remaining bricks blackened and fused by scorching fires. It might have appeared abandoned if not for the smoke curling up from ramshackle tarps thrown up over the remaining walls and the well-trodden path to the gloomy entrance. Iliana and Selene took their customary place at a booth near the middle of the building.

"Just two more years, Iliana. Two years and we'll have the coin to escape this dump of an empire."

"I counted everything again last night just to be sure I wasn't imagining it. We'll have to travel to the Opal Province if we're going to catch a ship, though. I've been asking around at the market, but no one knows of one that regularly makes landfall across the sea."

"That's the problem with this place. They think the forgotten gods favour this land. No one even bothers to dream that somewhere else could be better. Ignorant swine."

"We'll need to set up shop again once we reach the Opal Islands." Iliana set to neatly laying out her wares before her.

"Ooh! Maybe we should try calling it something new this time."

"Not again," Iliana moaned.

"I still think we should have called it 'Live by the sword, Die by poison.'"

Iliana gave her a quelling glance as Selene grabbed a fistful of poison-filled vials and draped them across her half of the booth.

"Or 'Pointy and Poison.'"

"'Extirpation Station' is ridiculous enough as it is. Don't push your luck."

"No promises." Selene smiled.

Customers began their furtive entrance into one of the many black markets of the Topaz Province. Some were hooded and masked, while others swaggered about, hair of the dog sloshing in their waterskins. Places like this were known strictly by word of mouth and often changed locations if officious sorts couldn't be bribed into turning a blind eye. Luckily, the Topaz Province had many officials with flexible morals and a love of gold.

"I'm looking for a very specific poison."

The upper crust affectation in the hooded man's voice caught Selene's attention. Beneath the rather obviously dirtied cloak, she caught sight of a clean silk tunic. Beautiful prey. It was clearly his first time in such a place. He carried himself too proudly, spoke too cryptically, wore clothes too good for any commoner, and his dyed leather shoes were too well made for a man amongst dregs. A lighter band of skin on his darker finger pointed to a missing ring. Perhaps a noble down on his luck, recently disinherited, his family crest repossessed.

"Well, I have a great variety here today. Something to kill silently? Gruesomely? Painfully? Or maybe you just want to teach someone a lesson? I have poisons that mimic any number of debilitating, humiliating or just plain unpleasant ailments. What did you have in mind?"

"I need something rare, lethal and exotic. Maybe from the jungles of the Emerald Province."

Selene hemmed and hawed for a moment, her heart racing all the while. Much as she would love to sell the man her newest poison at an outrageous price, a slithery feeling of danger crept down her spine. Another glimpse through a small part in his cloak revealed the glint of a breastplate. The magister's man?

Beside her, Iliana was chatting up a customer asking for a sharp sword, and not just 'normal sharp', but 'magically enchanted sharp'. Iliana's skill as a blacksmith was honed to exceptional degrees by her years of experience, making her blades the sharpest, her armour the sturdiest and her shields the best at deflecting blows.

Except her friend never boasted that her wares were enchanted.

Iliana fingered a blade beneath the booth.

"I may have what you need." Selene bent down, an eager saleswoman rummaging through her bags, and surreptitiously tapped Iliana's calf twice—their signal for danger.

"Ouch! Be a dear and hold this for me." Selene placed a small bottle on Iliana's side of the booth, "I think the bottle's chipped."

"Of course," Iliana replied.

Gods, she loved that woman's poker face. After years together and much practice, Iliana could finally bluff with the best of them, at least some of the time.

Beneath the booth, Selene had wiped the edge of Iliana's blade with a painful poison so intense the victim usually passed out before uttering a scream. The bottle on the desk would be for the man beside her, numbing his limbs and debilitating him with vertigo.

"This is a blade you may appreciate. Sharpest edge in the Topaz Province, guaranteed."

Iliana proffered it for the man, who foolishly ran his finger along the blade. He froze, mouth twisted in a scream that never escaped his lips before he dropped to the ground. Selene used the distraction to smash the fragile bottle of poison onto the hand of her own suspicious patron, whose face turned a sickly green as he clutched the booth. He fell to his knees but refused to collapse. Good. They needed answers.

Business went on as usual in the market.

It was that kind of place.

"How unfortunate." Selene pouted in mock sympathy. "Say, why come all the way here for *my* poisons?"

"Answer her or I'll start cutting off precious parts." Iliana held a blade to the slumped man's throat.

"R-retrieval of two bastards," he groaned.

"For what purpose?" Iliana asked.

"Don't know. Just know both Magister Amethyst and Magister Sapphire want a wayward daughter each. Big payday for whoever delivers."

Other vendors began to eye the two women. After all, it was that kind of place.

"Try it and you'll die choking on your own guts!" Selene glared the lot of the vendors into submission. Her prisoner's triumphant smirk at her threat was too much. He knew as well as she they would turn on her the moment she blinked. "These sorts of threats are always best punctuated by a good exemplar." And she made good on her threat. In seconds, their would-be captor was choking on thick, pink bile.

"I hate it when you do that," Iliana complained as she began packing up her side of the booth with neat precision.

"Whatever. Let's get out while we can," Selene retorted, sweeping her wares haphazardly into her sack.

The noble was still scratching at his throat in vain. Selene kicked him over as she walked out from behind the booth. No sense pitying a man sent to deliver them to certain death. Iliana stepped over him and cringed, almost apologetically. They left by the back entrance, blessing their luck—until Selene felt a pressure plate sink under her foot.

Before she could react, thick metal bars slammed down from above.

CHAPTER 2

Every day, Lethe, the Empire of Mages, teetered on the brink of chaos. Some days, Crown Prince Belisarius was required to do no more than soothe the ruffled feathers of a few nobles or distribute extra grain. Other days, maintaining the balancing act required drastic action.

Today was not a good day.

Prince Belisarius' heart raced as he read the reports in his hand, covering his dread with a grim scowl and a finger tapping impatiently on his desk. His dark eyes met those of his trusted praetor, Nicephorus, the highest-ranking minister in Lethe's sprawling bureaucracy. Nicephorus' own expression was carefully closed.

"You're certain?" Belisarius asked, praying it was a mistake.

"As certain as I can be without having each one examined."

Hopes dashed and bile rising, the prince took a deep breath. This needed to be contained. Quickly.

"How extensive is the corruption? How far from Nadioch has it spread?"

The praetor shook his head.

"We don't know the full scale. It seems as though it's limited to Magister Miroslav Diamond's family. Only those related by blood—his daughters—are affected. But I don't have enough reliable intelligence from outside the capital."

Belisarius could feel a headache blooming as he glared at the perennially empty desk beside his. If only his father had any skill in diplomacy and power games. While he was an excellent warlord, as an emperor he was lacking in many of the finer skills. Emperor Darius' idea of statecraft consisted of threatening to serve a dignitary his own liver. His solution to politics? To literally skewer a naysayer. While Darius reigned, the power of the crown was absolute, the opposition cowed. Now instead of ruling, Father frittered away his years in wine and women, and it was up to Belisarius to stem the tide. It had been his unspoken duty since he became old enough to understand his father's failings.

Nadia, his mother, had been the soft counter to his father's explosive personality. Her calm, steely determination had saved Lethe from ruination many times over. She was the one who had demanded the first noble hostages who would become the administration. She had established the bureaucracies that kept the empire running and won the nobles over. Nadia had, in truth, ruled while his father rested upon his laurels. It was she who had taught her only surviving child statesmanship and strategy.

Sometimes, Belisarius stilled reeled from her sudden and unexpected passing only a few years ago. Grieving her loss and abandoned by his father, the demands of ruling alone had been crushing—and still were.

Unlike the emperor, Belisarius hadn't been afforded the luxury of coming apart. Just three months after her death, Belisarius had suffered an assassination attempt. But not even that had been enough to rouse the emperor from his stupor. Now the prince's next great test was upon him.

If even the sycophantic Magister Diamond had the nerve to turn against the throne, despite living in the capital and ostensibly governing the province in which the imperial family resided, Belisarius might be facing the threat of a second Great War. Gods knew Lethe could ill afford another generation lost to war, famine and unrest. Even now, it was rare for any noble to have a grandparent, aunt, uncle or cousin, and few commoners who survived it had done so without wearing the indelible marks of violence and starvation. To contain this latest threat, he would need to be sly.

"How many unmarried men do we currently have in the upper bureaucracies?"

Nicephorus seemed bewildered for a moment by the line of questioning. He adjusted his imperial red pallium about his snow-white tunic, the most visible mark of his rank, before clearing his throat.

"In Nadioch? Or in each province?"

Of course, his right-hand man would know those numbers by heart. Nicephorus' competence was a balm for his dread.

"The capital."

"Nearly four hundred."

"Send invitations to every noble family in every province. Ensure they arrive by tomorrow morning at the latest. In two month's time, I am summoning at least one unwed woman of childbearing age from each household to be presented at court for the purpose of marriage. The magistri are to be commanded to send *all* unwed daughters of an appropriate age as candidates to marry the crown prince. Check the official genealogies to ensure we don't miss any, and have a blood ward created. Any woman who isn't related by blood to her patriarch should not be able to step into the palace." That precaution, at least, would prevent them from sending imposters.

"Your Royal Highness, isn't that a bit-"

"Yes, but it's the only way we can discover in one fell swoop how far reaching the rot is without arousing suspicion that we know they've used the ritual." Belisarius sighed. "If it's just one magister and a few minor nobles plotting against me, we might not be looking at more than a skirmish. But if multiple magistri are involved it could mean war. A bride show was tradition once. I will simply be resurrecting it."

"Ah." Nicephorus looked askance and smoothed out a non-existent wrinkle in his tunic.

No doubt he was pondering just how archaic the crown prince would appear in bringing back such a fossilized tradition. A bride show was little better than going to a horse market to check the teeth and hooves before handing over the coin. Not that the magistri could complain about backward practices, given their resistance to even the smallest of Belisarius' reforms. Still, not one among them would dare grumble about the prince's command, especially if they knew of the blood ward. They would be too fearful of appearing to cast doubt on the purity of their precious lineages and magic. Nicephorus knew all this, which was why he kept his counsel. He, like Belisarius, knew their options for luring every potential victim to Nadioch quietly and quickly were few.

"We may have some opposition to marriage partners for the beast mages in your service."

Those in Lethe whose magic presented in the simple form of beastly appendages found life to be particularly difficult. Despite having abolished castes decades ago, attitudes were glacially slow to change. Even now, beast mages were derisively called 'ferals'. It was Belisarius' long-term goal to change their fortune by electing those most suitable to high offices and to his personal guard. Their minor immunity to magic made them practical choices, and his imperial patronage served to bolster their numbers as scholars, artists, orators and chariot racers. But that was a problem for another day.

In this matter, compromise would only embolden the traditionalists. Elementalists—elemental magic elitists—needed to be brought to heel for his just society to take shape.

"Any family found to be complaining about such matters will have their titles stripped from them and given to more amenable relations, if any can be found. Their daughters, after being examined for the effects of the ritual, will still be required to attend, and if they do not wed, they will be found humble positions in the capital."

"I'll have the invitations written and sent out by the end of the day. My teleportation mages will ensure the magistri receive theirs immediately. Was there anything else?"

Belisarius sighed.

"Is my father sober today? I'll need to ask him some questions."

"He has not yet woken."

It meant he had not yet had the chance to drown in drink, but his praetor was too politic to say so.

"My thanks. Please see that the invitations are sent."

Nicephorus bowed and exited the room. The prince stood, and with great resignation, went to wake his father. It was easier to focus on his burning resentment of the man than the fear gnawing at his gut.

Belisarius was ushered into his father's chamber by two guards. The emperor was passed out in bed with two women only a few years older than the prince himself. They woke when he approached, and his glare was enough to ensure they left with haste. His father still stank of wine from the night before. Belisarius narrowed his eyes and tore the covers from his father's prone form. The emperor woke with a start, sending an empty bottle flying off the bed to shatter on the mosaic floor.

"Sober up, old man. I need information."

"Ah, keep your voice down, Belli. My head is full of bees." The emperor groaned, rubbing his temples.

Belisarius waited while his father put himself to rights and toddled over to a chair on the veranda. Darius had greying black hair and eyes the colour of blood, his skin the same warm brown as his son's. Belisarius stifled a scowl as he seated himself opposite him. Once, Darius had been feared throughout the land as the greatest fire mage of all time. At seventy, the emperor's figure was still trim, but starting to soften with drink and dissolution. He could well live another seventy to a hundred years, but if he persevered with this sort of lifestyle, he might only make it another ten.

As his father set about pouring himself a glass of wine, Belisarius placed his hand over the jewelled silver cup.

"I have no time to entertain a drunkard." Belisarius slid the cup aside on the glass table between them, boring his gaze into his father's. "Who knew about the Soul-Binding Ritual?"

The emperor's eyes cleared at the mention of that sinister family secret. He ran a shaky hand through his dishevelled hair and hunched forward.

"Blood relatives and a few others like Nadia, trusted advisors and the silver-tongues. It was strictly the fire mages amongst them who contributed their magic to magnify mine. Many of those relatives have since died, and all agreed to being silenced by the silver-tongued mages. Then, of course, there was Mercurius…"

Belisarius bit back a curse. Mercurius, the brother who had used a botched version of the ritual to kill nearly every sibling who might have become competition for the throne. He was a stain on the family history, the truth of his actions known only to a select few, and his execution a state secret.

"Is there anyone you suspect might profit by sharing our ritual with outsiders?"

"Is that what's happened to Lethe?" Darius sat back in his seat, shoulders slumped in despair.

"We've confirmed that Magister Diamond has used some perverse variant of the ritual on his own daughters. They live like the walking dead. I'm trying to discover who else might be using this variant to siphon the magic from their own kin. Mind and soul included this time, it seems."

A haunted look passed over the emperor's face. At least he understood the weight currently crushing Belisarius. The last time Darius had used the ritual, it had been to single-handedly turn the tide of war, and now outsiders had laid claim to it.

"Gods below. I always knew that one would come back to bite us."

CHAPTER 3

Iliana quickly learned to keep her own counsel. No matter if she begged, pleaded, swore or wept, her captors were unmoved, their pace relentless. Carted about like the vilest of criminals in a wooden prison atop a cart, robbed of her weapons and subject to threats, she curled up on herself. She hadn't even had the chance to say goodbye to Selene before they'd been captured. Magister Sapphire would drown her for sure this time, erase her like her mother and stepfather before her.

They kept to lesser used roads, skirting towns and marching through scorched ruins where only outcasts scraped by. Her captors were armed to the teeth, and bandits dared not approach their grim caravan. Iliana only wished she had the skill to conjure metal from the air, as Selene did her poisons. Alas, her captors kept even rusted nails well away from her, neutralising her only means of protecting herself. Iliana grew small inside her own mind, refusing to come out. If she were to die, she wanted to be somewhere else—somewhere safe.

It was inside those precious memories that she lived until she found herself in Magister Aristeo Sapphire's dungeon, being commanded not to die, but to obey.

Hot blood lashed Iliana on the cheek as a young girl lay screaming, strapped naked across a stone block and held immobile. Iliana shakily touched the blood, mind reeling. The heir to the Sapphire Province, Dominus Leo Sapphire, continued to whip his youngest sister without showing the barest hint of remorse. The magister, Iliana's birth father, leaned against the rough stone wall beside her prison cell and picked at his immaculate nails. Aristeo held up a hand, and Leo stopped, rolling his shoulders and neck, his blue silk tunic and leather boots splattered with red. If she'd had any food in her belly, Iliana might have thrown up.

"This will continue until either she dies or you agree to my terms. If she dies, rest assured, I have a great many more useless daughters who can take her place beneath that whip. You can stop this at any time."

The young girl's sobs made her throat ache and eyes sting. Unlike the men of Magister Sapphire's family, Iliana still had a heart. The problem was, they knew it, and they were happy to use it against her.

She turned to face this monster of a father. His bronzed skin, bright blue eyes and platinum hair were mirrors of her own, but that was where the similarities ended—physical and otherwise. He wore the beautiful embroidered silks and dyed leather of his station, while Iliana's rough, simple gown and sandals had been dirtied and torn from her captivity. His long, thick hair was swept gracefully back from his face and secured with an ornate gold clasp, while hers lay limp and greasy from days without a bath. When she answered, her voice was hoarse.

"Fine. I'll do it. Just stop."

The men looked at each other.

"I believe you owe me one warhorse and a chariot racing team for the Hippodrome, Father. Mira is still alive and your bastard has cracked."

The Magister's laugh echoed in the dingy basement.

"You have me beat, Leo. The warhorse and racers are yours." The magister turned to Iliana, the light in his eyes dying instantly. "One of the women will be down in an hour. You will learn to be a domina in the time allotted, or she will die in front of you."

The two made their way to the staircase.

"What about the girl?!" Iliana rattled her wooden bars with dirt-encrusted hands as they passed by their kin, sparing her no more than an afterthought.

"She will be left as she is. If she dies of her wounds, let it be a lesson. Had you agreed to my terms earlier, you might have spared her."

Iliana was left to stare into the agonized sapphire eyes of the dying girl as she slowly bled out.

"It's all your fault," the girl whispered.

Iliana shivered and could only pray that Selene found her own situation less dire.

Selene watched dispassionately from behind the metal bars of her cage as the magister's men rounded up her captors and her father electrocuted each one, blood, guts and fried gore flying. She supposed it saved her the trouble of making their innards melt at some later date. Father evidently wanted to impress upon her his power—both magical and political. He killed knowing he'd never face the consequences. Lucky, that. The only true shock of the day for Selene was the magister's short, flaming red hair—something she had not suspected was in her lineage.

Why he wanted her compliance so badly was still beyond her. She only hoped Iliana's father hadn't put on such a gruesome display to cow her. Her friend had been raised with love and care. This kind of mindless barbarity was beyond Iliana's scope of experience, even after years of selling at the black markets and dealing with scum.

Selene, like Iliana, had been born a bastard, her commoner mother tossed out after she'd given birth. But unlike her friend's skill with metals, Selene's poison magic was considered unsavoury, and her mother far less dedicated than Iliana's to making Selene a contributing member of society. While her foolish, heartbroken mother had drowned her sorrows in drink and the company of lowlifes, Selene had found herself subsisting on poisonous mushrooms and ordinarily inedible creatures. As she grew, so did her repertoire of poisons. Not even her mother's wastrel suitors had dared upset her.

She'd spent her youth travelling from village to village, selling potions no respectable person would offer, eking out a threadbare existence and dealing painful death to anyone foolish enough to try and harm her. Then, as if the heavens had finally decided she was worth noticing, a ray of sun named Iliana had looked her in the eye, spoken to her like a person, and invited her to share the cramped apartment she'd called home. To this day, Selene didn't understand why she'd done it, but she would forever repay that debt.

If Magister Sapphire was terrorizing Iliana, Selene vowed to kill him.

When her father was done his grisly chore, he turned his amethyst eyes on her, adjusting the military-style belt about his short purple tunic. Not a single drop of blood sullied his immaculate attire, his confident strides eating up the distance on the gore-strewn dirt road.

"Six out of ten. Points for the exploding eyes, but the jelly didn't fly nearly as far as the first one's fingers." Selene raised her chin, pointing out the relative distances of the two substances.

Selene's grin was hardly inviting when he stopped, a baffled expression on his face. Had he expected her to tremble or whimper? His ilk had come and gone all her life. He obviously wanted her alive for a time at least, else he'd have sent an assassin, and she didn't need examples to know the impact of lightning on a mage body. Had he expected her to beg for mercy on their behalf?

"Perhaps this will be less tedious than I had imagined," Magister Amethyst muttered as he approached the cage.

He stopped just out of range and stood upwind, safe from her poison. Selene bit back a curse. She really would need to learn to throw darts, as Iliana had insisted many a time. His calculating eyes searched hers.

"I have a task for you, bastard. If you complete it, I'll give you whatever you desire."

Selene raised a dark brow.

"And if I want to make your insides liquefy?"

The magister laughed uproariously as if she'd meant it in jest, wiping away a mirthful tear with a manicured finger.

"Ah, you really are mine. No, you damn menial scum, material things."

Menial. The favourite insult of elementalist pigs the empire over. So unoriginal.

"Can people be these material things?" Selene asked.

"As long as I don't care about their survival, yes."

Selene pondered his offer. Best ask for the moon first, and be prepared to haggle later.

"Then I want the royal copy of the Poison Compendium, enough gold to live like a queen until I'm an old hag, and I want Magister Sapphire's bastard daughter, Iliana."

"You want your companion? How sentimental." The magister's gaze turned predatory.

Selene slipped into his skin, that of a man who cared even less for mage life than she did, saw any emotional attachment as weakness—much as she used to—and ruthlessly exploited any opening. Her next words would be critical. Iliana was a whole province away, but in infinitely more danger if Selene didn't play this negotiation right. Thankfully she'd had a lifetime of dealing with dangerous men like him.

"I want what is *mine*. It's bad enough you had those men burn my stores of poison, but then you went and let my well-trained dog get sent off across the continent too!"

The Magister considered her, the predatory light dimming. *So easy to read*, she mused. Show him a reflection of his own pathetic self and he would see no faults, just someone to be bought off and bargained with—a civilized business transaction. Scum was scum, no matter how much wealth or power they possessed.

"When you've completed my task, you may have what you wish."

"Then as long as I can get that in writing, I believe we have an agreement. Now, Daddy dearest, what is it you wish of your sad little bastard daughter?"

CHAPTER 4

Belisarius' arrow whistled through the air and sank deep into the darting, levitating target. It dropped to the earth, inert.

The shuddering breaths of the horse, its hooves pounding on the packed sand of the training ground, drowned out the sound of his blood rushing to his ears. Though his marksmanship was flawless, his mind was in turmoil. The root of the corruption in his land was likely one of his closest living relatives, and it was all he could think about.

In days gone by, such a betrayal would have meant an instant and merciless death for the offender and any outsider who had discovered the secret. A quick interrogation from their silver-tongued mages would've found the culprit, as they had the power to tear the deepest secrets from a man with only a few spoken words. But just a few weeks prior, the palace's silver-tongued mages had collectively taken their own lives, leaving only the youngest alive and barely conscious. The timing couldn't have been worse.

Belisarius wondered if it was just paranoia, or whether he was right in finding the whole situation too suspicious to be a coincidence.

"You were slow."

"My shot was perfect," Belisarius retorted. *Gods below, if the traitors had wormed their way into the palace weeks ago...*

"And slow. You're distracted."

Marduk's eyes met the prince's, the intensity of his disapproval unwavering. The look suited him. As the strategos and thus the highest military official in Lethe, he needed to be able to intimidate any soldier with just a look. Of course, the man's physique also aided him in that regard. He sported the fangs, claws, horns and whip-like tail marking him as a beast mage, and a height boasting nearly seven feet of pure, lethal muscle. He was a prodigy in his own right, reputed to be the best weapons master in the empire. Even the emperor gave pause in Marduk's presence. Belisarius was lucky the strategos was also a close friend and confidant.

"You're impossible to please," Belisarius grumbled.

"I don't tolerate sloppiness in my soldiers. Just because I've taught you since you were a boy doesn't mean I'll tolerate it from you either, Your Royal Highness."

Marduk was twelve years the prince's senior, and had been his teacher and brother-figure since Belisarius had been capable of walking. The Empress Nadia had been the one to take Marduk into the fold of the imperial palace, against the protests of all the naysayers and elitists, thus earning herself and her son Marduk's complete devotion.

Belisarius sighed.

"I am distracted."

"Then get off your horse and sort it out. Target practice is for those with focus." Marduk signalled for a stable boy to take the reins of Belisarius' horse as the prince dismounted. "Should we discuss this?"

The invitations to the bride show had gone out just hours ago, and already the magistri had replied to confirm that they would be presenting all their unwed daughters of marriageable age. It would be two months before the show would begin and the palace had already ramped up its activity. Nicephorus had set in motion plans to hire a slew of new gardeners, servants, stable boys, seamstresses, cobblers, cooks, and even librarians and healers, all to cater to the enormous influx of arrivals to the palace. This would be the first such event since the empire had been established forty-five years ago. It would also be Belisarius's chance to show the magistri who it was they were expected to loyally serve, and impress upon them the wealth and might the throne wielded. If one of those magistri were aiming for his head, it was time to inform his strategos.

"Meet me in my chambers. I can't discuss this matter in the open."

Marduk nodded, following him as he wound his way through the palace corridors and up a winding staircase to the royal chambers. Belisarius sat in a chair on his veranda and waved at a seat opposite him. Marduk took it, somehow comfortably fitting himself in a chair he dwarfed. Servants in drab-coloured tunics appeared to wait on them, but the prince waved them off.

"I require privacy. Keep everyone out of my chambers until I've ordered otherwise."

They disappeared in moments, their soft-soled shoes making no sound on the mosaic floors.

"I need you to identify which of my immediate family has spoken of our tribe's ritual. I cannot guess who would betray us, which makes me ill-suited to discovering the culprit. I need your impartiality."

"Have you spoken to your father?" Marduk's eyes gave away nothing.

"Yes. He informed me that only those of our direct bloodline ever knew how to perform the ritual, but he could not give me a name of one he suspected. Mother knew but was never silenced. A few advisors knew too but agreed to be silenced. However, it has come to my attention that our ritual has been perverted, and we believe that it has been used by Magister Diamond on his own daughters. We suspect more of the nobles may also be involved. I have invited the daughters of all the magistri, and most of the nobility, to Nadioch on the pretence of selecting the future empress. Their attendance will allow us to suss out which families are guilty and which are innocent. Nicephorus believes he can determine this if he can see the women in person."

Marduk sighed, eyes faraway.

"This is the Soul-Binding Ritual you're speaking of?"

Belisarius nodded.

Perhaps this was a divine punishment for abusing the sanctity of the ritual, a corruption born from the greed which last tainted its use. Then again, maybe Belisarius was a superstitious fool to entertain the thought.

"Your late mother spoke of it to me, and had one of the silver-tongue mages ensure I could speak of it to no one but you, much as you had done to Nicephorus when he was sworn in as your praetor. It was part of my training to become your guard and tutor. I do not know the details of the ritual, but I do understand the effects well enough for me to be able to spot it were it to be used. The only relative of yours I can possibly see using the ritual is your uncle, Phokas, but he sailed away from Lethe when you were still a babe and has never returned."

"Why do you suspect him?"

All Belisarius knew of Phokas was that, while his mother was alive, she'd shipped goods and money to him across the sea.

"He never liked your father, always thought he wasn't good enough for your mother. When Mercurius attacked and killed your siblings twenty-eight years ago, Phokas blamed your father for it, said if he'd raised Mercurius right then none of it would have happened. He was your mother's favourite brother, so most of the time he could criticize the emperor without much in the way of retribution, and he doted on his nieces and nephews, so your father let it go. But when they died and only you survived, his grief was so great he claimed he couldn't remain. It's possible Nadia told him more of the ritual, or he uncovered more during the Great War. Both your parent's families were heavily involved with Darius' campaigns, after all, and no security is fool-proof. He is the only one among your relatives I can see having enough ill-will to risk the punishment for disclosing the ritual."

Few mages left Lethe, and those that did were usually either criminals or misfits. Had Phokas truly harboured enough animosity towards the emperor to leave? If so, why return now? Had Mother's death been the last thing holding him back from rebellion? Phokas could have known about the ritual, but he would not have been aware of the finer details, as only blood relatives of the emperor had been able to take part in it. Then again, the fact that someone of Diamond's ilk had used it proved his assumptions rested on shaky ground.

"Why did my father not mention this?"

"It was a dark time, Your Royal Highness, the darkest your mother or father ever faced. Perhaps he couldn't bear to remember it."

Belisarius pushed aside his anger. He was lucky Marduk had so readily supplied a name.

"Send one of your most trusted men to where my uncle lives across the sea, and bring him back if he is still there. Increase military presence throughout the empire and have them look for him here, if he has indeed returned. Have my mother's family watched as well. If any should ask about the increase in soldiers along the roads, tell them it is to ensure the safety of the bride candidates."

"At once, Your Royal Highness. I'll send Magister Opal's elder brother. He often delivered cargo to Phokas at the late Empress' behest. He should know where to find him. Have Nicephorus send along a spy as well. If Opal is in on it, the voyage might help expose him."

～≫≫ ≪≪～

Iliana peered through the crack of the open door as Magister Sapphire's heir, Leo, confronted her half-sister in the hallway.

"You stupid bitch! Are you trying to embarrass me?" he hissed.

"No, brother," Diodora replied, toneless.

Though Iliana flinched, hand going to stroke a dagger that was no longer at her hip, Diodora remained as still as a statue. Her half-sister's unnatural calm only seemed to inflame Leo's anger. He slapped her—hard. Diodora fell to the floor, a marionette whose strings had been cut.

"Don't ever interrupt me when I have company over."

"Yes, brother."

Leo scowled and stormed off. Diodora picked herself up off the floor and opened the door to Iliana's room. Iliana stumbled back. Diodora's lips curled up in a polite smile that never reached her lifeless blue eyes, a palm print reddening her cheek. It was as if she were missing some vital substance.

"Come, it's time to practice." Diodora guided Iliana towards the full-length mirror.

It was a luxurious item only a noble house could afford. Seeing her own reflection so clearly had only recently stopped disconcerting Iliana. As far as prisons went, Thalassa Keep was as luxurious as it was horrifying. Silent servants waited on her, silent seamstresses made her dresses and silent soldiers guarded her doors. Inside her cell, she was physically comfortable— she had a feather bed, daily baths and as much food as she desired. But every day she drew closer to the time she dreaded most.

"Your smile should never reveal your teeth. Show me what you've practiced."

Iliana dutifully grinned.

Diodora reported her every action to the magister. Any perceived failure, he'd warned her, and Mira would be strapped back onto that stone and whipped in front of her. As a mage born with a menial gift, the young girl was mockingly called 'ignoble' and treated worse than a mangy dog. It was a childhood Iliana had mercifully escaped when she and her mother had been cast out.

Diodora adjusted Iliana's expression and nodded solemnly.

"Hold that expression. It is the one you will wear at all times. Now, laugh."

Iliana did her best to imitate the laugh her noble sister had taught her. Diodora shook her head. Iliana's gut clenched, the sound of Mira's cries ringing in her ears.

"Like this." Diodora laughed quietly, the sound hollow.

Iliana suppressed a shiver and tried again. Diodora nodded.

"Smile."

Iliana obeyed.

"And if a gentleman approaches you, what should you do?" Diodora asked.

"Ignore him if he has not been properly introduced. Deny him my attentions if his title is illustrus or nobilissimus," Iliana answered.

"Correct. Now laugh."

The lesson continued until long after Iliana's facial muscles were screaming in agony and laughter had lost all meaning. When Diodora departed, it was a relief, even as a wooden bar was placed across her door to shut her in.

Tomorrow, they were headed to the capital.

Had Iliana focused solely on her own terror these past weeks, she might've simply thought her half-sisters dull, submissive and accustomed to taking abuse as their due. Both she and Selene had seen their fair share of such women, at the ends of their tethers, searching for one moment to strike back and even the odds of a lifetime stacked against them. Yet her half-sisters were like living ghosts, already dead and only breathing out of habit.

Stranger still, her sisters were nearly identical in their lack of expressions, and decidedly uninterested in complex conversation. Not one could speak of their tastes in anything from fashion to music, though they dutifully explained to Iliana what a proper woman's views on those subjects should be. It was a parade of terrible sameness. Only Mira, recovering from a whipping, had any spark of life in her.

Still, Iliana had persevered. Domina Roxane Sapphire, a woman of similar age and stature whom she'd never met, was the role she'd been ordered to play. Iliana had heard whispers amongst the servants outside her door that Roxane was bedridden and comatose, slowly wasting away of a mystery illness that the magister feared would ruin the reputation of his impeccably bred bloodline, should it ever come to light. Nobles were known to hide relatives considered imperfect in some way, sometimes refusing to ever let the poor souls leave their patriarch's home. Despite Iliana's dire circumstances, she pitied Roxane her lot.

Though Iliana wished someone would pity her *her* lot, as she and her unwed half-sisters had been commanded to present themselves before the crown prince as bride candidates. Magister Sapphire must have decided it was better to send an imposter than risk the public embarrassment of sending the real Roxane. If his scheme failed, only Iliana would face the legal consequences for imitating a noblewoman, her word meaningless against that of a magister. On pain of death, she was also to outshine her half-sisters to deflect the prince's attention from their shortcomings.

Iliana doubted the Magister meant for her to live much past the completion of her task. She would need to flee the capital—an effort which would be near impossible, as two of the magister's other sons were part of the imperial bureaucracy and would supposedly be keeping a watch on her.

Iliana curled up under the covers of her bed and closed her eyes, praying for sleep that never came.

When morning arrived, she and her sisters were bundled into the family carriage. Magister Sapphire swaggered up to the window and leaned in, his cold stare cutting through her heart.

"Ah, dearest *Roxane*. Should you get it into your mind that you might renege on your word, know that your sisters have been ordered to slit their throats with your knives. They understand it is a faster death than, say, drowning." Magister Sapphire smiled genially, patted her hand as her face went ashen, and then told the driver to make haste.

Iliana swallowed down her rising bile as the carriage lurched forward. She would be blamed for killing her five sisters and sentenced to death if she fled, imprisoned if the ruse were discovered, or face death if she returned. No matter where she looked, doom greeted her.

"How did he even find me?" Iliana asked no one as she hugged herself.

"How foolish. The magister has always kept eyes on his you, lest you cause him more embarrassment than your mere existence already does," Diodora replied, toneless as always.

A chill entirely unrelated to the summer breeze held Iliana firmly in its grip.

"Nasty little vermin." Selene spat on the paralyzed pest at her feet.

In the Amethyst Province, at Dragomire Keep, Selene had very dutifully learned her lessons, allowed herself to be tortured by current fashion and learned that anyone who didn't address her as 'Domina' or 'Your Resplendence' should be treated as less than nothing. She also held her tongue at the absurd amount of dragon-themed décor on display. It was unfortunate for the handsy servant beneath her heel that he had neither the benefit of Selene's recent education nor her self-restraint. Now, where to stash the bastard till he thawed?

"Domina Milena, it is time to practice your mannerisms."

Selene looked up into a set of amethyst eyes that would have been identical to her own, if only they weren't so damn lifeless.

"Drew the short straw, Carrot? Burgundy and Copper too busy?" Selene goaded.

Her half-sister betrayed no emotion at the demeaning nickname. Selene had expected women of the nobility to try to put her in her place, to use some of that wonderful noble education to cut her verbally, or simply treat her with a great deal of derision. Hells, their father was heartless—surely his daughters would exhibit some of his traits. But day after day, she tried to get a rise out of them without success. There was simply a wrongness to her sisters that Selene couldn't understand.

Carrot's eyes lingered on the servant before returning to Selene.

"This is improper conduct for a noblewoman, though you have dressed appropriately. Please put on your shoes and we will go for a stroll."

Selene would have expected her to speak with censure, but Carrot's voice was stubbornly hollow. She had three half-sisters in all, four if Selene counted the one she was meant to impersonate, and for the life of her she could not remember their names. So interchangeable were their expressionless faces and ridiculous gowns that she had taken to calling them Burgundy, Copper and Carrot, after the distinctive hues of their red hair.

Being a rather astute man, Magister Amethyst never allowed her within spitting distance of his stronghold. Selene was relegated to a cottage on the grounds, her abode facing the opposite end of the castle to where her father spent his days. Though if this gardener's cottage were any indication of what lay within the fortress, it was no wonder her mother had angled for the position of mistress. A soft bed, silk gowns, more food than she could eat and servants to wait on her. As far as prisons went, Selene had seen worse. While he had never permitted her to enter Dragomire Keep, she'd been allowed on the grounds so long as she was under supervision.

"Please state the list of noble titles and their manners of address," Carrot intoned as they strolled.

"Emperor and empress, addressed as Your Majesty. Crown prince addressed as Your Royal Highness. Prince or princess consort as Your Radiance. Magister and magistra as Your Grace. Dominus and domina as Your Resplendence. Illustrus and illustra are followed by nobilissimus and nobilissima, none of which have a stylized address."

Carrot nodded, adjusting Selene's posture as they walked.

"The plural of Domina?"

"Dominae."

"Dominus?"

"Domini."

"Magister?"

"Magistri."

Selene suppressed a bored sigh. All in all, she considered herself rather well behaved, given she was in reality a prisoner of her father's demands. Her task was to be well versed enough in noble customs and skills to pass as Milena, a daughter of Magister Amethyst. She was to display a penchant for mischief, outrageous enough to make her very dull half-sisters seem virtuous in comparison, directing the prince's attention away from them and towards herself at all times. From what she'd been able to glean, the real Milena was locked in her room, suffering from some potentially embarrassing illness the Magister wanted kept under wraps. The poor girl was probably pregnant and refusing to abort the illegitimate child. Daddy needed someone who could pass as Milena, without the baby bump, to show up for the prince's command performance. And if it all went sideways? Selene knew she would be the only one punished for it.

They promenaded around the lush grounds as Carrot pestered her endlessly about how she carried herself, or held the hem of her dress as she stepped over every puddle. As they passed a group of guards making their rounds, the soldiers stopped and bowed to Carrot.

"Curtsy, Domina Milena," Carrot said.

Selene reluctantly obeyed.

The soldiers weren't fooled by the false name Carrot used. Once the domina turned her head, they spat at Selene's feet and carried on. She caught snippets of their conversation.

"He's no mage at all. No one has ever seen him wield a gift."

"Yet the prince has the gall to force the magister to pay for his never-ending reforms. And he demands to see all the magister's daughters brought before him, as if they don't have suitors already. He's courting trouble."

Given how they openly mocked the prince, a punishable offense, her father must have said as much many times over. There was more to this whole business than met the eye. The importance of a quick getaway loomed large. Selene decided to put a little insurance in place against her father's inevitable betrayal, running her fingers along the neatly trimmed hedges as they passed.

She'd stated her demands and he'd agreed to them. It had all been very civil and neat—discounting the corpses of her captors, of course. But what self-respecting magister would make a deal with his nobody bastard and then actually bother to pay up if he didn't have to? People were scum. Based on that principle, he would betray her once she'd done as he'd asked and bury her body in some unmarked ditch at the first opportunity, allowing the true Milena to emerge from confinement when the time was right. She was no better than her electrocuted captors in his eyes, just slightly more useful and with a longer stay of execution. Besides, she could get everything she wanted when she was in Nadioch without his help.

Only a week later, Selene was sent on her way with Burgundy, Copper and Carrot, all neatly packed into the family carriage. There would be no teleportation mage to transport them, not when their journey was to be remarked upon and fêted throughout the province. Damn nobles and their damn performances.

Neither the magister nor magistra bothered to see them off. Selene looked at her very dull, silent sisters and sighed wearily.

"A domina doesn't sigh," Burgundy reminded her.

Oh, yes, this was going to be a long carriage ride.

Chapter 5

As they travelled through the Sapphire Province, evidence of the Great War was interspersed with the recovery. They veered around ghost towns hazy with lingering curses, passed great pillars of rock paused in the act of toppling watchtowers, and rolled through communities where paint flecking from the walls revealed the charred masonry beneath. Neat bridges, cosy towns and great swaths of vibrant green forest gave way to prosperous farms, vineyards and mills butting up against walled towns, which gradually increased in size and splendour. Everywhere their well-stocked caravan travelled, they were remarked upon and celebrated. When they finally arrived in Nadioch, located snugly in the Diamond Province, there was no question in Iliana's mind as to where she was.

The palace sat at the top of the high ground in all its dazzling magnificence, surrounded by innumerable lesser buildings as well as the high, imposing, fortified walls. Snow-capped mountains in the distance completed the perfect scene. Iliana had plenty of time to appreciate the views as their progress slowed to a snail's pace. Carriages from all over Lethe clogged every available road leading towards the palace while vendors plied their wares on either side of them. The streets simply weren't made to handle the congestion.

As they passed a vendor with jewel-encrusted daggers in their ornamental sheaths, hope flared in her breast. Iliana leaned out the window to get the vendor's attention.

"One of your daggers, the one with sapphires on the sheath, and the mother-of-pearl lacquered box to hold it. The driver will pay you," she said in her haughtiest voice.

"Your diction is excellent, but dominae have no need of daggers," Diodora intoned.

Iliana held her tongue to keep from making a remark about the daggers her sisters were holding. Instead, she made the first step of her escape plan.

"I am to stand out, Diodora," Iliana reminded her, accepting the dagger and box from the vendor. "To do so, I shall present the prince with a gift."

"Very well." Diodora nodded.

Iliana pretended to inspect the sheath, all the while enchanting the blade. Any man not of her blood who held it would be able to read her plea for help as it scrawled itself on the blade, only to disappear again when untouched. It was as complex a spell as the simple metal could hold. She only hoped it would reach the prince rather than one of the magister's men.

Their carriage driver rapped on the ceiling, startling her.

"Dominae, I've been informed by palace staff that carriages are being diverted to the Hippodrome to park, and their occupants carried in palanquins to the palace gates to avoid the wait. What would you like me to do?"

"A domina is to arrive at her destination in full splendour. A domina does not subject herself to commoners unnecessarily. We will remain in the carriage," Diodora pronounced woodenly.

"Yes, Your Resplendence."

Iliana held back a whimper. Her ass had gone numb from the carriage bench hours ago. She would have loved to have seen the Hippodrome, even from afar. Chariot racing was a thrilling sport, though she supposed the racing arena must be empty now if carriages were parking inside it. Unfortunately, the extra idle time meant she had longer to wallow in fear.

If she sought help from one of the men in the palace, would they help her? Or were they all as cruel as her father? Iliana's experience with nobles had been limited to her interactions with her family this past month, and she hoped they weren't representative. How far would the sympathy of a stranger take her, when she was in truth just a bastard daughter with no money, land, title or elemental gift to make her respectable in their eyes? Was her only hope to flee for the coast once this farce was over?

Much as she hated to admit it, Iliana had begun to rely quite heavily on Selene and her mad schemes. Her friend had a way of looking at a problem of any size and seeing it as just another quaint test of her sharply honed survival skills, damn the consequences. In that way, she greatly admired her friend's bravery. In contrast, Iliana had spent her life hiding as best she could. Sure, she'd learned how to live in an unjust, unpredictable world, but she barely kept her head above water rather than being master of her own fate. As she looked into the deadened blue eyes of her sisters and clutched the lacquered box close, she wondered if she'd begun to drown already and just hadn't realised it yet.

Even so, she had at least one card to play.

Sooner than she expected, they stopped at the palace entrance. With a flourish the doors of the carriage were opened and she was helped down the step, her thighs aching from disuse. The footman wore a dazzling, fitted tunic of deep red and taupe, his brown leather boots so shiny they nearly blinded. His perfectly manicured hand held hers with utmost confidence.

"Welcome to Nadioch, Dominae of Magister Sapphire."

Selene kept her eyes open and her mouth shut as she scoped out the palace, its fortifications and the positions of its guards, exits and servants' corridors. It was no easy feat, as every available surface was covered in busy patterns; mosaics under her feet, rich tapestries along the walls, painted columns, and gold and silver leaf glinting in the arched ceilings above. Knowing where to go in this maze could mean the difference between a clean getaway and capture.

First and foremost, she would find Iliana. If Magister Sapphire's daughters had been sent without her, then it was possible her friend was either still a captive or... dead. She tried not to dwell on that possibility. If nothing else, she could torture the information out of the Sapphire women. Once Iliana's location was certain, she would need to gain access to the library and steal the Poison Compendium, maybe even get her hands on a few rare poisons from within the palace itself. Then she'd take all the jewels her foolish father had sent with her sisters and buy passage off this rotten continent with her friend in tow.

Now that the unwed daughters of the various magistri had been gathered in a ballroom, separate from the lower tiers of the nobility, she had her chance to search for her statuesque friend. She wove through the crowd, catching the flavour of the gossip. A number of noblewomen had been barred entry to the palace, their parentage called into question by a blood ward ensuring they were of their fathers' loins. The gossipers tittered behind bejewelled hands about the loose morals of the soon-to-be-divorced illustrae and nobilissimae of the empire. Selene did her best not to roll her eyes.

There were only seven provinces; Ruby, Sapphire, Emerald, Diamond, Topaz, Amethyst and Opal. No daughters would be coming from the Ruby Province, as the prince held the title of Magister Ruby and, luckily for him, marrying cousins had gone out of style a few generations back. All in all, there appeared to be nearly thirty women vying for the position of princess consort. Selene pushed past nobles and their attendants, looking for Iliana, but she was stopped by the sound of a deep, bellowing horn announcing the arrival of the prince into the lavish hall.

Selene stopped in her tracks and curtsied as she'd been taught. When a royal attendant called for the women to raise their heads, she took in the appearance of the prince, as well as the men flanking him. He'd brought what seemed to be the highest ranking in his service. The big beast mage was obviously some military type, the stripes on his tunic and thick leather belt buckled with a large gold disk denoting his esteemed rank, while the others appeared to be advisors, their palliums perfectly arranged around their shoulders in varying shades of red. There was at least one man for every woman present. She wondered idly if the dominae considered anything less than the position of Empress rotten luck.

Her eyes fell back on the prince, a man she'd imagined to be portly, with arrogance woven into lines of his embroidered robe. Instead, she was forced to admit he was rather handsome, his dark hair and eyes complementing a terra-cotta complexion, his nose a touch long, his lips full. An appearance marred by the gaudy imperial red he wore, coupled with ruby accessories of every imaginable kind and even a few she'd never dreamed of. The other dominae were equally encumbered in their flowing silk gowns, weighed down by silver and gold embroidered patterns and twinkling jewels sewn throughout, every piece of jewellery on their persons heavy, ornate, and worth a small fortune. Anger blossomed in Selene anew. Even one of their ridiculous gowns would be enough to live comfortably on for decades. No one *had* to starve in Lethe, but the greed of nobles ensured there were plenty of empty stomachs to go around.

"We will now begin your presentation to the Crown Prince Belisarius Bloodstone, Magister Ruby, and future Emperor of Lethe, the Empire of Mages."

What pithy remark would she lay on the prince to make Burgundy, Copper and Carrot seem merely dull in comparison? A threat? Sexual innuendo? A bold challenge? Maybe all three? She also listened for Iliana, daring to hope she still lived. Each woman was introduced and allowed to curtsey, then the prince took her hand and kissed the back of it. A few short pleasantries were exchanged before the mechanical process was begun again. It was difficult to see the other women as they had shuffled out into a more or less straight line across the width of the room.

"Domina Milena Amethyst, Your Royal Highness."

Burgundy elbowed Selene, and she realised it was finally her turn. She curtseyed with the best of them and then raised her head. When the prince went to take her hand, she let her grin turn roguish.

"Only a truly bold man would kiss my hand knowing what I am. A poison mage has no use for a gutless suitor."

The best way to be eccentric in this crowded field? Admit to being ignoble and show not an ounce of shame about it. He rose a notch in her estimation when he didn't flinch or pull away. Instead, his eyes sparkled with amusement as his lips met her bare hand.

"And here I had assumed that it was *you* who had come to be *my* suitor," he said.

Her smile said that he must be a simpleton and her giggle was salt in the wound. If his odd expression was anything to go by, he was not used to women treating him like he was beneath them. Eyes slyly on him as he greeted her sisters, she measured him up. It was hard to discern his physique beneath all the ceremonial glitter and silks, but his hand, though perfectly manicured, had born calluses. He played the part of the consummate gentleman, unflappable and a smooth talker to boot. How much fun would it be to see him on his knees?

As she mused about how to bring the prince low, she heard the sound of Iliana's voice. Her heart leapt and she held back a cry of relief. She was alive! It took more will that she'd imagined not to push every person aside and leap into her friend's arms. What had the daft announcer called her? Roxane? Thank the gods she was in the palace and not in the Sapphire Province or worse. Iliana words were indistinct, but she presented the prince with a jewelled box. One of the prince's attendants took the gift from her while the prince thanked her graciously.

Selene could only imagine that Iliana had been forced into the same ruse. If she were to stand out from her sisters, what better way than to give the prince a gift, something the other dominae hadn't thought to do? But the longer she observed the other dominae, the more wrong her sisters seemed. Here were cheerful women with sparkling eyes, schemes in their smiles and every witty compliment rolling off their tongues. She would have to ask Iliana about it when she could. Unfortunately, the evening had only just begun. A gruelling marathon of dinner, dancing and games lay ahead, each preceded by a change of outfit. She sighed.

"A domina-"

"Don't," Selene hissed.

Belisarius nodded to the many dominae as his herald announced the end of the presentation and invited the women to prepare for the feast. They took their cue and sashayed past him on their way to the exit. The pompous poison mage winked at him before leaving, while the tall blonde who had given him a gift smiled shyly. The others had been perfectly polite beauties. It mattered not in the end. Nicephorus and Marduk had likely identified possible victims of the corrupt ritual. He invited them to his quarters as his attendants quickly stripped off his regalia and re-dressed him for the dinner ahead. When they were briefly alone, he began his inquiry, praying this whole ugly business could be concluded soon. He'd worked his people to the bone to set this ruse up in record time, but that meant his enemies had been given a whole two months to plan.

"What were your impressions?"

"Definitely all of Magister Diamond's daughters, but that was something we already knew. I suspect some of Sapphire's dominae too," Nicephorus replied.

"What was in the box Roxane gave?" Belisarius asked.

"It's being analysed by our curse mages. We'll know in a few hours if it's anything more than a trinket," Marduk answered.

"Marduk, did you sense anything in the other candidates?"

"Amethyst's daughters should be considered suspect."

"Nicephorus, I want you seated with the Sapphire women, and Marduk, you can take Amethyst. I've had the ballroom cursed so anyone under the influence of a complex spell will faint. Give everyone you suspect a dance partner at that time so that none of the women come to harm."

He could only hope the enchantment was finely tuned enough to detect the use of the ritual. It had certainly taken some doing to exclude all manner of common spells from triggering it. At times like these, Belisarius wished he were a curse mage, so that he could create the enchantments himself rather than having to rely on those not privy to his plot.

"Consider it done," Nicephorus replied.

"Easy for you to say. You don't need to make small talk with a poison mage," Marduk grumbled.

"That one certainly has a sharp tongue, I'll grant you. Show no fear." Belisarius grinned with a confidence he didn't feel.

Chapter 6

One of these things is not like the others.

Amongst the sparkles, silks and polite small talk of the noblemen and her sisters, the beast mage sat in his military leathers and coarse tunic, his knives hidden from more wholesome types. Thankfully, Selene was not at all respectable. She wondered just how far she could prod the enormous man who seemed not at all for chit chat. Given the other men at the table turned a lovely shade of green whenever she met their eyes, word had already spread as to her mage gift. Well, if she could not be loved, at least she would be feared.

"You have not introduced yourself."

"You may call me Marduk or Strategos," he replied.

So, this one was the top military commander of the imperial army. He suited the role.

"Then you may call me Milena. Tell me, Marduk, do you have a total of seven knives concealed on your person, or have I missed one?" She widened her eyes in imitation of innocence. One of the men in powder blue crossed with a bureaucratic red pallium choked on his wine.

The beast mage sized her up as if seeing her for the first time, narrowing his eyes. She supposed he frightened most with that glare, but there were scarier things in this world, and she had a part to play. Selene beamed in response.

"I believe your imagination has gotten the better of you, Domina. I am unarmed."

He wanted to play at being boring? The man was seven feet tall, crowned with horns, and he worked for the prince. Boring was simply not an option. How to tease him?

"Do you sharpen your horns, Strategos Marduk?"

"The only things I sharpen are my swords, Domina." His glare invited no further questions. It was a challenge she couldn't resist.

"Well, those and the seven knives on your person, correct?"

The rest of their table had gone quiet as they witnessed the spectacle. The beast mage harrumphed in reply. If she'd been the sort of woman to keep score, which she was, she would've awarded herself a point.

"While this has been a splendid chat, I'm here hunting an altogether different beast." Selene winked at Marduk. When she stood and walked behind him, his whip-like tail snaked out and grabbed her calf beneath her skirt. Naughty man! Now she was curious as to where he'd hidden it all this time.

"The crown prince is not to be disturbed during his meal."

Selene didn't have to lean down to whisper in the man's ear, such was his height.

"I suppose I'll just have to titillate him instead." She exuded a diluted poison from the skin of her leg. It would sting and burn, but nothing more. "Now, unless you mean to seduce me with that delectable tail of yours, you'd best remove it."

He loosened his grip but not completely. She went in for the coup de grace. She put her hand up against his ear, as if telling him a secret, and licked the shell with a poison that tingled. His tail jerked back, and she skipped off out of his reach.

It was time to be outrageous and eccentric. Time to play with the prince.

Iliana had never understood the urge to drink more than a glass or two of wine in a single sitting. Tonight, it was the sole balm to dull her crushing anxiety as she flirted with a nobleman named Nicephorus. He was *only* the praetor, the highest administrative official in the land, someone with the power to execute her many times over. Of all the gentlemen at her table, only his questions made her heart race. While the others chose perfectly neutral topics, the fair-haired, fair-skinned, green-eyed man's questions cut too close.

Surely, he knew her sisters were broken. He asked their opinions about art and literature, about their passions and interests. When they couldn't answer with anything more than vagueness, a strange expression would cross his face, and she felt the noose tighten around her neck. Desperate to keep his attention from wandering back to the lifeless eyes of her half-sisters, she monopolized his attentions.

She'd been forced to marshal her terror and use the best-known flirtation technique afforded a woman—to ask him all about himself and act fascinated. After a time, he stopped directing his attention toward her sisters and seemed genuinely pleased that someone found the minutiae of his job so compelling.

It was while downing her fourth glass of wine, and listening to the mind-numbing necessities of proper land management practices in the Emerald Province, that a ray of hope hit her square in the chest. Past Nicephorus' shoulder, an immaculately dressed Selene paraded her way to the prince's table. She fought back tears of relief and the sudden urge to sweep the miniscule mage up in her arms. *She's alive*! But what was she doing approaching the prince so recklessly? Surely, she wasn't meant to make unnecessary waves? Iliana's world tilted on its axis as her friend grabbed an empty seat from a nearby table, dragged it across the gleaming floors and sat herself down right next to the prince. Uninvited. Like a madwoman.

"Domina, do I have something on my shoulder?"

"Oh, no! It's just, um, I believe something rather strange is happeni ng..."

Nicephorus turned around with a puzzled expression and nearly fumbled the silverware in his hand, his face ashen.

"The poison mage," he gasped.

A pang of anger stung her then. Selene had spent a lifetime dealing with the revulsion of people like him. They had shaped how her friend viewed the rest of the world, had made her angry and bitter when she had so much love and kindness inside her. Iliana couldn't stop the acid dripping from her tone.

"What does her mage gift have to do with anything?"

"But she could-"

"Could what? What could any mage do, in a room such as this? There are servants, officials, guards and guests in every conceivable nook and cranny of this hall, keeping their eyes riveted on that very scene. I'm sure she's suffered plenty just by being born with that mage gift. There's no need for one more person to add their prejudices to the mix."

Nicephorus seemed torn between shame and an ill-concealed dread. He kept his mouth shut, as did the others at the table, but it was impossible to look away from the scene unfolding before them. It was beyond the pale in terms of etiquette. Iliana only hoped her friend had the moxie to pull off her stunt without losing her head. Impassioned speech aside, she began to break out in a cold sweat as nausea churned her gut.

"Tell me, Praetor, is the prince a generous or forgiving sort?"

Belisarius watched in fascinated horror as the boorish domina parked herself at his private table and grinned as though she'd just achieved some great coup. He prided himself on his reaction, which is to say, he remained sanguine and composed. He'd long known how high to arch his brow to indicate his displeasure.

"What brings the Domina Amethyst to my private table?"

"The view, Your Royal Highness. This is the best place in the palace for a love-struck young beauty to moon over the object of her affections."

Alas, she was immune to subtlety.

Cornered by the uncouth harridan, he refused to give her the reaction she so clearly sought. Never had anyone taken quite so much pleasure in displeasing him. If he remained cold, maybe she would eventually leave in boredom.

"And who would this young woman be?"

"I haven't a clue. I only supposed I might try blocking her view. Truly, I do you a favour. Whichever noblewoman here takes the greatest offense is the one most desirous of your affections."

"I don't believe I require your services as a foil in order to select my future empress." The bite in his voice transformed her smile from one of derangement to one of triumph. Damn her. Why was she doing this? To score political points against him by making him look foolish? It was certainly something a petty magister might cook up.

"Don't tell me—have you already fallen madly in love with me? Is that why you don't wish me to aid you?" She blinked in mock surprise.

Belisarius swirled the wine in his goblet, wistfully dreaming of throwing it in her face. Her shock might just make that political landmine worth it. If only he could wipe that smug, detestable smirk off her face.

"Tell me, Domina, were you raised by wolves or does your boorishness come naturally?"

At that, a very odd expression crossed the domina's face. It left him feeling a slight chill. It was gone in a moment, replaced by a leer.

"Ah, if only I'd been raised by beasts with parental instincts. Perhaps I would have learned how to properly appreciate the *attentions* of noblemen." She waggled her eyebrows in comic suggestiveness.

Belisarius was beginning to wonder if the woman in front of him was quite sane. Surely no well-adjusted woman of her station implied her parents were lower than beasts, and then made vulgar innuendos. Perhaps this was why no one had heard much of Magister Amethyst's youngest daughter. He had erred in not specifying that only those playing with a full deck need attend, and this was his punishment for demanding that *all* of the magistri's daughters must be present at his bride show.

"Dessert is served, Your Royal Highness."

One of the servants placed a small cake decorated in gold leaf before him, unruffled by the presence of the impudent woman seated beside him. How Belisarius envied him that quality in this moment. Resolved to ignore her, Belisarius went to take his fork in hand, but the domina had snatched it from under his nose, even daring to take a bite of his food. Just as he was about to lose his patience, she froze. The fork fell from her hand, clattering on the sumptuous tablecloth. Her eyes met his, wide with pain.

A whirl of blue skirts came barrelling into sight. His guards reacted as if Domina Roxane Sapphire were a threat, their spears raised.

"Your Royal Highness, it's poisoned. Whatever she ate is poisoned!" Roxane hissed.

"Keep your voice down." Belisarius glared at the blonde. She paled.

Domina Amethyst gasped and choked, her eyes streaming with tears. Roxane patted her gently on the back.

"Water," Milena wheezed.

One of the guards handed her a glass, and she drank as though parched, coughed a few times more and then breathed easy. Her eyes sparkled with wonder and delight as she stared up at the blonde.

"I think I just ate a mage." Then she turned bemused amethyst eyes on him. "And you, Your Royal Highness, have very refined taste in mortal enemies."

"Now that you've finished choking on my dessert, I believe you will explain yourselves." Belisarius regained control of the situation. "Send them to my parlour and have them wait for my arrival. Now, Domina Sapphire, you will escort Domina Amethyst as if assisting an ailing friend. You, Domina Amethyst, will act as if you've had a touch too much to drink. I don't think that should prove too difficult. Send for Nicephorus and Marduk when their absences won't be noted."

"Yes, Your Royal Highness," the guard replied.

"Toodles." The poison mage waved as she listed from side to side, playing her part.

Roxane whispered something panicked at her before the guard hurried them both away. The prince sipped his wine and contemplated the assassination attempt laid out before him. Was it happenstance that the only noble-born poison mage had sat down with him at just the right time to take a bite of the cake meant for him? Did he have more enemies than he thought, or was this attempt on his life related to the ritual? How did the poison mage fit into all this? He hoped the answers would be forthcoming. Until then, he would act as if nothing were amiss.

The wine soured on his tongue.

As soon as the guard escorted the two inside a room too opulent to be a humble parlour, the door was closed and locked from the outside. Even the looming threat of a royal interrogation couldn't dull Selene's excitement.

"Gods Iliana, I actually ate a poison mage! Do you know what this means?"

Iliana scowled.

"That the prince may be the one to behead me rather than my father?"

"No! It means I'm a top tier badass! Fuck, but that was painful. I only ever heard of *one* other poison mage surviving the concentrated poison of another mage, and when *he* died, a whole kingdom had to be abandoned!" Selene beamed. Truly, she was now a walking legend. No one would survive the blast radius of *her* death fog.

Iliana sniffed, tears streaming down her face.

"Gods, how I've missed you." She swept Selene up in a rib-crushing embrace.

Iliana's tears dampened her spirits and focused her mind.

"What did he do to you? What has he threatened?" Selene demanded.

"He's worse than a monster! All my sisters are to cut their throats with *my* knives if I fail to keep people's attention off of them or if I try to run away. He means to kill me when this is all over, I know it. Or worse." She shivered. "What I saw in that household... His son whipped his youngest daughter nearly to death in front of me just to get me to agree to this farce. Then they laughed about a bet... Now I'm forced to impersonate one of my sisters, and I'm certain the praetor knows. I haven't slept properly for two months, and I can't do this!"

Selene knew at that moment that Magister Sapphire had to die. He'd broken a part of her friend. She patted her hand and stroked her hair as Iliana barely held back sobs, all the while deciding he would make a fine first test subject for her most painful and lethal of poisons.

"His threats are meaningless. We'll deal with them together. The first chance we get, I'll slip into your room, knock your sisters senseless, and then we'll find every single knife of yours. We'll strip them bare and torture them for information if we have to, but when your sisters die, it won't be by your blades."

"Thank you," Iliana whispered between sniffles.

"Is that why you slipped a present to the prince? Were you going to ask that arrogant peacock for help?"

Iliana pulled away and wiped her tears, nodding.

"If anyone had the power to oppose the magister, it would be someone at the palace. I had no idea if you were… Anyway, yes, I enchanted a cheap, ceremonial knife to display a message when held. Even if he wouldn't help, imprisonment is better than death."

A skilled metals mage like Iliana could enchant a great many things into a metallic object, but metals, by and large, were only capable of holding one or two enchantments at most. Only the rarest of ores were capable of holding more, and only the Imperial Forge would ever have access to them, as Iliana had often complained to her.

"That's my girl. I bet that shit father of yours didn't even know that was possible, and didn't take any precautions against your mage gift. Lucky, that. Daddy knew nearly every poison mage trick in the book, but I still managed to put in a little insurance policy." She winked at Iliana, who seemed to be regaining her composure.

"Insurance?"

"Yup. If I croak, so will he, and every other trash person living in his castle and the surrounding area. I enchanted enough dormant poison there to make the whole place uninhabitable for a decade."

Iliana snorted, nearly back to her normal self. There were still shadows in her eyes. Selene wanted to watch the man who put them there die in the most spectacular fashion. She added it to her list of things to do before she left this rotten continent. They sat for a time in companionable silence.

"Wait, what was that about a whole kingdom being abandoned?"

"Ah, well, the thing about being a poison mage is that when you meet the gods, your body doesn't just decay like normal people. You produce this death fog. Most only make one that's about twenty paces across if they're competent at their craft. But if I survived eating the poison of another mage, then mine would be more like, you know, further than the eye can see on a good, clear day."

"Gods below, why didn't you tell me?"

"Well, it's kind of morbid. I figured I'd tell you eventually, but it never came up." Selene shrugged, a little embarrassed. It wasn't seemly for a mage to go around bragging about how many people she was going to take with her when she died.

"That's it! From now on, you will wear armour at all times! Do you hear me? I will not let you take out an entire province of innocents. You will live until you're an old woman, and I will let you die peacefully in an air-tight tomb. And that's final!"

"But what about my legacy? If I don't take out at least a whole province when I die, then who will remember me in infamy? I can't be remembered as the poison mage who survived eating another mage, and then die like some benevolent loser!"

"You can and you will."

"But my legacy!"

"Selene, no."

"But-"

"NO."

"Spoilsport."

CHAPTER 7

Behind the enchanted mirror hung on the wall of the parlour, Marduk, Nicephorus and Belisarius exchanged horrified glances. Not one of them knew enough about poison mages, it seemed. Given they had only just begun listening, Belisarius feared the amount of other vital information he may have missed. The men continued to watch as any semblance of proper conduct was discarded.

"You clean up good, you know. What do you suppose we should tell the snobs?" the poison mage asked as she flopped down onto a couch and began picking her nails.

"As do you. I was shocked to see you so clean. And by snobs, you mean the prince and his men? I don't know—the truth?" The blonde hiked up her skirts and sighed as she set her feet on a silver and glass table.

"Ha! As if those fancy pricks give a shit what happens to us. They're no better than our dear daddies. Iliana, don't forget what they're capable of—these are the same sorts we're dealing with. Besides, you know as well as I do that it's a high crime to impersonate a noble. We'd be lucky to avoid the dungeons."

"But can't we use them to, I don't know, keep the magistri busy while we get away?" She pulled off her shoes with a grimace and tossed them aside.

"Point them like an arrow? Well, maybe. It depends on how much they like their egos stroked. Shall we play at being damsels in distress?"

"Play at? Speak for yourself. Thalassa Keep was a place of nightmares."

The poison mage got up from her seat and sat next to the blonde, hugging her.

"If you don't want to relive the details, then don't. Just know that I'll kill him for what he did to you."

"It's not me who needs to be avenged. The real Roxane, I'm certain she's dying of some illness in her room or worse, and the magister is too embarrassed by her condition to have her healed. The rest of my sisters, they're treated worse than feral dogs, and there's something so *wrong* about them. It's like they're dead but haven't been allowed to die."

"Yours too? I've been trying to get a rise out of mine since we got kidnapped and I've got nothing to show for it. Trust me, I've gone to extraordinary lengths and I haven't even gotten Burgundy to twitch her lip. As for the real Milena? My guess is she got knocked up by the stable boy. But didn't you hear the gossip? The real reason we're here is because we share their damn blood. Anyone not related to their father couldn't even get into the palace."

"Her name is Burgundy?"

"Ah, maybe? I don't know. They all look so damn lifeless, I just kept calling them by their hair colours and now I don't remember their names. So it's just Burgundy, Copper and Carrot."

"You're unbelievable."

"Anyway, we doing the damsels bit? Weep over abusive daddies? Slip out the back while they pretend to have honour and all that rot?"

The blonde nodded. "Not like I'd be telling any lies."

"Oh, and if the questions get too detailed, just play dumb or distract them."

"Distract like crying?"

"No, a good interrogator will just wait you out. Better off just fucking one. Oh, then act really clingy, like you're going to get married, you have a list of at least twelve baby names in descending order of preference, and you want your room with him to be painted a very specific shade of yellow. Trust me, any sane man will literally be tripping over his own robes to get away."

The blonde guffawed.

"How in the hells do you scheme these things?"

The poison mage grinned.

"I've met a fair number of courtesans. They always had the best advice."

The three men listened as the chatter turned idle. Belisarius met the grim stares of his two closest advisors and friends. It was the best evidence they were likely to get in their investigation, and the most damning testimony—the daughters of the Amethyst and Sapphire magistri had been used as living sacrifices. At least two dominae were either dead or in dire condition, hidden away on the magistri's estates, and two bastards found to act in their steads in the capital. Whoever the two women in the parlour were, their familial resemblances to the magistri and dominae were uncanny, and they'd passed through the blood wards. Belisarius signalled for his friends to exit the small room so they could speak. An adjacent panel opened into the next-door parlour, and Marduk sealed the panel behind them.

"Your opinions?" Belisarius asked.

Nicephorus paced as he speculated.

"Bastards, most certainly. If we wish to punish the magistri openly, they make for poor witnesses, given they're unacknowledged and therefore guilty of impersonating nobles. For both to see something wrong with the dominae means it would occur to anyone who spent enough time in their company. It's possible then that the magistri never intended for their activities to remain hidden for long, or were caught completely off guard by the bride show. Given the poisoning, I think we should act as if the threat is imminent, Your Royal Highness. We should move quickly and with discretion. They need to be stripped of their titles and powers before they can threaten your reign."

"Marduk?"

"I agree. The three magistri pose a definitive threat, but have we caught them all? Diamond, Sapphire and Amethyst for certain, but what of the others? Are we sure that Topaz, Emerald and Opal are innocent? Three magistri pitted against you means war. And if war breaks out, are we certain the other magistri won't seize the opportunity? Right now, we don't even know who from your own family is involved. We will know for certain whose daughters have been affected after your ballroom stunt, though as we just saw, the magistri are not above inserting imposters. Until we know who is friend and who is foe, we should stay our blades."

Belisarius began pacing in the simple parlour. He'd lured his enemies' victims to the palace with only an assassination attempt to show for it. Now he needed to get his hands on the magistri without also inviting open rebellion.

"I believe we shall have to orchestrate a few betrothals—at least one for each family. Then the magistri and their heirs will be required to attend the wedding negotiations. Once here, they can be collared and imprisoned. When our silver-tongued has recovered, it will take only a few words from her to get the confessions we need."

"Who else would you like to involve in this deception? All told, there are currently thirteen women from the three provinces, the two imposters included."

"We need only the three of us for now. Only one woman from each family needs to be affianced for their noble fathers to be summoned to the capital. If we discover more in the ballroom, then we can invite more people in on our plans. Until then, I don't want to risk trusting anyone else. A poisoner just managed to slip past all our defences, after all."

"Then which noblewomen shall we pretend to court?" the praetor asked.

"Marduk and I shall take an imposter each. You will choose a fine Diamond. The metals mage would be a poor match for your gift, and the poison mage will likely be troublesome."

"I can attest to that. She certainly isn't shy about using her poisons, either. She even spotted each of my blades and made sport of telling me so." Marduk harrumphed.

"Do you think she's been sent as an assassin?" Nicephorus asked.

Marduk snorted, leaning against the wall. "If she is, then we should be so lucky. We'd have names and a paymaster. Something tells me *that* one can be bought, and there is nothing a magister can offer that we can't quintuple."

"I suppose if that's not enough, at least we know she cares for the Sapphire imposter. A threat against her would prove to be fairly effective," Nicephorus replied.

Belisarius heaved a great sigh. He knew which imposter he needed to court and he was already lamenting it.

"Marduk, you will be in charge of the blonde."

"Your Royal Highness, if the poison mage is a threat, you simply cannot risk it!" Former ease forgotten, Marduk stood tall and slammed his fist against the wall.

"We both know that if she is a threat, I am the only one with the magic to stop her. You heard her boast. We cannot risk an entire province full of innocents," Belisarius retorted.

"We cannot risk *you*, Your Royal Highness!" Marduk glared.

"I don't like it, but you are right, Your Royal Highness," Nicephorus cut in. "If you would allow me, I shall inquire as to how long it might take to construct an air-tight tomb." Nicephorus adjusted his pallium about his shoulders with a grim look.

"See that it's completed quickly." Belisarius nodded towards the door. Gods, he was going to live to regret this, he just knew it. "Now, shall we speak with our prospective brides?"

Selene ceased her banter with Iliana the second she heard the snick of the lock in the door. They rushed to right themselves, kick errant shoes under chairs and hide bare feet under artfully placed hems. Iliana caught the direction of Selene's gaze and watched with her as three supremely grave yet confident men entered the room. The only one of the three Selene had not yet had a chance to size up was the immaculate, green-eyed, blond bureaucrat. She disliked the man on sight. He dismissed Iliana without even a glance, preferring instead to glare at her with undisguised loathing. While it was natural to size up the threat first, he was a fool to discount her friend. Marduk, the tall beast mage, gave them both a proper once-over, assessing. The prince nodded to both Iliana and herself. Selene winked back.

"Rise for your prince," Nicephorus commanded when it became apparent neither were about to without prompting.

Selene placed her hand on Iliana's thigh, sensing her friend was about to obey.

"We'd love to, if only our feet were not so sore. Please sit, and don't loom so."

She smiled back at the officious man like a predator eying up its dinner. If they were seated, it would take that much longer for them to rise should Selene and Iliana need to flee on foot at this very moment.

"How dare you-"

"I dare because I am Domina Amethyst. A domina invited here for the purpose of marriage to your prince. A domina who has simply asked for your courtesy, while you insist on petty formalities."

While the man fumed, he kept silent. Marduk clapped him on the back and laughed. The prince kept a pleasant mask on his face.

"Let's sit as she suggests, friends. She is quite correct that we should do our best to act as courteous hosts while they are here for the bride show."

It didn't escape her notice that when the men sat, they were positioned to block the exit. The pair of couches the two groups sat at were a fair distance from each other, so any attempt to flee would be obvious and give the men more than enough time to see it coming. She didn't like this one bit. She could poison them, but before the big one skewered her with his blades? Debatable.

"Perhaps you would like to tell me just who it was that poisoned my dessert, Domina Amethyst?"

Now there was a topic she *did* like. Iliana's eyes often glazed over when Selene waxed poetic about her poisons.

"Would, but can't. I *can* tell you they've got serious coin. Not many people are willing to harvest the concentrated stuff coming from a poison mage's corpse. Of those that are, there are even fewer who can survive long enough to bring it back. And any that have won't be selling it for less than an emperor's ransom," Selene replied.

Iliana's hard squeeze on her thigh stopped her. Had she been too enthusiastic?

"Can you explain why I was saved from being poisoned by the *only* poison mage amongst the nobility?" the prince asked.

His pleasant face never slipped, despite the threat. It was a reminder that he was just another scummy noble. What did this peacock really want? If she knew, she could turn this situation to her advantage.

"What are you implying, Your Royal Highness? I simply think you're the luckiest man in Lethe."

When his polite mask was discarded, a shiver went down her spine. A paralyzing concoction coated her legs and the arm furthest from Iliana. He would be very sorry for the threat in his gaze.

"I'm implying that you're not who you pretend to be, *Selene*."

Damn. The first plan had crashed and burned. She shrugged, refusing to let him see her sweat.

"Oh, are we done playing that game? Very well. What do you want?"

"I want you to marry me."

It was the last thing she'd expected him to say. Her shock must have registered on her face, because a smug smile spread across the prince's.

"Are you entirely sane?"

"Selene!" Iliana gasped.

"What? He's all but accused me of poisoning him so I could play hero, and now wants me to make brats for him. Wouldn't you wonder if his brain had been replaced by slugs?"

"Damn it, Selene! He's the bloody crown prince! He could have you executed for saying that. One wonders about *your* sanity sometimes!"

"Only sometimes?"

Iliana muttered despairingly and put her head in her hands.

Marduk was the first to laugh outrageously, which had everyone looking at him with varying degrees of concern. Nicephorus cleared his throat and turned to Selene and Iliana.

"What the prince meant to say was that we would like to propose a rather lucrative business opportunity to you both. Neither of you are dominae, am I correct?"

Iliana looked at Selene, who shrugged.

"Maybe half-dominae? We're both illegitimate. It's not like we're playing at noblewomen because we wanted to, either," Selene added.

"Of Magister Sapphire and Magister Amethyst?" Nicephorus continued.

"Where the hells else would I get purple eyes from?" She rolled her eyes.

"And you are both aware that your half-sisters have had harm done to them?" Nicephorus asked.

"I guess? They're just wrong, somehow," Selene replied.

"Yes, but what kind of harm?" Iliana asked.

"You need not know of the specifics, only that in harming them, both of the magistri are guilty of casting foul magics, for which the punishment is death. In order to lure them to Nadioch, we are proposing a series of false engagements, the negotiations for which your families would be required to attend. Once they have been captured, your roles will be over, and you will be handsomely compensated," Nicephorus said.

"How handsomely? Because daddy dearest was very clear in impressing upon me that lightening can send bits of a person flying." Selene leaned forward. Gold was good. Certainly better than her odds of poisoning all three of these men without getting killed. She drew the invisible poison coating her skin back into her body.

"How will you protect our sisters? The magister has ordered my sisters to kill themselves with my blades the second anything suspicious happens. If my half-brothers have misgivings, I also believe some harm will come to us."

Sweet, kind Iliana. When would she learn? Selene stifled a sigh.

"You actually care? If they weren't so damaged, they'd treat you like trash," Selene pointed out.

"You didn't see what I did. They need help very badly."

Selene was about to unleash a tirade, but held herself in check. This was not the right place to tell her dear friend with her heart of gold what danger lay ahead in accepting this proposal. Not that they had much choice. As if a prince would allow mere castoff bastards to refuse a plan he'd already concocted to get what he wanted. Not when the alternative for them was a lifetime in the dungeons.

"We will remove all blades of your making from your sisters' persons and rooms between now and the end of the ball. I'll personally oversee the men in charge of keeping your sisters so busy they won't have the energy left to contemplate trouble. As for the sons of Magister Sapphire, they are under my employ and can be kept adequately buried in work. Is this acceptable?" Nicephorus asked.

"Yes, that would set my mind at ease." Iliana replied.

"Your friend seems willing enough, Selene. What will it take to get you to agree? I have very deep coffers." The prince steepled his fingers and raised a dark brow.

His confidence irked her. Fine—he wanted to play this game? Let's see if she could name a sum to beggar a prince.

"One million gold coins, a large, fully crewed, sea-faring vessel ready at a moment's notice, and the written promise that, if the situation becomes dangerous, we will be allowed to bow out and retain the entirety of our handsome compensation."

Instead of outrage, the prince simply stared at her, expression unchanged.

"And what, exactly, do you need all that for?"

"To get the hells out of this shitty empire, obviously," Selene replied.

The prince considered her for a moment, turned to Nicephorus, who nodded solemnly, and returned his steely gaze back to her.

"Done. I'm enchanted to meet you, my dear bride Selene. Or shall I call you Milena?" His wintry tone was at odds with his sweet words.

Her insides squirmed strangely when their eyes met. She turned from him to the man approaching, and did her best to ignore her inner warnings as the beast mage beamed down at Iliana. When he knelt before her, he reached for her hand, even then forcing her statuesque friend to look up ever so slightly. Iliana seemed to be somewhere between queasy and flustered.

Marduk kissed her best friend's hand and stared into eyes she knew to be as blue as the sky and a hundred times more captivating. Iliana's sapphire eyes spoke volumes, if you knew what to look for, and she looked like she was charmed by his actions. The beast mage needed to have his perceptive eyes removed. Selene's hackles were instantly raised.

"I hope you will not mind playing the part of my bride for a short time, Iliana."

It wasn't part of her better nature that rose to the fore when her friend blushed at Marduk's sincere gaze. Selene interrupted Iliana before she could reply.

"She won't, as long as *you* don't pretend to have honest intentions towards her outside this farce," Selene hissed, unable to stop herself.

"Excellent. Then we will have our guards escort you back to your rooms. The ball will commence shortly. We expect you to play your parts," Nicephorus warned as he rose, bidding them to do the same.

CHAPTER 8

Iliana had nearly perished as Selene had addressed the prince without regard to manners—or survival. She had envisioned their deaths at least a half-dozen times during the short negotiations. Instead of losing their heads, Selene had ruthlessly demanded more than an emperor's ransom in compensation. Iliana was reassured knowing her half-sisters would be safe now. But as Selene whispered when they were out of earshot of the guards escorting them, perhaps she herself was less so.

"We need help very badly. They're not offering mountains of gold as a gesture of generosity for our time, its fucking hazard pay! You think the magister isn't going to be ready for war the second he hears you're getting married to some lofty right-hand snob of the prince? If he comes to Nadioch, you had better believe we'll be in more danger than ever. A monster like him is going to assume you're attaching yourself to someone powerful in order to outmanoeuvre him. If I were you, I'd get a number of blades sharpened and be ready to run."

"Then why did you ask for mountains of gold and a ship?"

"Because they needed to think we wouldn't run until it got dangerous. What we need to do is prepare to run well *before* the magistri come to marry us off."

She kept this in mind as the beast mage named Marduk approached and kissed her hand before asking her to dance. When he led her to the floor, the couples around them did their best to shy away. Iliana smiled. At least she would have a dance partner she could look up to. And what an intimidating sight he was—seven feet at a guess, with horns and claws. His fangs were visible when he spoke, but it was his bold, rugged features, closely cropped dark curls and thick limbs of corded muscle that had her heart fluttering.

"I must confess that my dancing skills are rusty." He ground out the admission, a blush heating his tanned, olive-toned skin.

She nearly forgot her step.

"Well, I must confess that I didn't even know how to dance like this until a few months ago. I'm sure your knowledge of footwork with a blade in hand will help."

"And why would you say that?" he asked, his tone menacing.

She almost flinched. *No*, she reminded herself, *no more cowering*. As Selene had told her many a time, showing fear only whet the appetite of monsters. Iliana straightened her spine and forced herself to stare the enormous man in the eye. *He's just like a grumpy client. A grumpy, rugged, very strong client.*

"Because you have seven excellent blades on your person, and I can only assume it's because you know how to use them."

His thick, dark brows went from thunderous to shocked.

"I keep looking at you and assuming you're a proper noblewoman, but neither of you are anything of the sort. She said the same damn thing at dinner. Have I really fallen so far that little girls can spot my knives and make sport of me?"

Iliana hated it when someone called her a little girl. 'Little' had stopped being accurate after she'd turned nine, and the days of her girlhood had died with her mother and adoptive father. She was a master craftswoman, better than any man she knew, and she was sick unto death of everyone underestimating her.

"I am no little girl, and I can spot your knives because I've been taught to do so, Strategos. I can tell you that the knife at your shin requires a good sharpening, the one at your right hip is of the highest quality ore, and the one up your left sleeve has been enchanted poorly. I can tell you that because I am a master metals mage. You underestimate me at your own peril."

He closed whatever distance there had been between them, his hand hot and possessive on her back. Iliana truly felt it would be safer to flee from such palpable interest. She wished it were just a case of Selene's moxie rubbing off on her, but she had only her stupid temper to blame.

"Perhaps our time together will be more interesting than I'd assumed," he murmured, his deep voice sending a shiver down her spine.

His eyes pierced through her like one of his daggers. As he pinned her with that stare, she realised his eyes weren't black, but intensely dark green. A hand on her shoulder broke the spell.

"If I may?" asked Nicephorus.

He was polished and blinding in his white and green robes, the red sash pallium resting perfectly on his shoulders. Marduk nodded and handed her over to the Praetor.

"Until next time, master mage." Marduk winked.

Before she could figure out if he was being sarcastic or sincere, Iliana was swept away into the next dance by a man who knew precisely where to place his feet.

"I hope my friend has not frightened you overmuch."

"Oh, no. I'm fine, thank you."

His smile was both attractive and comforting. Safe.

"Please find it in your heart to forgive him. Being the strategos has left him very good at commanding men, but maybe less so at making small talk with young noblewomen."

"To which young noblewoman are you referring, Praetor?"

His smile was a balm on her tattered nerves. When he wasn't busy interrogating her or dictating good manners, he could be quite handsome. If he held her a little closer than the dance called for, she didn't complain.

The cavernous hall with its carved, painted columns was full to bursting with nobles dancing, making small talk or slipping off into the perfectly pruned gardens outside. An army of enchanted lights winked above, sparkling against the gold and silver painted ceiling and making the room as bright as mid-day. With the crush of bodies, only cooling spells kept the airy hall from turning uncomfortably humid in the summer heat.

"I would like to assure you that your sisters are being looked after by dashing noblemen under my direction, and they'll be assigned new servants I've handpicked for the task. Their rooms have been searched, and the knives have all been confiscated. For now, you need only concern yourself with enjoying your days here in the capital," he whispered between steps.

And just like that, a brutal burden lifted from her shoulders. She choked back tears of relief. Finally, there was a chance to escape the magister's cruel grasp without leaving dead bodies in her wake.

"Thank you, Praetor. You don't know how much that means to me."

He seemed genuinely pleased to hear it.

"It was nothing. Please know that you may come to me with any troubles you have."

"Ah, that would be very reassuring."

Iliana fixed a polite smile on her face. Sweet words aside, were she anyone else, would he even give her the time of day? Would he do anything more than report her for impersonating her sister? To men like this, she was just another disposable commoner.

"Yes, well I wanted to keep you informed. In a few moments some women may feel faint, your sisters among them, but it will pass and they will be safer for it, so try not to be overly upset when that happens."

"Is this part of your plan to bring the magistri to justice?"

Nicephorus smiled but kept his counsel. A slither of unease curled in her gut, but what could she do? Just as Nicephorus said, a few noblewomen did indeed lose their footing, but each and every one had partners who, to the last, gallantly lead them off the floor and brought them refreshments. Iliana relaxed her shoulders. She was about to tell Nicephorus something banal when she caught sight of the bewildered prince holding Selene in his arms—unconscious.

"Tell me, Prince, are you colour-blind?"

"I don't know why you would think so," Belisarius replied.

He looked at her as though she were spectacularly dull. It was a challenge Selene couldn't pass up.

"Well, I'm unsure how anyone could wear so much crimson without already being blinded to it. Perhaps you simply have very bad taste? Or would that be your seamstress? Do you even choose your clothes and dress yourself, or do you have people to do that for you?"

"Are you certain all those poisons haven't rotted your brain? I, for one, have my doubts."

She held back a snort. Insulting a man to his face had never been so much fun.

"If my brain is rotted, *darling*, what does that say about the man who wants me for his bride?" She blinked up at him.

"Don't let the momentary status go to your head. I'm not sure your ego would be able to fit in a ballroom as paltry as this." He rolled his eyes.

The ballroom comfortably entertained a thousand guests, of course, but she'd landed a blow. A prince rolling his eyes? It tasted like victory.

"You're right. Next to your conceit, there's very little room left to manoeuvre."

Black brows inched further down his forehead the longer she taunted him. Now his expression was anything but bored as a flush spread across his terra-cotta cheeks. In retaliation, he pulled her into a complicated set of steps she couldn't possibly keep up with. Hopelessly outmatched, she tried to slam her heel down on his toes, but the prince was fast on his feet, his rich, cheerful laugh at her antics spurring her anger. Then he upped the pace. It was all she could do not to trip. To finish, he twirled her with ease and posed her prettily for the final note. As their audience clapped politely, Selene's blood boiled. Only her long skirts had ensured she hadn't looked like a complete fool as she'd been tossed about. Worst of all, not a single obsidian strand on his head was out of place.

Just as the next song was starting, he turned a smug expression her way. She smiled back and then roundly crushed his toes with her heel. His momentary grimace was all the reward she'd get as he kept his hold on her.

"Allow me to escort you to the seats. You look like you could use a moment to collect yourself."

His triumphant expression galled her. She had a few poisons she hadn't tested out. Was it still treason if he didn't die?

"And you look like a wet bird tumbled out of a vat of red paint."

If her voice was more mewling than she'd meant, it was due to her laboured breathing and nothing more.

"Perhaps, but this bird is in high demand this evening, so be a good girl and try not to be too boorish while I'm away."

"I-" Overwhelming dizziness stopped her. The prince wore an uncharacteristically bewildered expression before he too began to swirl. "Dihya," she managed to croak out before she fainted.

⇝⇝⇝ ⇜⇜⇜

"Have you identified all of the affected noblewomen?"

Now that the festivities were over, Belisarius was ensconced in his study with a mess of papers before him. His ornate robes and heavy jewellery had been tossed aside and taken away by attentive servants long ago. Marduk was elsewhere, setting up a detail of guards to keep watch on the traitors' children round the clock.

"Yes, and it hasn't spread further than our first estimates. Diamond, Amethyst and Sapphire are the sole perpetrators. None of the lower nobility seem to be involved," Nicephorus answered.

Yes, it was *only* three magistri who were undoubtedly coming for his head. He supposed it could be worse, but could the remaining magistri be counted as allies? His spell for the ballroom had worked perfectly. If only it could've also informed him who he could trust at his back. Or if the latest thorn in his side was a threat too.

"What of the imposter? Has our curse mage been able to identify the spell Selene was under?"

When Selene had fainted, he'd feared the worst—that she'd been spelled into compliance with a plot against him. Aside from having a repertoire of lethal poisons available with a single flick of her wrist, if she were ordered to kill herself, the inhabitants of the palace, perhaps even the capital, would be doomed.

"It was an old memory erasure spell. Eagerly accepted, which she confirmed. There is no trace of compulsion," Nicephorus replied.

His gut roiled. What horrors could a woman with poison in her veins need to forget? And where had she even found a memory mage? They'd been a persecuted lot, and supposedly wiped out of existence centuries ago. Another lovely bit of unwelcome news for him to ponder in the early hours of the morning.

"She's awake and acting... in character. I don't believe she has recovered much of the sealed memories. She only reported strange memories of stealing an old woman's pies."

"I suppose we have that much to be grateful for." Belisarius sighed. Who could say what she'd kept bottled up? Would it be an axe waiting to fall? His plan could not afford mistakes. "Is there any indication as to the kind of memories she's had sealed?"

"His report indicated he could only feel a sense of great sadness. I've been told that being in proximity to your gift may gradually weaken the spell, but he couldn't say for certain."

"Send one of our spies to watch her from a distance and intervene only if she is in the act of sabotage. Otherwise, we can only hope her sealed memories won't interfere with our plans. What of the magistri? Have there been any indications they've begun to mobilize?"

"There has been no change within their borders of troop numbers or placements, neither has there been any indication of hoarding food, gathering horses or unusual financial transactions. However, our naval forces spotted a ship of foreign mercenaries entering our waters. There is no indication of which province they're sailing to."

"Inform them that they can sail back whence they came, or find themselves at the bottom of the sea. Under no circumstances are they to reach our shores."

Only Magister Opal and the imperial navy had vessels capable of making the journey across the open sea. If foreigner mercenaries had been hired, was Opal an accomplice, or was there a rat in his navy? Both? Another headache bloomed.

"Understood."

Nicephorus lingered tellingly.

"Was there anything else?"

"Perhaps this may not be the best time, but have you considered marrying one of the dominae from an ally faction? Both Emerald and Opal are well suited militarily and geographically to aid you if war breaks out. Opal contributes the most naval officers, builds the majority of our ships and has the greatest influence with foreign traders. The Emerald Province has the most defensible lands and has a great many gifted mages. It is also the only province that simply defended its territory during the Great War rather than becoming an aggressor. They have always been openly supportive of your reign."

"And this glowing review of Emerald has nothing to do with the fact that it is also your birth province?"

Nicephorus' green eyes sparkled, and he allowed himself a small smile.

"It has been fifteen years since I've set foot in my childhood haunts, but my position by your side has only strengthened Magister Emerald's trust in your capacity to lead."

"I shall give it a great deal of thought."

"Please see that you do."

CHAPTER 9

The sun had nearly risen, the palace preternatural in its silence. Doubtless, the staff of the kitchens had just begun their shifts to prepare for the prince's midmorning tea with the dominae. Guards blearily held their eyes open for the last hour of their rotations before they found sweet relief in their pillows. The very first of the birds were chirping.

It was the perfect time for a burglary.

Selene completed her morning stretches and donned the servant's garb that she'd snagged from a harassed-looking laundress. Inside the flowing robe she hid the sturdy metal bar she'd pilfered from the gardens she'd been forced to tour the afternoon before. Dressed and armed, she slipped through halls packed with tapestries until she reached the imperial library. A sleepy-eyed librarian manned a central desk, surrounded by unbelievably large tomes and a mess of scrolls.

"Do you know where I can find the royal copy of the Poison Compendium?"

"Chained Books, last shelf on the right. Wait, do you have permission-"

"Shhhh." The light sedative from her finger to his lips was all it took to put him to sleep.

She carefully guided his sagging head back down onto the pages of an open book. Flying on silent slippers, Selene passed row after row of chained books and scrolls sitting upon endless shelves in a darkened chamber. It was nearly a minute before she reached it, quickly spying the title. She took a steadying breath before taking out her bar and setting to work on the chain.

Prying it loose took much too long, and she was sweating with anxious exhilaration when she wrenched the connecting post out of the thick wooden shelf. One last tug, and the chain slipped free from its anchor. Not a moment too soon, as frenzied shouting echoed down the empty stacks. Selene assessed her options. Outrun the people rushing towards her, hide, or take her chances out the narrow window?

The window creaked terribly when opened, and the view was disastrous. An impossibly narrow ledge looked over a straight drop to the manicured lawns below. Hiding it was! After tossing her bar out the window, Selene scrambled up the ledges of the shelves and laid herself flat, making sure no fabric from her long tunic draped over the edge of the bookcase. She laid the book down carefully in front of her. The bookcases were incredibly tall, and it was highly unlikely even an average-sized man would be able to see her lying on top in the gloom.

Several guards burst onto the scene, surveying the damage to the bookcase and the chain's anchor lying discarded on the floor. The librarian peered out the window and blanched at the sight of her bar on the greens below, muttering as he swayed on his feet about her leaping with the book in tow. He ordered the guards to search the grounds, sending them off before following close behind.

Once quiet had descended amongst the musty leather and old parchment, Selene clambered down the bookcase. Book in hand, she casually slipped out of the library, using the billowing nature of her borrowed tunic and robe to hide the book against her stomach.

She was about to turn a corner back towards her room when a group of guards with another librarian in tow came storming down the hallway. Frantic, she stepped behind a tired-eyed serving girl heading for an alcove, ensuring her footfalls were silent. The servant created a small flame in her hand and pushed on the vase decorating the alcove. It swung inwards, revealing a narrow, winding staircase inside the walls. Selene crept in behind her before the entrance disappeared.

Everything truly was better in the capital, even the mages. Most elemental mages could only manipulate their element if it were already in front of them. Only nobles received the expert training to conjure it from nothing. Selene waited for a few breaths before trying to exit, but the mechanism was stuck. She cursed her rotten luck. She hid in the damp dark considering her options, the weak light of the magic flame ascending the staircase her only illumination. The serving girl soon found her destination and departed.

Selene scrabbled in the pitch black, hoping she'd be able to find the next alcove. One arm around her book, the other searching the outer wall of the spiral staircase, she eventually felt another lever mechanism. Was it the same exit the servant had used? It opened into a dim room, light snoring the only sound within. Selene snuck inside, unable to see more than thin strand of light not far from her. Just as she reached for that light, she tripped on a discarded bottle, falling face first. Instead of hitting a wall or the floor, her fall was broken—by a curtain? The sound of glass shattering and fabric ripping accompanied the blinding light of full morning.

"Ah, Belli, not now."

Unsure who Belli might be, Selene surged to her feet and rushed for the door.

"I'll return later," she whispered.

An old man grumbled and pulled the sheets over his head. The cavernous room screamed its owner's wealth and power, ornate in a way she'd never dreamed possible. Gratuitous use of the best oozed from every surface—silks that shone like polished silver, gleaming wooden furniture, rugs so plush she'd have slept comfortably on them, arranged between gold-flecked mosaics. There were gold and jewel-encrusted decorations, ceremonial swords, oil paintings and fine tapestries strung up along the walls. She'd thought the palace halls and her assigned quarters were richly decorated but she'd been wrong. The room was a thief's wet dream, and she didn't have time to swipe any of it. Just as she reached the door, a ball of fire slammed into the metal handle. Gasping, she leapt back from the searing heat.

"You're not Belli. What are you doing with that book?" the old man growled. He pulled the covers off and stepped out of the bed, glaring at her with his red eyes. An old warrior by the looks of his stocky body, softened from disuse and drink, his long, greying black hair and grizzled beard comically messy.

"Are you simple?! Obviously, I'm stealing it!" Selene snapped, royally pissed at being foiled by some grizzled old snob.

"And now you're trapped in here with me, thief."

The old man grinned. It was obvious he relished a good fight. Fire coated his palms, painting his golden brown skin in a hellish light. He was a competent fire mage. This might prove tricky.

"Wrong, you old lizard. *You're* trapped in here with *me*. Catch!"

Selene tossed the book straight at him. The old man snuffed the fire from his palms and gently caught it. As he was fumbling over it, she vaulted at him, her favourite paralytic coating her palms in less than a second. Noticing her charge, he tossed the book aside, but not fast enough. She smeared his right arm—his dominant, if she were correct. In seconds he would be stiff as a board and unable to direct his fire, though still able to breathe. Or so she thought.

"Fuck!"

He lit up his entire right arm in flames.

Instead of collapsing, he turned to her with a new light in his eyes, right arm hanging useless by his side and unable to produce flame. They danced around each other, avoiding any serious blows. The longer they dodged each other, the more evident it became that, useless arm or not, she would never get another direct shot at the old warrior. Her only chance at victory would be to play dirty. Just how she liked it.

Selene was sweating from the heat but grinning like a madwoman, an expression her quarry mirrored. As she dodged blows, she kicked off her slippers, allowing her bare feet contact with the mosaic floors, spreading a poison which required heat to activate. She only had one other poison that could be effective against a fire mage, but it was lethal, and she didn't want to murder a well-connected nobleman if she could help it. Killing nobles was a sticky business, after all.

"Is that all the heat a dried-up old goat like you can produce? Can't even hit a little girl. Fucking pathetic!"

That did the trick. Both his legs and left arm blazed with fire. Selene had to leap out of the way. The smell of burning cloth had her tearing off her robe and tunic, leaving her in nothing but a slip and her panties. Her clothes smoked and dissolved in flames. Just as she had hoped, her poison turned into a hazy smoke, rendering the old fire mage high on the concentrated fumes. His fires sputtered out, legs wobbling like jelly before he fell onto his rear, laughing hysterically.

Selene grinned and used two plates leftover from a meal on the terrace to scoop up her charred clothes and toss them into the fireplace. Shockingly, nothing else in the room had been set ablaze. Perhaps an enchantment spared them? As the old man tried to hold in girlish giggles, she retrieved her book and tried the door handle. It was hot but firm to the touch. The doors were immoveable. The metal handles had melted down the space between the doors and hardened, effectively sealing her inside.

"Fuck!"

Selene ran for the alcove and pushed just as the serving girl had done before, but it wouldn't budge. She threw herself at it to no avail. Trapped.

"Does that sometimes," the old man giggled. "Guess you're stuck with me, ha!"

Selene stalked out onto the terrace to see what opportunities she might have, but, to her great dismay, it looked out over the very garden in which she was supposed to drink tea shortly. That garden was also very, very far below her.

"Going to jump in your undergarments?" the old man teased her.

"Never stopped me before." Selene sighed.

"Oh, just sit and have a drink with me, thief. For that inspired bit of trickery, you can have the damn book."

Selene's interest pricked up at that. She placed the book in a corner of the veranda.

"Help me to the seat. There should be a bottle of the good stuff in the oak chest over there." Selene complied, helping the old man sit. "What's your name dear girl?"

From dirty thief to dear girl? She might have to use this poison more often. She poured them both a glass of spirits.

"Domina Milena Amethyst, at your service," Selene replied, holding out her hand.

The old man nearly choked on his liquor. She smiled with more than a hint of sass.

"Explains the sticky fingers, I suppose," he grumbled. He took her soot-stained hand in his and kissed the back of it. His grin was wolfish when he replied, "Darius Bloodstone, Emperor of Lethe."

❧ ⤛⤜

The most accomplished musicians played stringed instruments at a volume sure to please the ear without the need to strain one's voice. All manner of neatly planted foliage bloomed around them, their fragrant flowers scenting the mild mid-morning air. Prince Belisarius sat at a table with a pristinely white tablecloth and perfectly arranged silver teacups, holding court with the eldest Dominae Topaz, Emerald and Opal, sipping delicate tea and making entirely decent conversation. Domina Emerald had the warm, deep brown skin and glittering green eyes of her line, her black hair swept up in intricate braids. Topaz had the distinctive amber eyes, copper skin and dark hair of her father, while Opal had a spell-binding opalescence to the whites of her black eyes along with her blue-black hair and fair skin. Though their figures ranged from petite to voluptuous, each was charm and femininity personified. Not a one used light mage charms to enhance her beauty.

Domina Topaz was smooth with her compliments, Domina Opal quick with her wit and Domina Emerald enlightening with her keen insights. Each noblewoman shone in her own way without losing ground to the other two. Glittering jewels and fashionable dresses had been chosen with military precision for their desired effect. Perfect etiquette, politic responses, practised laughs and mannerisms—these were their weapons of choice. It was nothing less than a true battle for his attentions and affections. He sat with the very crème de la crème of noblewomen.

Belisarius was also enormously bored. These were the very same conversations he'd had a thousand times since he was old enough to understand how this marriage game was played. It was why he'd eschewed personally meeting with noblewomen most of his life. As their conversations played out, a great many predictable, meaningless words were spoken, many from him. It was nigh impossible to discern the real women beneath the polished dominae in a forum like this.

At least everyone partaking in this tea had the good grace to ignore the raucous, bawdy laughter emanating from the emperor's veranda. It was an odd sound this time of day. His father rarely woke before noon, and only bothered with female companionship after dark. At least the emperor seemed to be in good spirits. Whoever the woman was, Belisarius might need to take note of her and ensure she made herself available more often. While he resented his father for shirking his duties, he had no desire to see him suffer misery and loneliness.

No, only one thing truly marred the event. The poison mage hadn't bothered to show her face. Her attendance had been mandatory. Belisarius couldn't falsely affiance himself to her if it was known that she had failed to attend these gatherings. The metals mage had shown up and was dutifully taking a stroll through the gardens on Marduk's arm, while the eldest Domina Diamond was staring with deadened eyes at Nicephorus and exchanging banalities.

In only a short time he would need to announce Selene as his princess consort. She needed to plausibly claw her way to the top of society—and ostensibly his notice—before then. Being the only domina not in attendance, her absence was palpable, her disrespect once again blatant and public. No self-respecting man would choose such a harridan for his wife. As the work required for his plans to succeed grew, his mood darkened.

When the event ended, he saw all the dominae off and promised each a dance after dinner. He sent a glance Marduk's way, then to his praetor. The strategos nodded and kept Iliana behind with him. Once only the three men and Iliana remained, Belisarius dropped the polite mask.

"Where has your friend gone? I doubt she would leave you behind, but I could be wrong."

"I don't know. I've already explained to Marduk that I am not her keeper." Iliana raised a defiant chin, her spine ramrod straight.

When would these women stop giving him a headache? The blonde was supposed to be the more reasonable of the two. He pinched the bridge of his nose and took a steadying breath.

"Find her and place her under house arrest. She doesn't leave her room without an escort and she will attend every scheduled event. She will behave like a domina, one attempting to garner my affections. Have one of the royal tutors drill etiquette into her skull until her ears bleed. If she refuses, she'll not receive a single coin of compensation and will be thrown in the dungeons," Belisarius ordered Marduk, who bowed.

Iliana gasped and glared at Marduk, stomping on his foot in a fit of pique. As she spoke, she punctuated each of her sentences with a disapproving poke to the man's chest.

"How can a man of your stature be so spineless? You're not even going to argue about how ridiculous his reaction is to Selene not attending a single tea party? I thought you had a better head on your shoulders."

"There is nothing I've said which has been out of line, Iliana. Your friend agreed to my terms. She should know to obey them," Belisarius huffed.

"With all due respect, Your Royal Highness, she agreed to be a false fiancée, not obey your every whim. She's not a beast to be tamed. As it stands, your orders make you no better than the magistri."

The metals mage must have a core of molten iron to defy him so, her blue eyes flashing with ill-advised anger. Belisarius glared but she refused to back down.

"I am nothing like those monsters," he ground out.

"You are cut from the same cloth so long as you see us as tools rather than people." Iliana glared, curtsied indignantly, and excused herself.

"Shall I arrange tutors for the both of them?" Nicephorus narrowed his eyes at her retreating form.

"No. Just have Selene found." Belisarius sighed.

Gods, had he just been told off by a young woman? It shamed him to have lost his cool so quickly. That damned poison mage kept finding her way under his skin.

His father's howls of laughter caught his attention once more.

"When you find Selene, bring her to my study. In the meantime, I need to find out whose company my father is enjoying so much at this hour," Belisarius mused.

"Your Royal Highness." Both Marduk and Nicephorus bowed in unison.

Belisarius made his way through the gardens, ascending the staircases to reach his father's rooms in record time. The guards were nowhere to be found, but Father often dismissed them when he wished for privacy. As he reached the doors, he kept his mage gift close to his skin, aware of his unfortunate tendency to dispel enchantments. His father's room had been made fire-proof for good reason. Once there, his bemused curiosity vanished, leaving fury in its wake. He stood at the entrance to his father's inner chambers and listened to none other than Selene trading stories with the emperor.

"...and then, this handsy servant said, 'a bitch like you should know her place.' So I told that little slime, 'yes, it's standing above you with my heel on your throat.' And then bam! He fell like a toppled tree! Guess where my heel was?"

"On his damn throat! Ha!" The emperor laughed.

"Is it true you literally skewered a man in a debate? Because I've always had this glorious image in my head. Please tell me it's true."

"Darling, I didn't just skewer him. I did it with my own damn scept re...while it was on fire!"

The two were overcome with a fit of laughter. Belisarius' jaw locked up with the force of his clenched teeth.

"This is some seriously good shit, Darius. A girl could get used to this."

"Only the finest fire brandy for my future daughter-in-law."

"Oh please, as if Prince Stick-Up-His-Ass would actually marry a girl like me. Besides, Iliana and I are setting sail in style when this whole thing is over with, never to return."

"Don't spoil my fun, little girl. That's an imperial edict!"

"Alright, so you can come with us. Think of it—no more stuffy empire. Oblivion as our oyster, waiting for us. I'm taking enough of your money to keep you in silks until you're a dusty old skeleton anyway."

"Ha, yes, I'd heard as much! The praetor looked a bit green around the gills over it, too."

Peals of laughter had Belisarius clenching his fists until the bite of his nails nearly drew blood. He went to rip open the door only to find it an impossible task. He pounded on the wood.

"Open the damn door!"

"Can't! It's welded shut!" Selene called.

"Belli? Is that you?"

"You know, I've been meaning to ask, but just who in the hells is Belli?"

Belisarius concentrated his anger and kicked the doors apart. Luckily, the metal was still warm and pliant. They flung open, the sight greeting him enough to get his blood boiling all over again. Neither were properly dressed. Both were covered in soot, their hair wildly unkempt. His father sat in a pair of singed pants, while Selene wore nothing more than a slip barely covering her lithe thighs. He tore his gaze away to find a bottle of expensive spirits on the table, half empty.

"Belli, my boy, you didn't tell me you had such a lively fiancée!"

"What are you doing here?" Belisarius growled at Selene.

"My goodness, *Belli*, get your mind out of the gutter. There's a perfectly reasonable explanation." She waggled her brows as she played with the disastrously short hem of her slip.

"Please, enlighten me," he ground out.

"Well, I was stealing a book and wound up here, where Darius attempted to capture me. I ended up poisoning him, but he'd welded the door shut at that point, and the servant's entrance doesn't open, so we decided to have a few drinks and trade war stories. See? Perfectly reasonable."

"You poisoned *my father!?*" Belisarius stomped further into the room and grabbed Selene by her arms.

"Oh, please. His arm will thaw out in an hour, and the other one was just a teensie, weensie psychoactive poison that wore off ages ago. Stop being so hysterical."

His father waved it off like it was nothing.

"She gave as good as she got. I gave her the book as a gift."

He glowered at Selene. She shrugged.

"You're incorrigible! I'm attempting to prevent another Great War, and here you are playing the thief and cavorting with my father in your undergarments instead of living up to your end of our bargain!"

"Gods below, I missed a fucking tea party! If your empire crumbles because I didn't sit nice and pretty with Domina Jewel Snob So-And-So, talking ponies and flowers, this whole damn continent is doomed anyway. Besides, I can be a shameless hussy with anyone I want!"

"Not while you're living in this palace you won't be! That event mattered because your absence showed how little respect you have for me in the most public of forums. If this ruse is to work, you have to at least *pretend* to be someone I might consider an appropriate wife! That means you act like a gods-damned noble, attend the events and, yes, talk ponies and flowers with every airhead in the palace if the situation calls for it!" He rounded on her, gripping her slim, bare shoulders in his hands.

Selene sneered, undaunted.

"As far as I see it, that's your problem, not mine. If you weren't such an arrogant bore, you'd see that the one who has to act like the love-struck fool to pull this off is you—not me. I played my part as the eccentric daddy hid away all those years. Be a bit fucking odd if I change my personality now. My deal with the magister means I get up to all the antics and make my sisters look like well-mannered dolls in comparison. Don't want to start a war? Don't try to change the script I've been given."

Belisarius released Selene as if stung, glaring as he wrestled with his anger. He hated it, but she might actually be right. Everyone had witnessed her shocking display the night before.

"Belli, don't be a brat. If you can't stomach the thought of being an actor on this stage you've set, then devise another plan. Otherwise, what the girl says makes sense. Hells, if you don't want to play at being in love, *I'll* play the part."

Not his father, too? When would this nightmare end? Selene gasped in mock shock, a hand on her chest as she fluttered her lashes. Belisarius looked away from that damn slip, resolving to ban the use of such thin, sheer materials in their future construction.

"You dirty old goat. You think you could keep up with my wild ways?" She eyed Belisarius with what could only be described as evil glee. "How would you feel about calling me *mother*?"

A moment of gut-wrenching horror at the thought changed his mind. Gods save him, he should never have conceived this awful scheme. But no matter how he thought about it, there was no other way to peacefully lure the magistri to Nadioch—not unless he also wanted them at the head of their own armies, or at the very least, ready to openly commit regicide.

"I *feel* overcome with my love for you, dearest Selene." He ground out the words as if he were chewing glass.

"Good! Because if we're going to do this, I have a few ideas."

Belisarius' soul withered ever so slightly to hear it.

CHAPTER 10

Nicephorus' world was composed of castoffs. He'd spent his life tediously sewing all the disparate pieces into an effective whole, as if putting together an ugly patchwork quilt. The sprawling, complex bureaucracy on whose apex he stood had been built using superfluous sons, noble bastards and other talented men denied the position of heir or lacking the prized elemental magic championed by the elites of the provinces. Even in the palace, bureaucrats not extensively trained in some martial skill or another were considered beneath noblemen who'd never worked for the benefit of the people a day in their lives.

Meanwhile, due to the prince's reforms, his bureaucracy ensured clean water flowed throughout Lethe via aqueducts, the price of bread was kept reasonable, intracontinental trade blossomed, legal disputes were settled quickly and fairly, and banditry and piracy were kept to a minimum. Yet it was never enough. No matter how brilliant their minds or how useful their interventions, convincing large swaths of the illustri and nobilissimi of the merit of the reforms proved difficult when their chief concerns were for the opinions of the magistri, who by their nature despised any change to the status quo. Given these headaches, the very last thing Nicephorus wished to add to his extensive daily workload was playing nanny to an unpredictable, antisocial poison mage.

Nicephorus pulled a cord of black silk hanging from the ceiling of his office. A series of pulleys alerted the correct branch of government of his need. As if emerging from under the surface of a placid lake, a mage stepped from the shadows in the corner of his office. His uniform was dark, a veil concealing his features. He was the logothete in charge of spycraft and security at the palace, an executive bureaucrat serving directly beneath the praetor.

"Domina Milena Amethyst has wandered off. Please locate her and notify me of her whereabouts. Be cautious and do not approach her. I'm told she can be quite lethal."

"I'm sure we'll find her shortly, Praetor." The shadow mage bowed, disappearing into darkness once more.

Moments later, a knock on his door interrupted him from the report he was reading. The flushed face of a young notarios, the pale pink stripes on his tunic denoting him as the lowest bureaucrat on the rungs of the governmental ladder, peered into his room. Nicephorus frowned. The boy's manager, an asekretis, would have to teach him proper protocol. No one was to disturb the praetor so casually.

"Pardon the intrusion, Praetor. But I just saw Domina Sapphire working at the blacksmith's without an escort."

Nicephorus jumped up from his seat, his expression grim. He could feel a headache beginning to bloom behind his eyes. What was so difficult about playing the part of a pampered noblewoman? Apparently, he would need to mind two mages today.

⪼⪼⪼⪥ ⪤⪻⪻⪻⪻

Iliana hated the cumbersome, bejewelled skirts she was forced to wear to these damn parties. She reflected on this as she turned her back to the prince and his men to make her exit, nearly tangling her legs and tripping like the fool she was. Gods only knew how much her latest fit of temper would cost her.

She stomped up steps and took a calming breath, trying to walk with her usual gait down wide, extravagantly decorated corridors where nobles sashayed over floral mosaics without a care in the world. Upon returning to her suite, five sets of deadened eyes and an eerie silence met her in the shared parlour of Magister Sapphire's daughters. Each engaged in the quiet, feminine pursuits of needlepoint, painting and reading etiquette manuals. Iliana envied them their skill with the needle and thread, but little else. Their eyes drifted from her back to their activities without comment.

Her frustration at this ridiculous farce was beginning to grate. Obediently following the dictates of both magister and prince, she was forced to be a puppet, commanded to dance and entertain on a whim. It was suffocating. She needed to get the hells off this damned continent, to leave the foolish political games for the nobles to fight themselves. Better they bloody each other's noses than bend her till she broke. Not even the supposedly level-headed strategos had raised his voice in her, or Selene's, defence.

Selene was obviously doing as she pleased, which was no different than usual. Iliana only hoped the prince decided not to let his anger dictate his decisions. She sighed. Her hands itched to create something, to lose herself in something familiar and reassuring. She shut the door to her own separate room and squeaked in surprise when the prim servant girl stood and greeted her.

"I'm sorry, I didn't see you there."

Entirely unfazed, the girl smiled.

"Is there anything I can help you with, Your Resplendence?"

Maybe it was time Iliana began doing as she pleased, consequences be damned. Her sisters were in no danger, and she yearned to make something that might one day gut a man just like the magister. Or teach a lesson to that blockheaded strategos.

"Yes. Help me into some sensible clothes. I'm going to visit the smith."

Decision made, the serving girl helped her out of her complicated, bejewelled dress and into a nondescript frock. Thus garbed, she wound her way through the palace unmolested. Iliana had spotted the smoke of the blacksmith's workshops on her first tour of the palace grounds. Now she simply had to convince them that a magister's daughter was both capable and determined enough to be there.

If the results of this farce weren't so essential to the peace and stability of Lethe, Marduk might have laughed at the prince's predicament. Having just met Belisarius on his rounds, Marduk had been informed of the latest development. Unfortunately, the poison mage had been quite correct. A change in character drastic enough to meet the prince's requirements would raise suspicions higher than the eyebrows Selene already elicited with her current behaviour.

Of the three of them, Marduk felt he had the most enviable assignment. He neither had to spar with a harridan nor make polite conversation with the living dead. He even found himself perversely charmed by Iliana's fits of boldness. As he headed towards the sparring grounds, he noticed an unusual gathering of men peering into the smith's workshops. Had the old man finished a new sword? Marduk couldn't help his detour.

"You can feel the difference in weight, can't you? It's perfectly balanced. Now try hitting the target," Iliana said.

"Five silvers says it's as off as the first."

"I'll take that, I say it hits closer."

"I'd say you'll be out five silvers. Old man couldn't hit the side of a barn if he tried."

Marduk watched, arms crossed, as Iliana coached the old blacksmith into holding a dagger and aiming for a target across the workshop. The entirety of the shop had ceased work for the spectacle. Marduk almost felt sorry for the girl. The man's aim was legendarily bad. Still, he would be here to salvage the situation when it—

The dagger sank into the centre of the target. Shocked silence reigned.

"And that, gentlemen, is the power of a master metals mage. There is simply nothing superior to a well-enchanted blade."

Excited chatter drowned out what Iliana said to the blacksmith, who gazed up at her with profound respect, shaking her hand. Good gods, blades that never missed their mark? Arrows that always found their target? The possibilities were endless. Marduk's mind buzzed with the potentials. Plot or not, he wanted this mage, even if she did have a tendency towards inadvisable outbursts when angered.

"Domina Sapphire, a moment of your time," Marduk called, voice and body cutting through the crowd.

Men parted with respectful mutters of *'Strategos'*. Iliana looked up, her painfully plain dress smeared with grease and grit, hair swept up, platinum tendrils slicked against her tawny skin. One such tendril curled down her neck, inviting the eye to follow it to her cleavage. Which was substantial. He swallowed back a sudden hungry pang.

She blushed, fingering her plain dress, her brow knotting.

She turned to curtsy to the workmen.

"Gentlemen."

They bowed en-masse, some more clumsily than others.

"Visit anytime you wish, Domina."

She nodded, giving Marduk her hand, her fingers curling in on a gasp as she caught sight of the dark smears on her hands. He took her hand anyway, tucking it into the crook of his arm. If that meant her hip occasionally brushed against him, he was not one to complain. She was quiet, refusing to meet his eyes. He supposed she might think herself in trouble.

"How are you with a sword?"

"Passable, I think." She raised her pale brows, her tone uncertain.

"And with a sword you enchanted personally?"

Her gaze turned shrewd. Good.

"Why do you ask?"

"Because I'm willing to offer you a lucrative contract with the Imperial Forge if you can impress me with your very best enchanted bladework."

"And what would I need to do in order to impress you?" she asked, eyes wide as she leaned into him.

Too close. He could feel her every soft curve. He cleared his throat.

"Show me something I've never seen before."

Iliana chewed her full, bottom lip, wetting it with her tongue. Did she know what she was doing? Gods help him if she did.

"Deal."

She stopped, held out her hand and shook his with confidence. He couldn't wait to see what she was capable of.

⟫⟫⟫⟶ ⟵⟪⟪⟪

A trickle of sweat ran from Iliana's hairline down her neck. Her hands touched the blade in front of her, her magic pulsing through it, remaking it as though it were being forged anew. Even quality metal like this could only handle a few enchantments in total before crumbling or shattering. Her magic was, as most magic, a matter of willing it into existence and endless practice. For enchantments in particular, her specialty, it meant giving an object precise, simple instructions—if this, then that. And every metal and alloy spoke a slightly different dialect. Iliana prided herself on knowing them all. She'd heard some in foreign lands had to speak or write their spells, but in Lethe, it was all about intention made manifest, her magic the language and the speaker.

This enchantment had to be truly impressive to win a contract with the Imperial Forge. Their metals mages set the standards throughout the empire, and they had access to rare ores with boundless possibilities and languages she'd never heard. Undaunted, she knew her strengths. She just needed the right amount of drama. The last exciting thing that had shaken the world of enchanted blades had been rust-proofing steel decades ago. Iliana suspected the comfort of guaranteed patronage at the Forge dulled their minds. Setting the first blade aside, she picked up another.

Iliana enchanted the second blade with a special something she'd mused about. Never having wielded it in practice, it was a gamble, but with the right amount of luck and bravado it could work. Enchantment complete, she rose from her seat beside the rack of weapons, picking up her first blade and stepped into the sparring ring. Her opponent was an ebony-skinned, green-eyed young man in his leather practice armour. He was tall, well-muscled and lean. The way he held himself and moved suggested he could balance on the head of a pin and strike fast. Thankfully, she only needed to be able to parry a single blow for this enchantment to work.

"I want to see the difference between a standard sword from the armoury and your own work." Marduk turned towards his man. "Treat this seriously, but do not harm the domina."

"I would never dream of it." The young man raised his chin, affronted.

Marduk clapped him on the shoulder as he exited the ring.

"Just a caution, Julius—she has no formal training."

"Understood." He nodded.

Damn! For this to work, she needed him to truly swing at her.

"If you're too soft, I'll cut right through you," she taunted.

A mischievous grin lit the man's face, transforming the seriousness of a soldier into one of delight. He was dazzling.

"Begin!"

He lunged. Iliana only managed to parry at the last moment, but it was enough. She had sensed enough of the other blade's enchantment to get an idea of what she needed. As they circled each other she added a little extra something into her own sword.

"Come on now, I'll even let you get a free hit in. I swear it on my honour." He bowed.

Iliana was sure her grin was anything but ladylike.

"Honour is for the dead!"

Iliana rushed him, swinging her sword down on his. He blocked it in just the way she predicted he would. His grin was wiped clean off his face when her blade cut through his in an instant, forcing him to leap back before her blade went through him just as easily.

The young man looked at her, looked at his half blade, tossed it aside and marched towards her as tense silence consumed the arena. He dropped to one knee before her.

"Marry me."

The silence broke to the sound of hoots and shouts. Iliana blushed and scowled. She was here to showcase her work, not flirt with soldiers, no matter how handsome or talented.

"Don't jest. It's not amusing."

"But I-"

"Alright Julius, thank you. Domina, I believe you enchanted a second weapon. I would be honoured to be your opponent this time." Marduk pulled the man up and delivered him to the ribbing and jokes of his comrades. The green-eyed soldier appeared crestfallen.

Iliana took a deep breath before she nodded. It would do her no good to be beset by nerves now. This time she would need all her focus. Placing the first blade back in its stand, she picked up the second. Her showstopper. She squared her shoulders, ready as Marduk was handed a regular sword. Silence enveloped the crowd once more.

"I will go slowly."

"It's your funeral," Iliana bluffed.

All those hours practicing her poker face with Selene had been worth it for this moment alone. His genuine smile nearly struck her dumb. Her heart skipped in her chest, and she had the strangest urge to smile back. Perhaps the soldiers of the imperial army were chosen for appearances as well as skill. They circled, and, true to his word, his swing was something she could parry, if that had been her intent. Instead, she allowed the metals to smash before unleashing the enchantment in the blade. Startled cries erupted from the crowd as the blades, once solid, liquefied, melded together and gathered on Iliana's hilt to create a sword twice as long and wicked-looking.

Marduk was left holding a bladeless hilt. She pointed her blade at him. With all the showmanship she could muster, she raised her chin, a small smile curving her lips, brows ever so slightly arched, her tone politely bemused.

"Have I impressed you?"

Raucous cheers erupted from the soldiers. Marduk tossed his hilt on the ground and grinned, the look in his eyes wild.

"May I?" he asked.

Iliana handed him the reformed blade. He whistled as he swung it experimentally.

"It's a thing of beauty."

Iliana did her best not to preen too obviously at his praise.

"It's the first time I've experimented with that enchantment. I'm pleased that you approve."

He stared at the melded blade anew and tested its weight.

"The contract? It's yours—if you want it."

Iliana smiled and curtsied. It was all she could do not to squeak and scream and jump with excitement. Her inner metals mage drooled at the prospect of playing with rare ores. Rumour had it they could hold endless enchantments.

"I'll give it serious consideration."

Just as Marduk was about to speak, a twinkle in his eyes and a roguish grin making her heart flutter, a familiar voice cut through the animated conversation of the sparring grounds.

"Domina Sapphire, may I interrupt?"

Marduk watched as the praetor looked Iliana up and down, glaring, his lips curled in disgust. His hand shot out from his pristine robes, demanding hers. She curled in on herself, shoulders tight as she catalogued every supposed fault in her appearance. Trying to tuck her wild platinum locks away only made the state of her hands clear, and in attempting to hide them in her skirts, her eyes tracked every dark smear and wrinkle in the fabric. The master metals mage shrank as she held out her hand like a misbehaving child.

Usually, Marduk got on well with Nicephorus, but this scene struck him as profoundly ugly. Just seconds ago, she had been full of deserved pride, vibrating with barely concealed excitement. Now that woman had been washed away, found wanting by someone wholly unappreciative of her gifts. Even his men had gone silent, their gazes burning holes of distaste into the person of the praetor.

"My apologies, Praetor. Domina Sapphire was busy leaving us in awe of her skill. I would be honoured to escort Her Resplendence to her next appointment."

Marduk stepped forward and snatched her hand out of the air before it could reach that of the praetor. He tucked it into the crook of his arm once more, his free hand covering hers. She would be under his protection from now on. If the praetor wished to criticize and belittle her, he would have to go through Marduk first.

Clearly displeased, Nicephorus dropped his hand, his smile tight and unconvincing.

"Very well. If you would please follow me."

When Iliana's hand tightened on his arm, a little flutter of warmth bloomed in his chest. He felt even taller than his seven feet as he walked behind the praetor, a talented beauty on his arm.

Chapter 11

Belisarius sighed, pushing away from the reports littering his desk. After news of Iliana's gift to him had spread, his other bride candidates had made a game of it, hoping to earn themselves his favour through increasingly elaborate tokens of affection. The latest and most extravagant gift had come from Domina Opal. Being the only daughter of a magister had the advantage that all her father's efforts were focused solely on her, rather than spread out amongst several daughters. Consequently, Belisarius was now the owner of an ill-tempered griffin.

Lethe kept to itself, and so mages generally had little knowledge of or contact with the creatures and peoples of the other lands. From his recollection, griffins were noble beasts capable of communication with other species. This one only shrieked indignantly. He would have to find a way to return it to its own lands without causing offence. Yet another task added to his growing list of responsibilities.

It was a strain to reign in his wandering mind as the praetor addressed him in his study, giving him the most succinct summation of the many goings-on of the empire.

"The horses have been prepared, Your Royal Highness," Nicephorus announced after one of the notarios whispered into his ear.

"Hopefully this activity will prove to be less fraught with complications than those of the past few days," Belisarius grumbled, shoving unwelcome memories of Selene's smug grin from his mind.

A mounted hunt would appeal to the more athletic of his prospective brides. He had no need for a woman who couldn't handle more than the occasional ball. The responsibilities of an emperor required stamina. The position of empress would be no less exhausting. The solitary nature of a hunt would also ensure he'd be unable to accept further gifts. He should be relieved, yet something sat ill with him. He paused in the act of standing.

"Your Royal Highness?" Nicephorus asked.

"Do they even know how to seat a horse?"

"To whom are you referring?"

"Our false dominae. You don't suppose they know how to ride?"

Nicephorus' hands tightened perceptibly on his sheaf of parchments.

"I must confess, I am unaware of the extent of their educations in that regard. Given what we know, it is unlikely."

A farmer might have occasion to use an ox, a wealthy merchant a horse, but the imposters were neither. Belisarius groaned. How in the hells was he to make this charade work if Selene appeared to fail every test?

Sweat broke out across every inch of Selene's skin as fear quickened her breath. It was as tall as a mountain, and doubtless had maimed at least a few of its former riders. She took a cautious step back. Marduk ran his hand along its wild mane. When it tossed its head and whinnied, she flinched. Selene was terrified of horses. Evil beasts.

She'd tried to convince herself, with the help of at least half a bottle of Lethe's finest wine, that given enough libations, she'd be able to approach the damn creature. Except being a poison mage meant the desired effect would never occur and even in her panic she well knew it. If only she'd raided the royal stores of poison, she might've found one that acted long enough for her to mount the terrible creature. Iliana, the traitor, had been cautious at first, but seemed to get the hang of it just fine, making Selene feel even more foolish. A cruel torture invented by the prince, that's what this was.

"I will do you anything you want, just don't ask me to get near that thing." Selene backed away, keeping her eyes on the horsey threat.

"Bucephalus is a fine horse and very even tempered. I've already assisted your friend and given her a quick lesson. Iliana was able at least to trot along quite well with very little trouble. Many of the women will use this as an excuse to flirt with the noblemen. You needn't do any more than that today," Marduk replied as he checked the straps on its saddle. Yes—he would need to do that, so when the beasty inevitably threw her, her ankle could tangle in the contraption. Then it would drag her to her death.

When Marduk approached with the outrageous intent of seating her atop it, Selene skated out of his reach.

"I won't do it."

"What could you possibly object to? Surely the fearsome poison mage isn't terrified of horses?"

"When you've been run out of as many towns as I have... Let's just say, I've got a taste for just how unpleasant it is to be hunted on horseback. Besides, I can see it's got an evil streak. Just look at those shifty, horsey eyes! It's going to try to eat my fingers and toes, I know it!"

"This isn't negotiable, poison mage. Once you're on his back, you'll realise how ridiculous you're being." Marduk shifted side to side, arms akimbo, doing his best to corner her.

When his arms shot out, Selene ducked, dove between his legs and scrambled up, running as fast as she could manage. Thank the gods riding outfits necessitated form-fitting trousers.

Marduk was hot on her leather heels. When she turned a corner, she nearly ran over Domina Opal, along with a group of the other dominae. Being equivalent in height and surprisingly nimble, the island domina turned deftly out of Selene's way. Her dark brow arched over black eyes with opalescent whites. She wore a red long-sleeved tunic over fitted silk trousers, her jet hair swept painfully tight up off her face. Only her red-painted lips provided colour to her otherwise porcelain-like paleness.

"Domina Amethyst!"

Selene spared a single glance as Marduk stumbled to a stop in front of the gaggle of highborn women. They busied themselves gasping and squeaking their indignant surprise. Knowing he was unlikely to plough through them, Selene fled. But soon, she found herself out of earshot and out of places to run. Horses lined the stable on both sides, all popping their enormous, terrible heads out to see who had been causing the commotion. The better to bite her, she was certain. The only stall without one was at the very end of the hall. She slid under the raised door and came face to face with something quite unexpected.

Iliana carefully guided her horse to stand beside the others. The dominae were in fine form, resplendent in their long-sleeved, embroidered silk riding outfits, sitting atop their beautiful mounts as though they'd been born there. It was as she sidled up amongst them that she caught the flavour of their gossip.

"Did you see her? She was positively spooked. I don't think I've seen anything so disgraceful in some time."

"Well, perhaps not since the first night when she swaggered up to the prince like a barbarian."

Giggles rippled out.

"One should really pity the esteemed Magister Amethyst. I heard he's kept her hidden most of her life. Her sisters may be dull, but at least they've managed to comport themselves like dominae. I doubt we'll hear much of Domina Milena once the princess consort has been chosen."

Iliana wanted to open her mouth in protest, but she was cut off by the fanfare of the prince's entrance onto the grounds. His riding attire was smartly done in red and black, his long black hair braided and pinned. His horse was enormous, its jet coat glossy with health. The prince was kitted out with bow and quiver.

"Good afternoon, dominae. Today's activity is a horseback hunt. There will be a prize for the woman with the most impressive kill—a private dinner with the man of her choosing. Those who do not wish to partake are free to ride along the more tended trails to the East of the hunting grounds. If you wish to participate, please let your attendant know, and you'll be provided a bow and quiver with twelve arrows. Each set of arrows will have uniquely coloured fletches in order to pair each huntress with her kill. The competition will last three hours or until your quivers run out of arrows, whichever comes first. Happy hunting, my dear dominae!" The prince turned away before commanding his steed to dash into the woods in the distance. The picture he presented had a great many of the women sighing with appreciation.

A flurry of activity accompanied the prince's departure, with many of the dominae deciding to compete. Iliana wondered if maybe the coloured fletches had been chosen in order to prevent a nefarious thinning of the herd. There was questionable wisdom in sending out a few dozen women with weapons into a thickly wooded area, especially when every one of them was hunting for beasts as well as a particular husband. Deciding discretion was the better part of valour, Iliana opted to trot along safer paths. She only hoped Selene would decide to do likewise. Whenever she deigned to show up, that was.

Chapter 12

"Filthy fucking mages."

The stable smelled of fresh hay. Her own ragged breath was the only sound. Dim light filtered through windows too high for her to clamber through. Only Selene and the griffin were present in the stall. Had she just hallucinated? It didn't feel like she'd come into contact with a novel poison, but she patted herself down all the same.

"Lost something, you dumb cow? Do cry for me. I've been longing to taste mage tears."

The griffin lay on its stomach, its birdlike forelimbs folded in front of it while its leonine half lounged behind, its enormous wings folded up to cover most of its large body, fur blending seamlessly into feathers. Its head sported a wicked beak, intelligent eyes, sharply pricked, tufted ears, and, if she wasn't mistaken, small, curled horns growing out behind them. It was magnificent to behold after all her years devouring whatever information she could about life beyond Lethe. Had it truly spoken?

"Gods, your face looks stupid. Bring it closer, you plain creature, and I'll rearrange it for you." It leered at her, its lion's tail waving slowly from side to side.

"You know, I've either struck gold with a new hallucinogen, or griffins can speak," Selene mused, studying the creature before her.

"Domina Amethyst!" Marduk roared in the distance.

Selene jumped, just barely stuffing down an undignified squeak.

"Let's make a deal, griffin—you hide me in your wings, and I won't poison you into compliance," Selene whispered, grinning like a predator, hoping to intimidate the great beast.

"Come closer, and I'll rip out an eye, you smelly cretin!" the griffin hissed.

"Poison it is!"

Selene inhaled deeply and blew out a strong sedative, instantly knocking out the beast. She hurried under its wing. Just in time. The strategos' footsteps thundered on the wooden planks outside the griffin's stall. Frustrated thumping accompanied the shrieks of demon horses.

"Fuck!" Marduk swore, the pounding of his footsteps growing dimmer by the moment.

A few more beats of silence, and Selene felt safe creeping out from under her makeshift hiding spot. It was not a moment too soon. The griffin was rousing. When it eyed her, she jumped back. It leapt at her, shrieking anew. Only chains kept it from mauling her.

"You little heathen! You dare to use your filthy magics on me?! If not for these damned chains, I'd tear you limb from limb!"

"Gods, calm down already. Most sedatives don't kill, and you're obviously fine. Besides, you called me a dumb cow. Be grateful I didn't dose you with poison oak."

The creature blinked, startled. It stopped trying to pull free of its chains and sat up, smoothing its feathers. It stared down its beak at her with cautious superiority. Gone was the vicious mockery in its voice, replaced with an air of refinement.

"You can understand me, girl?"

"Unless this is all some brand-new poison I'm enjoying?"

"Unlikely. You know, I didn't take you for the type."

"What type?"

"A murderer and a thief."

Despite her initial success, Iliana was unable to convince her horse to do as she wished. The honey-coloured mare had decided that it very much liked the flowers bracketing the gravel-lined leisure path. Branches of trees reached overhead to provide dappled shade. In the distance, a field opened up. Nobles trotted along crystalline brooks and perfectly tended hedges as their servants hurried along on foot at respectful distances. Despite trying to discreetly pull the reigns and whispering threats, the beast was implacable. Other noblewomen were beginning to comment as they passed, giggling as Iliana's back was turned by her mare's positioning. At least they couldn't see her mortified blush. The strategos had taken the time to teach her how to mount her horse and guide it gently, but in his rush to give Selene the same lesson, he'd forgotten to teach Iliana how to dismount. Selene's instinctive fear of horses must be catching. The ground appeared to be quite a way down, and Iliana feared having the recalcitrant animal throw her for trying to dismount awkwardly. Images of the horse taking off while she was still attached ran through her head. It was true no one could die of embarrassment, but the last thing she could afford to do was make more of an ass of herself than this horse already had.

"Stupid strategos. Stupid horse."

"Don't blame the beast for your inexperience, Domina."

Iliana gasped and tried to turn around. Her blush deepened as Marduk kept ducking back into her blind spot as she looked around her other shoulder. She growled, crossed her arms and refused to try again. His laugh was deep and rich as he took the reins from her hands and guided the horse along the path. The stubborn beast acted as though it had always been as sweet and biddable as a loyal dog.

Marduk was resplendent in his riding gear, his tanned skin and corded muscles on full display. The military stripes on his tunic and the large gold buckle of his belt denoted his rank, but it was the awareness in his eyes and his precise movements which would have given him away were he to discard the vestments of his station. Or perhaps she had simply taken to staring overlong at him. In her defence, there was a great deal of him to ponder.

"You never showed me how to dismount. I've been stuck sitting here like an ass," Iliana complained, trying to steer her thoughts better than she could her horse.

"You can blame your friend for that. I've been trying to hunt her down since I left you. To think a person can be so scared of a horse," Marduk snorted.

"Selene has many faults, but that isn't one of them. Running for her life while being chased by mounted men is hardly likely to have endeared them to her." Iliana's reply was icy. She would not tolerate people mocking her friend.

"You always come to her defence. Have you considered that she might have been in the wrong on those many occasions?"

"I'm not a fool, Strategos. But if you purchase poison to supposedly kill rats, and then decide that the rat in need of killing is a spouse or parent or rival, is it really the poison's fault? I make blades for a living, yet no one categorically sees me as a murderer. Am I to blame for all the blood a blade sheds in the hands of another? Surely you know those prejudices are just excuses used to shift blame to people without power."

"While I agree with your general sentiment, I very much doubt your friend marketed her poisons as anything so innocent as rat poison or insecticide." Marduk arched his thick brow.

Iliana tried to appear affronted and serious, the better to hide her cringe. Selene's merchant smile slipped into her mind's eye, along with her usual spiel to customers: *Silently, gruesomely or painfully, we have the perfect lethal poison for you! Humiliating, debilitating or just plain unpleasant, poisons to teach 'em a lesson they won't soon forget. Get them here!*

Iliana steadfastly refused to admit as much to Marduk. Best to change the topic.

"Will you be so good as to show me how to get off this horse?"

Marduk laughed, winking at her with a knowing grin.

"We can go down the path to where the trees are thicker. There won't be so many prying eyes."

"What is the domina doing with a *feral*?"

"If *my* father caught me with a beast mage, I'd be disowned."

"Shh! Isn't that the strategos?"

Marduk's back straightened at the insult, his dark eyes narrowing. Disbelief had Iliana in its grip. Her anger towards him melted away in an instant, replaced with a fierce protectiveness towards the one man who had shown true respect for her skill.

Here stood the most powerful strategos in the empire, a weapon's master and a prodigy, and petty noblewomen without a single accomplishment between them dared to spit on him for being a beast mage? It made Iliana's blood boil. If only she'd had a few darts on her person. She supposed she'd have to settle for words. She painted a beatific smile on her face, placing her hand on his cheek.

"My dear strategos, please try to forgive them their ignorance. I'm certain that when the prince hears of their impertinence, he will see that their families are dispossessed. Have mercy and allow them one last day to enjoy their noble lifestyle."

Marduk's eyes widened. A slow, harsh smile lit his handsome face. He took one of her hands in his and kissed the palm.

"Domina Sapphire, your beautiful smile could sway even a heart of stone. I will allow them one last day of ignorant bliss. The gods know they will spend the rest of their lives in mindful penance." He shot the women a lethal glare before they galloped off.

Marduk said no more, leading Iliana's horse onto the secluded path. When they were out of earshot and sight of the main path, she touched his shoulder.

"Are you alright, Strategos?"

He answered without bothering to face her.

"I have thicker skin than you might imagine, and require neither saving nor coddling by a woman more than a decade my junior."

Iliana bristled. Thick skin, her foot! Well, if he wanted to take out his frustrations on someone, he could find another target. She'd met a great many men who were charming enough until they were rendered aid by someone they saw as their lesser.

"Fine! Would the prickly old geezer help this needless busybody off her horse?"

Marduk's stony gaze had her realizing her mistake. Gods, she needed to sew her own mouth shut. She'd gotten brave, seated tall atop the horse, forgetting just how intimidating the he could be. The only solution was to brazen it out.

It was harder than she'd imagined. His large hands made her feel entirely too petite as he assisted her. When her hands braced on his wide shoulders, she did her best not to meet his eyes. Was it her imagination, or had he set her on the ground altogether too slowly? She stood tall and held back her embarrassment, but when she chanced a peak at his face, his intense gaze had her heart fluttering.

"I said it wasn't required, not that it wasn't appreciated."

"Oh," Iliana replied, swallowing.

Was that a tree at her back? Her cheeks heated, and she wished she could crawl under a rock and hide. He lifted her hand and bushed his lips across it, his eyes never leaving hers. She was pinned to the spot.

"Thank you. But I don't want you to needlessly entangle yourself with the wagging tongues of arrogant noblewomen. Not on my account."

"I'm no noblewoman. What do I care if they speak ill of me?"

"You do yourself a disservice, but I-"

He was interrupted by a dark shadow passing quickly overhead. Iliana looked up instinctively. The tail end of large, dark wings flew overhead.

"Wow," Iliana breathed.

"Surely you've seen a winged beast mage?"

"Well, yes, but the magistri are adamant about not allowing them to fly in their provinces. I'm used to seeing wind mages. It's really a thing to behold when you can see them in all their glory," Iliana replied, still gazing skyward.

"All their glory, eh?" Marduk grumbled. She blinked, and the pain in his eyes was gone. Had she imagined it? "So, you'd fancy a ride through the sky?"

"Oh, no. I've never been good with heights," Iliana replied.

This beast mage was all over the map today. One minute he was all business, the next teasing, then cold, then hot, then sullen. For some reason, her reply seemed to make him feel better. How had he ever become the strategos with such a mercurial personality?

"Why do you look so happy to hear that?" She raised her brow.

"I was just thinking I'd rather not have my soldiers flying you about."

"Are you saying I'm too heavy?" Iliana scowled.

Marduk laughed—again. Apparently, she provided him with no end of amusement.

"I'm saying I don't want to share you with any of them."

"Oh," Iliana replied, cheeks heating once again.

He was standing altogether too close. She could smell his oiled leathers, feel the heat of him. Her waist burned where he'd had his hands on her, strong and sure. What would it feel like to have him trace his calloused fingers along her neck, her cheek, her lips?

"Indeed," Marduk grinned.

When he leaned in, butterflies fluttered restlessly in her gut. She was in definite danger of feeling a bit too much attraction for the handsome mage, torn between a desire to kiss him and the urge to flee. She'd always dreamt of leaving the continent and the fear of her father behind. The last thing she needed was to feel tied here, to know her life could be in danger at any moment, death as swift as a flash flood. But as Marduk slowly leaned closer, his dark eyes softening, the time to dither slipped from her grasp. Whether it was ultimately fortunate or unfortunate, she would never know, but a distraction came on swift wings.

The branches of the canopy creaked in a turbulent wind, the beating of immense wings audible. Amidst the clamour, Iliana heard feminine shrieking. An enormous dark shadow bearing a breath-taking wingspan flew overhead.

"I'm sorryyyyyyyy!" a feminine voice howled pitifully, quickly fading into the distance.

"Selene?"

"Fuck."

CHAPTER 13

"Are you suicidal, or just stupid?" Selene demanded.

"I beg your pardon? I'm neither! I'm from a noble lineage. Can't you see how beautiful my plumage is? Well?" The griffin extended his wing pointedly.

"Stupid, then. I'll have you know, all my murders were committed in self-defence only. That aside, if you knew all that, why in all the hells would you say as much? I'm pretty sure other murderers would just slit your throat, fancy feathers or not."

"I did stay quiet while I was on the pirate's ship that brought me here, but that's because they'd have just as soon eaten me as sold me." The griffin shivered, his feathers ruffling. "The stench was nigh unbearable," he said, haunted.

"Is this a griffin thing, or a *you* thing?" Selene asked.

"How discerning! As you suspect, I was cursed by a member of the fae race when I spurned his advances. I haven't been able to take on my common form or communicate with decent sorts since. My life has been one tragic mishap after another. But surely, you'll help me change this? You may have shed blood and lifted a pretty bauble here and there, but you're noble, just like me. Will you help me communicate with your kind and break this curse?"

Selene had discerned no such thing, other than that the creature before her was an idiot. Even in the isolationist empire, mages knew that fae were bad news, to be avoided at all costs. Still, he could be useful.

There was a mounted hunt to win, and she refused to ride a demon horse creature. Why not this griffin instead? He could kill something really impressive for her.

"You know, the only thing I'm shocked about is being the first noble you've met who can understand you. Plenty of thieves and murderers among them. But far be it for me to turn down an opportunity like this. What are you called, griffin?"

"I am known as Renfreid, Lord Renfreid. And you, Lady?"

Selene thought on this. According to rumours, knowing a being's name was all the fae needed to lay a spectacular curse. If her name got out in connection with some disgruntled fae, she might find out whether the conjecture was true. Thankfully, she had another she could use as cover.

"Domina Milena Amethyst." Selene curtsied prettily despite her riding attire. "Now let's come to some sort of arrangement, shall we?"

⟫⟫⟩ ⟨⟪⟪

Belisarius had just been informed of Selene's undignified absence from the hunt by one of Marduk's soldiers, who then took off with a bow and launched himself into the sky with a set of feathered wings. While a respite from dealing with Selene's antics was welcome, the thought of spending dinner making more meaningless conversation with another domina had him dreading the evening ahead. At least with Selene, he didn't need to pretend he was enraptured by the conversation.

As the sun drifted through the heavens, the hunt was nearly over. Belisarius took one of the rougher paths back to the castle, a winding, mulchy trail for his horse to trot along, one of his favourites. The sounds of gurgling waters brought him back to the days of his childhood when he, Mother, Father and Marduk would picnic nearby. He emerged from the canopy of thick, dark pines to the sight of a familiar stream and its rocky shore.

In the middle of the stream stood Domina Opal, her riding pants rolled up to reveal pale, slim legs. She held an arrow in her hand as if it were a spear, entirely absorbed in her task. Her horse was off drinking in the distance. In a flash of movement, she jabbed the arrow down and came up with a speared, wriggling fish. When she caught sight of Belisarius, she quickly replaced her sheepish grin with a straightening of her spine.

One of the younger bride candidates, beloved on the islands, Belisarius had taken care not to cause her offense. The culture of the Opal Province allowed their women unprecedented freedoms compared to the women of the continent. Noblewomen of his court often called them wild, immoral and hopelessly masculine. Perhaps, if she won the competition, he would have the chance to ask her about it while gently prying into her father's loyalties.

"Your Royal Highness, I apologize for appearing before you in such a state."

"I take no offence, Domina. In fact, I'm impressed by your skill. Perhaps I'll have the honour of your company tonight?"

With a cheeky smile, the domina placed her hands on her narrow hips.

"I should think so. I've managed to kill two coyotes this afternoon."

Belisarius nodded at her triumph. Two coyotes was a noteworthy kill for a domina. Perhaps he might find an ideal bride during this deception after all.

"Impressive. Would you do me the honour of accompanying me back to the palace, Domina?"

She blinked in surprise, the opalescence of her eyes making them appear even larger in her heart-shaped face.

"I would be delighted, Your Royal Highness. Please, call me Charis."

"Then, Charis-"

A crashing roar echoed out of the woods on the far side of the brook. The domina's horse pricked its ears, sniffed the air and bolted. Belisarius had to fight an equally unsettled response in his own steed. Whatever it was on the other side, his horse was spooked.

"Domina, grab my hand. We must leave!"

Her barefoot pace was slow on the slippery rocks along the shore. She grabbed his hand just as a bear, twice as large as any he'd seen, crashed out of the forest. Belisarius helped her swing up onto his horse as the bear rushed at them. They made it as far as the bushes before the horse's hindquarters were swiped by a massive paw. The horse turned, reared up and clocked the bear in the face with its hooves, throwing Belisarius and Charis to the ground in the process. Belisarius recovered from the fall first, pulling the domina up along with him as he dashed towards the treeline, ignoring his hurts. The pained screams of his horse rang out, and he prayed to all the gods that its death would give them the head start they needed.

"What are you doing?! Aren't you a fire mage? Just kill it!" the domina screamed.

If only it were that simple. He kept his own counsel and continued to pull the domina along as fast as their legs could take them. They managed to get to a clearing on the other side of the strip of woods before crashing branches signalled the bear on their heels. When he dared steal a glance behind him, he could see the beast gaining fast. He had only a small dagger on his person, his bow useless without the quiver that had been secured to the saddle of his horse. So be it. He turned around, pushing the domina onwards.

"Go! Reach the soldiers and tell them to call for a healer! I'll buy you time!"

He didn't bother looking back as the bear bore down on him. Gods, he only hoped there would be enough of him left for the healers to piece back together. Prepared for the worst, he pulled out his dagger, the drumming of his heart drowning out the din. The creature was massive, maddened, weeping burns between patches of singed hair.

As the beast closed the distance, enormous raptors' claws tore down from the sky, catapulting the bear aside, gouging out chunks of meat. Before the bear could recover, a vicious beak lashed out, ripping the bear's thick, bristled throat. The bear dropped to the ground, gurgling. When it weakly tried to rise, the raptor's claws viciously pushed its head down into the bloodied grass. The griffin shrieked in triumph.

"What a rush! I take back what I said about you, Renfreid. No over-stuffed chickens here."

Belisarius couldn't believe his eyes, let alone his ears. Selene sat atop the griffin, clutching what appeared to be small horns behind its pricked, tufted ears. Her hair was in wild disarray, as were her riding clothes. When she turned to him, her eyes were bright, her limbs trembling.

"Oh! Didn't see you there, Belli! I hope this one counts towards the contest." She winked.

"Thank the gods," he said under his breath. If not for this barbarian woman, he'd have been bear food. He supposed he would need to swallow his pride where she was concerned, given that she'd saved him twice now.

"What was that? Oh, never mind. Let me introduce you to Lord Renfreid, a griffin of noble lineage. He and his people would be more than grateful if you would hear him out."

With that the bells rang out, signalling the end of the hunt.

"This had best not be some elaborate prank, Domina Amethyst," Domina Opal hissed in her ear.

"Get ready to make your apologies, Domina Opal. Not every noble-woman is capable of giving the prince a diplomatic cluster-fuck as a gift. You should consider yourself outdone in that regard," Selene replied.

Domina Opal's painted lips thinned into a red, mutinous line. Selene had dramatically swooped onto the hunt's display stage on the back of a griffin, both prince and mauled, slightly burnt bear corpse in tow, wowing the crowd and dismounting with a flourish. Domina Opal had been relieved that the prince was unharmed, then apoplectic that Selene had dared to commandeer her gift to the prince for her own advantage. Sour grapes, as far as Selene was concerned. Even now, Domina Opal openly doubted the tale of a noble, shapeshifting griffin, cursed to remain in only one of his forms, unable to speak with anyone but Selene.

Selene had made very clear to Renfreid that there would be no mention of the particulars of the curse once he was freed from it. He'd agreed, and she'd made one-sided introductions to everyone gathered in an antechamber not far from the stables. Unlike most of the palace, this room was decidedly bare, having only a simple pattern painted on the walls in place of the usual overwhelming colours, patterns and glitz.

Only the emperor had managed to greet the griffin without looking or sounding at all doubtful. The small group of mages shuffled, uneasy, waiting for the spell to be broken by Lethe's best curse mage. The prince, emperor, praetor and strategos, along with Domina Opal, her oldest brother Admiral Zephyros, Iliana and Selene herself all stood at a distance guaranteed by the curse mage to preclude them from catching any of the spell's backlash.

"It is done," mumbled the elderly mage. "I hesitate to say this, but a kiss is required to undo the curse in its entirety, otherwise it will reassert itself in a few days."

Before anyone could reply, Domina Opal shoved Selene forward without anyone being the wiser. Her only reprimand was her older brother's narrowing eyes.

"How sweet of you, Domina Amethyst. No need to be shy, please step forward."

Vindictive bitch!

Still, it was no great burden to kiss the beak of the creature that had let her feel what it was like to fly. All quiet chatter ceased when she approached the griffin.

"Don't look so hard done by, I'm hardly going to bite."

"I seem to recall threats about faces being rearranged."

"Bah, you lot aren't as bad as I'd expected. I mean, you're still a bunch of weird prudes, but some of you have your charms."

"Good to know."

Selene put her hands up and pulled down the griffin's head so that her lips could reach his beak. Once they had, his form imploded into smoke, reforming into the shape of a man. Selene stepped back. He was not just a tall man, but a very naked, very lovingly sculpted man. Renfreid had slightly pointed ears and his hair resembled a lion's mane of red-gold feathers, his skin a warm copper tone. His wicked grin was just a little infectious. He burst out laughing, picked her up by the waist and twirled her around before kissing her passionately on the lips. Selene pushed him away.

"You taste like burnt hair."

"And you taste like freedom, little mage."

He placed her down on the floor. Selene revelled in the stunned looks of those gathered. The first to speak was the emperor himself.

"Please accept my apologies for your troubles in my realm, Lord Renfreid."

"No apologies necessary, Emperor Bloodstone. But perhaps you would avail me of some hospitality before I return to my people?"

"It would be my pleasure to show you all the charms my empire has to offer." The emperor nodded, turned on his heel and walked to the door. "Starting with clothes. Please, follow me."

Renfreid smiled, patted Selene on her head and paused before a very ashen-faced Domina Opal. When he leaned down and whispered in her ear, she seemed to regain some colour in her cheeks. Satisfied, the griffin-turned-man all but skipped after the emperor.

"Please forgive us, Your Royal Highness. If we'd had any idea-" The admiral knelt before Belisarius, his head down, dragging the domina to kneel beside him.

"Rise, Admiral Opal, Domina Opal. This was an entirely unprecedented affair, and one which turned out to have a great many silver linings. Had it not been for Lord Renfreid, I'm certain I would be a dead man. Know that I bear neither you nor Domina Opal any ill will."

"Thank you, Your Royal Highness."

Both siblings bowed deeply before excusing themselves. Nicephorus led the elderly curse mage to the door, thanked him for his service, and inquired how his students were progressing before the door closed on their conversation. Iliana turned to Selene and pulled her up in a fierce hug of her own.

"You really are loved by some strange god, Selene."

"I know. He might have lint for brains, but gods, did you see the size of his-"

Marduk cleared his throat before she could finish. Selene stuck out her tongue at him.

"What? Was I not supposed to notice the godly appendage on display? Bad domina, bad!"

Iliana snorted with laughter, failing to keep it concealed.

"If—if you'll excuse me." Iliana curtsied, trying not to let the giggling escape. Before the prince could even nod, she'd dashed out of the room, no doubt so that she could snort and chortle without this serious, boring lot of gentlemen.

"Your Royal Highness." Marduk bowed and left the room.

Only Selene and the prince remained.

"Thank you," Belisarius said, his voice soft.

"Sorry, what was that? I think I heard gratitude, but I'm not certain."

"Thank you, Selene. Had you and the griffin not intervened, I would be dead."

His sincerity stopped her next taunt before it could roll off her tongue. When he approached, he took her hand and kissed the back of it, like she was a proper noblewoman. His eyes were dark pools, drawing her in. Before she did something she regretted, she pulled her hand from his and backed away.

"Uh, sure. I'll see you at dinner, I guess."

Selene tore off, trying to outrun the strange fluttering in her chest.

CHAPTER 14

Sneaking about a busy palace was a lot harder than Selene made it out to be. This was especially true when one was significantly taller than the average woman. Wearing clothes dirtied by sweat, grease and grit among the ornate finery probably didn't help matters. Nevertheless, Iliana persevered, doing her best to disappear into the busy tapestries and hide behind overflowing vases nearly as tall as she.

Iliana's furtive trips to the forge were saving her sanity amidst the overwhelming decadence of noble life. From the time the sun rose to long after the stars had come out, some stranger was touching her, speaking with her or expecting something of her, and through it all she was to be composed and docile, a perfect conversationalist and flatterer. There was a serving girl to wash her, comb her hair, choose her clothes, change clothes, apply make-up, brew her tea, even brush her teeth if she so desired! Noble women lived like extraordinarily pampered pets. Every aspect of their care was seen to, and in return, they were expected to be perfectly companionable every moment of every day. She didn't know how they could stand it. It was its own kind of hell.

Not for the first time, Iliana envied Selene the outrageous behaviour expected of her. So far, Selene had poisoned several servants who had come into her room without enough advance notice. Gossip about the harridan Magister Amethyst had hidden away for so long was dominating conversations amongst the noblewomen. Some had even wondered aloud exactly why the prince had not sent her away yet.

Though, given her own experience earlier in the day, Iliana suspected that gossip would soon begin to swirl about herself and the strategos. As far as she could tell, she was the only one amongst the dominae who had even spoken to the beast mages within the prince's closest circles of power.

She touched her lips, wondering what his kiss would've felt like, if his stubble would have distracted her from the feel of his tongue, or if the bite of it would have made his kiss all the sweeter.

But her daydreams came at an inopportune time. Convinced the hallway was deserted, she'd allowed her mind to wander. She didn't notice until it was too late that the eldest Domina Emerald was striding towards her with purpose, her green silk gown flowing about her ankles, her bejewelled slippers winking up at her from below. A gold and emerald necklace, earrings and hair pins framed an undeniably beautiful visage with full lips and high cheekbones. Two palace servants, in drab grey and trained to be unnoticed, trailed at a respectful distance.

"Domina Roxane? A moment of your time."

Iliana almost didn't stop. She still wasn't entirely used to hearing that false name.

"I'm afraid I'm rather dishevelled, Domina Zoe. Perhaps we can have this discussion at the ball in a few hours?"

"No, we cannot. And please do not use my name so freely. You may be a Domina, but you still possess menial magics. It would be unseemly for an ignoble to presume herself on the same level as an elemental."

Instead of bowing and scraping as she'd been taught, Iliana stiffened her spine and held her tongue. Though Domina Emerald might be a refined beauty with a flawless dark complexion, piercing green eyes and fashionably swathed in the finest silks, at heart she was what her parents had taught her to be—an elementalist. Even within the highest ranks of the nobility, a twisted pecking order persisted. Iliana refused to bend to it. She would stand tall and proud despite it all, as Marduk did.

Domina Emerald bristled. The proper protocol had not been followed.

"Since you seem to be of a mind to pursue a gentleman befitting your circumstances, rather than aiming unbecomingly for the prince, I propose we make allies of each other. You have enough sense and daring to put unsuitable women in their place, like you did to that ridiculous Amethyst creature on the first night. In any case, I should very much like to make it known what I have just discovered. Of course, as the future empress I cannot be seen speaking of such things, you understand?"

More curious than acquiescing, Iliana nodded her head. The domina was not one to be indirect, nor one to mince words. A relief, given some of the conversation Iliana had been privy to. She briefly wondered how much power one needed to feel so free to discuss one's motives.

"When I become empress, should the rumours ever get back to you, I will protect you and yours completely. As for what I just saw... well, it shouldn't take long for word to spread."

"What about your servants?"

Iliana nodded to the women who stood at a distance with serene, downcast expressions on their faces, giving away nothing. Why was it nobles always forgot the presence of their servants? Domina Emerald smiled and crooked her finger. Iliana obligingly leaned down so that the woman could whisper in her ear.

"Only I witnessed the event. Dominae Opal and Topaz in a lovers' quarrel. Apparently, rumours about the islanders being voracious in their sexual appetites are true. Domina Topaz was often invited to the islands in the past, and it seems she is displeased that Opal has rejected her advances now that they are no longer girls. I will ensure that they are the candidates selected amongst the finalists. Opal may be a serious contender, but Topaz only wishes to prevent her paramour from marrying out of her reach. When we three are selected, you will winnow the field by spreading the tale. Once I'm the only serious candidate left, I'll be empress, and you'll be handsomely rewarded. What say you?"

"I do so love an intrigue," Iliana replied with a practiced smile, careful not to reveal her displeasure.

Domina Emerald would assume she'd agreed, and by the time the woman would expect Iliana to do as she'd been told, she would be on a ship full of gold halfway to another continent. The domina beamed, her eyes sparkling like the glittering jewel of her province's namesake. Was it a trick of the light, or a spell? Iliana curtsied a polite farewell as Emerald sashayed prettily down the corridor, her servants following silently after.

Noblewomen liked to fight just as underhandedly as common ones. Exactly how Domina Emerald planned to ensure only those she wanted were chosen during the final selection was beyond Iliana. The strings the Emerald Province pulled must be truly entrenched for her to be so certain of herself, because if there was one thing Emerald projected, it was absolute confidence in herself and her position. Whether or not such pride was justified was something only time would tell. Iliana shivered, hoping she would be well and truly gone before Emerald expected anything of her. A powerful woman like that was unlikely to suffer those who disappointed her.

"Domina Amethyst, I regret to inform you that the Poison Compendium is imperial property and belongs in the chained books section under strict supervision. I must ask that you relinquish it."

Selene kept her gaze on the page before her. It bore a precisely rendered picture of a rather noxious weed that grew in damp conditions, which caused severe gastrointestinal problems in anyone unfortunate enough to ingest it. It was one she'd made a tidy profit selling in the past. Who didn't love inflicting explosive diarrhoea on their least favourite neighbour? She licked her finger and placed it on the page directly on the picture, depositing a sample of the poison as she did so.

When she looked up at the middle-aged, immaculately groomed, bespectacled librarian, she raised an imperious brow. There were several more librarians, but they stood several paces behind the one who had spoken. As far as she knew, the man before her was neither a dominus nor anyone of any consequence. He had a great deal of gall, to speak to a domina in that way. That simply wouldn't do.

The imperial library was dimly lit by enchanted lights and the odd narrow window. Selene had found herself a small sitting area near a display of ornamental armours and blunted, showy daggers. She would know, as she'd tried to steal a few. Though few nobles were about, Selene was not about to lose face to an impertinent nobody. Burgundy had taught her better.

"The Poison Compendium belongs to the greatest poison mage in the empire. If you feel differently, try to take it from me."

She could see a bead of sweat trickling down the small section of his neck, visible above his high-necked scholar's robe, the simple silk hems denoting his station. When he didn't make his move, she resumed her perusal, turning the page slowly, relishing the power. She could get used to this.

He stumbled forward in an ungainly fashion, grabbed the book from her hands, and snapped it shut as he lurched backward, wary. She made sure to use her most unsettling smile. By the time he looked down at the pale pigskin cover of the book, the poison she'd slathered over the leather had seeped into his hands. He cried out, dropping the book and backing into his posse of followers, staring at his hands in horror as they blistered.

Selene rose prettily from her seat, bent down, and picked up the large tome to resume her reading. When she was seated once more, she raised a single brow at them.

"If you have complaints about your affliction, take it up with the emperor, since he was the one so kind as to gift me this book. Now run along, before I decide you deserve more than boils for your disrespect."

The librarians were quick to flee, stumbling over each other in their haste to get away. One of the men, his dark, messy hair streaked with grey, his robes too big for his lanky frame, seemed paralyzed by the sight of her. She snarled at him. He didn't need to be threatened again. It calmed her to know she was once again alone.

Iliana had complained about the sheer amount of time in forced company, and Selene tended to agree. She'd taken care to train the servants to leave her well enough alone unless and until she requested assistance, but outside her chambers it was a different story. It was beginning to fray her nerves to have this many people so often buzzing about her when she was swathed in silk skirts and weighed down by jewels.

Though she'd taken to carrying a poisoned dagger beneath her skirts at Iliana's request, she didn't feel safe in the palace, not least due to the fact that the weak-willed first son of Magister Amethyst, Theodore, had been trying to speak to her since the hunting competition. She'd been dodging him since he'd shaken her hand, told her she'd grown into a fine woman, introduced himself as her brother and tried to wink conspiratorially at her in front of a crowd. Had he not possessed a remarkable resemblance to their father she would have doubted his parentage, so hapless and inept he'd been. No wonder her father had chosen his second son as his heir. Even at thirteen, little Dimitri was the perfect bloodthirsty soldier. She'd seen her fair share of stray cats unceremoniously dumped in her short time at the magister's, their charred little bodies visible under the paltry amount of soil thrown atop them. She really hoped she'd get the chance to kill that little shit. Alas, it was the older brother that assailed her now.

Theodore approached her carefully, looking around often to assure himself they were alone. The dominus was doing his best impression of a skittish mouse navigating a pit of vipers. When he finally came near, he stood awkwardly in front of her, rocking on the balls of his feet and swinging his arms. His attempts at nonchalance were failing so miserably it was painful to watch. If she were the sort to feel pity for noble, wealthy, idiots, she supposed his performance might just arouse a flicker. No doubt his peers made sport of eating him alive. His presence was quickly turning tiresome. She glared up at him.

He cleared his throat uncomfortably and approached her, doing his best not to make eye contact for too long.

"Can you tell me what has become of my sisters? The last time I lived at home they were...different. Also, what has become of *my* Milena?"

Selene couldn't help the confused tilt of her head. Had the magister not seen fit to at least tell this bumbling creature to keep his mouth shut? If not, she would have to reconsider her estimation of the magister's intelligence.

"Don't you already know?"

"Well, no. Father threatened me with death if I didn't stay silent. But even Sonya won't tell me, and she always used to tell me everything..."

"Sonya?"

"My third youngest sister, her hair has the most blonde in it of us all," Theodore replied, equally confused.

"Oh! You mean Carrot. I doubt you'll get much out of her. She's pretty fucked up. As for Milena, you'll have to ask the magister. Long story short though, if you don't already know, you don't need to know. Understand?" Selene did her best to use the smile she'd been taught meant *go away, I'm finished with this discussion*. Sadly, she'd either been unable to reproduce it faithfully, or her half-brother was a little thick. Her coin was on the latter.

"How can you say that? They're my beloved sisters and something is wrong with them! Can't you understand?" His eyes misted.

Selene growled at the dominus. This twit wanted her to care about some drama she wanted no part of? If he'd been so concerned, why hadn't he gone to the magister to complain? His timidity rubbed her the wrong way.

"What I can't understand, Theodore, is why you believe a bastard your father tossed away like trash would give a damn about some pampered breeding sows and his biggest disappointment. If you care so damn much, grow a pair and confront him. But we both know you won't. It's why you're standing there, hoping I'll coddle you and make it better, all so you can go back to what you're good at—being a spineless, spoiled child."

He froze, stunned, before he hunched his shoulders to lick his wounds. She wasn't particularly proud of herself, but it would be better this way. Maybe he would manage to keep his head when Daddy was executed by the prince for whatever crime he was guilty of. Unless this was an elaborate ruse, Theodore probably hadn't been invited to take part in the plot.

"You... You're just like *him*."

Selene smirked. If she were their father, Theodore would be dead, not dealing with hurt feelings.

"If I start caring for the opinions of useless brats, I'll let you know. Until then, fuck off."

Chapter 15

The flickering candlelight was magnified by magic, bathing the grand, airy ballroom in sunny mid-afternoon brightness despite the late hour. Every column was sculpted and lavishly painted, every arch decorated with a stunning mosaic. The ceiling glittered with embedded crystals and the floors were of polished, veined marble. Servants in drab greys carrying drinks and delicate appetizers wove through the throngs with the equal and confusing abilities of being seen by, and invisible to, the nobles gathered. Silks, jewels and dramatic, colourful fashions were on full display.

Selene's fingers itched to pocket a bauble or three as she considered her list of reliable fences for high-end goods. Temptation was getting the better of her. As she approached the backs of the wallflowers on the edges of the revelry, she heard a familiar voice.

"Domina Emerald, you look lovely."

Despite his words, the praetor sounded anything but pleased. Interest piqued, she crept as close as she dared to Nicephorus and Domina Zoe Emerald, the better to eavesdrop.

"I do so hate your practiced smile, cousin."

"Then all my effort has been worthwhile. How may I assist you this evening?"

"Do not pretend you are unaware. I will be empress, and I expect you to expend your considerable resources to assist me. I have already taken care that my sisters do not interfere. I am working to ensure there are no other serious contenders as we speak. What have you done thus far?"

"I'm pleased to report that I've yet to lift a finger."

"Do not toy with me, Nicephorus. The war may have forced our families to merge, but you are from the subordinate branch. You will assist me, or I shall be forced to inform my father."

"The Magister has always coddled you and supported your ambition, but I won't tip the scales in your favour. If you wish to become empress, then you must do so on your own. I won't corrupt the grand, meritocratic vision of the late Empress Nadia with nepotism."

The domina laughed, as practiced as it was vicious.

"Meritocracy is the lie told to the ignorant masses of ignobles, menials and ferals so that they remain content."

"My bureaucrats are-"

"From noble houses exclusively, and the second sons and other castoffs at that! Pretending otherwise is wilful ignorance. The best and brightest run the provinces, the dregs serve under you and the rest resort to manual labour, I suppose. But never mind all that. I did not come to you to rehash old arguments. Support me now, and you will get your hands on those bright minds. Otherwise, you will find your office diminished in importance once I am empress."

A short silence preceded the praetor's reply.

"Win the prince's heart, and I'll move my chess pieces in your favour."

"Very well, but I will remember your reluctance. Good evening, cousin."

"Good luck."

Given how much Nicephorus disliked his cousin, the domina rose a notch in Selene's estimation. Zoe was still an entitled elementalist, but she was a noblewoman who took what she wanted, consequences be damned. She had the confidence of any magister, but also the pride. The empire regularly punished driven women like her. Although if there was one woman likely to take the seat of empress through sheer determination, she'd place money on Zoe. Poor Belli had no idea of the storm he'd unleashed.

Iliana had a newfound respect for noblewomen. Her evenings were beginning to take their toll. Every day, a new marathon of social events stretched into the wee hours of the morning. She'd been dancing with strapping soldiers and dashing noblemen for much of the past hour, passed from one set of arms to another in seamless transitions. Her shoes were already uncomfortable, and her back stiff from tensing, worried she might fumble the steps or forget to flirt with the appropriate amount of ladylike witticism. She found herself wistful for the days she would spend hours at a forge, breaking her back over swords and knives and shields, sweating from the molten heat. She prayed dinner would be served soon, or some kind soul would take pity on her and invite her to discuss inane topics near the refreshments.

"Domina Sapphire, you're looking rather weary. Would you like to accompany me off the dance floor?"

"I would be elated, Strategos."

Iliana smiled up at her saviour. The strategos cut a rather imposing figure in his formal military regalia. His genuine grin was a balm after all the forced smiles and chatter of the evening, his eyes sparkling with mischief.

"You're in high demand this evening," Marduk remarked.

"I could stand to be a little less popular," Iliana griped.

"And here I thought you might enjoy the attention. My soldiers are all too eager to show you their best. I'm certain at least a few are serious in their interest."

"You sound almost jealous."

"I do not often meet women of your calibre. I find myself reluctant to share your time."

"Flattery will get you everywhere, Strategos," Iliana teased.

"Will it afford me a private dinner? No one looking over your shoulder, ensuring you've used the correct utensil or judging your every spoken word, guaranteed. As long as you don't find my company too onerous, that is."

"Are you quite serious?" Iliana asked, clutching at his arm. Cautious hope made her desperate. The idea of slipping off her bejewelled shoes and enjoying some private time with the charming beast mage sounded divine.

"Deadly."

"What about the banquet?" She looked askance.

"I do not believe we will be missed," he whispered conspiratorially.

"Then I will be glad that it is not only my friend who benefits from a private dinner with her suitor."

His broad smile made her heart flutter. *Oh no.*

"Follow me."

She nodded. It occurred to her that perhaps her evening with Marduk might prove to be just as taxing on her heart as the dancing had been on her body. She resolved to spend the evening figuring out just what she wanted to do with her growing fondness for the big man.

Selene had watched contentedly from the sidelines while Iliana found herself the belle of the ball. Man after man propositioned her to dance, desperate to charm her. She'd slipped off somewhere with Marduk not long ago. Selene didn't like it, but Iliana could gut a man if the situation called for it.

Selene did her best to blend into the scenery, happy to listen to the buzz of gossip around the refreshments. In the distance, the prince gamely fended off insistent elder magistrae, likely trying to negotiate the seat of empress for their daughters. He looked like he might need saving. Selene sat back to enjoy the show as the women drew closer, encircling their prey. She wasn't the only one watching the scene with interest.

"What I don't understand is why he hasn't dismissed the ignobles among the bride candidates," a nobilissima standing by the punch said.

"I confess I'm equally puzzled. Surely only the elementals should've been considered from the start. Anything else is an insult."

"Exactly! I know there aren't any fire mage noblewomen of high enough rank outside his family, but really! It's vulgar for menials to parade about as if they deserve the title of domina, let alone empress."

Selene eyed the women to her side. Not a one was more than a nobilissima, and it showed with the inferior charms they wore. Light mages often created various charms to disguise the odd imperfection, a wrinkle here, a pimple there, but they were easily caught out in flickering candlelight. Truly competent light mages could change the likeness of an entire feature; lips made plumper, cheekbones slightly elevated, a double chin faded to nothing, and a flickering light wouldn't show any tell-tale signs. But such things cost a great deal of money, and the nobilissimae beside her were failing to hide their flaws, physical and otherwise.

People were scum, no matter how much money they had to waste on frivolous charms. The proof was in the pudding, or in this case, the noble. To compound matters, a nobleman convinced of his own self-importance swaggered over to her as she sipped wine beside one of her dead-eyed sisters. He made an ass of himself with a single sentence.

"I'm sure a poison mage like you rarely gets many offers to dance, so, shall we?"

Anger coiled in her gut. She'd spied him across the ballroom making some kind of boyish dare with his fellows as they pointed at her like schoolchildren, hoping they would keep to themselves. Perhaps he needed reminding why poison mages were universally feared and loathed. He should know to speak of poison mages in hushed tones well outside of earshot.

Alas, he was ignorant.

While she'd been warned against killing nobles, no one had forbidden teaching lessons. Selene smiled and held out her hand, all the while thinking of a list of poisons that might just do the trick. From across the room, his comrades were overcome by amazement.

As a dancer the man was subpar. He pulled, guiding her closer to his group. So be it. A good teacher was more than capable of handling multiple pupils. Before the song had even ended, she was surrounded by his leering friends. Unfortunately for them, all she had to do was breathe.

Her mere presence was too much for one, who opened his vile mouth first.

"So, is it true that anyone who puts their cock in you will die instantly?"

"Is it true you're all infertile?"

"What about garden slugs, do you eat those?"

"You know, our garden is infested with those slimy creatures, care for a feast?"

Several sets of gleaming eyes were trained on her. While a gently bred noblewoman might run from this pack of snide bullies and their cruel questions, embarrassed and ashamed, Selene would not.

"Boys, boys. If you want to know, then lean in." Selene crooked her finger, luring them in. "The one and only thing you must remember about poison mages is not to piss them off. By the time you've finished your insults, you're doomed."

"I don't-" One of them started as his face turned a delightful shade of green. He did his best to hold it in, but it would be nigh impossible to prevent what happened next. One of her most potent emetics would help wash the filth from their lips. He lurched away from the group before he vomited.

"Oh g-" And another splattered his friend with half-digested appetizers.

Selene was already far enough away from them as they took turns collapsing into a pile of their own sick. As petty revenges went, this one was quite the spectacle. It reminded her of those fancy fountains in the middle of wealthy towns, except it was much more satisfying. She stifled a laugh as horrified nobles hastily vacated the area while servants tried to remove the men from the room. It had not gone unnoticed that she had been in a close huddle with them only moments before.

Ah, sweet, terrified, respectful distance. How I've missed this.

Instead of heading back towards her sisters, she sashayed her way to the prince. Rudely inserting herself inside the tight, claustrophobic circle of older women, Selene grinned when it loosened up as they realised who, or rather, what, she was. So laden with jewels it was a marvel their necks hadn't snapped under the weight, each refused to acknowledge her, silently sipping wine. An ignoble domina without her parent or brother in tow was beneath the notice of an esteemed magistra. Unfortunately for them, Selene was becoming adept at these little power plays.

"It's so very disappointing when young men *drink* to excess, don't you think?"

Each of the women understood the implicit threat. Widening their eyes in horror, each stared at her beverage as if worms writhed in their crystal cups. Selene rarely saw dignified women make such hasty retreats, but to their credit, they made it look graceful.

"You really do know how to clear a room," the prince sighed.

"One of my many fine talents."

"Lucky me."

"And here I thought you'd be grateful. They looked like they were ready to sink their teeth into you and strip your bones clean. Who knows? If I'd left you to them, you might've found yourself enjoying a stable of concubines twice your age."

He hid his laugh with a more dignified cough.

"Would you accept a dance as thanks?"

"Certainly."

As their dance commenced, the other nobles seemed to take their cues. The men had been removed and the mess cleaned, so there was little left to gawk at. Except the woman who'd caused it, having just sent a group of magistrae running, now twirling in a prince's arms. Point to Selene.

"Do I need to know what you did to those nobilissimi?"

"It was no less than they deserved. They almost hurt my feelings."

He gave her a look which clearly indicated his doubt. She gamely ignored it.

"So how is Lord Renfreid? I didn't see him. Did you forget to invite him?"

The prince almost—*almost*—sighed.

"I'd almost forgotten about him. As it is, our resident griffin is busying himself exhausting every courtesan in Nadioch, male and female, all at once. At this point, they're plying him with wine to try to slow him down. Does everything you're involved with turn into some twisted, chaotic circus?"

"Only the fun things."

The prince bit down on his smirk.

"So, where did you say this orgy was being held?" Selene asked.

CHAPTER 16

Belisarius watched with some dismay as the poison mage dug into her dinner with extreme enthusiasm. He'd only just managed to convince her that attending an orgy would be considered beyond the pale, even for the now infamously eccentric Domina Milena Amethyst. It did irk him that she'd seemed so keen on it. She'd grudgingly resigned herself to a dinner with him instead. So much for enlightening conversation or even refreshing banter.

"Please feel free to show some eagerness. Your sense of decorum is overwhelming."

She rolled her eyes.

"Noble etiquette is performance, Belli. Is there really any point to pretending around you? Even the servants have made themselves scarce."

They'd done so because he'd insisted on having a very private dinner with the woman in front of him. At least for this part of his ruse, he needn't make a fool of himself in public.

"Was your life before this so very different? Surely even a commoner eats with some propriety."

"Says the man who has never known hunger. Look, can I be honest here?" Selene asked, exasperated, gesticulating with a piece of meat speared on her fork as she pointed at him.

"When are you not?"

"None of us dirty commoners bother to eat tiny morsels one at a time, nor do we waste time eating slowly. First, a meal like this is one I'll never see the like of again. Second, if I ate like a noble, the food would be cold before I even finished it. You only pick at your food if you don't like it *and* aren't grateful that it's there. As far as people like me are concerned, it's noble etiquette that's got the whole business wrong."

Though he'd never seen the hungry masses, it stung that she might think he didn't know there were plenty out there. He'd set up public baths and charitable centres to distribute oil, bread and watered wine on a regular basis to those in need for this very reason. She could cast stones all she liked, but she'd never been tasked with solving issues of this magnitude.

"Are the charitable centres not to your taste?"

She rolled her eyes—again. He gripped his fork harder than was necessary.

"You mean aside from the fact that going to one puts a damn target on your back for every predator in town? Pimps, loan sharks, traffickers, cultists, you name it—they're watching the line and picking out the weakest and most desperate."

Had he hoped for an enlightening conversation? Gods below, sometimes he wished he were a little more circumspect in his wishes. This was the first he'd heard of such a thing. He would have to figure out a better method. Perhaps he'd been looking at this whole situation wrong. Who better to interrogate about the circumstances of his people than one used to living amongst them? He was not so proud he couldn't admit to having a blind spot or two.

"And if you were in a position to change Lethe for the better, what would you do?"

"Raze it to the ground," Selene muttered between bites of her bread.

"I'm asking seriously."

He hated this woman's tendency to spit in his face. She paused, looked up at him and tilted her head.

"Do you actually care what I think?" She sounded doubtful.

"I'll certainly take it under advisement. As you can imagine, I don't often have an opportunity to discuss the state of my empire with anyone but noble-born advisers."

"Well, except Marduk. Any noble beast mage is killed the moment they're born," Selene replied matter-of-factly.

Something dark wriggled in his gut. He wondered if her mage gift was actually the ability to magnify every area of society he felt powerless to change fast enough. He didn't trust himself not to argue with her, so he just nodded. She seemed satisfied, closing her eyes and wrinkling her brow in concentration.

"I'd probably start with women being able to own property. Can't tell you how many dogs I had to defend myself from who hoped I might be desperate enough to pay rent with sex. Then education for commoners—all of them. Iliana wouldn't be a master metals mage if her stepfather hadn't decided to teach her everything he knew. And when this is all over, you should put a woman and a beast mage in charge of Sapphire and Amethyst. Be nice if you could punish elementalists for being scum, but that might be too much for a fire mage like you." She grinned, daring him to say differently.

"Oh, well, if that's all," he huffed, sitting back in his seat. "Do you know how much push-back I'd receive from the magistri and other nobles over such radical proposals?"

Just the sheer number of objections he would need to overcome to even suggest such things made his head ache. He'd have to cash in every favour ever owed to his family to get a single idea realised. Not to mention, allowing every noblewoman to own property would throw the succession of every major household into question and upend the social fabric of the empire.

Selene slammed her hand on the table, scowling.

"Oh, excuse me for being a *radical*! Live long enough on the fringes and you're bound to pick up a few vulgar ideas! That aside, two of the magistri are already plotting against you. What do you care if the rest get their *feelings* hurt at this point? You have an entire bureaucracy of hostages from every snooty family in Lethe nestled securely in Nadioch. If they don't like it, you can always dispossess them of their ranks and lands. Then they'll be damn grateful for my ideas." Selene harrumphed, her arms crossed, cheeks tinged pink. "Do what you want, or not, as the case might be. I'm leaving this shit place soon enough anyway."

He'd hurt her feelings. And he felt... bad about it, which was an odd thing given she never seemed to care about offending anyone else. It wasn't as if the ideas weren't worthy of consideration. In fact, they had merit. He'd asked her opinion and then insulted her for it. It was incumbent on him to be a gentleman about it, however belated.

"I'm sorry. I shouldn't have belittled the advice I asked of you. It was not well done on my part."

"No, it wasn't," Selene grumbled, pushing food about her plate. "If you're not careful I'll spread awful rumours just to teach you a lesson. Perhaps I'll start calling you Prince Two-Pump as punishment."

"That's hardly necessary." He gritted his teeth, regretting his apology already. Damn it! What more did she want from him?

"Didn't anyone teach you how to play dirty? The first rule is however hard someone hits you, hit them back worse. Darius must have taught you something." She raised a brow.

"I regret to disabuse you of the notion, but it was my mother who attended to most of my education. The rest was in Marduk's hands," he replied lightly.

"Maybe that's your problem. No one's afraid of you because you didn't learn to be scary enough. Have you considered doing a couple public executions?" she asked, swirling the wine in her glass.

"I have no desire to rule as my father did, Selene. My enemies will be dealt with harshly but justly." He narrowed his eyes.

"Sure, until that isn't an option anymore. What I don't get is why you don't just march on the magistri. Their armies are nothing compared to yours. Or just send a couple assassins," she scoffed, leaning back in her seat, arm flung over the top.

"And then how many people become collateral because of a few criminals? There is no need for widespread suffering if the problem lies with a select few. As for assassins, the risk of failure igniting a war is too great." Belisarius shook his head.

"If you say so." She sipped, appearing unconvinced.

Thankfully a polite knock on the door to their suite prevented an awkward impasse in their conversation.

"You may enter," Belisarius called out.

Several servants began clearing off plates and cutlery, replacing them with lightning speed and setting down the dessert course. They bowed, leaving the room in a swirl of dull, monochromatic clothing. Selene's eyes glittered at the sweets on display. If she'd wiped away drool he wouldn't have been surprised. It was almost cute.

"Looks delicious, but are you sure you should be eating that? I heard it'll go right to your thighs, and let's just say, you don't need it." Her fork slowly, unerringly, reached for his portion.

He retracted his former thought. She was a harridan, through and through. His thighs were perfectly proportioned! He slapped down her hand, her fork clattering on the embroidered tablecloth.

"As Prince of Lethe, I'll eat whatever I damn well please."

"But yours looks bigger than mine! At least give me a piece so we're even," she whined.

"No! Keep your thieving hands to your own dessert."

"I seem to recall these thieving hands saving your ungrateful life." She pointed at him.

He arched his brow, cut off a large portion of the pie and made to give it to Selene, whose smirk was equal parts bright and smug. Just before it reached her plate, he bent over the table and popped it into his mouth. As he sat back, he relished the look of utter betrayal, her mouth agape. The sight was almost as delicious as his dessert.

"Mmmm. Possibly the best piece of pie in the *entire* empire," he crowed.

"Monster!"

Just as he was about to laugh, a horrible feeling of disorientation came over him. The floor rose up to greet him. Selene raced over and licked his fork. Was now really the time for such pettiness?

"Shit! I know this one."

Fuck.

Had he really just eaten poison? It was just his luck. Was someone trying to frame Selene for his murder? He gasped, his heart pounding wildly as breathing became a chore.

"Tell anyone I can do this, and I'll kill you." Selene warned as she hovered over him. Splitting his tunic in half with a concealed knife, she placed her hands on the bare skin of his throat and chest. "Why the fuck isn't this working?!"

Belisarius put all his effort into dispelling the mage gift he habitually kept himself cloaked in. Panic swelled as he failed to drag in a single breath.

"There! Okay, this is going to hurt, so brace yourself and try not to scream too loudly."

Fire consumed every particle of his innards. He fought to control his gift from reasserting itself as Selene worked. Sweat soaked his body from the strain, but at least he could breathe, however laboured. Just as quickly as the pain had come, it vanished, leaving him winded and shaky. Above him Selene toyed with a blue liquid coating her palms. Within seconds it seemed to vanish into her skin. She breathed a sigh of relief.

"Sweets really will be the death of you, Your Royal Highness. It would be safer if I ate them all from now on." Her half-grin was sympathetic, at least.

He tried to laugh but coughed instead.

"So, you can cure poison too?" he asked, his voice hoarse. Belisarius put his palms on the floor, pressing them into the mosaics hard enough to stop his hands from trembling.

Her eyes were deadly serious as her finger touched his lips. He held his breath.

"Hush! Never say it. It's against a poisoners' code to save someone from a fellow practitioner."

"Then why do you even know how?" he asked, holding back a shiver as she removed her hand, brushing his lips.

"I had to. What if Iliana accidentally got into something?"

The notion struck him as so ridiculous he couldn't contain his mirth. He gasped for breath between peals of hysterical laughter. When he finally calmed down, the reality hit him. Gods below, he'd been so close to death. Twice in one day was enough to undo any sane man. First a bear abused by fire and whipped into an unholy rage, loosed upon his hunting grounds, now poison.

"So, what did someone try to kill me with this time?" he sighed.

"You're taking this better than I expected." Her brows were pinched. Perhaps she too questioned his sanity.

"What choice do I have? I can hardly go crying off about the unfairness of it all." He ruled an empire. Assassination was par for the course, whether he liked it or not.

"True. This one was a depressingly common berry. You can find it throughout the capital region. I'm sure even those hacks in your poisoner department have tasted it once."

So, whoever wanted him dead was wealthy enough to afford the deadliest poison, but too lazy to go the extra mile on the second try? What in the hells was he supposed to make of that? And not only that, but he couldn't get the bear's burns out of his mind. No one had found any evidence of a fire in the forest and he certainly hadn't attacked the bear himself. Someone had deliberately frenzied the bear, as if it were a beast set to take part in gladiatorial combat. It was simply too much of a coincidence for it to rampage on one of his favourite trails. Had the burns only been to enrage the bear, or had it been an attempt to make it appear as though he'd fought back and failed? Worse, did someone know he couldn't conjure flame to protect himself, or were they merely testing him?

Belisarius set his unanswerable questions aside. He would simply have to be grateful he'd survived. Who had the time to think up all these elaborate assassination attempts? He rolled onto his side and hauled himself into a seated position, leaning against the leg of the table. Selene stared, rapt by his bare chest.

"Is there something wrong?"

"Hmm? No, nothing. So I was thinking we should really get the rumour mill going. I tore your clothes, and you look like you just finished a race. I think you should definitely rip my clothes off."

"Uh…"

The sight of her in that illicit little shift, toying with the hem as she'd mocked him, crept unbidden into his mind. Perhaps he would hold off on ruling against the thinness of the material. For now.

"You're right, too dramatic. Perhaps just a sleeve?" She smiled, crawling over to him.

Heat crept up his cheeks. He cleared his throat before doing as she'd asked.

"Best muss my hair as well, Your Royal Highness," Selene suggested, using the chance to crawl closer.

"Right," he replied, swallowing tightly. Why did she make him so nervous? Something predatory in her gaze heated his blood. Ensnared by her amethyst eyes, he could smell her delicate floral perfume, feel her breath against his skin. Belisarius reached out and began pulling pins from her hair, letting the silky brown strands free. A mistake. She looked like she belonged in bed.

"The paint on my lips," she breathed, her nose almost touching his.

"What about it?" His eyes unerringly found her lips. Soft. They looked soft.

"It should be on you."

He bit back his instant agreement. Breaths mingling, he had several wicked thoughts as to where she should mark him. He fought to keep his cool.

"I'm sure it's not necessary." His voice was huskier than he'd meant.

"Don't be silly. What kind of tryst doesn't include a few kisses?" She flicked her eyes to his and licked her lips.

Rational thought fled.

"I... uh..."

"Exactly."

She ducked her head and began a slow trail of kisses up his chest, one hand resting on his hip, the other braced behind him. The view from his vantage had him envisioning her lips trailing lower. Her hand moved up along with her lips, her little nails scoring his pectoral, lightly grazing his nipple. Everywhere she trailed her nails, lips and tongue followed. Why was he resisting the strange pull she had on him?

When her lips met his jaw, he threw in the towel, turned his head and kissed her soundly. He thrust his fingers into her hair, holding her. She deepened the kiss, brazenly stroking his tongue with her own. Soft lips, hot little tongue, cruel, grasping hands—he was undone. Inflamed, he matched her fervour, blood pooling in his groin. Visions of hauling her close, skin pressed to skin, were thwarted when she pulled away.

"I-I think that should do it."

"Not nearly," he growled, reaching out for her.

She ducked out of his hold and stood, shaking out her dress and refusing to meet his eyes. Gods, but he wanted more. He ached to flip her on her back, retake control, make her ache in turn. She looked like she wanted it too, her cheeks flushed, gaze hungrily skating back over his body. Needy. He had to close this bewildering distance.

"See you, uh, tomorrow." She waved awkwardly, all but sprinting for the door. She was gone before he could even reply.

When he calmed down enough to realise what he'd just been about to do, he groaned. He really had lost his sanity.

"Fuck."

The room was decorated with intimacy in mind. The lighting was dimmer, unenchanted candles providing the illumination. Rose petals were strewn across the marble floor, a few artfully arranged on the small table in the middle of the room. A sideboard with dishes kept warm with lidded trays occupied one wall. Calming, pastoral tapestries decorated the others. It was altogether more than Iliana had expected.

"What would you have done if I'd said no?" she asked. She was more than a little taken aback. This was the most sweetly, and most impressively, anyone had ever tried to woo her.

Marduk shrugged.

"Given the food to the knights in training. Made sure the candles were blown out."

"Are you trying to court me, Strategos?"

"Is it working?"

"I'm undecided," she replied, blushing.

"Then perhaps the promise of a meal to be enjoyed without being on display will sway you. Come, take a seat. Feel free to kick off your shoes. I can tell they're hurting you."

He held out her seat for her and helped her to get comfortable before seating himself. She slipped out of her pinching, extravagant footwear.

"This is very kind of you, Marduk. Thank you."

"I imagine it isn't easy to adjust to the very strictly regimented life of a noblewoman, given your relative freedom before. Though the circumstances for this charade are troubling, I want you to know you can be yourself when it's just you and me."

Iliana sipped her wine and wondered at her good fortune to have had her lot thrown in with his. It was a damn sight better than she'd imagined when she'd arrived in the capital, fearing for her life.

"Why would you go to the trouble? I'm a bastard, and of a criminal, no less." She feared his answer.

"Is it so strange that I might sincerely enjoy your company?"

"What about the fact that we're leaving once this is over? Are you just looking for a... a momentary affair?" She braced herself for the worst. Iliana liked this man. She didn't want to be nothing to him.

"Would that be so awful, if we enjoyed ourselves?" Her heart sank. "Besides, the future is hardly set in stone. Perhaps I'll decide to join you on your journey. Gods know, I won't be able to show my face in polite company once you leave my innocent reputation in tatters." He winked.

So, it was just a tryst he wanted. It hurt. Did she want more of him, as impossible as that would be? She set it aside as best she could. It wouldn't do to dwell on what couldn't be.

"I highly doubt a strategos is allowed innocence of any kind," she said, her tone light.

"My hands may be bloody, but my heart is as pure as the driven snow." He placed a hand over his heart.

Iliana let out a splutter of laughter, then covered her mouth with both her hands. She had a rather unfortunate habit of snorting as she laughed. It was hardly something one wanted to show off to a man of his station, no matter how silly said man was behaving. Marduk smiled and reached across the table to remove her hands from her face.

"You don't have to hold back your laughter."

"It's not a very appropriate laugh."

"No, it's not," he agreed.

"Hey!" She tried to pull her hands out of his grip, but he couldn't be moved.

"Fear not, dear woman. I'm told my snore could wake the dead."

"Snoring, you say?"

"Yes. I also steal all the covers. No one is without their faults."

He released her hands and grinned. She felt the loss of his warmth keenly.

"It hasn't escaped my notice that you've only mentioned things having to do with one's bedroom, Strategos."

"I don't know what you mean. Perhaps you were picturing what we might do. *If* we were in a bedroom. But we're not, so you should try to resist the temptation to imagine it," he replied with all the cheek he could muster while he cut into his steak.

Iliana chortled with laughter. After a while, Marduk couldn't hold back his own guffaws at her snorts. By the time they'd both stopped laughing, Iliana was wiping tears from her eyes and suppressing giggles. As she looked across the table at the man before her, she realised it might be impossible to avoid a bit of heartbreak over him, no matter what she chose to do.

Chapter 17

Selene shot out of bed, back slick with sweat, heart hammering in her chest. A dream of riding atop a beast mage's shoulders, clutching spiralling black horns, had warped into a nightmare of screams and ash and agony. Ripped apart at the seams, she felt herself unravelling. She patted her body, trying to reassure herself she was indeed whole.

Flooded with adrenaline, Selene stared wistfully at her pillow. A few hours more till dawn, the sky was still a murky blue. As she slowed her breaths, her mind wandered. Thus far, she hadn't bothered to learn much about the magistri. Given the interesting tidbit she'd learned about Emerald's history, it might be in her interest to go properly armed into any future dust-ups with the dominae. She dressed herself simply, stealing out of her rooms. Her destination? The library.

A man with longish, dark, unkempt hair was the only librarian on duty. His robes appeared worn, a touch too big for his tall frame, obscuring whatever physique he hid underneath. As she got closer, she noticed his skin was a light brown, and that his dark hair was streaked with grey. He shelved books silently, unaware of her.

"Librarian, I want help finding a book."

"Oh my!" He jumped, dropping his books, his rough voice at odds with his delicate appearance. "Please, forgive me, I didn't hear you approach. What is it I can help you with, Your...?" He looked up at her from his position on the floor, gathering books under one arm.

"Domina Amethyst. And you can help me find books about the noble houses and their current members."

"You've come to the right place!" he beamed. "We have detailed genealogies, some of which include mage gifts and miniature portraits. We also have official and unofficial histories, as well as..." He leaned in conspiratorially. "...a rather scandalous book of gossip."

"I'd like to see all of them. What was your name?"

"Azar, Your Resplendence."

"Thank you, Azar."

"It is my pleasure. I presume you're hoping to go into battle well-armed with knowledge?"

"Something like that."

"Very good. I'll retrieve the materials at once."

Azar bowed and scuttled off. Once the rumours got going, she would need more than her standard go-to of revenge-poisoning her opponents. Much as she hated to admit it, that wasn't always going to work in her favour. Not with women who spoke as if their tongues were lethal weapons. Selene needed to know enough about them to play a noblewoman's version of 'dirty' if she wanted to keep her full monetary reward.

Early morning rays reflected off walls of white stone, streaming through tall, pointed windows open to the elements. Plants grew in a haphazard arrangement, their vines scaling the walls. A single butterfly fluttered about, unperturbed by the visitor to its quiet haven. Belisarius placed the bottle of ceremonial wine at his feet. The secluded, serene garden enclosure had been created for just this purpose. Words learned long ago rolled off his tongue.

"To the gods, forgotten by foolish mortals, I beseech you. Protect this insignificant man, whose ancestors you saw fit to liberate from the old world. Grant me safety as you granted them your boundless world, Oblivion, formed by your decaying souls. Accept my meagre offering and rise from obscurity."

As he finished his prayer, footsteps sounded behind him. It was disrespectful to turn away in the middle of supplication; some said dangerous, too. In a moment that never failed to strike a chord of fear in his heart, no matter how routine, the bottle sank into the earth, leaving undisturbed soil in its wake. Offering accepted, the prince let out a pent up breath and turned to the interloper.

"One wonders if they didn't want to remain forgotten, why they didn't at least tell us their names."

"Good morning, Father."

Darius stood before him properly—if simply—attired in a short, military-style tunic of imperial red, leather boots polished and gleaming, no hint of drunkenness or hangover. Even his long hair and cropped beard were properly groomed, the scent of sandalwood soap drifting on the breeze. It was a rare sight, and before noon at that.

"I heard what happened the other night. You're lucky the girl was there. The magistri and their benefactor are getting desperate to try the same thing twice," Darius remarked, only his white knuckles betraying his worry.

Belisarius nodded. He'd been close to his father, even idolized him as a boy, but that had changed when Mother died suddenly and unexpectedly three years ago. As Darius abdicated all responsibility and wallowed in self-destructive misery, Belisarius had been left to grieve alone and shoulder the weight of Lethe. Despite sharing the pain his father felt, Belisarius couldn't find it in his heart to forgive him for the abandonment, nor the broken promise to rule side-by-side until Belisarius' own coronation. He was only two years from the age of thirty, when he could be crowned while his father still lived. It was an extra bitter pill to swallow, with Selene's remonstration ringing in his ears that a lack of fear on the part of his enemies was at the root of it all. It was the fear his father had always commanded in the hearts of the nobles that he'd needed, and Darius had never once offered it.

"I can only hope that my praetor's spies and investigators are competent enough to uncover the poisoner's trail. Until then, a prayer to the forgotten gods can't hurt. What brings you here?"

"I wanted to see you were okay for myself. First the hunt, then the poison. Yesterday must have been difficult."

Anger scalded Belisarius.

"I'm in perfect health, as you can see. Was there anything else?" he asked, striding towards the exit where his father held himself awkwardly. Darius reached out, a hand on his arm.

"I would like to help you. Is there a part for me in your game?"

Belisarius ground his teeth. So all it took to garner his father's co-operation and attention was to be nearly assassinated—again? Had the attempt on his life not long after Mother's funeral not been enough? Where had this fatherly concern been when Belisarius had needed him in his grief? He'd fended off nobles alone as he'd stood at his mother's freshly erected mausoleum, and he'd do it again now. Perhaps if he'd been a better son or a more practical man, Belisarius might have accepted the olive branch, but the days when he could look at Darius without bitterness were few and far between. This was not one of those rare occasions. He tugged his arm free and swept by his father, refusing to meet his eyes.

"I've no need for unreliable players. If you'll excuse me, I have matters to attend to."

CHAPTER 18

Never had a more cruel torture been devised. No poison, however painful or paralyzing, was a match for what had befallen Selene. Tea time. Instead of playing with or harassing Belisarius, Selene had been forced to have polite conversations with the pretty Dominae Emerald, Opal and Topaz. The powers that be had decided it was time to single out serious candidates for Belisarius' hand. Seated with that short, exalted list, Selene wished she could just put these incredible bores to sleep and wipe her hands of the drudgery. But much as she wanted to, she couldn't. That officious snob, the praetor, had threatened her with monetary losses. Curse her lust for gold!

Each wore an embroidered silk gown in the colour of their jewelled namesake, the bright, saturated hues clashing as badly as their personalities. Had they been men, Selene wouldn't have been surprised if they'd come away wearing each other's blood instead of pretty baubles. The assumption that their dismissal might offend her was laughable. She'd remained silent, sipping her tea while the three women ignored her to trade witty barbs back and forth. Given what Selene knew about a potential war in the near future, it all seemed trivial.

Thus far, Selene's personal favourite was the tall, beautiful Domina Emerald, cruel and unrelenting with her verbal assaults. Opal obsessed over proving her intellect and political savvy, while Topaz crowned herself queen of the backhanded compliment. It was like watching a pack of wild pups working out the hierarchy. Now, where was it that she'd last seen wild pups? Something half-remembered and warm seemed just out of reach.

"Then let us settle this deadlock. Domina Amethyst, what say you?"

Her musings were interrupted by three sets of politely determined eyes. What exactly had they been going on about? Did it matter? Selene wished she could spend her time with the griffin, who at least told funny stories before disappearing with another lusty mage on his arm. If Belisarius weren't such a jealous prude, she'd have taken the griffin up on the invitation in his eyes. It had been an age since she'd had a good tumble with a handsome man. But it was warm brown skin she imagined running her lips over and silky black hair she wanted tangled in her greedy fingers. *No, stop it!* Now was not the time to go off imagining ridiculous things.

Selene cleared her throat.

"While vaguely amusing, your prattle is beginning to bore me. Can't you just slap each other to decide who will win this competition?"

Their indignant gasps were all but choreographed. She'd bet good coin they were practiced, at least.

"Spoken like a truly vulgar woman. I cannot fathom what the prince sees in you," Emerald seethed.

"Haven't you heard? The prince seems to appreciate the... flexibility of her mind." Topaz smiled with derision.

"Perhaps the domina knows where the bodies are buried. Nothing else can explain why such a barbarous creature was included among the top candidates," Opal opined with suspicion.

A few thoughts crossed Selene's mind, most of which would lose her a substantial amount of gold if she chose to follow them. Others might lose her considerably less, but would be oh so satisfying. Reining herself in, Selene put her cup to one side, stood and wiggled her fingers. The three dominae watched her with a mixture of disdain and wariness, leaning away as she approached. She sauntered around them, hand gliding across the backs of their plush chairs. Domina Opal, with that strange fire in the whites of her eyes, flinched as Selene cupped her cheek. Topaz shot killing glances her way.

"Isn't the reason obvious? Your fear of me proves the power I hold."

"How dare you threaten a proper domina that way! And an elemental one, no less. If you didn't have your title, a crass menial like you would be whipped for such a thing," Emerald scolded, ire plain.

Topaz's silent glare threatened murder, while Opal held herself still as a statue. Selene released Opal's face as the domina flushed with embarrassment, and turned to Emerald.

"Do you deny it, Domina Emerald? Have you honed your gift, or have you honed your useless social graces instead? Have you been content to let the men of your family hold every last ounce of true power?"

"My power lies in my impeccable bloodline and position in society. One word from my lips and you would become a pariah, even more so than you are already." Emerald raised her chin.

"And is that meant to intimidate me? Do you think the emperor fears the wagging tongues of other nobles? True power simply crushes those beneath it," Selene countered.

"I shouldn't have to remind you, but the emperor is a man. Have you forgotten that the late empress held sway over the nobles because of her intellect? Her power to persuade all she spoke to? The late empress was a paragon of a feminine strength and virtue. You fall dangerously short of the mark." Emerald raised a brow, looking down her nose at Selene, a faint sneer twisting her full lips.

"What would you even bring to a marriage with the prince? If words are so very important, convince me your candidacy is superior," Selene goaded.

"My province-"

"No, not your province. It belongs to your father, and in future, to your brothers. What good are you to the prince without your family's connections, and the powers of your male relatives? Or is that everything you are and have allowed yourself to be?" Green eyes glared back at her, but the domina was silent. "And either of you? Do you have an answer for that question? Have either of you developed your gifts past the level of a simple party trick?"

"The imperial army is led by a respected strategos and manned with legions of soldiers. An empress is not meant to fight. We don't live in a bygone era of savagery, Domina Amethyst. A civilized society is no place for that kind of mindset. If you truly wish to live as some warrior queen, there are a great many barbarian nations across the seas," Opal replied, her composure regained.

"How long ago was Lethe engaged in a bloody war?" Selene smiled. "How long ago was it that traitors infiltrated the palace and slaughtered the prince's siblings?"

The women looked at each other, searching the others' eyes for a rebuttal, but in the end all they could muster was contempt. Pathetic!

"We are, each of us, born with the potential for great power. Only fools cultivate helplessness," Selene said.

"A domina is hardly helpless. No one exists alone unto themselves. We are members of powerful, wealthy, respected families who would come to our aid with weapons drawn were we to ask for it. We have the support of entire provinces behind us. What good is one mage against an army?" Domina Topaz retorted.

Selene fumed. These women needed to be educated properly. They'd been wrapped in the safety of their names their entire lives. Not one had survived hunger, violence or neglect. Given their outlooks, none of them would survive any true conflict. When she was gone, they would need to start thinking like survivors if they wanted to be more than a pretty face on the throne.

"And which army would dare march against a husband of mine when I can personally decimate an entire city with a flick of my wrist? If I were bloody-minded, I wouldn't tolerate competition for the position of empress. But you are right. We live in a civilized society, so instead, I allow you your pretty words. But let's not pretend. We all know that if it came down to it, I could crush each of you beneath my feet. That is power, dominae, and never forget it. The men in your families certainly haven't."

"I need not listen to such blatant threats against my person. I will make it my business to teach you what it means to be a pariah." Zoe Emerald glided towards the door, all huff and indignation. The others followed suit, wordless and refusing to look her in the eye.

Selene turned to their retreating forms and smiled. "If the peace of the empire were to fracture, what good would your social standings do you? Would it protect you from the ugliness in the hearts of men at war? Would you even be able to defend yourselves from an enemy soldier? A common criminal? Your power is a delusion, feared only by those who are equally powerless. When I become empress, not a single man will object to my husband's plans because of the power *I* will bring to bear. He'll never need to lift a finger. What would anyone with real power have to fear from any of *you*?"

When the door closed, Selene sighed and rolled her shoulders, stretching her neck. She'd never been forced to play nice with so many people for so long. Selene congratulated herself on her ability to clear a room—and her schedule, too! Maybe she should treat herself? There were several hours until the evening's festivities. It seemed like fair compensation after the tediousness of the afternoon tea. But first, she needed to get rid of another irritant. Selene breathed deep and released her favourite paralytic into the air of the room. It wouldn't kill, but it would lock up the joints something fierce. In short order, a man dropped out of a shadow in the corner of the room, dressed in a dark tunic with two white, vertical stripes, a silver belt buckle and black, shiny boots. Military, or spy?

"A shadow mage. How predictable." She crouched over him.

"Domina Amethyst," The man replied with a stiff nod, his dark hair cropped short and his face clean-shaven.

"Are you a dirty voyeur, or were you ordered to follow me?"

"Which answer is less likely to get me decimated by a flick of your wrist?" He grinned with gallows humour, his grey eyes sparkling.

"Oh! I like that attitude of yours. Given you're still alive, you must know I suspect you're a lackey of the prince or that stuffy praetor. So, which is it?" She smiled, poking his cheek.

"Praetor. On order of the prince."

"I appreciate your dedication to your job, but if you intend to spy on me, I'll have to put an end to that. It'll take the fun right out of skulking about the palace causing mischief if I know you're there."

"I've been prepared to die in service to the throne since I entered the palace. Do what you have to."

"Silly shadow mage. I'm not going to kill you, just slow you down. Now that I know you're out there, it would ruin this new game between us if you die." Selene stared at him with what she hoped was her best deranged leer. The man began sweating profusely. She kissed his cheek before standing, shaking out her skirts and turning to leave.

"Enjoy that one, my shadow, and be sure to tell your replacement I'll be waiting for them."

With that she left the room. She knew exactly where she wanted to go to relax, now that she had no one following her.

Prince Belisarius rubbed his aching temples. If the rebel magistri didn't kill him, then the bloody poison mage surely would.

"What exactly did she say to the other dominae?"

"In essence, that they are candidates for empress because she allows it, and that if she so pleased, she could end their lives. She made sure to impress upon them that they were powerless, and that she would be chosen as empress because of her overwhelming strength, that their family names were less than useless to you."

"Tactically speaking, she's not wrong," Marduk replied.

"The future empress will not be chosen based on her ability to murder countless innocents!" The praetor fumed at the strategos.

"So the dominae chose to pit their wits against Selene's bloodthirst and found themselves wanting. That is hardly surprising. Were any harmed?" Belisarius asked, exhausted.

"No, but Domina Emerald made her complaint to me personally. Additionally, Selene is now wandering the palace unsupervised. She detected and compromised my spy."

"The shadow mage?" Marduk raised his brows.

"Don't sound so impressed! It only confirms what we suspected about her criminal leanings. The imperial poison mages assure me my spy will recover in a few days," Nicephorus replied, caustic.

"Inform the rest of the espionage unit to locate her but not to approach her. Have each of them carry an antidote for paralytics and purgatives. If that is all, I'm going to take my leave. I'll think on a suitable punishment for her threats."

"Your Royal Highness," Marduk and Nicephorus chimed in unison as Belisarius rose.

In his rooms, attendants stripped him of his ceremonial robes as his headache kept up its relentless pounding. He needed to restore himself before the evening, when he would be forced to play the part of a besotted suitor to that harridan. The need to do so galled him. Days of acting like a fool in public, all to be rewarded with her smug smile. How had Magister Amethyst not killed her himself?

Worse still, she'd been standoffish since their kiss. One which had left him reeling—and thinking about it far too often. He wanted another taste of her tart mouth, wanted to punish her with his tongue for flirting with the griffin, and wanted her begging for mercy in the most sensual of ways. *Enough!* The buzzing in his head intensified. He hadn't invited a woman into his scheme—he'd unwittingly recruited a demon.

"Are the amenities at the hot spring prepared?"

"Yes, Your Royal Highness."

"I do not wish to be disturbed. By anyone. Anything short of war can be handled by either the strategos or praetor."

"Understood."

The tension slowly drained from Belisarius' shoulders the closer he got to the sole oasis within the palace—a hot spring, off-limits to any not of royal blood. It was covered by stained glass and home to fragrant, tropical plants curated for both their decorative and restorative properties. The steam was funnelled away to heat the floors of several royal apartments come winter. It had been one of his mother's private projects, and it never failed to relax him. Stripping off the last of his clothes, the prince entered the grand chamber.

The palace was full of useless simpletons. No self-respecting poison mage collected thousands of poisons and failed to sample the wares. Only self-loathing types were in charge of the imperial vault that hoarded them. Selene incapacitated most of them by combining several poisons they were unlikely to have ingested. Two had managed to fend her off, but they were too old to put up much of a physical fight. In the end, she'd been able to sample a number of new beauties before she'd needed to beat a hasty retreat, stuffing a bottle or three in her skirts for good measure.

They should be grateful for her time—education of the ignorant was considered a virtue, after all.

It was that same hasty retreat which put her in a bit of a predicament. She had lost herself in an unfamiliar section of the palace, using a number of servants' stairwells before thinking better of it. Now enclosed in a hot spring garden, a stained glass roof dimming the interior, finding the exit was taking time and she was getting overheated in her heavy beaded silks. As she wandered through it, stripping as she went, she bundled her clothes under one arm. It was too damned hot to be wearing much of anything in a place like this.

Just as she'd spotted the exit, it appeared someone was entering through it. She hid behind foliage, spying his backside as he passed—truly a feast for the eyes. His long dark hair swayed as he strode by, lovingly sculpted musculature on display; thick thighs, powerful shoulders and a pert bottom. Thankfully, he wasn't the perceptive sort, allowing her to look her fill. Adjusting her garments under her arm, Selene crept towards the exit. A bottle fell from her bundle, crashing noisily on the rough rock floor, shattering splendidly.

Her last greedy impulse had doomed her.

As if he were part beast, the man leapt from the spring and was upon her before she could flee. He pinned her to the ground, cheek shoved onto the smooth stone. A very embarrassing squeak made its way out of her before she realised he was touching her bare skin. Poor fool didn't know what was about to happen to him.

"Delectable rear or not, I'll have you begging for mercy if you don't unhand me *now*."

"Somehow I think not, Selene," Belisarius growled.

Disbelieving her ears, Selene craned her neck to the side to catch a glimpse of the man holding her captive. And what a glimpse it was! Who knew the peacock had the body of a demigod? She'd seen his bare, chiselled chest but this was something else. A mind-blowing, sculpted masterpiece crouched atop her. Thoughts of licking those slick muscles crept unbidden into her mind. She'd always been weak to the fit ones.

Damn! No!

He was a peacock first and foremost! His impressive manhood came into view, nestled in a 'v' of dark curls. Selene sucked in a breath.

Her mouth watered. She grew slick with desire.

She would never admit to it.

"I think I need to insert lye directly into my eyes," she mumbled.

"Of course, it would be *you* who worms her way into a forbidden area! Which of my people did you poison to gain entry?"

She almost snorted. Forbidden indeed.

"I got lost! Would you let off? If you don't-"

"What? What will you do? Poison me? I dare you to try."

Selene grinned.

"My pleasure."

But nothing happened.

"The fuck-"

"I am the *one* man you can't use your damn poisons on. Care to try a different tack, *darling*?"

She paused to think.

"I am but an unarmed, weak young woman being manhandled by the prince of Lethe. One who is suffering from a ruinous lack of undergarments. Whatever shall I do?" she simpered.

"Have you never taken any matter seriously in the whole of your life, woman?!"

He pressed her further into the floor. Her nipples hardened. She very seriously considered the state of her sanity in that moment.

"Well, you're not an antidote mage, or whatever those flunkies call themselves these days. The hell kind of mage are you?"

"Answer my question!"

Gooseflesh rose where his hot breath fanned across the back of her neck.

"I very seriously want you to let go of my arm. It's damned uncomfortable."

The prince grunted in anger, releasing her. She turned around to find he'd grabbed a towel to cover himself, but only just. Most everything else was bare to her hungry gaze. Unfair.

Damn! Focus! He was crossing his arms and glaring, his partially wet hair glistening jet black on his chest. She wanted to sink her teeth into his perfect pectoral. Fuck it, she needed to either poison him or ride him, maybe both. She tried the first but was unable to produce it. The mystery deepened.

"You've got range too. Damn, that's impressive."

"Did you just try to poison me *again*?"

Wait a minute. He didn't even know when she was trying to use her magic? Could he really be that rarest of rare mages?

"You're a negation mage, aren't you?" she gasped.

She'd known about only one such mage, and he'd been the best assassin people only ever whispered about, able to overcome any mage, no matter how powerful, simply by being in the room with them. He never allowed a target a fair fight, disabling their magic and overpowering them with weapons, poisons and anything else he deemed necessary. Those in the criminal underworld referred to him as *The Negation*.

"How in the hells do you know about negation mages?"

"Only the best assassin ever is a negation mage. How else would I know about them?"

He was only momentarily bewildered before a scowl overtook his features once more. It mattered not. Her eyes had other things to look at, like the line of dark hair leading to an impressive royal sceptre.

"*Was* the best assassin. He took on the wrong contract and died before divulging the name of his paymaster."

"*You* killed The Negation?" Her respect for him trebled, which still wasn't particularly great, given he'd started off so low. Yes, that was why she only saw him as the peacock, dripping wet and too masculine for his own good. Did he really need the towel?

"Is that what he called himself? Yes, after a fashion." He sighed, looking exhausted. "Why was I angry with you?"

Selene shrugged, sitting attentively.

"So how come I didn't die from eating poison that first night? How did I even remove the poison the second time, now that I think about it?" she wondered.

"I don't erase a mage gift, I suppress the outward expression of it. I can't stop your body from absorbing poison—just producing it. As for the other night, I held my gift in check long enough for you to help."

"Interesting..."

So, it was like something he unconsciously conjured at all times? It had range, so it also worked in a certain radius.

"Just leave. I'm not interested in whatever escapades you've embroiled yourself in now. If you've harmed someone, inform an attendant of their predicament. I wish to be left alone," he sighed.

He turned, removed his towel and slipped into the waters of the spring. Selene saw no reason to go—not yet. How could she, when the greatest tale never told had been hinted at so maddeningly just now? Besides, he was naked and she was needy.

"I don't hear you leaving, Selene." His voice was whip-like.

Selene stripped off the last of her clothes and dashed under the water in the spring. Belisarius seemed too stunned to speak.

"I'll leave when you tell me how you killed him. Promise," she replied with as sincere a voice as she could muster. The longer she stayed in the spring, the more her muscles unwound. No wonder he kept this little gem to himself. Looked like she'd just found her new favourite spot in the palace.

"Fine. I killed him with a knife. Happy?"

"Getting there," Selene sighed, relaxing into the warmth. "So how does that work anyway? An ignoble mage as prince of an empire full of elementalist pricks? Why let them get away with the snobbery?"

"Very few know what my mage gift is, and everyone else assumes I command fire, as all my siblings did. There's no reason to disabuse them of the notion when all it would mean is more resistance to my reforms. Contrary to your opinion, both laws and minds must change before the last hateful remnants of the caste system die. And if you hadn't noticed, the most important men at my side are decidedly *not* elemental mages."

"Be hard to hide it once you get married. I can guarantee the dominae think you're a fire mage." Selene drank in her fill of his slick body. Seated on a nearby stone bench, her nipples just covered by the depth of the water, she caught his eyes snaking down before he looked away guiltily. She licked her lips, his eyes tracking the movement.

Fearing she'd liked his passion too much for her own good, she'd run the last time. She couldn't keep him, after all. Not that she'd wanted to. But this time, she cast aside those fears. Hunger curled low, making her ache.

"Cross that bridge when I get to it," he said.

Selene sauntered closer, this time sitting up so that her breasts were mostly bared. His eyes widened at the sight. The tendrils of steam were not quite so thick here, and she could see a blush across his cheeks.

"Is this your twisted way of trying to seduce me?" Belisarius asked, voice gone husky.

She liked the sound of that. And his delicious muscles were begging for it.

"It could be, if you wanted it," she replied, excitement pulsing through her.

How long had it been since she'd been able to really let loose with a man? Years? Ever? To never need suspect a man of only wanting her for the thrill of danger her gift posed? The idea was heady. She found herself wading closer to the prince, watching as the scowl melted off his face and lust darkened his eyes.

"If this is your idea of a prank-"

"Promise you'll spank me?" she asked with a sassy smile, reaching out for him.

Grabbing her outstretched wrist, he jerked her against his body, water sloshing with his quick movements. His other hand gripped her thigh, pressing her hips to his. Her free arm wrapped around his slick shoulder, nipples grazing his chest as her core rubbed against a thick shaft. Perfection.

"A spanking would be the least of your worries."

"Less talk, more seducing."

Selene kissed him—hard. He released her wrist, and she wrapped that arm around him, too. His hand skimmed down her back, his kiss punishing. Fingers kneading her backside, he ground himself against her. The tingling shot down to her toes. She nipped his ear, licking and kissing her way down his neck as his harsh breaths sounded in her ears. When he pulled her away, she groaned in denial. She'd almost had a mouthful of his perfect chest.

His lips found hers again, and she became vaguely aware that he was lifting her out of the waters and positioning her on a plush towel. No matter how eagerly her tongue greeted his, Belisarius punished her, claiming her. When he finally let her up for air, hot, hungry lips worked down her neck as he crouched over her, refusing to let her move. He sucked on her nipple, dark eyes lost to some primal need as he gazed back up at her. Then he bit down gently, sending a bolt of lust straight through her.

She took hold of him, revelling in the feeling of hot, soft skin stretched tight over rigid steel. His fingers found their way to her core and stroked her mercilessly. Leaving her breasts behind, he kissed his way down her body to where his fingers tortured her in the best way.

The sight of him between her thighs, his long black hair trailing across her stomach, hand gripping her hip—it was a wicked, waking dream. His tongue kept her on the edge of sanity as he filled her with his fingers. She lost all control, choking on her pleasure. But he wasn't done. Slowing his erotic onslaught, he proved immune to begging, bargaining or threats, refusing to be rushed, not until she saw stars a second time. Every sensual nerve alight, breathless from pleasure he leaned over her, his mouth glistening from his task. He took her hand and placed it back on his shaft.

"Do you want this?" he asked, dark, sensual promise plain.

"I want it now!" she cried out, beyond shame or games of one-up-manship. She ached.

Selene guided him into her, stretching deliciously. When he thrust, she moved with him, desperate to feel every inch. Her nails scored his back, legs locked on his hips, frantic to have more of him. Every stroke lit her senses on fire. He angled himself, hitting her just right, wrenching a sharp gasp from her. Reclaiming her mouth, he branded her with his tongue as he took his due. When his lips left hers, his thrusts turned frenzied, dark eyes wild and fierce. She drank in the sight of him as he followed her to completion.

They lay tangled, gasping as if they had just run for their lives. Her fingers threaded through his long, silky hair as she breathed in the scent of him. His eyes found hers, searching for something she couldn't name. Grinning like a fool, she pulled him down for soft, lazy kisses. Eventually, he pulled away, helping her back into the spring when her shaky legs refused to cooperate. Coaxing her into his lap, his chin resting on her head, they simply sat. His arms encircled her and she sank into him, flush against his smooth, warm skin.

Neither said a word.

Chapter 19

The ballroom glittered with the flickering flames of hundreds of candles held aloft in chandeliers. Elegant chatter, the clinking of glasses and the soft music of stringed instruments created a constant, low buzz. None of it could distract Iliana from her friend's odd plea. Having just finished a round of dancing with the increasingly popular griffin, Selene had been deposited close at hand. Dressed in purple silks and glittering jewels, Selene looked as though she belonged in this overcrowded noble party. Her words, however, did not.

"I need to make Belisarius forget we fucked."

"Wait, what happened? How? I thought you both despised each other."

Iliana had noticed that the prince no longer had a cold and haughty disposition when he danced with Selene. He'd been almost tender, playing his part to utter perfection. Perhaps his acting was no longer just that.

"Well, I was busy furthering my education, and I bumped into him in the bath. Anyway, he looks amazing naked, and I couldn't help myself. The problem is now he's being... *nice*."

Selene spoke the word like it was the filthiest thing to have ever crossed her lips. Iliana could barely contain her snort of mirth. Selene could handle death and mutilation with aplomb, but an affectionate look had her running?

"Don't laugh! It's so humiliating!"

"Which part? The sex or his change of heart?"

"Obviously the feelings bit! The sex was top five, easily," Selene replied with all seriousness.

"Selene, this isn't a problem." Iliana crossed her arms, mulish. She would take no part in a scheme so hare-brained.

"He hasn't even insulted me once since the sex! Not once! It's weird, and I need to make it stop," Selene whined.

"Have you ever considered that maybe he finds himself attracted to you, and now wants to have a better relationship?"

"Gods forbid!" Selene shuddered. "I don't do *relationships*."

"I beg to differ. We are best friends, are we not? That is a relationship, and you've been a true if eccentric companion without any ill effects."

"That's not the issue. Wouldn't you find it odd if the strategos suddenly started treating you like a noblewoman? It's the same thing!"

Iliana really wanted to knock actual sense into her friend, but could see it was not a fight she would win this day. She held her tongue regarding the strategos, whose attentions and respect she liked very much. Perhaps participation was the best way to mitigate the impending silliness. Iliana sighed, certain she would regret this come morning.

"What did you have in mind?"

"Well, you see, I pumped one of those pathetic poison mages they keep locked up here in the palace for information. One eventually squealed about a private garden, which is rumoured to have a flower that causes one to forget. It's my best shot at fixing this situation."

"You want to scour the Imperial Gardens, which are enormous, for a rumoured private garden, with a rumoured flower that *supposedly* removes memories?" Iliana asked, incredulous.

"These are desperate times, Iliana."

"I'll only help you look for a bit tonight. If we find nothing, you agree to call off this scheme and figure out a better way to handle your interactions with the prince. Deal?"

Selene held out her hand.

"Deal."

No sooner had Marduk taken his eyes off the blonde metals mage than he'd lost her—not an easy feat for a man who could see over every head in the ballroom. Normally, he would just follow the scent of her, but every woman in attendance wore heavy perfume as a matter of habit. It was hell on his keen senses. Was that her sneaking out to the terrace with the poison mage? Marduk rushed to follow. He was certain this would end in confrontation with the tiny terror herself, but he refused to allow Iliana to be caught up in dangerous mischief if he could help it.

The metals mages of the Imperial Forge were highly suspicious of an outsider joining their ranks, galled by the aspirant's gender, and had taken to eyeing him mutinously over his insistence that Iliana be made a member. In the end they would relent or find other employment, but he could ill afford for his star candidate to find herself in hot water with the prince or praetor.

Once free of the hell of the ballroom, Marduk tailed the two friends on their stroll through the gardens. He didn't expect to hear much from them he hadn't heard before, but one new development caught him off guard.

"What would be so terrible about being romanced by the prince?"

"It would be weird. For everyone." Selene crossed her arms.

"I don't know. He had an awfully besotted look on his face when the two of you danced earlier. *He* hasn't acted awkwardly." Iliana tweaked her nose.

"It was awkward *for me*," Selene growled, batting her friend away.

"You can be such a child sometimes. Most people would be happy to find someone they both liked and had chemistry with."

"But I don't like him. We just had sex, that's all!" Selene gesticulated, arms wide.

Marduk nearly faltered in his next step. As it was, he barely stopped himself from crunching rather loudly on the gravel. It couldn't be true. Belisarius had never taken anyone but the most professional and circumspect of courtesans to bed. He'd never laid a finger on any noble-born woman the whole of his life, bastard or no. Until this scheme, he'd kept all interactions with noblewomen to the absolute minimum, the better to avoid a marriage not wholly of his choosing. But what if it weren't some idle boast? The thought was unsettling.

So much for the punishment Belisarius had meant to dole out to the tea party terror! Though as he reflected, it all made a certain sense. Selene wound Belisarius up like no one else. She treated him without respect, laughing in his face when he made threats. Perhaps the novelty of the situation was what attracted him? Belisarius was a late bloomer in many respects, romance included. There had yet to be a woman he'd ever had inordinate interest in. If that had changed, if Selene had decided to remain in the empire... His eyes flashed to Iliana, the way the moonlight made her hair shine like spun silver, the graceful sway of her full hips, the beautiful lilt of her voice. Desire and hope made his heart ache and soar. *No.* He crushed the dream. He couldn't afford the luxury of such thoughts.

Marduk placed his next step as silently as the last, determined to get to the bottom of it all.

"Mmm-hmm. Top five, I believe you said." Iliana smiled, finger tapping her lips.

"You're enjoying this, you cruel hussy!" Selene pointed an accusing finger at her.

"Even if you somehow pull this off, I intend to remind you of it daily till the end of time. I've never seen you squirm like this before. You eat toads, worms, snakes and slugs in front of me without batting an eye, but something about the prince sends you into a fit."

"One makes me strong, the other-"

"Makes you feel vulnerable?" Iliana leaned down, face to face with Selene.

"I was going to say makes my skin crawl." She pushed Iliana's face away.

"You know what I think?" Iliana asked, catching up to her friend.

"Don't want to know," Selene grumbled, arms crossed again.

"I think you're scared because you do like him, if only a little. You've had this merry look since you first baited him. I think you enjoy tweaking his nose and getting into fights with him. Obviously, he's just as twisted as you, since he seems to enjoy it just as much."

Marduk was torn between hoping Iliana had the right of it, and fearing that she did. He couldn't help the spiral of his thoughts. It would mean she might stay. It would also mean he'd been a colossal fool, trying to woo her into his bed instead of trying to fully win her heart.

"Belisarius is just a peacock, nothing more!" Selene stopped in her tracks, stomping her foot.

"Is it Belisarius now? It seems the peacock has just the right feathers to attract *you*, Selene." Iliana twirled a lock of platinum hair around her finger.

"I'm not talking about this anymore."

Selene put her hands to her ears, which only made Iliana laugh heartily and sing taunting children's songs. Every so often, the two would peer into various flower beds. Selene would comment on whatever flora could be used to incapacitate and then Iliana would taunt her about the bouquets the prince was sure to give her. What on Oblivion were they up to?

"So, what are we looking for? Do you even know what colour it's supposed to be?"

"White. I heard it's supposed to be small, white and luminesce slightly."

"Are you sure they didn't send you on a snipe hunt? You *did* just poison them and then raid their collection," Iliana pointed out, peering over a tall, sculpted hedge.

"Oh, I'm sure. I told them I'd be back with sharp blades if they steered me wrong."

"Honestly, there should be a sign around your neck warning innocent people about you."

On that, he and Iliana were in complete agreement.

"Nah, then I'd lose the element of surprise."

Marduk didn't know how he felt about this new development between the prince and the poison mage. While it might be good for Marduk, it would throw the whole of the empire into chaos if he were serious in his intentions. Nicephorus might even die of shock. That aside, how was the flower involved? Was there some lethal plant on the grounds? As Marduk mulled it over, the pair stopped in front of a heavy gate. It led to the late empress' private gardens, sealed since her death.

"That's an awfully big lock for a garden, *wouldn't you say*?"

"Gods below, don't rub it in. I was sure this would all be for naught, and then you'd have had to own up to your feelings."

"Not while I breathe! Now, if you would, my darling friend?"

"Fine, fine. Just promise me that if you can't help yourself again, you'll deal with the outcome like a grown woman?"

"It won't happen again. It was temporary insanity."

"Isn't everything you do temporary insanity?"

With a single touch the lock opened and fell to the ground with a heavy thud. Marduk did a double-take, mentally revising a list of security measures for the locked doors of the palace. Iliana and Selene unwound the chains threaded through the bars, as though they'd done it too many times to be concerned. Marduk's worry grew. If he didn't interrupt this soon, Iliana might give the Imperial Forge good reason to reject her candidacy.

"The metal feels creaky, so let's be quick about this before someone investigates the sound."

"I need only a moment!"

The doors screeched open, leaving his ears ringing. Marduk and both women cringed at the sound.

"Quickly!"

Marduk followed, careful not to touch the gates as he entered, his footsteps silent.

"I think I found it!" Selene whispered.

Marduk crept through a garden overrun with tiny white flowers. They reflected the light of the moon, emitting a warm luminescence. Empress Nadia had used her mage gift to create all kinds of botanical wonders, but he didn't recall these. Many of her little refuges had been closed after her death, neither the prince nor the emperor able to bear the sight, but it troubled him that Selene had wanted to find this very place.

"What are you waiting for? Collect one so we can go."

"I'm curious…"

Selene plucked a flower and popped it in her mouth. Her eyes glazed over. She shook herself, then returned her gaze to the flowers at her feet.

"Oh! Found it! I'm curious though…"

"Wait! Selene?"

The poison mage grabbed another flower and ate it. Her eyes had another faraway look before she came back to herself. Iliana lunged to grab Selene's hands in hers and peered, concerned, into her friend's face.

"How did we get in here?" Selene asked. "Never mind. Look, it's the flower! Time for a sample."

"No! You've already eaten it twice. Don't you remember?"

Marduk blood ran cold. What in the hells *was* that flower? He did his best not to step on any, lest he contaminate his boots with their poison.

"Don't try to trick me, Iliana. Just because you want to amuse yourself with my situation, it's no reason to be a spoilsport. We found this place in a single night, fair and square."

Iliana picked Selene up in a bear hug, pulling her away from the flowers. Good girl. It was the right move. Hopefully, that would be the end of it. He would inform the prince of the danger and perhaps have the whole garden ploughed under and the earth salted.

"You've already eaten these things twice, and the second time you bent down for more because you couldn't remember you'd already done it. Obviously, it does what you were told."

"But poisons shouldn't affect me like that... If I can't remember it, how am I supposed to use it? You're sure I've already eaten it?"

Selene stared wistfully at the flowers while Iliana looked ready to burn them to ash. Marduk shared the sentiment. What was a man without his memories, after all?

"I'll let you have one more, but first, a precaution."

"What do you have in mind?"

"Take off your slipper off, grab a rock, and then put it on again. If you can't remember having done so, then I'll take you out of here even if I have to drag you. Agreed?"

"Fine."

Selene did as she was asked, grimacing as she yanked her bejewelled slipper back on. But there was a craftiness to her visage. Marduk was surprised Iliana hadn't hauled her out for that look alone.

"Did you hear that?" Selene asked.

"What?"

"Go look around the hedge. Has someone found us?"

"I certainly hope not." Iliana picked up her skirts and headed straight for Marduk. The second Iliana's back was turned, Selene plucked as many flowers as she could and crushed them in her palms, trying to fit even more before stuffing them all into her mouth. Marduk decided to make himself known at that moment.

"Strategos! I didn't see you there." Iliana smiled guiltily as she posed, trying unsuccessfully to obstruct his view.

"Please don't try to fabricate some story. I've been following you since you left the ballroom. Save your outrage for your friend, who has just swallowed two handfuls of those flowers."

"Gods below! Selene!" Iliana whipped around in a flurry of skirts and tore her friend away from the garden altogether. "Selene! Selene!" Iliana snapped her fingers in front of vacant amethyst eyes.

When Selene recovered from her stupor, the look on her face was utterly devoid of her cynical air. She stared up at Iliana with wonder and awe, eyes wide and a girlish smile lighting up her features. The words out of her mouth made Marduk's heart freeze in horror.

"Wow, you're pretty. Are you here to be my new mom?"

It had been an age since the emperor had joined in any official festivities. Darius saw little point in making pleasant chatter with nobles who would just as soon belittle him behind his back. However, since he'd met Selene, he could feel that old need for fun and mischief surface. He'd had one of his servants regale him with tales of all her antics in the palace. Darius had howled with laughter when he'd heard what she'd done to the praetor's spy. The parlour in which he'd been found would be off limits until someone could deep clean the carpets.

"Father? What brings you to the ballroom, and in full royal kit?" Belisarius asked.

"Came to see my future daughter-in-law. Where is that minx?" He smiled, slapping Belisarius on the back.

"Probably threatening to murder another bride candidate. I've sent some of our other spies to keep a watch on her."

"I'm surprised the rest of them haven't found a way to disappear before being assigned the task." He chuckled.

"The night is young."

Darius patted his son's shoulder and went to seek out Selene. In an instant Belli was swamped with female attention. He was a good-looking sort, but Darius always knew when his son was simply wearing the mask of the politician.

None of the dominae fighting for his attention held sway over his son's heart. Darius supposed that was one of the hazards of growing up royal—you were desired for all the wrong reasons by all the worst sorts.

Darius had been lucky to find Nadia when they were young nobodies, relatively speaking. Even as a girl, Nadia had been a powerful plant mage, often called upon to help the harvests of powerful neighbours. As a minor noble with more siblings than she could count, she had also often played the peacemaker. Darius had been the sixth child of a third wife of the King, often left to his own devices, a prince in name only. Those were easier times. He wished Belli could've lived like that, a real childhood, a life where he could fuck up now and then without the weight of an empire on his shoulders, where he could've fallen in love ten times over with pretty girls who only wanted him for his smile.

He hoped Selene would be just that woman for Belli. She clearly didn't want his son for his crown or power, and he'd never seen Belli so flustered over a woman before. Yet she wasn't anywhere to be found. The eyes of predatory nobles on his back made his skin crawl. Fuckers were always scheming with their false smiles and hungry eyes. Even now, one or two hoped to throw their daughters at him. Frustrated, he marched back to his son's side. Dominae excused themselves prettily and retreated.

"She's not here." He crossed his arms, slouching in defeat.

"I suppose your plans for mischief have been ruined." Belli raised a brow.

"I hope you at least have some fun with her, Belli. You could use an uncomplicated bit of fluff."

Belli looked at him oddly, grip tight on his glass of wine. Darius couldn't help teasing him.

"And who knows? Maybe you'll give me a couple of grandkids to play with. I won't mind if they're not legitimate. I'm not picky."

His horror was stark, if fleeting. Darius stifled a snort. Then Belli narrowed his eyes when one of Marduk's men whispered something in his ear.

"It seems she's found mischief all on her own."

Iliana paced back and forth, anxiety ratcheting up every few minutes as Selene failed to recover her faculties. She'd screamed and complained about how her clothes and shoes hurt, then that she was hungry, then that she wanted to play. She was seated now, stuffing her face with cake and explaining that her mother never made her cake or much of anything really, and that she'd learned to catch frogs for supper. It was a depressing window into Selene's upbringing, but not unexpected, given the few tidbits she'd told Iliana over the years.

"Who else can we ask about those flowers? Surely someone remembers?"

"I've sent someone to ask the prince and the emperor."

"I wanna play piggyback. Let me hold onto your horns," Selene demanded, her arms outstretched towards Marduk.

"Finish your cake first," Marduk replied, unease plain.

"Okay." She grinned.

"How could the poison mages in the palace not know more about it?" Iliana's hands shook as her heart raced.

What if Selene never recovered? She didn't want to lose the woman she loved like a sister. How would she look after her if they didn't receive payment for their charade? Iliana didn't even know who she could ask for counsel on caring for adults with these kinds of needs. Overwhelmed, tears threatened.

"I think you overestimate how much importance has been placed on their department over the past several decades."

"But she's never been under a poison's influence this long before. What if it's irreversible?" Her voice wavered, emotion choking her.

The door swung open before Marduk could reply. Both the prince and emperor stormed inside, imperial red robes fluttering, their brows knotted with concern.

"What happened? Your message was cryptic at best," the prince asked.

"She's eaten a large quantity of poison and she can't seem to recover," Iliana replied.

The prince looked at Selene, who was stuffing her face with sweets, and then back to Marduk and Iliana. Selene was wearing a large, loose nightgown, her hair in disarray and her face and fingers covered in bits of cake. She had to admit, it didn't *appear* particularly alarming.

"Please explain yourselves. I was under the impression she was in dire straits."

"Your hair is pretty. Why do you wear so much red?" Selene asked him as she licked frosting from her fingers.

"Gods damn it, Selene! I have had enough of your games!" the prince bellowed.

Selene cowered, curling into a shivering ball, eyes wide with terror.

"I'm sorry! I'll be quiet! Please don't hurt me!"

"Don't scream at her!" Iliana shot back, putting her arms around her friend.

"Your Royal Highness, to the best of our abilities, we've determined that Selene believes herself to be five years old," Marduk said to a bewildered prince. "This occurred after she ate a large quantity of white flowers from one of the late empress' gardens. Given this prolonged state, we'd hoped that either yourself or the emperor might know something about this particular poison."

"She'll recover," the emperor replied, pained.

"When?" Iliana asked.

"Given her tolerance to all manner of substances? A few hours maybe." The emperor had a haunted look as he gazed at Selene.

"How do you know this?" Belisarius asked, suspicious.

"Another time, Belli." He shook his head. He knelt before Selene, his eyes soft. "Dear girl, don't pay too much attention to that loud boy. No one is going to touch a hair on your pretty head. If you'd like, I could tell you some of the very best bedtime stories in the whole empire."

"You promise?"

"I promise."

Iliana wasn't sure why the emperor would have known about the poison, but she was grateful. She would have to wait and see if Selene recovered. For now, she allowed herself some optimism.

CHAPTER 20

It was easily the worst headache Selene had ever experienced. Confused by shifting dreams of warmth and horror, she woke groggy and uncertain. War drums were beating in her head, made worse by the expectant, hopeful, terrified looks of the gathered crowd. If only she could hide in a dark, quiet place. But the sun's glaring rays bored mercilessly into her eyes like a hundred tiny lances. The glares of the praetor, strategos and prince competed for piercing potential.

"The fuck is going on?" she moaned.

"Thank the gods, she's normal!" Iliana smiled and hugged her.

"Celebrate in whispers!" Selene hissed.

"What do you remember?"

"Leaving the ballroom? Did we get into a bar fight? Please tell me we fleeced someone out of some gold." Nothing else would make up for her aching head.

"No, you went looking for those white flowers in order to-"

Selene launched herself from her makeshift bed and pressed her hands across Iliana's mouth, pounding head be damned. There was simply no way she would allow any of these men to know what she was about, least of all the prince. At least he was back to glaring. Perhaps she needn't seek out those flowers after all.

Why were her hands so sticky?

"Not another word, dear friend."

Iliana's blue eyes were all mischief. This boded ill.

"But don't you want to know what you did after you ate those flowers?"

"I'm sure these esteemed gentlemen have better things to do with their time than listen to our antics, don't you?" Selene warned.

Her heart sank when Iliana's smile deepened. Gods below, had the prince seen her in some embarrassing daze? For some reason, the idea was unsettling.

"Oh, these esteemed gentlemen were full witnesses to your antics. No need to be shy." Belisarius had a look of unholy glee in his dark eyes. A mortified scream was trapped in her throat.

"Those flowers had you convinced you'd become your five-year-old self. We spent the night entertaining a toddler until you passed out," Iliana replied cheerfully. "I hope this teaches you a lesson in not putting strange things in your mouth."

Selene only just stopped herself from sneaking a glance at Belisarius. She didn't care what he thought. Nope. Not in the slightest.

"You're enjoying this, damn you," Selene grumbled, clutching her head. "Don't look so smug. Even though I can't remember a damned thing, I promise to be shameless about my conduct as soon as this headache fades."

"Your Royal Highness, allow me to escort her to her rooms so that she might spend the day in quiet reflection. There is nothing of import scheduled that requires her presence. Perhaps you should take this time to look over some of the documents my agents have collected." The praetor's glare at her was censorious.

As soon as Belisarius turned to leave, Selene stuck her tongue out at the praetor.

"Perhaps you will allow me to escort you to your rooms?" Marduk asked of Iliana.

"I will," Iliana replied.

It was just the praetor left. Lucky her.

"So, what did you want to say that you couldn't in front of your master?"

"If you're going to act like a complete fool, do it out of sight of others. I'm deducting one tenth of your reward for your behaviour. If you want it back, then don't cause any more trouble."

"That threat would be a lot more credible if I didn't have our agreement down in writing, Praetor," Selene replied, full of vinegar.

"You are nothing more than the illegitimate trash your father thought to cast on our doorsteps. The punishment for impersonating nobility is ten years imprisonment. It was your good fortune the prince could use you for the betterment of the empire. Don't think you're good enough to be breathing the same air as the rest of us."

"You done? Don't need to spit at me, do you?" Selene sneered. She was used to dealing with people who only saw her as a thing that didn't meet their expectations.

His green eyes turned sharp and cold as he grabbed her arm. His grip was stronger than she thought it would've been. Perhaps he wasn't just a paper-pushing weakling, mage gift aside.

"I've already heard whispers of your conduct with the prince. Don't go getting ideas. There is no place for such an unsuitable empress, least of all one as barren as a female poison mage."

Yet another expectation she couldn't meet, but that one hurt, leaving a raw ache in her chest. She refused to show it. She raised her chin.

"It sounds like someone has been a good little researcher. Well, you're not the only one who got to know who they're dealing with, *berserker*. Best hope I don't slip you a butter knife at the next tea party. You wouldn't want to lose control, would you?"

He released her as if burned.

"That's immaterial to this discussion."

"Which do you think is more pathetic, Praetor? A barren poison mage, or a berserker too weak-willed to pick up a blade? At least I don't use the prince's gift as a security blanket against my own nature."

Nicephorus' glare was glacial, his white-knuckle fists shaking with rage. Job done. It was the least she could do after his vile comments.

"I'll see myself to my room."

⤐⤐⤐ ⤏⤏⤏

As Marduk ushered her into her family's suite, the deadened, silent stares of her sisters drew him up short. It was unnerving, to be sure, but Iliana had learned to suppress the shiver it sent down her spine. She'd learned to suppress a great deal recently.

"Perhaps this is not the most restful place, Domina. Could I interest you in a peaceful getaway for the day?"

"Oh! Are you certain? I wouldn't want to impose if you have a busy schedule."

There was no chance a day in his presence would be close to soothing if her fluttering heart was any indication.

"It would be my honour." He kissed her hand. "Change into something comfortable and leave the rest to me."

Giddy and flushed, Iliana nodded, waiting for him to turn the corner before she rushed to do as he suggested. It was a relief to be helped out of her evening gown and heavy jewellery. She washed up in a basin and had the serving girl pin her hair in a loose style to give her aching scalp a rest from the previous night's updo. As she waited in the parlour, her sisters quietly turning the pages of a book or embroidering simple patterns, Diodora touched her elbow. Iliana swallowed her squeak of surprise.

"A feral is an inappropriate suitor for a domina, even a menial one," Diodora intoned.

Iliana narrowed her eyes.

"How dare you call him that! He is a kind and honourable man and he is the strategos. I don't care what's been done to you, you have no right to look down on him like that."

Diodora tilted her head, her placid expression never changing.

"It is my duty to teach you how to behave as a domina. A domina does not associate with fer-"

Iliana put her hand over her half-sister's mouth.

"Stop! I will not hear another vile word of it."

As if her task were now complete, Diodora turned away without comment and continued to sew the same, simple pattern on the silk square before her.

Marduk's arrival couldn't come soon enough. When he knocked on their door, she was glad to take his arm and be free of the place. It wasn't until they were walking along a gravel-lined path some distance from the palace proper that the tenseness left her shoulders. Iliana resolved to banish her troubles from her mind. No more of Selene's hare-brained schemes. No more slander. No more sisters. Just her, the warm sun on her skin and Marduk, a picnic basket in one arm and her on the other.

"How are you faring? I can't imagine it's easy being here." Marduk broke their companionable silence.

Iliana felt herself tense anew, gut churning with anxiety. What a perfectly horrid question, and yet no one had bothered to ask her before now. She'd stood against the unrelenting onslaught of her situation, but now she faltered. Suddenly, the walls she'd built around herself crumbled.

Marduk must have sensed it. He stopped in his tracks.

"Whatever it is, I'll fix it."

Tears stung her eyes. How long had she been desperately holding herself together, hoping someone would offer to take all her woes away, soothe her hurts, make it better? She was no longer a child, and yet her childhood was the last time she'd felt truly safe. How weak and foolish it was to wish that someone would protect her. And yet it didn't stop her from wanting it very badly.

"I...I don't think you can. And besides, you have problems of your own. You don't need to shoulder mine." Iliana pulled on his arm, urging him to keep walking, eyes turned from his.

"I can carry more than you think, Iliana. If you need a sympathetic ear, I'm here."

She took a deep breath. The man at her side twisted her in knots. She wanted him to be her protector, but he had offered her no more than a toss between the sheets.

"Truthfully, so much is awful here. The nobles delight in cruelty and pettiness, the servants are forced to act like furniture, my sisters' conditions scare me and yet they say the most hateful things. Selene causes mayhem, which I suppose is par for the course, but I worry for her all the same. She's not nearly as invulnerable as she appears. And every day, I fear my father will try to kill me."

"Has he threatened you?" Marduk's brows furrowed as he drew her closer.

They turned off the manicured footpath. A dappled, vibrant canopy stretched overhead, the trail sloping upwards.

"Not...recently."

What could she really call a lifetime of being terrorized and hunted? She'd had to flee every town she'd settled in the moment he'd tracked her down. Nowhere was far enough for Magister Sapphire to lose sight of the daughter he'd failed to drown.

"Do you not wish to discuss it? We don't have to, if it's too difficult."

The sound of flowing water had her gripping his arm. She held her breath as the trail opened up, a narrow stream intersecting it. Iliana stopped him. Maybe if he saw her as damaged, she could free herself of her illusions about him. The truth was always the best way to have a man running in the opposite direction.

"The creek by my childhood home wasn't much wider than that, maybe as wide as I am tall. Even in Spring, with heavy rainfall and the snowmelt from the mountains, when it breached its banks, the water never made it to town. But when the magister heard of my neighbours boasting of my skill at my stepfather's forge, remarking on the similarities in our appearance, he... he destroyed the town. He sent a giant wave and swept it off the map. I survived because I was in the forge that night, and I turned all the metal into a ball and sealed myself in. When I emerged, everyone was dead or gone. And now he tracks me down no matter where I run. He doesn't need to say anything, but he has always threatened my life."

Except Marduk didn't turn away, or make false promises.

"And this is why you wish to leave Lethe."

"Yes."

Marduk let go of her and jumped across the stream, basket in hand. He put it down and turned to her.

"You're right, I can't fix that."

Her heart sank. Best to have this part done with now.

"I can't fix the cruel nature of the world we live in, or change what a monster the magister is, nor can I change what's happened to you."

And yet, he leaned across the stream, his hand outstretched, eyes solemn.

"But I can be someone you can lean on, for however long you wish it. I can listen to your worries, and take you away from those cruelties, even if it's just for a short while. When you need a place of peace and safety, I can be that place for you."

Iliana bit her bottom lip to keep it from trembling.

"Please don't say things you don't mean. You only wanted me for a bit of bed sport, remember?"

His hand curled into a fist and dropped to his side.

"Do you want my honest answer to that?"

Iliana nodded. She'd had her heart stomped on a time or two. She'd survived it before, and she would survive it again. Bracing herself, she met his eyes.

"I know a good woman when I meet one, and you're better than I could ever dream of. I didn't think you would ever want more than bed sport from me. You're breathtakingly talented, endlessly kind, you're strong, brave, and you're the most beautiful woman I've ever seen. And your plan is to leave Lethe. I've not asked for more because I assumed you could not, or did not want to, give me more."

Heart pounding out of her chest, she swallowed her fears, letting her hopes eclipse them.

"And if I wanted more?" she whispered.

"Whatever you want of me, whatever you need of me, I would be honoured to give it to you."

Iliana's face heated as her hopes soared. Her tongue was frozen, words impossible to form. Tentatively, she reached out her hand. His grip was sure, and when she leapt, he was there to ensure she made it across. He held her a little longer than necessary and it warmed her heart. He kissed her hand, retrieved the basket and led the rest of the way, a small smile turning up the corners of his lips.

When they reached the end of the path, it was to a stunning sight. Below, the river valley behind the palace opened up, a panoramic view of rolling green hills, lush forests and the mountains in the distance.

"It's beautiful," Iliana gasped.

"And so far as I know, no one else knows of this hidden gem. I come here when I need an escape. Now, whenever you need it, you'll have a place to escape to." He squeezed her hand.

"Thank you," she whispered.

Usually the schemes and plots were Selene's domain. This time, it was Iliana's turn. At first, Iliana had thought her desire to stay on at the palace and let Marduk romance her was pure girlish fantasy, one with a predetermined end. But if Selene had formed an attachment to the prince, perhaps everyone could be happy. All she needed to do was make her friend realise it.

Iliana gazed into Marduk's dark eyes and gave in to hope. He wanted more than just a bit of fun, and she was ashamed not to have realized before now. It was in the way he defended her to the praetor, in how he never failed to respect her skill, in how he absent-mindedly stroked her fingers whenever she put her hand on the crook of his arm. She'd never been a stranger to the admiring glances of men, but Marduk looked at her like she was the sun and the moon.

He laid out the picnic, his voice calm.

"In a few days, there is to be a play at the Odeon as well as chariot racing in the Hippodrome—Reds versus Greens. Would you like to see one of them? With me?"

"I would. The races, that is. I have always wanted to see them." Iliana's eyes sparkled with excitement.

"A woman after my own heart." He smiled, patting the space beside him.

She decided she very much liked the idea of being more to this man—here, in Lethe. All she needed was a plan, and a bit of luck.

CHAPTER 21

The birds had only just begun chirping in the weak, early morning light. Though the dawn had proved cool, the day promised to be a hot one. Famous actors had been scheduled to enact a gripping tragedy in the Odeon, while the imperial Reds and the provincial Greens were slated to race in the Hippodrome not far from the palace. Not that Selene would get the chance to enjoy any of it, if what she was hearing were any indication. She and the other finalists, Opal, Topaz and Emerald, had been hurriedly assembled in a cavernous ballroom in the twilight hours before dawn. Today they were to undergo the final competition of the bride show. She couldn't believe Belisarius had failed to warn her before having the praetor drag her from her rooms.

The prince, decked out in a gold-embroidered imperial red tunic and robe, stood before them with an apologetic smile on his face. Selene planned to make him deeply sorry.

"Dominae, please forgive me for disturbing your mornings. I wanted to give each of you as much time for this last test as possible. An empress is required to gain the support of other nobles in her role of supporting the emperor. In the worst of times, she must convince enemies and antagonists to support her, regardless of their differences. In this last test, the four of you will compete for each other's vote for the position of empress."

He pulled out four small orbs from a cloth sack, each a different colour—emerald, opal, topaz and amethyst.

"The rules are simple. No physical harm may be done to gain a vote. You have one vote, but you need not vote for anyone if you choose not to. You must retain your vote and gain the votes of two of your three competitors to win, and you cannot change your vote once it is cast. Each of you will be given an orb, the colour of which corresponds to your family house. It will change its colour only if it is given willingly to the woman of your choice, when it will change to reflect her family's namesake. All votes must be cast by noon. If no winner is chosen, I may decide that I've nominated inferior candidates. You'll have use of the antechamber to my left. No one will enter once the competition begins, and no one will leave until it is finished. Only the four of you will know what is said or done once the doors are shut. Good luck."

Not a one could hide her own brand of shock as they were given the aforementioned orbs. Topaz was the only one who appeared unconcerned. In fact, she appeared downright gleeful as the doors to the lushly appointed antechamber were closed, her amber eyes glittering with triumph.

Once the door locked behind them, Selene's blood boiled as her mind raced. That damn peacock of a prince was going to feel her wrath when this was over. No one had told her she needed to do anything but play her part and not kill anyone to get her gold. Selene swore to find a way to poison the prince, negation gift or not.

The first to break the silence was Domina Zoe Emerald.

"If you would all take your seats, I believe we have some serious negotiations to attend to." Even tired and thrown off her game, Domina Emerald cut an imposing figure. She motioned to the four sumptuously decorated chairs seated around a circular table.

"Yes. Best get on with this." Domina Topaz's smile was bright.

Selene and Domina Opal seated themselves without further comment. As if in on the scheme, each woman's servants had selected a gown whose colours and patterns clashed with the other three. Inside, Selene was screaming. Aside from threats of painful death, how was she going to win over women she'd spent her time dismissing and insulting? Emerald cleared her throat politely and spoke with utter confidence.

"I will get straight to the point. I *will* be empress. While I have no notion how Domina Amethyst made her way into our number, I can say with confidence that you, Charis, and you, Mina, are here due to my careful efforts. I expect the two of you to cast your votes for my candidacy, and I should hope I do not need to say aloud why."

Opal and Topaz paled, their expressions horrified. Opal swallowed hard and schooled her features, a hardness making the whites of her eyes glitter with her namesake's fire.

"So you expect to win with veiled threats, Zoe? You're not the only one who has gathered information on the others. Do I need to mention the name of a certain stable boy who made your acquaintance in your seventeenth year?" Opal relaxed in her seat, chin raised.

"How dare you make such baseless accusations, Charis!" Emerald stood, her hands fisting at her sides.

"When your family turned him out without reference, he came to work in our stables," Topaz replied with quiet fury, her smile sinister as she steepled her fingers.

Selene vaguely remembered some gossip to that effect from one of the books she'd read. Most mages had a contraceptive spell inked on their bodies to prevent pregnancies, so there was rarely any evidence of youthful affairs. It allowed for a great deal of fun to be had by the lower classes, and discreet dalliances among their noble counterparts. It was only ever a problem if you forgot to get the spell re-applied. However, it was the secrets both Opal and Topaz seemed to harbour that Selene wasn't privy to.

"Okay, I understand the dirt on Emerald, not that it amounts to much. But what in the hells are you threatening Opal and Topaz with?" Selene asked Emerald.

"Don't you dare!" Topaz slammed her fist on the table.

"Your reign will be turbulent if you speak a word," Opal threatened. Emerald smiled cruelly.

"If you wish to keep your secrets buried, you will cast your votes in my favour."

Selene watched her gold disappear as Opal and Topaz looked at each other in angry resignation.

"Did you two commit treason or something?" Selene asked. She had to do something, anything, to keep Emerald from getting their votes.

"No!" Topaz replied, horrified.

"Never!" Opal growled.

"Did you kill someone together?" Selene continued.

"Of course not!" Opal rolled her eyes, exasperated, as Topaz shook her head.

"Then I really don't understand why you're worried about her threats."

"Of course, the walking scandal doesn't understand! How could you ever understand what it's like when no one expects anything from you?!" Topaz snapped, her eyes shining with unshed tears. "You know what, Zoe? Fuck you and your gods-damned superiority complex! I'll tell her myself!"

"Mina, you don't have to. She has no right to know." Opal tried to soothe her, but Topaz slapped her outstretched hand.

"Fuck you too, Charis! You sent me away! You threw me aside because I loved you, and all you wanted was a plaything! I only came here to keep you from finding the man you obviously wanted instead!"

"That's not fair! I sent you away because I had to, because my father wouldn't let me love someone I couldn't keep! And I can't keep you!"

The revelation felt almost anticlimactic. Selene was well aware that same-sex relationships were frowned upon amongst the nobility. But to the lower classes, who couldn't inherit property and who weren't expected to produce heirs, it was hardly a punishable act. It wasn't even illegal. If the griffin guest from a foreign kingdom could openly have wild orgies in the palace with anyone he pleased, it was hardly worth mentioning if one domina desired another. Selene was about to say as much, but Domina Emerald cut in before she could speak.

"And neither of you will live it down if the nobility of Lethe know the two of you were lovers. You especially, Mina, would be lucky to be married off to some beast mage son of a tenant farmer. So cast your votes. No one else need know your secrets," Emerald promised as she leaned back in her chair, triumphant.

"No one in my province gives a fuck who I bed. It's only you continentals who can't accept people as they are. I won't vote for you," Opal retorted, crossing her arms.

"You're correct, no one expects an islander to act as a good and moral daughter. But Domina Topaz is not an islander, and her father is a strict traditionalist. You may be able to hide your shame across the narrow sea, but Mina cannot. Perhaps you no longer love her, but surely you care enough not to sentence her to a life rotting away of neglect at best, or suffering abuse at worst."

Opal and Topaz exchanged a troubled look. Topaz turned away first, producing her orb.

"Mina, don't," Opal pleaded.

"She's right. My family will never forgive me if they knew," Topaz replied.

As she stretched out her hand to give Emerald the orb, Selene caught her wrist and held it tight. She couldn't let this go south for her. Emerald's threat to the other women was more potent than any poison Selene could temporarily dose them with. She would need to rely on bravado and half-truths to see her through this challenge.

"Before you do something foolish, hear me out."

"I hardly think I need the advice of a madwoman," Topaz retorted.

"Then how about the promise of a future empress?"

"What could you possibly promise me? In spite of the attention the prince pays you, no one seriously thinks you could ever be empress," Topaz scoffed.

"Really? And how many other dominae has the prince begged to visit him in his chambers? How many other candidates are already seen favourably by the emperor himself?"

Shocked silence reigned. Emerald recovered first.

"You lie! The prince has never taken a noblewoman to his bed!"

"Well, I don't know about his bed, but the hot spring was a more than adequate place for fucking. If you don't believe me, ask your cousin. Or ask the librarians about the book His Majesty gifted me with," Selene replied, haughty. She could see the tide turning. Opal and Topaz were beginning to see her in a new light.

"You can't possibly believe these delusions of hers." Emerald slapped her palms on the table.

"Maybe she's lying, maybe not. Either way, I'll hear what she has to say. Speak your piece, Milena." Topaz clutched her orb close.

"I've already had discussions with Belisarius about reforms I want enacted. The most important is for women to be able to acquire and inherit property and titles. With your support," Selene nodded to both Topaz and Opal, "I may be able to convince enough of the noble families to pass it. And if women can own their own property..."

"A woman need not marry a man if she so chooses," Topaz interjected, her amber eyes bright.

"I could inherit the Opal Province," Opal mused, a covetous expression on her face.

For a moment, silence, as each woman contemplated what their lives might look like. Topaz pursed her lips, her eyes closing and her shoulders slumping.

"That's impossible. None of the magistri would agree, your father included," Topaz sighed.

"You're right, which is why the first man to publicly object in court will die by my hand," Selene smiled.

"You wouldn't!" Emerald objected.

"I would," Selene retorted, resting her hand on Emerald's. Emerald glared, tearing her hand away. "Zoe—may I call you Zoe? I wasn't being modest when I said before that my power is as real as it gets. I'm the most powerful poison mage in Lethe. When I'm empress, I'll be above the law, and my reforms will pass. It will go more smoothly with the support of the provinces, but either way, it'll get done. People who get in the way of what I want tend to perish. I expect there to be objections, but I have no doubt there will be far fewer once the first dissenters die, vomiting up their liquefied innards."

"These are just grotesque fantasies! What you envision is simply untenable! What if your father is the first to object? Or Magister Topaz? What will you do then?" Emerald asked, gesticulating in her fury.

"Zoe, if you knew my father, you'd understand the bastard has it coming," Selene replied.

"What you're saying is madness. You would become a social exile," Emerald huffed.

"They don't seem to think so." Selene nodded to Opal and Topaz. Emerald obviously feared she might walk out of the room without the votes she wanted. "Do you *actually* hate my reforms? With your ambition, you could rule the Emerald Province outright. I would even voice my support if you wanted to stake your claim."

"Why are you even doing this, Amethyst? You don't need the throne like I do! I'll never rule in my own right, reforms or no! My brother would die before giving up his rights, you insufferable fool!" Emerald looked about ready to slap Selene, desperate horror and fury in her gaze.

"Guess you'd better get serious about cultivating your gift then, eh?" Selene winked at Emerald before turning her attention to Topaz and Opal. "When I am empress, I will raze Lethe down to the bedrock. What sprouts from the ashes will be a new empire that doesn't just tell women to look pretty and breed when we're told to, with whomever we've been sold to. In my Lethe, you'll have the power to choose your own fate. So, given your options, who will you vote for?"

Belisarius paced, every grain that fell into the bottom of the hourglass ratcheting up his unease. He only hoped Selene was up to the task. Nicephorus had insisted on the final test to find a proper prospective bride for when all the madness finally subsided. Feeling much too dutiful, he'd agreed.

The thought of Selene loosing made him ill. Belisarius wanted her. He wanted all her brazen, wicked recklessness, all her smug grins, her every cry of pleasure, every insult, every fight and every moment of peace she allowed him. But he dared not admit it, lest he speak into being something that could never be. Or lest he receive another lecture from his praetor.

The thought of wedding someone else filled him with existential dread as it never had before. It was folly to think he might have Selene. Besides his own minister's objections, he didn't even know if the poison mage would stay once the magistri were caught. For all he knew, she considered him no different than any other she'd lain with. As he paced with increasingly undignified and obvious anxiety, the last grain of sand fell from the top of the hourglass. The antechamber doors opened and his heart stopped. Belisarius schooled his face and posture into a calm poise that bore no trace of his inner turmoil.

"Who have you elected as the winner?"

"I believe I have met the conditions for victory, Your Royal Highness. I have held onto my vote and gained two others."

Selene grinned her thief's grin, holding out three purple orbs for inspection. When he stepped down to take them from her, a burden lifted from him. Thank the forgotten gods—she'd won. When she placed them in his hands, however, a new problem arose. Selene pulled him down, ostensibly to kiss his cheek, but what she hissed in his ear was anything but amorous.

"You'll pay for tossing me to the wolves like that, Belli."

There had never been a more important battle, nor one Marduk felt less prepared for. Truly, the invitation had slipped out of his mouth. Today he dressed simply, but as one fit to accompany a domina in his box at the Hippodrome; a lightly embroidered silk tunic with his military stripes, a sturdy leather belt sporting the gold decorative buckle denoting his rank, and fine leather boots that had been polished to gleaming. He'd even checked that the short hair around his horns wasn't curling oddly.

Now that Iliana was returning his affections, he found himself stricken with nerves. Her every smile stripped intelligent thought from his mind, the thousand questions he wanted to ask disappearing before they could reach his tongue. The sight of her covered in grease and grit made his heart race as much as the icy blue silks and dazzling gems did. Shy and bold, beautiful and brilliant—and everything he'd never dreamed he could have. He prayed that today, he could tell her just how serious his intentions were.

They toured the market erected outside the Hippodrome, her hand placed properly on his arm. No more than pleasant small talk had been exchanged as they looked for treats to share while watching the games. He could feel himself losing momentum.

"Was there anything you wished to see before we enter?"

"Is there anyone selling enchanted weapons?" Her eyes glittered with excitement.

He chuckled at her enthusiasm. Sometimes he forgot how much more could be had in Nadioch, how much grander it was than the backwaters she'd been forced to hide out in. Or how much had cropped up the last few months, especially now that it teemed with nobles here for the bride show.

"There are a few worth seeing."

As they wove through the crush of stalls and customers, Marduk spotted a man tailing them. Though dressed in fine silks, there was something in his bearing that struck Marduk as off. His footsteps were like those of a blade master—sure, balanced, all while he kept them un-erringly in his line of sight. He could be one of the praetor's. Nicephorus had been quite emphatic that Marduk ought not to entangle himself with a woman of low social standing and questionable judgement. Had the praetor gone so far as to send a minder, or was Marduk's paranoia well-founded?

"You've gone quiet. Is something the matter?"

"We're being tailed. I'm not sure of the man's motive."

Iliana stilled. He bit back a curse. The last thing he wanted to do was frighten her off. But when she looked up at him, all he saw was determination.

"The blade up your sleeve. Hand it to me discreetly. If you throw it, best that it hit the mark in this crowd."

He slipped it into his palm and placed it under hers as it rested on his arm. He could feel the heat as she remade it between their palms. It amazed him still, this woman's power.

"My necklace is made of a sturdy metal coated with silver. I can change its shape if need be."

"You never cease to amaze. There's a crush ahead. Perhaps we can lose him in it."

"Unless there are a great many men of your stature in the capital, I doubt it," Iliana quipped, giving him a wide, convincing smile.

Marduk laughed, but his smile was savage. Threaten him, or put Iliana in harm's way, and the malefactor would pay in blood.

"He's gotten close. Allow me to deal with him, Domina."

"Shall we turn and face him?"

"On three, but stay behind me. One. Two. Three."

His movements were practiced and smooth as he turned to face their pursuer, pulling Iliana behind him. One of her hands gripped the back of his tunic while the other swung up to her necklace.

"State your business, cur, or I'll have your head!" he growled.

He noticed the eyes first. Deadened. Determined. Unfazed by the attention of those around him. It was the look of a man whose only task was that of ending lives and he didn't care who knew it. Not one of the praetor's men. When his gaze slid over to Iliana, Marduk lunged, dagger in hand. He was not strategos for nothing. He sank his blade into the man's neck and tore it through flesh. It felt easy—too easy.

Instead of the spray of blood he expected, it was as though the man's image dissolved. Iliana's shriek alerted him. As he turned, white hot pain exploded in his gut. The attacker stood before him, unharmed, holding the hilt of the long blade currently residing in his midsection. Too late, he realised the mage's gift—teleportation.

"Filthy animals should know their place," the assassin whispered, twisting his sword.

"I concur."

Like some avenging fury, Iliana appeared behind the man, every last trace of sweetness gone from her mien. Rage, fearsome and awe-inspiring, radiated from her sapphire eyes. She was out for blood.

The jewelled hand of a noblewoman joined that of the assassin on the hilt before the metal turned liquid, sending an icy chill through Marduk's insides as it flowed from his wound and shackled the teleportation mage's wrist to Iliana's.

"Stupid bitch!"

The assassin struck Iliana with his free hand as Marduk fell to his knees. Eyes riveted to the scene as Iliana struggled with the mage, he tried to get to his feet. He had to protect her. In a moment, they could be anywhere in the empire. But most mages couldn't teleport freely while in great pain.

Marduk pulled a blade from his other sleeve and rammed it through the man's boot and foot, planting it between the cobbles, ignoring the agony in his gut. The assassin screamed. Marduk held in his own innards with one hand while the other kept him from crumpling completely. Blood pooled beneath him as more surged up his throat. Gods below, he didn't have much time.

The assassin went for another blade with his free hand.

"Run!" Marduk howled.

The effort cost him. He coughed crimson as more slid through his fingers and pooled beneath him. He couldn't die. Not until she was safe.

"No," she said, as quiet as she was vehement.

Metal turned to liquid again with a flash of her eyes, solidifying on the assassin's hand. Now devoid of weapons, he made as though to strangle Iliana. She caught his metal-coated fist in her hand. Agonized screams rang out. A wet crunching sound later, and blood rushed down the assassin's arm as he fell to the ground, cradling a crumpled metal stump in place of his hand.

"Fucking whore!" The assassin spat.

Another shriek tore from his throat. The stump had contracted in size.

Vicious, glorious woman. Dark crept around Marduk's vision.

"Shut your filthy mouth, or I'll take more than just your god's damned hand!" Iliana shouted, ripping the dagger from his foot and dragging him away.

Touching her necklace, she fashioned a collar with inverted spikes and a set of chains ending in a stake. She promptly collared the assassin with it and then drove the stake firmly into the ground, using the grip of Marduk' own dagger as a hammer.

His vision went spotty. She rushed to his side, her steely eyes turned watery. No—he didn't want her to cry. He tried to reach up to wipe her tears but didn't have the strength.

"I'm so sorry. It was the only way I could get the blade out without doing more damage to you. Are you bleeding too much?"

"You're like a goddess of war," he whispered.

"Oh gods, did he hit something vital?" Iliana turned to the crowd, shouting for a healer.

"I think I'm in love." His words slurred.

He fell to his side, unable to hold himself up any longer.

"No! Don't leave me, Marduk! Please, stay with me!" She cupped his face with her calloused palms, tears falling in earnest, then turned back to the crowd with an agonised roar. "Gods damn it, get me a fucking healer!"

He supposed, if he must die, at least he would do so in the arms of a beautiful warrior.

Chapter 22

Nicephorus was ushered into the prince's office as stone-faced guards clutched their spears outside. Belisarius' hair was dishevelled along with his robes. The darkness in his eyes reminded Nicephorus of the look the emperor often wore before he was about to sever heads.

It was incumbent upon him that in dark times such as these, he was flawless in his duties and steady in his demeanour. The prince uncharacteristically held a bottle of spirits in his fist as he glared into the dying embers of his fireplace. That was almost as worrying as his foul mood. The empire couldn't afford two drunkards in charge. Nicephorus owed it to the late Empress Nadia, his saviour, to see that her beloved son did not follow in his father's footsteps.

"Your Royal Highness, while I was looking over the strategos' work I noticed a recent report he hadn't yet had a chance to read. It's regarding your uncle's whereabouts. I'm sorry to inform you that he passed away a few years ago. The local authorities believed the fire to be the work of a band of brigands that had been active in the area at the time. Neighbours reported he died trying to protect the other occupant of the home."

"Thank you, Nicephorus. Is there anything to report from the interrogation of the assassin?" Belisarius asked, his voice gruff.

"Nothing particularly helpful, Your Royal Highness. He has said that he cannot identify his employer, only that he was paid a great deal of money to kill the strategos."

Belisarius sighed heavily and placed the bottle on the table beside his chair.

"The magistri are getting more brazen. Had a healer not been so close at hand, I might have lost both a strategos and a close friend today." Belisarius turned bloodthirsty eyes on him. Nicephorus suppressed a shiver. "How soon can we lure those snakes to the capital? I believe I'm done waiting for more knives in the dark."

"We can announce the engagements as soon as the end of the week," Nicephorus answered, tallying the costs associated with what would need to be glorious displays of wealth and pomp. The Purples would need to race the Reds in the Hippodrome, an epic romance would need to be acted at the Odeon, gifts arranged for all the noblewomen, grain and libations offered to the people of Nadioch, a grand sacrifice made to the forgotten gods, and those were just the peripheral matters. He would have the estimates on paper within the next few hours and set his people to the task of preparing the most magnificent party held since the official coronation of the first emperor and empress. A shame it was all for a ruse.

"Prepare the invitations. I'm eager to end this rebellion."

"As you wish, Your Royal Highness." Nicephorus bowed, glad to be quit of the scene and his prince's barely banked fury.

The shadowy pests had begun carrying antidotes for paralytics. Selene put her latest tail into a deep and profound sleep. It would be a miracle if he woke at all over the next day. Task done, she made her way through a series of servant hallways and darkened corridors until she stood before the personal chambers of Strategos Marduk. The guards allowed her entry.

Selene had visited multiple times during the day to comfort her friend. Iliana had sobbed, inconsolable at the beast mage's bedside, refusing to leave until he woke from his healing coma. His blood loss had been profound, and he was lucky that the best healers in Lethe had been only moments away. In the dark of the night Iliana slept soundly in her chair, her head and arms resting on the bed, never leaving his side. It made Selene almost queasy with the thought of what she needed to do next—killing a strategos could mean her own execution. But no one played with her friend's heart and lived.

No one.

Selene kissed her friend's cheek, ensuring Iliana would sleep without waking for an hour at least. If she played this right, no one would be the wiser.

Sensing the threat, the beast mage opened his eyes, squinting blearily.

"Don't move, Strategos. You've only just begun recovering from a mortal blow."

"Poison mage? What are you doing here?" He rubbed his haggard face.

Selene's eyes flicked to his other side. Iliana's hair appeared as spun gold on his sheets in the dim candlelight. Marduk made as though to touch her.

Selene hissed.

"Don't-"

His hand stopped mid-air, eyes turning sharp as he returned her hard stare.

"Don't touch her, Strategos. If you do, I won't be held responsible for what happens."

"Don't threaten me, girl. Even half dead, I'm more than a match for you."

"You're only digging your grave deeper."

"Explain yourself, or I will show you who here is digging her grave."

Selene glared back at the strategos, her pulse pounding in her ears. She approached him around his enormous bed as she spoke, coating her skin in a neurotoxin. It was rare enough that few knew how to search for the signs of it. Hopefully, by the time anyone suspected foul play, Marduk would already be on a funeral pyre.

"When we began this farce, it was obvious you had designs on Iliana. I understand. She's beautiful, talented and sweet. However, we made ourselves clear. We're leaving this wretched continent. You couldn't let it be though, could you? You've been seducing her with lies! She may be a genius with metals, but she's naïve at heart. I've watched her shed tears at your side all day, crying over the bullshit you've been telling her, and I'm putting an end to it. Better you die a hero in her mind than live on as one of her ugly regrets. Make peace with the gods, Marduk. It's the only mercy I'll be showing you."

"Do list these lies I'm accused of telling, Selene. I understand your protectiveness of Iliana, but you're speaking nonsense," Marduk har-rumphed.

He was significantly less intimidated than she'd expected him to be. It made her pause.

"You've been taking this charade too far! It's obvious Iliana has devel-oped feelings for you, you crook. I've heard that you're promising her a position with the Imperial Forge!"

The man at least had the decency to blush at the accusations.

"Are you her mother? Gods below, to think I need to explain this to you."

"Don't explain. Pray. You'll be meeting the gods soon enough."

Marduk levelled her with a glare.

"Listen up, poison mage, I'll only be saying this once. I intend to marry Iliana in truth, if she'll have me. She may be more than I deserve but I will spend the rest of my days ensuring she wants for nothing. And I've not told her any lies in our time together. Her position with the Imperial Forge was earned through her exemplary skill, and every compliment I paid her could never live up to all that she is. Now, begone to whatever lair you've conjured for yourself."

Selene stilled, digesting the information. Perhaps she should poison him anyway, just to keep Iliana to herself. But she couldn't. If even half of what he said were true, he was precisely what Iliana had always wanted. Selene's nails bit into her palms with her restraint, her eyes stinging. She didn't want to give up her friend, but Iliana's happiness came first.

"If you've lied, you'll die slowly and painfully of a poison no one will ever identify," she hissed.

Marduk snorted, then groaned in pain as he cradled his stomach. Selene, perhaps uncharitably, hoped his wound had opened and he bled to death.

"If you're that upset about me ruining your plans to leave Lethe with Iliana in tow, why don't you just stay? Perhaps you really could be empress. With your reward, you'll certainly be as rich as one." He smirked, then muttered, "And you're bloodthirsty enough to rival Darius himself."

"Go fuck yourself, Strategos! I hope she says no!"

"We'll see." He closed his eyes, a stupid, satisfied smile on his arrogant face.

Unbelievably, the man fell asleep in her presence. So much for his sense of self preservation. It was a nasty parting shot for him to suggest someone like her could be empress in truth. As she gazed at Iliana's sleeping face, something tight and painful bloomed in her chest. Would Iliana really abandon her to marry the strategos?

Dust motes danced through the beams of sunlight escaping through the thick curtains. Iliana woke to one such beam blinding her into wakefulness, her only rewards a crick in her neck and screeching pain in her lower back. Marduk watched her silently, his expression serious.

"You're awake! How are you feeling? Do you need me to get the healer?" she asked, flustered. She shot out of her chair, opened the drapes fully and busied herself tidying his bedside.

Marduk held out his hand. When his calloused fingers closed around hers, she was struck again by how large he was.

"There's no need for the healer. I'm comfortable at present."

"Ah. I see. That's good then. Perhaps a cup of wine? I could bring you some food?"

Something about his gaze sent a swarm of butterflies fluttering madly in her stomach, her pulse pounding in her ears. Surely, after he'd watched her maim a man without batting an eye, his view of her had dimmed. Selene could get away with that level of violence and shrug, but Iliana had always been reserved about throwing her weight, or her magic, around.

Then there was the matter of her having defended him. Some men, while grateful to be alive, might be too proud to handle such a thing gracefully. She feared it might be enough to put him off her at last.

At the time she hadn't even considered such things. Her mind had been too busy shrieking like a vicious harpy that her man was hurt, and that the one who'd done it must be made to scream. She supposed it was too late to put that foolish bit of animalistic instinct back into its cage.

When she looked at the great big man sitting tucked into his oversized bed, her heart felt too big for her chest. He might have professed certain sentiments the day before, but he'd been close to death by blood loss and might not have expected to live. While she wanted to hold those words close to her heart, and the memories they'd made in their secret getaway, she knew it was a foolish thing to do.

His eyes softened the longer she stared at him. Was that pity shading the dark green? She hoped his rejection would be quick so that she could slink away to lick her wounds.

"Iliana, please sit still for a moment. I wish to talk with you."

"A-alright."

She tried to harden her heart for what was to come. It stung more than she thought it would. He had seemed so different from the men before.

"Yesterday, you saved my life. I will forever be in your debt. Thank you."

"You would have done the same for me." Iliana replied, subdued. He seemed to be working himself up to something. It boded ill, just like her roiling gut. Though she supposed if she threw up on him when he finally broke it off with her, it would be just what he deserved.

"Nearly dying puts a few things in perspective," he mused, gazing out the window.

"Mmm," Iliana murmured, not trusting herself to speak. Was he really going to drag out his rejection?

"It strikes me as a coward's impulse to put off important conversations. Death might have robbed me of the opportunity to have those, and I'll be damned if I let another moment pass without saying what needs to be said. Lest you think I'm speaking rashly, I want you to know that yesterday's events have very little bearing on what I have to say."

Marduk paused to look her sincerely in the eyes, his rough hands swallowing hers. She didn't even trust herself to make a peep. She couldn't swallow, couldn't breathe, emotion choking her. This was it, the end. Her naïve, girlish fantasies would be exposed to the glaring light of day for what they were. She should have known no one would want her and her baggage. No man would ever really recognise her talents, would respect her for them, would want her to be more than something pretty on his arm, would feel alright with being saved by her. What an easy mark she'd been. She was going to live to regret giving away her heart so easily.

"I love you, Iliana, and I would be honoured if you would consider being my wife in truth."

No, that wasn't right, was it? Was she so hurt that she was imagining hearing what she wanted? Stunned, she didn't realise she'd held herself still and silent for quite so long. Not until she saw the hope bleed from Marduk's eyes.

"Wait!" she cried, her hand reaching out to touch his chest. "I—yes, I love you, too. I want to marry you, too."

Warmth flooded her cheeks, her heart hammering. She laughed and launched herself at Marduk. He wrapped his arms around her and kissed her. His rough stubble abraded her lips but she didn't care, not once the first, smooth slide of his tongue met hers. She didn't know where she ended and he began. She'd never felt so light and yet so grounded. Tears of joy streamed down her cheeks.

He groaned. She gasped.

"Oh! I'm so sorry. Your injury, I forgot." She tried to pull back, but he held on, firm and unyielding.

"Your touch is healing in its own way. Don't go."

Iliana was suddenly very aware of the situation. She was astride his thick, powerful legs, dress rucked up to her thighs, arms tangled around his neck and shoulders, her breasts mashed to his chest. Despite his pain, he was not unaffected, his eyes unfocused, breathing ragged and an unmistakable hard member poking her. Nothing short of a thick blanket could hide her blush. The only thing that made her sudden embarrassment easier was that Marduk, too, was blushing. He scratched the stubble on his chin ruefully.

"I must confess I have no ring to give you."

"A ring? Oh, yes, a ring! I confess, it had slipped my mind as well." She smiled shyly.

"I will rectify that immediately," he assured her, wiping the remnants of her tears.

"Mmmhmm," she replied, her smile growing in time with his discomfort.

"I apologize for that. You deserved a more thoughtful proposal."

He blushed, chastened. It made her bold.

"Marduk?"

"Yes?"

"You can make it up to me by kissing me."

And so he did.

CHAPTER 23

The jaws of Belisarius' trap were drawing closed. The magistri had been summoned to Nadioch to negotiate the engagements and attend the false weddings. Had Marduk not been attacked, the prince might have been more confident in his plans. Marduk and Nicephorus stood before him in his study as Belisarius contemplated throwing his weight around for the first time since he'd taken the reins of power.

"Since this latest attack, I've begun questioning my confidence in our original plan and my reluctance to having more than a handful of people know my motives."

"Did you have something in mind?" Nicephorus asked eagerly.

"I don't want any more surprises if we can help it. We've resisted speaking with the Diamond, Sapphire and Amethyst women in any capacity because we assumed they couldn't be of help in their current conditions. However, given Sapphire's daughters had been given strict orders to commit suicide under certain circumstances, they may have the ability to understand complex orders. I want them questioned by our silver-tongue mage regarding the magistri, their plans, any changes to their routines, any new guests, everything. The young silver-tongue has recovered enough for that, so use her. Can you arrange this, Nicephorus?"

"I shall draw up a list of questions we will want answers to." He nodded.

"It goes without saying, I want each of them incapable of revealing any details of their interrogations to anyone else."

"Of course."

Belisarius turned to Marduk, his heart in his throat. He'd almost lost his oldest friend. He'd spent the night of Marduk's attack hovering on the edge of panic, praying not another loved one would be cruelly taken from him. But Marduk had survived the night and was on the mend. A few days had passed, and Marduk had been sufficiently healed by the court mages. It was a relief to see him without the pallor of pain.

"I want you to choose two of your most trusted naval commanders. Have each take a complement of ships and officers on the fastest, most secretive route to the harbours of the Sapphire and Amethyst provinces. Lock down their harbours and march on their castles. When the magistri arrive in Nadioch, if things go poorly, I don't want them to have a chance to flee in any direction. I want them surrounded, blockaded and their strongholds sieged and warded against escape, if necessary. Meanwhile, I want you to have the imperial forces ready to defend the palace. Send an extra detachment to the Ruby Province as well. If the traitor among my family resides there, I want him dealt with."

"I will have the ships provisioned and ready to set sail by dawn tomorrow," Marduk replied.

"See that you do." Belisarius dismissed them. Nicephorus didn't waste a moment as he hurried from the room. But Marduk lingered, watching the praetor's retreat. "Was there something you wished to tell me?"

"It's about Iliana. I've offered her a position at the Imperial Forge. Her enchantments are brilliant. If we're to provision our ground forces, I want her enchantments on all our equipment."

"Brilliant? That's high praise."

"She can enchant arrows never to miss their targets, swords which consume those of the enemy, blades so sharp they cut through steel with ease. I want her working on these and new creations."

"Gods below." Belisarius couldn't hide the hoarse croak from his voice.

Such things could change the face of battle in the empire. Even a small force could turn the tide with enchantments like those. As such, if she, or her creations, fell into the hands of others, Lethe could once again be consumed by another Great War. An unsettling thought for the future.

"One mage cannot enchant the weapons of an entire army overnight. At present, have her focus on the arrows for the archers remaining in the palace. But keep this a secret. If things do go badly, neither she, nor her weapons, can fall into the hands of our enemies. From now on, I want her here at relevant meetings, and I want her security to be a high priority."

With a mind for unconventional weapons, her ideas could help shape his plans. Thank the gods Magister Sapphire hadn't realized her talents.

"I understand, Your Royal Highness." Marduk replied.

"And Marduk?"

"Yes, Your Royal Highness?"

"I..." He paused, unsure how to tell his oldest friend and the only brother he'd ever known how much he'd feared losing him. "You're not allowed to die on me."

"I wouldn't dream of it. If that is all, I'll see to my tasks."

Marduk smiled as he rose and bowed before leaving.

The next few days would be busy and tense, but the true test would come when the magistri replied to their invitations. Either they would revolt, which would mean war, or they would walk into his trap. But even if they came, he would not relax until he had their heads on pikes and he knew none of their blindly loyal allies or other opportunistic nobles would take up arms. Worse, he feared he was missing vital pieces, not least the name of the mastermind behind it all. It was the attempted assassination of Marduk that didn't fit neatly to their pattern thus far. How many more enemies had Belisarius failed to spot?

The magistri had been obscenely quiet. Had their daughters not been summoned, Belisarius might never have discovered the second and third players in this plot. Intelligence reports came to him daily informing him that neither the Amethyst nor Sapphire magistri were marshalling forces or making any moves whatsoever. Diamond was acting as carefree as he usually did, betting exorbitant sums on the chariot races and spending money he probably didn't have.

Had the attack on his strategos been a desperate gambit to weaken him? Even under interrogation by the silver-tongue, the assassin had provided no useful information. Was there yet another enemy he hadn't considered? Aside from the emperor, the entirety of his family resided in the Ruby Province, banished from Nadioch in the wake of his siblings' deaths to prevent ambitious relatives from setting their eyes on a weakened throne. Their communications, associations, grudges and ambitions had been discreetly analysed by Nicephorus' men, all without producing a viable suspect for the role of traitor. It was enough to make him tear at his hair.

Belisarius rose from his seat and stretched his aching back. It was nearly time to change for the evening's festivities. He had a few hours yet to rest his body and mind. Using a private passageway, he made his way to his chamber, glad that he'd told his servants to leave him be until it was time to be presentable.

"Your secret exit is behind a tacky sculpture? That's just sad, peacock."

Belisarius cursed. How in the hells had she snuck in here? She laughed at his glare. Gods, it rankled. And yet, the sultry promise in her eyes had him strung tight with anticipation.

"What did you steal today?" he asked, removing his robe.

"Nothing... yet," she replied slyly. She wore a thick cloak clasped at her neck. Beneath, he glimpsed a tantalizing hint of gauzy fabric.

"I'm shocked. Has my palace run out of shiny baubles to tempt you?" he asked as he removed his tunic, see-sawing between desire and annoyance.

"Oh, I'm not interested in baubles today. My prize is something else."

"I'm sure you're dying to tell me what it is," he replied, his back turned. As her soft footsteps grew closer, the dull thud of heavy fabric hitting the floor made him catch his breath. She leaned in, the heat of her thinly clothed skin and pebbled nipples against his back setting him aflame. Her whisper in his ear made him ache.

"Well, I had planned on sullying the royal peacock's virtue."

He turned to the sight of her unlacing the ties on her nightgown, cloak at her feet. Her nipples grazed the fabric in hard, darkened points, the sheerness of the gown hiding nothing. Had she really worn that through the palace corridors? His hands fisted at his side to keep from dragging her to the floor.

"What says the peacock? Are you ready to be ruined?"

Belisarius lost himself in her amethyst eyes. Except there were dark smudges beneath them. He was about to ask, but the last tie had come undone and her gown slid to her feet. Bold and unashamed, she stood before him. When he stepped forward and pulled her close, her hand slid to his leggings, diving beneath the fabric and gripping him in her small hand.

"Don't call me peacock," he growled as she stroked him.

"Do you want to experience bliss?" she asked, ignoring his command as she stroked him harder. "Let me poison you."

No man in his right mind would agree. Unfortunately, he was not in his right mind, because he was very close to agreeing to potentially dying of a poisoned cock. He must be mad.

"I promise to ruin you for every woman that comes after me," she whispered, her eyes dark with lust as she gripped his hair in her hand, anchoring him. He hated it as she tugged on his hair, and yet he loved the sting of it. He rid himself of the last stitch of clothing.

"Do it," he commanded.

She smiled, and then the most rapturous sensation sent him to his knees.

"What-" he gasped.

"One of my favourite poisons, highly diluted. Do you like it?"

Sweet merciful gods, the barest breeze had him close to spending. He gripped her hips with shaking hands, his fingers probably bruising her backside as he caught his breath. She would not gain the upper hand. He jerked her close and spread her thighs for his tongue. But when he found her sweet centre, his tongue was coated with the same wicked brew as his manhood. Wild, mad, perfect woman.

"I've always wanted to see you on your knees," she purred, stroking her fingers through his unbound hair.

"I will make you beg for mercy." He didn't even recognise the timbre of his voice as his lips tingled with her poison. He would not lose this game between them.

"Promises, promises." She gasped as he dragged her to the floor and set to fulfilling his vow to turn the tables.

If this tide of madness had dragged him under, he never wanted to come up for air again.

⇝⇉ ⇇⇜

"Praetor, a word," Marduk called as he caught up to Nicephorus in the halls.

"Strategos?"

"There is an issue I wish to discuss with you. Shall we walk?"

"Lead the way. Is there some aspect of the prince's plan which bothers you?"

Marduk shook his head.

"Nothing so grave. In fact, I'm relieved he's willing to make better use of our military in this affair. I am certain Admiral Opal is keen to impress him after the fiasco with the griffin. No, what I wished to discuss is less to do with military matters, and more to do with personal concerns." Marduk paused.

"Go on," Nicephorus said. His eyes dimmed and shoulders slumped, eager statesman no more. Here was a man who felt himself a captive audience.

"It has come to my attention that the prince is spending his time with the poison mage, outside of what this plan calls for. I had hopes you might warn her, lest she start believing herself to be a true candidate for empress. My wish is that you will let her know, in the strongest possible terms, that her ignorance of all matters of statecraft makes her the very last choice for even the role of concubine. Can I leave this matter to you?"

"If even the esteemed strategos sees that she has begun deluding herself, then I'll make it a priority to see that she is dissuaded."

Nicephorus' eyes turned icy with determination. The suggestion that Selene should be punished for her temerity fell on fertile ground. Marduk almost felt sorry for her.

"I'm glad to hear it. I knew I could count on you. If you'll excuse me, I have ships to provision and troops to ready." Marduk bowed.

The praetor bowed and hurried off to his own tasks. Marduk grinned and made a quick stop at the chambers appointed to Iliana's family. Iliana made her way out into the hallway to speak to him.

"Your devious little plan is already in motion."

"*Our* devious plan, Strategos. Who was it that said an asymmetrical attack was the better choice? I know Selene. Whatever the praetor scolds her for, she'll do it all the more just to make a point," Iliana replied, hands on hips.

"Kiss me, you minx."

Iliana blushed, looking back and forth down the hallway for privacy's sake before kissing him softly on the lips.

"Now go back to whatever it was you were doing. I have an appointment at the library."

"What could you need from the library?"

"Books on statecraft, obviously." Iliana winked before disappearing back into her chambers.

As Nicephorus and Domina Daria Amethyst descended the stone steps, the natural light grew progressively dimmer. Wall sconces lit the way, casting harsh shadows like a grasping embrace. The cool air chilled, the scents of dark earth and damp rock pervaded. When they reached their destination, one hand politely tucked under the other's arm, they stood in the deepest of the dungeons.

"If you'll come this way, Domina Amethyst."

Nicephorus led the dead-eyed woman to a room hewn out of solid rock warded against all outside magics. Inside sat a white-haired girl with intelligent amber eyes and an ashen cast to her light brown skin. A guard had his hand placed on the metal collar around her neck.

The silver-tongue mage and her minder were here to assist him in his investigations into the Soul-Binding Ritual plaguing the noble houses. Before the current spate of troubles regarding the Ritual, most of the silver-tongue mages had committed mass suicide by poison, leaving only the youngest alive. Although previously housed in the secure wing of the palace, since their deaths, she'd been secured in the dungeon to limit access to any who might provide poison in future. Her minder was one of the Unhearing Knights, their order formed to defend against and capture the mages, acting as their guardians, caretakers and jailors when the situation called for it. He communicated by sign language, which

Nicephorus, along with most of the rest of the palace, was well-versed in.

"Which soulless bitch is this?"

"You're speaking to Domina Daria Amethyst. You know how this works. Ask her my questions, nothing more, or your minder will activate the collar and you'll go without supper." Nicephorus turned to Knight Marius to sign.

"She is only to command the Domina. If she attempts to do otherwise, collar her.

Marius nodded solemnly.

"Sure thing, berserker scum. Wouldn't want my imprisonment to be barbaric, would you?" the silver-tongue spat.

Marius slapped her up the back of her head. She scowled at him, but all the young knight did was shrug. He was more than capable of reading lips, as the silver-tongue well knew. Nicephorus seated the domina before seating himself at the head of the heavy table.

"Who performed the ritual which took your gift from you?" Nicephorus asked.

The silver-tongue sighed before locking eyes with the noblewoman across from her and repeating the question. Nicephorus felt the pull of the enchanted words, no matter that they were meant for another.

"Father performed the ritual," the domina replied.

"Who taught your father the ritual?" he asked, the silver-tongue repeating faithfully.

"I don't know."

"Did anyone you thought suspicious stay in residence before or after the ritual?"

"There was a man in a mask who visited often before, but I wasn't to greet him or introduce myself."

"Do you know why the ritual was performed on you?"

"Father said he needed power that surpassed the emperor's, and that I would provide it for him in lieu of an advantageous marriage."

"What became of your sister Milena?"

"Milena hasn't woken since father used the ritual on her. She was the first. Father said he had fixed the ritual after that. Now we are to call the illegitimate daughter, Selene, by that name."

Nicephorus sat back in his chair and bit back a frustrated sigh. It was much the same story he'd heard from Magister Sapphire's daughters. The first daughters had been sacrificed to an imperfect ritual, leaving them in comas. After that, a long pause had taken place before the rest of the women were used as living power sources for the magistri, and, in the case of Magister Sapphire, his adult heir as well. Magister Diamond's daughters had been the last to be so abused, and had been wholly unable to answer complex questions.

"Does your father know Magister Sapphire has done the same thing to his daughters?"

"Yes. He informed me that he knew I would be able to walk and speak after the ritual because Magister Sapphire had already been successful on his second eldest daughter, Diodora."

It was the strangest aspect of this investigation. Three separate magistri were conspiring together. Each magister was an ambitious man in his own right, and not known for especially close relations with the others. Why would they assist each other, knowing only one of them would be able to claim the empire in the end? Was it a gentleman's agreement to return Lethe to the status of separate and distinct kingdoms once more? Did they plan for a free-for-all once the current emperor and prince were out of the way? None of the dominae were any help in discovering the reason behind it all. Thwarted, he turned to the silver-tongued mage.

"That will be all. Ensure she cannot discuss what has occurred here."

The mage glowered at him before turning to the domina.

"Do not speak of what you've exp-" In an unexpected jolt, the silver-tongue mage leapt across the table, grabbing the domina's head between her hands, locking her crazed amber eyes with the passive purple ones. She whispered too quickly for Nicephorus to follow. The knight hauled her away, snapping her collar shut, sealing the mage's ability. Whatever had been said, he only hoped they'd interrupted it in time.

"Have you been compelled, Domina?" Nicephorus asked, his heart hammering wildly in his chest.

"I don't know," she replied, toneless as ever.

Just what he needed. Yet another complication. Nicephorus turned his rage on the white-haired creature before him.

"What have you done?"

"Why don't you ask one of the other silver-tongues? Oh, wait, they're all dead."

"You will be punished for this, Alexandra."

"I'm already being punished! I dared commit the offense of being born. What are a few lashings compared to a lifetime in prison?"

"You should be grateful you were allowed to live at all! No one else suffers your kind to be born!" he shouted.

Nicephorus turned to Marius and signed.

"Take her to her quarters. I'll decide on her punishment later."

"Understood. Should I have one of the other knights keep an eye on Domina Daria?" the knight asked.

The praetor sighed, aggrieved, and shook his head.

"My spies will keep an eye on the domina."

Marius nodded and dragged Alexandra from the room, a wild smile on her face.

"Domina, it is time we left."

The domina obediently placed her hand in the crook of his arm as they left the dungeon and ascended the stairs. Brooding on difficult females, he now had the unenviable duty to lecture the prince on his sudden, inexplicable fascination with the one running wild in the palace corridors above. Sometimes, Nicephorus wished his obligations weren't quite so thankless.

CHAPTER 24

Darius sat in companionable silence with his son, tumbler in hand, alcohol untouched. The days when Belisarius sought him out had been fewer and further between since Nadia had passed, and he wanted to be fully present for the rare occasion. He knew he hadn't done right by him, and that their subsequent estrangement was due to his absence. He also knew that nothing he could say would make up for that, so he'd resolved to try now, in these rare moments when Belli let him in.

Today, Belisarius had asked to see him, a troubled look on his face. They sat on the veranda in Darius' chambers, ostensibly playing a game of chess, the warm scent of flowers drifting by on the evening breeze. Belisarius had been losing terribly almost as soon as he'd placed his first pawn.

"I've just spoken with Nicephorus. Rather, I have been *spoken to* by the praetor."

His son's eyes were dark, frustrated.

"Is it the magistri?"

"No. The military manoeuvres seem to be going off without issue. I don't believe the magistri know what's about to befall them." He waved it off.

Darius smiled knowingly. If not politics, it must be love. Nothing else could distract his serious son. Had his late bloomer finally found himself tangled up in troubles of the romantic variety? Darius hoped so.

"I did wonder when you might have these sorts of troubles. Honestly, I was shocked you made it out of your teens without once being struck."

Belisarius put his head in his hands and groaned.

"I must be a fool. I'm surrounded by advantageous matches, each one beautiful and flawless and entirely suitable. But instead I'm drawn to a harridan who delights in spitting in my face and driving me mad. Why can't I be rational?"

Darius' first impulse was to have a good laugh at his son's torment. Belli had spent his whole life either coolly, politely rejecting the advances of noblewomen or sending companions away who thought *they* at last had claimed the heart of a prince, rather than just a night in his bed. He had never, to Darius' knowledge, been pricked by more than passing fancy or easily appeased lust. Dutiful prince that he was, he'd probably never imagined being overcome by love. Reining in his first impulse, Darius gave voice to what he hoped Belli needed to hear.

"Why not her? Why can't the prince fall in love? Are you not made of flesh and bone like the rest of us?"

"I am responsible for the empire. I cannot afford to get carried away by...this. When the rebellion has been crushed, I will need to consider marriage in truth. I *want* to. If this has taught me anything, it's that I need more allies. That never used to be a problem. I've known my marriage would be political my whole life. Except now..."

Darius' heart ached. A father should be able to give his children everything he'd had and more. Belli deserved the same wild, passionate, enduring love Darius had shared with Nadia.

"Now the thought of other women is detestable? Unbearable?"

It could be no other way for a man in love. Belisarius nodded, shame twisting his features. Shame that shouldn't be there. Darius took a deep breath.

"Your mother was in your position once. I was nothing more than a brawler, a reprobate and a flirt. I believe she used those exact words, actually. I lured her from the arms of a more suitable, upright, proper nobleman all the same. Nadia never regretted following her heart, Belli."

Please follow your heart.

"It's not about me, don't you understand? The empire demands-"

Darius slammed his fist on the table, knocking pawns, knights, kings and queens from their squares and interrupting Belisarius.

"Fuck the empire! I ruled as the tyrant who made even stones bleed, and the empire survived. After all the work you've done, all your reforms that have made life better, don't you deserve some small happiness, independent of how it benefits anyone else?"

Belisarius needed to learn to be selfish. But the very suggestion had his son's eyes turning stormy, his lips thinning in a furious line.

"The empire survived because mother dedicated her life to tending it. How can I betray that effort by letting my emotions get the better of me?"

Darius sighed and fixed his son with a hard stare. Is that what Belli had thought all those years? It hurt his heart to know his own son thought so little of him, and that their teachings were now preventing him from having something good and real in this life of games and artifice.

"Listen. Your mother and I ruled as a team, always, in everything. Who do you think helped my campaign against the other kingdoms? Who do you think had the idea to use the Ritual to ensure victory? Which of us do you think first showed absolute cruelty, then the possibility of mercy? The answer is *both* of us. Behind closed doors, your mother could be a hot-headed tyrant, same as me. It was only outside that we appeared any different. Did you think any action we took was not first discussed in detail? Hells, even that leech I skewered was someone your mother and I thought needed to disappear to keep the peace. Your mother was a wicked genius, Belli, and I loved that about her. I was the spear, the tyrant, the distraction. Nadia was the shield, the politician, the strategist.

Without her wisdom, my strength, and our shared vision, none of this would have been possible. We both kept the empire from crumbling."

Belisarius was quiet for moment, as if coming to terms with this new view of his beloved, virtuous mother. He had only known her as a loving, protective presence in his life; someone who challenged him intellectually and taught him the intricate dance of court politics. Perhaps his son didn't understand that all the violence and threats over the years had been the result of both their calculating minds.

"I still find myself with the same problem. I cannot make Selene into a politician. I must marry someone who can take on that role."

Darius guffawed at that, which left Belli with a very sour look on his face.

"You don't need another politician by your side."

Darius raised his hand to forestall the objections.

"You're already a consummate politician. If I didn't know better, I'd say you were a silver-tongue. What you need is a tyrant. The more fearsome, the better. Let the nobles come begging for your mercy after speaking with your wife, and let them be grateful to you for your benevolence, however small and sparing. You are respected by many, but they must also fear you. Let them believe you are the only thing keeping them from suffering at your wife's hand."

Belisarius mulled it over, his eyes widening as he took a reluctant shine to the idea. Good. Darius pressed the advantage.

"You will be emperor one day very soon. You, not the praetor. His advice is valuable, but at the end of the day, it is you who rules over Lethe. If you truly desire the poison mage, then the two of you must find a way to make it work."

A knock at the door interrupted the intimacy of the moment. A servant entered and bowed deeply. The mask slammed down over his son's face.

"Prince Belisarius, I've come as you requested to remind you of the evening's activities."

"I will be there in a moment."

The servant bowed once more and left the room. His son's mask slipped as he smiled. A real smile.

"Thank you, Father."

Darius' heart warmed. When Belisarius left the room, he sipped his drink. There was always the possibility that the poison mage had no desire to remain by Belli's side. Only time would tell. For everyone's sake, Darius hoped she stayed.

Domina Emerald had made good on her promise of pariah status. While noblewomen had avoided Selene before, they now made exceptionally wide berths around her person. The noblemen very carefully kept their eyes averted or set their gazes above her small frame. Aside from the prince, only Lord Renfreid bothered to ask her to dance with any frequency, and even then, the griffin was much too absorbed making up for lost time between the sheets. She did her best not to roll her eyes. This was far preferable to having to sit and make nice with snide strangers or banter with condescending gentlemen. The only women who dared sit next to her were her sisters. Thankfully, they were all being dutifully escorted by Nicephorus' lackeys. But tonight she could use a distraction, and there were precious few.

Selene's dreams had become disturbingly vivid. Faceless women would hold her tight until fire engulfed them and darkness swallowed her whole. The past few nights the dream assaulted her whenever she closed her eyes, and not even her time in Belisarius' bed could give her a peaceful sleep. The nightmares gnawed at her heart like a rat chewing its way through a wall, filling her with dread. Last night, she'd woken to her own screaming. She was being torn apart at the seams by something she couldn't touch, couldn't fight. Whenever her mind wandered, she found her hands touching her chest, fingers probing for a wound that wasn't there. She was so tempted to tell Belisarius about it, for fear it was some kind of curse he might be able to dispel. But every time, she held herself back. It was one thing to share her body, another to be vulnerable.

Her anxious spiral was interrupted when Burgundy was placed beside her, her minder making noises about refreshments. Normally, they sat in companionable, if awkward, silence. Tonight, that changed.

"Have I misbehaved?" Burgundy asked in her dull tone.

"How the hells would I know? Pretty sure you're incapable of it."

"Father would be angry if I did."

"Father is a sick fuck, Burgundy. He doesn't care about you."

She seemed to actually be thinking this over.

"He cares very much about Dimitri and about his guest in the mask."

"Yes, he would care about his heir. The little ghoul is very much a chip off the ol' block. Who's the guest though? I don't remember seeing anyone arrive while I was there."

"He lived with us for some time, though he does travel often. I don't know his name as I was never properly introduced."

"That's your problem, Burgundy. No bloody curiosity. Guy in a mask lives in the same house, and you don't even ask his name. Whatever they did to you really messed you up."

Burgundy stared blankly at Selene.

"You're creepy as hell when you do that, you know? When you get un-fucked, I hope you're as much of an asshole as the magister is. We'll spit on his grave together. No, stop looking at me like you're deciding which expression you're supposed to use. Gods, this is why I don't talk to you. I'm leaving now, goodbye."

"Have a pleasant evening."

Selene spotted Iliana near the refreshments and nonchalantly made her way there. She'd been warned against too much public interaction between herself and Iliana, but Selene missed her. It had been getting harder and harder to get a spare moment with her friend as the pace and duration of these damn parties had ratcheted up in anticipation of this evening's announcement. Iliana was also spending an inordinate amount of time in the company of the strategos, which boded ill for their plans to sail away once this was over. Selene couldn't shake the fear something painful was stalking her, waiting for her to slow down so it could rip her apart. Her need for comfort was like an ache.

"Domina Roxane, how lovely to see you here," Selene intoned prettily. Iliana's eyes sparkled back at her.

"Indeed. And what a wonderful night it is. I haven't much time, but I wanted to tell you that I've been proposed to! By Marduk! And I said yes!" Iliana replied gleefully.

The air rushed out of her lungs as her heart squeezed painfully in her chest. The blow hurt more than she'd expected. Would she be leaving Lethe alone? Selene refused to linger in Nadioch like an unwelcome guest of a happy couple, no matter how much she loved one half of it. Her lonely future stretched out before her.

"Domina? A moment of your time?" A dashing, dark-skinned soldier in his ceremonial kit approached Iliana and extended his arm.

"Of course, Julius." Iliana smiled back at him before turning to Selene. "I'll see you soon, Domina Milena." She winked as the soldier led her away.

Fucking strategos! She really should have poisoned him. Now she was going to be alone. Again. Iliana was clearly over the moon for the meat-head and there was nothing she could do or say that would change it—short of murder. That damn, gnawing rat tore another chunk out of her heart. And yet, despite her pain, it felt like doom still awaited her. What in the hells was wrong with her?

Selene searched for Belisarius. Perhaps being in his arms would provide some small comfort. He was in conversation with a group of older women—magistrae, if the sheer number of gems dripping from their persons were any indication. Selene put on her fake smile and prepared to wade into the melee, though the charade made her feel fragile, like frayed rope forced to hold an impossible weight. Before she could interrupt the congregation, Nicephorus stepped into her path, grabbed her hand and dragged her into a dance.

"Don't harass the magistrae. The prince will require their help when this affair is over. One will likely be his future mother-in-law. He doesn't need you mucking about in the affairs of the empire."

"Don't threaten the servants. Don't poison the poison mages. Don't call the dominae weak snobs. Don't speak with Iliana in public. Gods, do you ever stop nagging?" Selene mimicked him in the least flattering way. His scowl had her grinning. If comfort was off the table, maybe some sparring with the prickly praetor would soothe her.

"I wouldn't need to nag if you were even half as cultured as the servant who cleans the latrines."

"There were latrines? I've been shitting in the garden this whole time. Silly me."

Nicephorus' face briefly twisted in horror before he realised the ruse. That he'd mistaken her jibe for truth spoke to how he regarded her. She hadn't realised her opinion of him could get any lower, but here he was, lowering the bar yet again.

"If you weren't required to appear in public, I would have you whipped."

"Is that what tickles your fancy, Praetor? It figures someone as repressed as you would-"

"Shut up, you swine," Nicephorus hissed. "When this affair is over, you had best run for the docks rather than stroll. Our agreement covers only your payment, not the condition you need to be in to receive it."

His grip turned punishing on hers. She dug her nails into his hand in retaliation.

"It's always threats with you. You know the only real threat in this ballroom? Me. Your spies are too afraid to get within spitting distance. I'm having a great time finding new ways to incapacitate them. And here you are, acting like you're better than me, all the while knowing that the only man you consider your better can't keep his hands off the poison swine. The situation is *delicious*."

Red crept up the praetor's neck. Victory.

"Crow all you like. The crown prince has never allowed himself to be swayed by the wiles of a woman, and, for the good of the empire, he never will. One of those weak snobs, as you call them, will be his wife, have his children and rule Lethe with him. All while you become no more than a distasteful memory. You're nothing but an uncultured, ignorant troll without enough knowledge of politics to qualify as a stable boy, let alone a lowly concubine. In every way that matters to the prince, you are inadequate."

Before Selene could reply in kind, the music stopped, and Belisarius made his way up to a throne set on a dais. Her anger simmered beneath the surface of a polite smile cracking at the corners. What a shit night this had proved to be, and it was only half-over.

The emperor had joined the show, seated to the right of the throne in one of his own, his face a stern mask. At least she had Darius' company to look forward to.

Belisarius cleared his throat.

"First, I wish to thank everyone for gathering here tonight. As you know, this bride show has been my honour to host. Not only have my talented bureaucrats and soldiers found wives, but I too have met my match here." The crowd murmured politely before he continued, "Please greet my fiancée, and your future empress, Princess Consort Milena Amethyst."

Polite clapping accompanied the lethal stares and shocked murmurs of a great many men and women in attendance. Zoe Emerald's face had turned ashen, eyes wide. A servant stealthily removed the wine glass from her trembling fingers before she lost her grip. Magistra Emerald in particular looked like she was plotting murder. Selene shrugged off her immediate fear, straightening her spine and plastering on a beatific smile, all the while imagining everyone writhing in pain beneath her feet. Some congratulated her, most simply did their level best not to bare their fangs. Nicephorus wore a politely bland expression.

"If you wouldn't mind escorting this uncultured troll to the empress' seat, I shall endeavour not to murder you and everyone else here with their false smiles and hollow congratulations."

He escorted her with all due haste. In moments Belisarius took her hand in his, kissing it politely. A little mischief twinkled in his dark eyes. Selene grinned, grabbed the front of his robe and pulled him in for a searing kiss. His shock was gone the instant her tongue swept across his lips, and then it was all she could do to keep her hands where decency demanded. If their kiss went on a little longer than the crowd expected, the onlookers kept their mouths shut. When their lips parted, a faint blush crossed his cheeks, his hands fisted in the material of her dress slowly releasing her. She had to admit that she did, indeed, like him ever so slightly. He was great fun to tease, a good lay, an excellent kisser and handsome. If only he didn't have that damned crown.

Even if it was just for show, she imagined briefly what it would be like to be his bride in truth. It was a silly fantasy. A man like him would never want a woman like her to be his wife, let alone in charge of an empire. A sometime lover was as close as she would get. Her eyes swept the room, and her grin turned predatory. *Eat your hearts out, snobs.*

When he led her to the empress' throne, she sat prettily as they had planned. The nobles were allowed to step close to the dais and give their congratulations. Belisarius handled all the small talk, which gave Selene the chance to size up the well-wishers.

A nondescript man with blonde hair, a ruddy complexion and pale eyes, maybe a few decades her senior, bowed deeply to both herself and the prince. She thought nothing of him until she heard his voice.

Then her night truly went to shit.

"I am unutterably pleased that you have chosen a beauty from the Amethyst Province, Your Royal Highness. My people will be delighted to hear the future empress is one of their own."

Agony lanced Selene's heart, her nails digging into the arms of the throne, a scream trapped in her throat. Memories washed over her, her seams torn asunder. The thing haunting her had pounced, mauling her innards. A gaping hole was all that remained of her heart, and through it, waves of grief and molten anger spilled through. The name of her foster mother, the mother of her heart, rang out in her mind. Dihya. She nearly choked on her fury as memories of warmth and love were replaced by those of despair and hopeless wrath. The memory spell she'd paid so dearly to have placed on her had just broken. Selene struggled to keep her breathing normal as a dark and terrible pain crystalized into something hot and sharp, and pointed directly at the man before her. The emperor seemed to sense her bloodlust, his warrior's instincts turning his body to face hers. She held herself in check, but only just.

"Forgive me, but I didn't catch your name," Selene said, her voice low and cool.

"I am Illustrus Maksim Ignis. The pleasure is all mine." He bowed again.

She was not mistaken. A monster in silks stood before her.

"Illustrus Maksim, I seem to recall that about ten years ago, you expanded your territory. You used fire to thin the woods and discourage bandits, did you not?"

"I'm pleased to hear you remember it, Your Radiance. Yes, we had trouble with a few tenants who refused to leave, but in the end, we were successful in transforming my land into productive agricultural properties."

"Did you know one of those tenants you evicted was none other than the Knight Illustra Dihya Arcus, also known as the Terror of the Skies? She was a hero of the Great War."

She'd been Selene's hero, her saviour, the only one who'd shown the starving brat she'd been true and abiding love.

"I had no, uh-"

"And that she was killed in the fire you set on her home? One she had been rewarded with as payment for her services."

"You did *what* to my knight?" The emperor shouted, slamming his fists on the arms of his throne.

"Your Royal Highness?" The man pleaded with Belisarius.

But Belisarius barely spared him a glance as he placed a hand on hers. Selene's fingers ached with the need to strangle the man. He'd killed the only person she'd ever considered a mother. If it weren't for all the people here, she would have tackled him to the ground and torn open his throat with her bare teeth. She still might.

"Is this true, Sir Maksim? Recall that you are speaking to the crown prince."

"It was a horrible tragedy, Your Royal Highness, but the land was mine to claim."

Belisarius turned his eyes to Selene's.

"He has admitted his crime, Princess Consort. What should his sentence be?"

CHAPTER 25

Fucking pies. Gooey, moist, fragrant, fucking pies. They'd tempted Selene once upon a time, and now it was all she could do to swing the axe up high and maim the target beneath her, failing to suppress it all.

With hindsight, she could see that the spell had been disintegrating since that first night in the ballroom. It was little things in the beginning. Dreams and wisps of memory. Then nightmares and dread. Her impending solitude, combined with that pig's voice, had been enough to finally tear the spell asunder. It might as well have torn her in two. She struggled to make sense of the broken orphan she'd tried to forget, and the woman who cared for naught—the woman the spell had allowed Selene to become.

The worst was that, when Iliana had come to her wondering why she looked like shit, she'd bitten her only friend's head off. Iliana's wide-eyed hurt had made her gut churn. Another person she loved—disappointed. Selene hated herself for it, but hadn't been able to keep the vile anger in check—about Iliana leaving, about Dihya, about being so fucking alone. Gods below, she wished she could've taken it back. All of it.

Unfortunately, she knew herself too well now. She needed another memory mage. While a lesser woman might choose to drink to forget her pain, it didn't work on a poison mage. Selene preferred the fix that would keep her functioning, anyway. At least her birth mother had taught her one thing in life—never let your shit drown everyone around you. And so she hoisted her axe up high above her head and used every ounce of her strength and anger and sadness to bring it down, trying to remember and to forget.

Dihya, a war hero, discharged and forgotten in her backwoods cottage, had caught Selene stealing a cooling pie. She'd enfolded her in great, broken wings and brought her into the only loving home Selene would ever know. Dihya had civilized her as best she could, taught her to read, to curse, to fight dirty, and eventually how to be part of a family. Selene might have lived in that damn run-down cottage until she had been as old as Dihya herself, had it not been levelled by an arrogant illustrus looking to plant another crop of fucking wheat. Maksim had threatened them for weeks, but Dihya hadn't been frightened, and Selene endeavoured to follow her adoptive mother's lead. She'd been away at the market selling potions when the illustrus had struck.

In the end, Selene had been helpless to do anything but watch as the last of the fires licked up the cinders of the great wooden beam that had stretched from one end of the cottage to the other. The detritus of their lives together had been scattered amongst the ashes; the singed remains of a toy, bits of broken pottery, a piece of a warped comb. She'd called out Dihya's name until she was hoarse and the sun had set on that cool autumn night. Forced to cling to the warmth that emanated from the wreck, she had curled up in their former kitchen. When the biting winds woke her in the morning, she was covered in the swirling ashes, and lying next to the broken horns of her beloved mother. Only Dihya had sported such fierce, curling horns in life. Dihya had died in that house, and taken Selene's heart with her to the grave.

Rip.

Hoist.

Swing.

Crunch.

On and on it went, until her arms and legs trembled from the strain. Sweat dripped down her face and stained her back. She hoped it would mask her tears. She'd always prided herself on caring so little for anything that nothing could hurt her. Now she knew she was just a vulnerable hypocrite. Self-hatred poisoned her as no toxin could. She'd known love so boundless that the grief nearly killed her, and instead of honouring that love, she'd let her weakness triumph and chosen to run from it all. Dihya would've been so disappointed with her.

Rip.

Hoist.

Swing.

Crunch.

"Has your memory spell broken?"

Selene ignored Belisarius. She couldn't handle him seeing her this way.

"I've known it was there since the night you fainted in the ballroom. I fear my gift might have weakened it."

Did it even matter? The damage was done. Any anger at him was eclipsed by the hatred she felt for herself.

Rip.

Hoist.

Swing.

Crunch.

"Come to bed, Selene," he whispered in her ear.

"Busy," she replied, nearly out of breath.

Rip.

Hoist.

Swing.

Crunch.

Before she could pull the axe out of the mangled target, his larger hand grabbed hers, pulling it away from the handle. He easily twirled her around to face him, pulling her close. His eyes were black as night, and his hair took a sheen from the stars in the sky. His lips crushed hers, and her battered heart and body responded. Damn him.

"I'll make you forget," he promised.

Maybe a distraction was what she needed. She kissed him back.

"Don't be nice to me," she breathed between kisses. Lust she could handle, but she feared kindness might brand something indelible into her.

"Never."

Belisarius woke when he sensed Selene had left the warmth of the bed. He'd taken her until they both collapsed, and then spent the night with her in his arms. The rightness of it convinced him to be brave. He watched for a time as she gazed out at the early morning sky, her expression mournful, wiping errant tears as if swatting flies, her only covering a simple shift. He hated those tears as much as he understood them.

When he sat companionably across from her on the veranda, she closed up her expression. He hoped one day she wouldn't feel the need to do so. Maybe she would remain in the capital long enough for him to see that day. He took a deep breath and offered her his heart.

"I want you to consider staying here."

Fuck. That wasn't precisely what he wanted to say. Selene stared, brows furrowing with puzzlement.

"Of course. Isn't breakfast on its way?"

He bit back a groan of frustration.

"I meant in the long term. I would like you to stay with me, here in Nadioch, even after this is all over."

Selene stilled. Her eyes misted, lost and vulnerable. Gods he wished she would let him hold her. She turned away, a neutral mask in place when she spoke.

"I'm sure your praetor would strenuously object."

"The praetor doesn't decide my future, or yours. Would you like to stay here, with me?" he asked.

He couldn't remember the last time he'd felt so exposed. It was as terrifying as it was necessary. If he wanted a real relationship with her, he knew he would have to be the first to bare his soul. Her prickly, defensive nature demanded nothing less.

"I..."

"You don't need to answer right away. Think it over and-"

"I would."

His heart skipped a beat, and then beat so fast he was certain it would fly out of his chest. His smile was irrepressible. Selene blushed, then growled.

"Stop that. Don't get a fat head just because I said I'd stick around. If I do, you'll have to do something about that green-eyed bastard. The last person who pissed me off as much died."

Belisarius didn't like the sound of that. Had Nicephorus been excessively antagonistic? No longer.

"I'll see that his attitude changes."

Selene nodded loftily and then began fussing with her hair, the red creeping down her neck and up to the tips of her ears. He found it endearing, watching her badly hide her self-consciousness in his presence. A facet he hadn't seen yet. When she stopped mid-stroke of a strand, he could see that her mind was buzzing.

"Speaking of attitude adjustments, do you want me to make good on my insurance policy against Magister Amethyst?"

"Your what?" Belisarius asked, blindsided.

"I figured he'd try to kill me at some point, so I seeded his estate with enchanted poison. If I die or stop holding it back, then they'll bloom and kill everyone on the estate. Probably all of the surrounding land as well, and perhaps the nearest village, if the winds are just right."

"I'd, uh, prefer not to endanger innocents if possible, but I'll keep that in mind," he replied, wondering at his own sanity for wanting her still.

"If you say so. When this is over, can I have Magister Sapphire?"

"We will need him alive to interrogate him and formally sentence him."

This was not how he'd envisioned their conversation going when he'd lain awake in the night, planning how to ask her to stay without scaring her off with words like *relationship* or *permanent*.

She waved her hand lazily in the air.

"I mean after that. I have business with him."

"When he's no longer of use, then you may do as you like," Belisarius replied. Magister Sapphire was to be sentenced to death anyway. It didn't matter who had a hand in it, just that it was done.

"Excellent. Also-"

A loud and urgent knocking interrupted her.

"Your Royal Highness, I have news that cannot wait," Nicephorus called.

Selene's eyes narrowed, an angry cat, hackles raised.

"Would you like me to see him in another room?" Belisarius asked.

Selene blinked in surprise, face heating once more. He couldn't wait to start using this in the games they played. If every kind gesture flustered her, he was going to undo her with chivalry. She cleared her throat and raised her chin.

"No, do let the man in to see his prince," she purred, relaxing into the seat.

"Come in," Belisarius called back.

Nicephorus rushed into the room, messy piles of correspondence still cradled in his arms, his robes and pallium askew and his long blonde hair dishevelled in its braid. It was only once he stopped that he realised Selene was also present. She smirked triumphantly and waggled her fingers in greeting.

"What is she doing here?"

"Selene is here because I invited her. What is so urgent, Praetor?" Belisarius' tone brooked no argument.

Thus prompted, the praetor ignored Selene and reported his news.

"Four of your relatives have left the Ruby Province and cannot be located. Two uncles and their eldest sons. They appear to have left suddenly last night. This may be the source of it all, Your Royal Highness," Nicephorus hedged.

"Spare no expense in finding them. I want them alive. Understood?"

Nicephorus bowed before running from the room. Despite the ugliness of the betrayal, Belisarius felt better knowing who the perpetrators were. He could finally stop looking at his family and wondering who among them hated him so bitterly that they would risk the stability of the empire to harm him.

"You're strangely happy for a man who was just informed his family members helped commit terrible crimes."

"This rebellion has been taxing. Knowing we've identified all the conspirators is a relief."

"And you expected some of your family were in on it?"

"Unfortunately," Belisarius nodded. "Someday in the near future, I will tell you the whole of it."

"I look forward to the full sordid tale." Selene smiled.

CHAPTER 26

Two brothers. Two nephews. It was a hard blow. Darius had little in the way of family left. But something didn't sit right with Darius. There were too many puzzle pieces shuffling around. The emperor had been up late the night before, dealing with the fallout of Illustrus Maksim's admission of murdering a former knight in her own home. Illustra Dihya had been his bravest beast mage, and his most deadly, until her wings had been wounded beyond repair. The anger at knowing she'd died because of some mewling brat had kept him up until long after the sun had risen.

He'd just received word of family members fleeing in the night, like rats abandoning a sinking ship. There would be nowhere they could go. No ship would take them, and no province would shelter them. Exhausted by his own anger, he sank into his bed. Without Nadia, the damn thing was too big, too cold. He wondered briefly what she would have done.

Nadia had always had a soft spot for family. It had been difficult for her to see reason when kin was involved. She might have pleaded that they receive some sort of punishment short of death. Even when almost all of their children had been killed by Mercurius, she had only reluctantly agreed to have Mercurius executed, and only after he'd forbidden her further experiments with the memory flowers. It had been months after that dark day before they could speak to one another. He knew his surviving son had no such blind spot, and for that he was grateful. With thoughts of his wife swirling in his mind, Darius drifted off to sleep, no closer to solving the puzzle in his mind.

Despite its cavernous size, the stark, unadorned room was all tight angles and nearly airless. Windowless walls ensured the only lighting came from enchanted wall sconces. Having been assured that fresh air was, in fact, being circulated through vents improved neither the condition of the room nor Iliana's mood. She sat at what could only generously be described as a desk, beside her more arrows and arrowheads than she'd ever seen in her life. The scale of her task was daunting—to enchant each one to find its mark. Ilana had lost count of them somewhere around two thousand. She only knew that no matter how many she'd done, it was only a fraction of those that remained. Hours of drudgery and exhaustion dragged at her. Working for the Imperial Forge was a sight less glamorous than she'd been led to believe. The room was hot and stifling, the lighting was giving her a headache, and her back felt like it was on fire.

"Work for the prince, he says. The praetor won't be able to naysay our engagement, he says. Fuck! Would it kill them to let some damned air into this bloody tomb?!"

"Is that unladylike language I hear? Tut tut. Your class is showing."

Iliana started, falling off her stool in shock.

"Selene? Where are you? The storehouse in under heavy guard."

"I'm in a vent, but I'm a little stuck. A hand?"

Iliana looked up to see a slim hand waving out of the vent. Given the ceiling was lower than most, she didn't need to stand on top of anything to reach her friend. Iliana raised her arms, grabbed Selene's above the wrists and pulled. In moments her friend was freed, along with a rush of blessedly cool air.

"They have you working like a dog in here, don't they?" Selene remarked as she looked around, squinting in the dim light.

"I'm to enchant the lot of them. I may go mad before the end." Iliana swept her hand across the room.

"I'm not sure I follow. Is this voluntary on your part, or do I need to have a second and final discussion with your... man you intend to keep?"

Iliana didn't like that Selene was hostile towards Marduk. She supposed it would be a slow process to reintroduce them as friends, like trying to get two angry cats to sit peaceably together.

"Yes, I agreed to this. It's in case our fathers decide to come with their armies. Wait, did you say *second* discussion? What happened during the first?"

"Oh, you know, there might have been some dick measuring, I may have nearly murdered him. It's okay though, we worked it out," Selene remarked casually as she ran her hands over the fletching of the arrows arrayed throughout. "But that's not important. I had a hell of a time finding you, and an equally difficult time getting here. Why are you under lock and key?"

Iliana wanted to scream, just a little. She would have to confront Marduk about this later. She could picture the conversation now.

"So did my best friend try to kill you?"

"Oh that? Didn't seem like a big deal. Just another day, right?"

"As long as you're not upset about her homicidal tendencies..."

"Not to worry. It keeps things interesting, doesn't it?"

Stubborn fiancé. Stubborn friend. She did her best to push those angry thoughts away.

"No one is supposed to know that the arrows are enchanted, or how I do it. The prince wants this very hush-hush. Also, it is not okay that you tried to murder Marduk. I'm going to marry him soon, and I want him unharmed."

"It's not like I didn't have a good reason," Selene muttered, chastened.

Iliana waited, her arms crossed and her brow raised.

"Okay, okay, I thought he was lying about his feelings and the job at the forge. I figured it'd be better if for him to die than break your heart and stomp on your dreams."

Selene set her lips in a mulish line, daring her to disagree with the assessment. Maybe Iliana was a touch mad herself, because it warmed her heart a little to know Selene cared as much as she did. She grabbed Selene up in a fierce hug.

"Agh! Ribs!" Selene wheezed.

"You're so cute sometimes. But he was telling the truth."

When Iliana set Selene down on the floor, she was given a baleful glare by her friend.

"You know, everyone looks at you and thinks you're perfectly normal. You want a good job, a good man and a good home. But I know very well you would have made a special dagger with his name on it if he'd been lying. You have patience in spades, but when it runs out, well, you're scarier than me."

"And don't you forget it." Iliana winked. Very few things made her truly angry. But after losing her mother and stepfather, she simply didn't tolerate threats to the safety of people she loved and valued. While she might not have killed the strategos had he been lying, she would have been sorely tempted to leave him a few important bits short.

Selene's swam with guilt as she played with her hair.

"I'm sorry I yelled at you the other day. You didn't deserve that."

"Are you going to tell me why?"

"The memory spell I had on me broke and forced me to relive some painful things." She hugged herself, eyes askance.

Iliana could see her struggling to think of a way to explain it. The dread in her eyes was real. All Selene had ever told her was that she knew she'd had a memory spell placed on herself and she'd done it willingly. Also, she'd warned her not to dig into it. Iliana had speculated about what a woman who personified the saying 'devil may care' felt the need to forget, but she decided it was none of her business and a moot point. Now that the spell had broken, she could see the turmoil. For the first time, behind the brashness, there was distinct vulnerability. Loss and grief hid behind that shield of emotional invincibility. Not for the first time, Iliana wondered if the woman she'd come to know had slipped so far into pretending nothing could hurt her that she'd truly believed it herself. At least until something finally came along to shake the foundation of that belief. She reached down and put a hand on her shoulder.

"You can tell me the details some other time when you feel ready. I accept your apology."

Selene's anxiety seemed to vanish before her eyes.

"So, what's this hush-hush business you've been conscripted to do?"

"You remember when I toyed with the never-miss enchantment on those darts so we could clean up at the taverns?"

Selene's eyes went wide and she swirled around, looking at the armoury anew.

"It's better than seven out of ten? You perfected it?"

Ilana nodded proudly.

"And you negotiated per arrow, yes?"

"Uh."

Selene groaned dramatically.

"What do I always tell you? If they want it badly enough, you should make them bleed gold for it. Never mind. We'll renegotiate. I can't believe no one told me about this. You'd think Belli would've mentioned something given I fucked him nearly blind. Damn ingrate."

"Not going to go running for memory flowers this time, are you?" Iliana teased.

Iliana could've sworn Selene flinched. She started toying with the end of her long braid. It wasn't just the vulnerability that was new. Had

Selene caught feelings for a man? Iliana made heroic efforts to repress a shout of excitement. Her plan could finally start to take shape.

"Not for that, no. He even wants me to stick around."

"That's good news...right?"

"I don't know. What does he even want from me? We both know I insult him just to see that little vein in his neck pound. I'm stealing things these days just to see if he notices, so we can argue about it later. I've threatened enough noblewomen to burn every bridge in the empire twice over. The rest of the time, I'm testing how many of the praetor's spies I can poison or evade. I mean, I know I'm a great lay, but you can see why I'm confused, right?"

Iliana was beginning to see why the praetor always had a short fuse over matters concerning Selene. As for the prince, she wasn't certain of his intentions. He must at least be quite infatuated with her friend. Iliana had come to know the open secret of the prince's aloofness towards women from the many gossiping noblewomen she spent her evenings with. But the emperor himself seemed to have taken a shine to Selene. Surely that meant the old man approved of how close his son had gotten to her? If Iliana could nudge her in the right way, maybe there was a chance she and her friend could be happy in Nadioch together.

"Selene, I'd bet good coin you're the first person outside his family that just treats him like-"

"A hot piece of ass?" Selene smiled winningly.

"I was going to say like a person instead of a prince." Iliana frowned. She thought Selene's lack of any sense of deference was just a touch suicidal, but for whatever reason the gods had smiled upon her. It was very much in keeping with Selene's approach to things to career through life balanced on the edge of a knife. Perhaps, like herself, the prince was captivated by the promise of madcap adventure in her grin. "But I suppose the more important thing is, do you like him enough to want to stay?"

She watched as Selene played with her hair. Again. It shocked her to no end, but Selene was well and truly infatuated. Iliana kept her poker face studiously in place.

"I maybe want to keep him," she mumbled shyly.

Iliana bent down so her eyes were level with her friend's and placed her hands on her shoulders. This was just the chance she'd been hoping for. She'd anticipated that a good dose of the praetor's warnings would push Selene further into the prince's arms. It seemed to have worked.

"How badly?"

"I'm not sure I follow."

"Do you want to share him with some other woman who considers herself your better?"

"Of course not." Selene frowned.

"Then become empress in truth. You're more than ruthless enough to outcompete any of the other women who want him. And I know just the thing to help you tip the scales in your favour."

Selene was pleased to find that pretending to be the fiancée of the prince, however temporarily, had its benefits. Private rooms with personal spaces free from the empty expressions of her sisters, a terrace that looked out onto the gardens, a slew of servants who didn't need to be taught to keep their distance unless summoned, and fancy seats at both the Odeon and Hippodrome.

A dressmaker had come to take measurements and hold up what seemed like millions of swatches to her face—all in imperial red, of course. A jeweller had been next, then the shoemaker, then a perfumer, and on and on it went until she declared herself done with the business. She supposed Belisarius wanted this to seem as real as it got in order to lure the magistri peacefully to the capital, their spies reporting back that she was being pampered in the extreme. Selene allowed herself a girlish grin while imagining herself in one of those dresses. With Iliana's skills playing a role, Selene had no doubt their fathers would be swiftly cornered and imprisoned.

She'd managed to keep herself so busy during her days—and Belisarius busy during the nights, and sometimes mornings and impromptu afternoons—that she scarcely had time to think. Even now she devoured books on history, statecraft and the economies and peoples of the provinces. If she was going to stay, she reasoned she should at least be able to offer an educated opinion here and there. Iliana had helped, curating a whole host of books for her to read. Belisarius would find her new knowledge impressive, maybe even consider her a real candidate for empress. He already knew she was strong and ruthless enough, but she would prove she was clever, just as Iliana had suggested.

Selene clawed her way to her goal with the same ferocity that she protected her nascent hope. It was all that stood between her and the pain in her chest whenever she thought of Dihya. It was tolerable, so long as she surrounded herself with busyness, Iliana, Belli and Darius, things she hadn't had years ago when the wound had festered, nearly killing her. She reasoned she would be able to keep it together long enough not to need a memory mage immediately. But if the time came, where to find one this time around? The wily mage had erased their image from her mind along with her pain, but even now their identity was a mystery to her.

A knock on her door roused her from her musings. Another perk of being an especially honoured person in the palace? The library brought whatever she wished directly to her.

"You may enter."

Selene recognised the man holding the precarious pile of books and scrolls once he set them down on the table before her.

"Would you like me to place these books on your shelves, Princess Consort?"

It would take some getting used to, hearing that title without the instinctual suspicion that it was spoken with derision. Now that she was a royal fiancée, she'd received more than an upgrade in her living quarters. Bloody nobles were circling like a pack of hungry dogs, flattering her or insulting her, usually both at the same time. No wonder Darius killed one every so often.

"You may leave them here, Azar."

The librarian smiled and bowed.

"I'm honoured Your Radiance remembers my name."

"How could I not remember the name of the only librarian who doesn't cower in fear before me? Why is that, I wonder?" she asked as she glanced at him. There was nothing especially notable about him—average build, average looks, better than average sense, light brown skin, salt and pepper hair and robes too big for him. He wore a small earring in one ear; a charm, perhaps?

"I believe Your Radiance only punishes those who are rude. Am I wrong?"

Selene wondered how it was that a man his age could appear so innocent. Was she excessively jaded? Surely not. If the part of affable academic was all an act, he deserved extra gold for the performance. Either way, he was the only librarian who dared come within spitting distance.

"No."

The librarian smiled amiably.

"Is that a charm in your ear, Azar?"

Startled, his hand protectively cupped his ear. He bowed deeply.

"I apologize, Princess Consort. Please do not ask me to remove it. I was disfigured as a boy, and it is the only thing which has allowed me a normal life since."

"No need to worry. It was simple curiosity, no more. What have you brought with you today?" Selene asked.

His family must have spent a fortune on a charm so well-crafted, or been owed an enormous favour by a powerful light mage. He seemed relieved that she'd not pushed any further, and smiled. She could play nice when other people were nice.

"You'll find some of the most highly regarded books on leadership, statecraft and warfare among those I've selected. Given your new role, I've also taken the liberty of adding the few tomes available on the lands beyond Lethe. The thin volume on the top here is also quite rare, and has one of the few surviving tales of our ancestors' transit to this world from the old. While it isn't necessary reading, I've always thought it a shame that there aren't more mages who have had a chance to read it."

"That is very thorough of you. Why aren't you the head librarian?"

"I'm not worthy of the praise, Princess Consort. I'm just an extra hand hired to help out during the bride show."

"Have you enjoyed your time in the palace?"

"It has been trying, but also quite educational. I had hoped to remain in Nadioch from here on."

"Then I'll make sure you're kept on after the bride show, Azar."

"I am most grateful for your generosity, Your Radiance."

"What kind of princess would I be if I didn't reward valuable service?"

Selene allowed the librarian to leave. According to her books, in addition to leaving her detractors trembling in fear, she was going to need to build up a group of people entirely and exclusively loyal to her. Today it was the librarian; tomorrow, who knew?

Chapter 27

Why did the damn hallways have to go on endlessly? Why were there all these useless rooms between her and the sweet relief of her own bed? Iliana trudged to her new room, given to her now that she was officially Marduk's fiancée. Unlike Selene's rooms, Iliana's was decorated exclusively to her own tastes, without care for how the servants might think of her. It was simple, spacious, comfortable, and littered with design sketches for her projects instead of overwhelming tapestries and overstuffed vases. Except it was also too damn far. Drained, aching, she'd only just finished the unending task of enchanting the arrows. If she never saw another, it would be too soon. Now, all she wanted was to collapse into her feather bed and silk sheets. Instead, she found herself blindly walking into a rather impressive chest.

"Iliana? Are you alright?"

As she looked up, she realised she knew that impressive chest very well. Concern radiated from Marduk's dark green eyes.

"I need sleep. Everything hurts," she muttered.

He swept her up in his arms, relieving the aches in her legs and feet. If she weren't already set on it, that kindness alone would have convinced her to marry him.

"Your wish is my command." He smiled.

She was beyond any feeling of embarrassment as the nobles they passed gasped or giggled, such was her fatigue. Her head resting on his chest, she let the sound of his heartbeat and the warmth of him soothe her. He navigated the remaining maze of corridors and covered walkways with ease, and they entered the part of the palace complex reserved for commanders of the military and their families. Of all the buildings, Marduk's was the largest, with several grand rooms branching off a well-tended central courtyard. Once inside, he instructed the servant to prepare the bedroom and leave. Gently placing her on the cool sheets, he removed the shoes from her swollen feet and tucked her in.

"When you wake, we'll have something to eat. Sleep well." He leaned down to kiss her brow.

She hated the sight of dark circles like bruises under his eyes, his shoulders slumped with fatigue. No doubt he too had been run ragged preparing for the potential of another war. Worse, the dangers wouldn't necessarily end if the magistri were captured. The nobles of their territories might seize on the situation either out of crass opportunism or blind loyalty. She'd been treated to every doomsday scenario courtesy of her honorary place in the prince's meetings. Iliana touched his cheek, his stubble scraping her fingers.

"Stay. You need the rest as much as I."

"I'm not sure-"

"Right now, neither of us has the energy for anything else. Don't be stubborn."

Marduk grinned boyishly.

"Don't be so certain of that."

Iliana rolled her eyes and began drifting off. Marduk slipped under the covers next to her and kissed her head before settling. Iliana fell asleep to the sound of his slow, even breaths, cradled against his chest, his arm protectively embracing her.

When she woke, the last glorious rays of sunlight were streaming into her room, painting the sky in a thousand shades of orange. She felt refreshed, though the tangled mess of her dress had given her new kinks in her back. A small table by the window was already piled high with fruits, cheeses and meats, and a bottle of wine with two glasses nearby. She poured herself a glass. Her only complaint about the room was that the bed was unnaturally high and large, to accommodate Marduk's frame.

Splashing caught her attention. Had her fiancé decided to take a dip in the bath? She crept to the door of the luxurious bathroom and spied her man enjoying the steaming waters of the smooth brick pool. She was enjoying the view profusely until the steam cleared and she noticed two jagged, upraised scars along his back. Iliana gasped at the unexpected sight. The door swung open on its hinge.

Marduk turned and grinned.

"Spying is a bad habit, darling."

When he saw that it wasn't embarrassment that had surprised her, the humour bled from his expression. His lips thinned, his eyes averted.

"You had wings," Iliana finally managed to choke out. "Who would do such a thing?" Horrified tears welled up in her eyes.

"The same kind of man who would slaughter nearly a whole royal family," Marduk replied. He turned from her and wrapped himself in a towel, refusing to meet her eyes. "I'm sorry you had to see that. I hope you can overlook it in the future."

Iliana was rooted to the spot. Gods below, the assassin who had murdered the imperial children nearly three decades ago...Marduk would have been no more than a child himself. The barbarity of it made her ill, until blistering anger replaced it. How many had made him feel like less of a mage for having lost his wings? Even now, the great strategos stood before her, ashamed of his scars. She placed her palm on his warm, wet chest before he could pass by her, stopping him in his tracks. She forced him to meet her eyes.

"I believe you were about to coax me into the bath with you, Strategos," she purred.

His eyes widened with disbelief.

"I believe I was about to let you," she continued.

Marduk tossed his bundled clothes aside. She flicked her eyes to the towel at his waist. It disappeared like the rest. Iliana began pulling off her simple frock.

"I was going to extract promises from you for every article of clothing I removed." She plucked at the ties lacing her slip. Marduk swallowed, his eyes riveted to her chest as she slowly exposed it. "You were going to agree to each and every one, naturally."

She pushed him farther, until he was ankle-deep in the pool. Left with only a thin slip, Marduk drank in the sight of her with stark greed. She didn't mind in the least. She was enjoying the view. Rarely had she met a man so well built. Broad shoulders, thick arms, muscled thighs, an impressive chest, and a trail of dark hair that led straight down to a prize that had her aching with anticipation. Thank the gods this was not her first time, or she might have looked upon him in trepidation rather than abject lust.

"And then?" he asked, his voice husky. Her own greedy stare had not gone unnoticed.

"I was going to demand you keep your first promise."

"Which was?"

Iliana removed her last article of clothing, baring herself in front of him. She could see he was wound tight as a bowstring with need. For that matter, so was she. It was hard to keep her thoughts organized at the sight of him. She wanted him so needy for her that all thoughts of shame or sadness were banished for good. There was no room for those things between them.

"A massage. I'm sore, and, well, you've nothing else planned for the evening."

He blinked owlishly at the unexpected request. Only the tips of her fingers were touching his chest, urging him deeper into the pool. He grinned, clasped her forearm and pulled her into the water, bodies fitting snugly against each other. Her breath hitched at the insistent length of his erection against her hip. She blushed at the needy ache it inspired. Grabbing him by the horns, she pulled him in for a kiss. His tongue met hers and she melted against him, his calloused hands wandering down her back to squeeze her rear as his tail snaked around her thigh.

"You go grabbing a man by the horns, and he's going to assume you're only interested in a certain kind of massage."

"If you keep talking, I'm going to assume you don't know how."

Brow raised in challenge, he pulled her into the deeper part of the pool. She noticed then that his claws were missing, filed down.

"Marduk, your claws..."

"They'll be back within a day. Did you really think I'd forgo the chance to touch you?"

Setting her on a stone bench, her breasts above the water, he pulled her legs apart to stand between them. It was all she could do not to moan at how wide he spread her. One hand of his braced against the edge of the pool while the other unerringly found her core. A soft kiss coaxed her to take hold of his member. As she revelled in the velvety feel of him, he teased her cruelly with rough fingertips and soft caresses. Swallowing her cries of impatience, she wrung groans from him in turn. Marduk's thick fingers speared her, and suddenly his attentions kept her dangling on the edge, driving her half mad as he stroked her. Lust and need made her bolder. Iliana grabbed him by the horns and bit his lip.

"Harder!" she commanded, breathless.

Kiss harsh, he acquiesced, sending her over a blissful edge crying his name. Her body limp and exquisitely sensitive, heart racing and breathless, she wasn't the least bit bothered by the smug smile on his rugged face. Marduk gathered her in his arms and carried her to the bed. Set down on cool sheets, she stared hungrily at his straining erection. Need flared anew.

"Do you know what your second promise to me was?" she asked playfully.

Her legs dangled over the edge of the bed, and she had to crane her neck back to look him in the eye. He leaned over her, forcing her further back until her shoulders pressed against the covers. His sweet, slow kiss scrambled her thoughts. She pulled him closer, taking him in hand once again as he teased her tight nipples between his fingers. Her legs wrapped around him of their own accord, urging him to grind against her.

"I have a sneaking suspicion I know what you want," he murmured with a playful twinkle in his eye.

When he pulled away, she nearly begged for his return. Refusing to let him get too far, she locked his hips in place with her legs. He chuckled softly, grabbed her thighs and pulled them further apart. Exposed, he began the deliberate, tortuous process of grinding his erection against her. Iliana couldn't stop the helpless moans from escaping her lips. Though his expression was fierce, his voice was calm, controlled. She loved him for his gentleness, but she craved his fire.

"But I can't be certain. What is it you want?"

He increased the pressure, hitting her just right, robbing her mind of reason as she clutched the sheets between her fingers. She'd been mistaken, thinking she could control this game of seduction, but she'd never enjoyed playing the fool more. Bucking her hips against him, chasing that glorious feeling, she was about to reach the peak again when he eased the pressure.

"No!" she cried, thwarted.

"You have to ask for what you want, Iliana." His whisper drove her mad.

His horns were too far away for her to grab. She unlocked her fingers from the sheets and made to show him, but he caught her wrist and forced it above her head, shaking his head. His tail circled her thigh where his hand had been, keeping her pinned.

"Use your words."

"You! Please!" she begged, her free hand snaking around his head, fingers sinking into his short curls.

Marduk obliged, pushing himself into her inch by glorious inch. She'd never felt so full, such delicious, exquisite friction, the ache finally sated. At least until he drew out of her, unhurried. She flexed her thighs and angled her hips, forcing him into her faster than he'd meant. Their eyes met, and Iliana exulted in the moment his control gave over to wild need. When he filled her to the hilt, he increased his tortuously slow pace, faster, harder, until they were both lost to all sense and reason, just sweet friction, slick bodies and devouring kisses. He was everywhere, devouring her in the best possible way. Her world narrowed to the feeling of building ecstasy, and it didn't take much to send her over the edge again. Marduk followed her, his groan of pleasure sending a hot frisson down her spine. His breath was as ragged as hers. His kiss was as sweet as his lovemaking had been fierce.

"I love you, Iliana," he growled.

Heart fluttering in her chest, her smile was inescapable.

"I love you, too."

Iliana woke to a knocking at their door. Marduk roused, his arms having cradled her in their sleep.

"I'm sorry to disturb you Domina Roxane, but your sister, Domina Diodora, is saying she has urgent business with you," the servant said from the other side of the door.

"I'll be out in a moment," Iliana yawned.

"What could she want at this hour?" Marduk grouched from beside her, burying his face in her hair.

Iliana turned to kiss him on his cheek before swinging her legs over the side of the bed. A delightful twinge gave her a slight hitch in her step as she padded silently on the cool stone floor to where a simple robe was hung. She wrapped it securely around her waist.

"I'm sure it's nothing serious. I'll be back soon."

Iliana stepped out into the receiving parlour, a simple room with simple, plush furniture, martial-themed tapestries and a mosaic of sea creatures beneath her feet. Diodora sat stiffly in a chair, a cup of untouched tea in her hands, the room bright with magic sconces. When she stared at Iliana, it was with those familiar, deadened eyes. She appeared as if she'd just come from a ball, her platinum hair swept up and festooned with jewels while the sapphires at her ears, neck and wrists sparkled. Diodora mechanically placed the cup on a nearby table, stood, and smoothed out her embroidered silk skirts before approaching Iliana. When she was a few paces from her, Diodora spoke.

"Have you truly lowered yourself by sleeping with a beast mage?"

Iliana froze, dumbstruck by the vulgar question. It was all the more bewildering coming from the prim and proper lips of her half-sister. So neutral was her tone that Iliana wasn't even certain if her sister felt the disgust she implied. There was no reason to respond at all charitably.

"I think it would be best if you left, before I find something sharper than your tongue to cut you with."

"I am to assume that means you have."

Iliana almost didn't catch the quick movement of Diodora's hand thrusting out from where it had been hidden behind the flowing skirts of her evening dress. In it, she held a wicked blade of sharp glass in a cheap wooden handle. Without metal, she hadn't sensed it. Iliana deflected Diodora's hand with an unpractised swipe of her own, narrowly sparing herself a dagger deep in her gut. Iliana cried out.

Blood bloomed across the gash on Iliana's stomach.

Marduk burst through the bedroom doors, brutally shoving Diodora away. Her half-sister flew into the table, splintering the wood, and crumpled onto the floor. Once he could see she was down, Marduk looked over Iliana, panic in his eyes.

"Are you hurt?"

"No... I... I think it's just a scratch," Iliana stuttered, shocked by the sudden violence. Not once had she seen any of her half-sisters move with such speed.

Marduk inspected her belly and nodded. He marched over to Diodora, kicking away the blade. He knelt down and heaved her up by the fabric of her dress, the many sapphire pins and jewels she'd decorated herself with strewn across the mosaic floor. His glare sent a shiver down Iliana's spine.

"Why did you attack my fiancée?! You'd best answer before I decide to send you to rot in the dungeons for the next few decades!"

"Father said that the family would be disgraced if she were intimate with you. He told me to kill her, and then myself, if that happened. It would lessen the scandal. No domina in her right mind would wish to be tied to a beast mage, and any magister who allowed it would be ridiculed."

With a spiteful glower at Diodora, Marduk called out for the guards.

"Send her to the dungeons for questioning. Have someone get a message to the praetor and the prince that we must meet immediately." He turned to the newly arrived servant. "Call for a healer. My fiancée has been attacked."

When it was just the two of them, Marduk pulled her into a tight embrace. The sound of his wildly beating heart was the only indication of his terror. Lucky that. Iliana shook.

"Starting tomorrow, you're getting lessons in combat."

Iliana buried her head against his chest, trying to ignore the fiery sting across her belly as she shook harder.

"It's safe now, my love," he cooed.

Except it wasn't. Tears welled in her eyes.

"I-I shouldn't cry. It's not even close to the worst cut I've ever had." She choked, her voice watery.

"If you come apart, I will hold you together." He ran his hand down the length of her hair, over and over.

Her lip trembled. In moments, she was nothing but a vibrating mess. She supposed it was too much to hope they would get out of it all unscathed. No matter where she went, her father tainted it, stealing her joy. But there was nowhere left to run, not if she didn't want to carve out her own heart by leaving Marduk behind. She wouldn't do it! He'd taken everything from her, but she wouldn't let him take Marduk too.

"I hate him! I just-I just wanted *one* place where I could feel safe. He took it from me. He stole it again!" Iliana sobbed, hands fisted in his robe.

"He didn't steal our love, or our lives. He failed. You won this battle. You belong here, and he can't take that from you, Iliana."

She came apart then, tears soaking his robes. But through it all, he kept his promise—Marduk held her together.

CHAPTER 28

The days before the magistri's arrival had seen a whirlwind of activity unprecedented in the history of the palace and Nadioch. It been cleaned from top to bottom, made to sparkle, and then polished again for good measure. Fresh flowers hung from every available perch, tapestries seemed to have mated and produced offspring overnight, and the only scent from the stables was that of freshly groomed horse and new hay. The streets of Nadioch had been festooned with flowering plants, bright ribbons and palace personnel distributing grain, booze and tasty treats. Every magister had outfitted their chariot team in outrageous costumes and had them running races nonstop in the Hippodrome while magistrae were patronizing every heart-pounding romance play in the Odeon. The ordained path of the honoured magistri's carriages had been laid out with extra finery, and the cobbles swept so clean they could be eaten off of with more confidence than the local taverns' crockery.

Everywhere, the sounds of music and revelry could be heard late into the night. It wasn't only the prince who had secured himself a wife, after all. A great many other noble families had nuptials to plan, and each magister had a son or daughter who had found someone to bring home during the bride show. Overnight, dress makers and florists and wedding planners were so thick on the ground, you couldn't go more than a few steps without bumping into at least one of the three. Every inn for miles around was full, as was every home, apartment, spare room, barn, stable, shed and dingy hole. Anyone who could lay claim to any spare inch of space was raking in coin from visitors. So were the taverns, shops and entertainers.

Selene was greatly disappointed not to be a part of it all. She knew she'd have sold out of her wares quickly enough. *Got a new son-in-law who needs to disappear? Did some vixen sink her claws into your man? Hoping to inherit that property before the kids come along? Poisons for every occasion! Discounts for multiple purchases! Debilitating, humiliating or just plain unpleasant. Poisons for all!*

She heaved a sigh and got back to her books. The more she read, the more she realised there was no manual on how to rule. You could be a feared tyrant, a wily trickster, a beloved paragon, but nothing ensured you wouldn't meet your end. Selene began to understand just how precarious any monarch's life was, and how useless all those dominae would have been to Belli. He needed someone like her who could terrify the nobles like Darius did. She could find her place here in Nadioch, in the palace, by his side. Though she knew it was dangerous, she nourished the bloom of hope within her.

"Princess Consort, Domina Roxane is here for you."

"Show her in," Selene replied, putting down her book.

Iliana entered, an anxious wobble to her practiced smile. Selene sent the servant away, and soon her friend released the stiffness in her shoulders. Selene patted the seat next to her on the long couch. Iliana sat and hugged her, burying her face in Selene's shoulder.

"I'm scared of what happens when the magistri arrive," she whispered.

"If they so much as break wind, they'll be made into pincushions with your arrows. Your sisters are already locked up for good measure, and the spare domini are under kill orders if they start looking cagey. It's going to be okay," Selene murmured, rubbing her back in soothing circles.

"What if they hurt Marduk?" she choked.

"Tell him to use the praetor as a shield," Selene muttered. Green-eyed bastard still glared at her like she was dung on his boots.

Iliana giggled irreverently and then sobered.

"Your father can use lightning." Iliana's eyes tightened at the corners.

"Want to hear a secret?"

"What?"

"Belisarius is going to make their mage gifts irrelevant."

"He's that strong?"

"He's a negation mage," Selene crowed proudly.

"A what? I thought he was a fire mage." Iliana sat up, interested.

"Mage gifts don't work around him. The magistri won't even conjure a spark before they're neutered."

"No wonder you're so relaxed."

Selene shrugged.

"You know, you never got around to telling me what your memory spell was about."

Selene paused, prodding the wound in her heart. It was still tender and fresh, but the unutterable pain no longer plagued her every waking moment. Maybe that meant it was time to talk about it. Dihya hadn't raised her to run from her problems, or her demons. She took a deep breath before she began.

"It all started with a pie cooling on a windowsill, and a very hungry little brat."

When the day of arrival dawned, the streets were empty of revellers, musicians, and all but the most stubborn merchants. The skies were as dark as dusk, the clouds a steely grey, heavy with sheeting rain that washed away any evidence of yesterday's frivolity. Thunder rumbled down from the distant mountains, the only sound outside that could be heard above the din of the deluge. Despite the gaiety of the occasion, sombreness permeated the very air, as thick as the blanket of humidity which had settled on the capital.

Damp earth and beeswax candles scented the air of the large audience chamber in which only the most important individuals were present. Belisarius surveyed the throne room, decorated heavily with imperial red and flashing gold. Storied tapestries hung on the walls, sandwiched between painted columns with mosaics both under foot and glittering above in the arched roof. The magistri of Emerald, Opal, Topaz and Diamond were already in attendance, seated at the long tables to the right of the dais, along with their heirs and un-affianced daughters, while the tables to left were populated by the highest ranked officials, some with their new fiancées.

None of the magistrae were in attendance. At any one time, they, their husbands or their heirs were expected to be within their provinces. Events of this magnitude at court were considered to be the purview of men.

On the dais, all bedecked in imperial red, Belisarius sat between his father and Selene, who was perfectly playing the part of princess consort. When this was over, Belisarius hoped to convince her to take on the roll in truth. He reached over, placing his hand on hers, and squeezed. How far they'd come from their first meeting.

Refreshments were being served while a small string quartet tried gamely to be heard over the sounds of the rain and simultaneous conversations. Without too great a delay, a servant whispered in Belisarius' ear that the magistri had arrived and were ready to be presented. He fought back his dread as the great doors creaked open to reveal the traitors and their heirs, striding forward with confidence.

"Magister Aristeo Sapphire and his heir, Dominus Leo Sapphire. Magister Grigori Amethyst and his heir, Dominus Dimitri Amethyst."

Belisarius scrutinized the magistri as they approached the dais to greet him formally. Sapphire had a certain brash swagger to his stride, mirrored almost exactly by his son, a spitting image of the tall, bronze-skinned, blue-eyed, white-haired father. Beside him, Amethyst had a quieter, if no less deadly, air about him. If only for a moment, he saw the same predatory gaze Selene often sported. Grigori's small grin at the sight of her beside Belisarius did nothing to disguise the fire in the magister's eyes. The young Amethyst heir had perfected the look of a noble stricken with a terminal case of ennui. Both possessed shockingly red hair, alabaster skin and below-average height. Magister Sapphire was the first to reach the dias, his long strides eating up the distance. He and his son knelt respectfully.

"May the forgotten gods see fit to remember you, Emperor Darius, Prince Belisarius."

Both Belisarius and his father nodded solemnly, repeating the gesture when Magister Amethyst gave the same greeting.

"May the forgotten Gods see fit to remember you, Emperor Darius, Prince Belisarius. Dear Milena, you do our bloodline proud."

While the two men knelt before him, Belisarius stood. The room quieted.

"Magister Miroslav Diamond, would you and your heir, Dominus Philip Diamond, join the Magistri Amethyst and Sapphire before me?"

Magister Diamond's lightly tanned skin went ashen as he stood, a slight wobble in his knees. Both he and his heir knelt behind the other magistri.

"Esteemed guests, these men and their heirs kneeling before the throne do so as traitors to the empire and users of foul magics. Guards, collar them!"

At the announcement, the tables of the magistri erupted in protest and shock. Only the Sapphire heir attempted to lash out before being subdued. With mercifully little resistance from the rest, the magistri and domini were collared with magic-suppression collars, reserved for the worst of criminals and silver-tongue mages. Magister Sapphire appeared furious, Amethyst unperturbed and Diamond on the verge of vomiting.

"Explain! What is the meaning of this? What proof do you have of these charges?!" Magister Topaz shouted.

The outburst wasn't unexpected. Topaz had historically been on good terms with both Sapphire and Amethyst, his province nestled between the two. Aside from the jolt of seeing his equals so reduced in public, he was no doubt gravely concerned about the continuity of revenues he garnered from the duties he imposed on traffic between the two larger provinces.

"Hold your tongue, Topaz, or I shall take it from you!" the emperor shouted back, looming to punctuate his threat.

Once again, silence reigned. Belisarius held out his hand to Selene, who calmly stood and took it. Marduk escorted Iliana to the step below the dais, resolute beside her.

"On threat of death, the woman beside me was forced to impersonate Domina Milena Amethyst, who currently sleeps in a coma, locked away on the Amethyst estate, a victim of foul magics. Explain, for those present, your situation," Belisarius said.

The eyes of the crowd went to Selene. Only the slight tightening of her hand in his signalled her unease.

"My name is Selene, a poison mage and bastard daughter of Magister Amethyst. I was kidnapped and forced to impersonate Domina Milena Amethyst and ordered to keep the eyes of the prince off my sisters, who are all victims of foul magic. The magister made very clear what the cost of defying him would be when he murdered the very men he hired to kidnap me."

"We cannot take the word of a self-proclaimed bastard of no repute over the word of an esteemed magister, Your Royal Highness. A man has every right to do with his daughters as he sees fit," Topaz interjected.

The prince gave him a wintry glare before turning to Iliana. What Topaz said may have been the case legally, but there was no excuse for the use of foul magics.

"Strategos, if your fiancée would be so kind as to further illuminate the situation?"

Iliana's face paled, but he was glad to hear her voice didn't waver. He could feel Selene's grip on his hand tighten once more.

"My name is Iliana. I'm a metals mage and bastard daughter of Magister Sapphire. I, too, was kidnapped and forced to impersonate my half-sister, Domina Roxane Sapphire. While imprisoned in the Sapphire estate, I came to understand my sisters were victims of foul magics. The magister said that my half-sisters would slit their throats with my knives if I tried to escape before successfully keeping their conditions unnoticed by the prince."

"What is this foul magic the magistri are accused of committing, Your Royal Highness?" Magister Emerald asked, sanguine as always.

The prince was deeply glad that Emerald was a cooler head in this situation. Thankfully, the man cared blessedly little for the fates of anyone unconnected to his province.

"Domina Daria Amethyst, step forward. Domina Chrysanthi Sapphire, step forward. Domina Galena Diamond, step forward."

The three women stood and obediently approached, each curtsying low, their hollow stares identical.

"Dominae, I command you, as your crown prince, to perform your mage gifts for those assembled."

"I cannot, Your Royal Highness." Chrysanthi replied first.

"And why is that?"

"My mage gift was given to my father, the magister."

"Dominae Amethyst and Diamond, are you similarly incapable?"

Both Daria and Galena replied in unison.

"Yes, Your Royal Highness."

"And what reason did your father have to do this to you, Domina Amethyst?"

"I was to give him my magic in lieu of an advantageous marriage, so that he could become a king."

Whispers raced through the small crowd. Hostility, disgust, horror and predatory glee manifested themselves in those eyeing up the accused magistri. No doubt a few cared less about the accusations than the opportunities for expansion that their imminent sentencing might bring. Belisarius supposed that was better than using the opportunity to rebel.

"Of course, I wouldn't ask my esteemed guests to believe such serious accusations without some modicum of proof. Praetor Nicephorus, if you would bring forward the proclamation orb?"

"Your Royal Highness, I have it here." Nicephorus produced the orb from a velvet sack and gently unwrapped the cloth around it. It sat like a crystal-clear melon, cushioned by the fabric in his hands. Only the palace possessed such a rare object. Its sole purpose was to determine the gift of the mage whose bare skin came into contact with it—a reflection of their very soul.

"Allow Magistri Emerald, Topaz and Opal to touch it so that we might ascertain for all those present that it functions properly."

"Yes, Your Royal Highness. Magister Emerald, if you would be the first to honour the prince's request?" Nicephorus asked.

The magister placed his hand on the orb which instantly flashed green, indicating the magister's command of earth. Emerald nodded, pleased with the result. The praetor repeated the process with Opal, the orb flashing silver, indicating his command of wind. Finally, when Topaz placed his hand on it, the orb turned pitch black, indicating his command of darkness itself. Thus satisfied, the prince spoke his next order.

"Praetor, have the daughters of Magistri Amethyst, Sapphire and Diamond currently present touch the proclamation orb."

"Domina Daria Amethyst, if you would begin the process?" Nicephorus asked while holding the orb in front of her for the magistri to see.

When she placed her hand on it, the orb remained crystal clear. The unharmed dominae gasped with horror, while their fathers' eyes went wide with shock. As Nicephorus repeated the process with each ensorcelled domina, the shock turned to outrage. The implication of the orb's clarity was impossible to deny. The women had been rendered soulless. It was the very foulest of magics, a crime worse than murder. A man may do as he wished with his daughters, but these acts were as perverse as they were taboo, and there would be nothing to stop them from doing the same to their peers. Or so Belisarius hoped they would believe.

"Given the evidence before you, do any present wish to plead for clemency on behalf of the criminals?" Belisarius asked.

Resounding silence was the answer he'd expected, and it was what he received.

"I, Crown Prince Belisarius Bloodstone, Magister Ruby and future Emperor of Lethe, hereby sentence the Magistri Sapphire, Amethyst and Diamond, and their heirs, to death, for crimes against the empire and the use of foul magics. Take them to the dungeons to await their executions."

CHAPTER 29

Marduk held the slipper-shaped oil lantern high, illuminating the stone steps in the inky darkness where the sconces failed to reach. Having just left his relieved and thoroughly sated fiancée in their apartments, he had set his mind to the task ahead. Behind him, Belisarius and the emperor followed. Though their steps were light, both having been trained as warriors, their descent into the dungeons was anything but quiet.

"You had best pick new magistri before the night is out. Topaz was all but salivating at the chance to expand his borders. Emerald too, for that matter, though the cold bastard managed at least not to be too obvious about it," Darius grumbled to his son.

"One problem is solved, and another three rear up their heads. I should have planned for this. I've been so focused on the traitors I failed to properly plan for the instability resulting from their arrests," the prince griped.

The long staircase down to the dungeons was probably the most private part of the castle. Sound didn't travel, and the passage was too narrow, the walls too thick for anyone to be inconspicuously spying. Marduk supposed it was the best place for the prince to air his doubts. Though he didn't think Belisarius need worry on that account. No doubt Nicephorus already had lists of worthy candidates in mind.

"They had best watch their cups over the next few days. Given the distaste they showed your fiancée, I would be shocked if they left Nadioch in good health," Darius mused.

"She is not my fiancée in truth. I have only just received her promise to remain in the capital after this situation is concluded." Belisarius sighed.

Marduk noticed then that the emperor had stopped in his descent. He stopped as well, turning to look. Fury twisted the old man's face.

"Have I raised a fool, then? What are you waiting for?"

Belisarius' face changed from irritation and exhaustion to wrath. It was not unlike the expression on the emperor's face. Marduk stifled a sigh as the two prepared to butt heads. Belisarius turned to face his father and shouted.

"Perhaps if you'd been more of an emperor these past few years, instead of drowning yourself in distractions, I might have more time on my hands to pursue her! Instead, I spend nearly every waking moment desperately keeping Lethe from collapsing into violence! You have no right to judge how I conduct my affairs!"

Marduk almost wished he could leave father and son to fight it out. It was a long time coming, this quarrel of theirs. Belisarius had gone from respecting his father before Nadia's death, to festering resentment of the man who raised him. The Emperor had done himself no favours in that regard by acting the part of a wastrel and abandoning his responsibilities to his grieving son. No son had loved his mother more than Belisarius had loved Nadia, and he might always hate his father for finding even fleeting comfort with other women mere weeks after she'd died. Still, as painful as it was to watch, he had to make sure neither did lasting physical damage to the other. Unfortunately, the psychic damage had already left permanent scars.

"I know I've behaved poorly, Belli, but I have every right to comment! I am your father and still the emperor! If you don't give her an official status now, then she will never command the loyalty of anyone inside or outside of the palace. They will always treat her as though she is beneath them. If you wish to keep her, then do not fail her!"

"Do not speak to me of responsibilities. You haven't lifted a finger since mother died."

The emperor's shoulders stiffened, his anger melting into despairing resignation.

"I have failed at a great many things in my life. I only wish you would see that I want you to do better."

Belisarius glared, turned on his heel and continued his way down the steps, passing Marduk by. Marduk waited for the emperor. When Darius noticed him, he seemed surprised.

"I leave the interrogation to the two of you. I'm not sure I'd be of much use."

Marduk nodded, his face neutral. It was painful to watch two men he cared about make so many mistakes and hurt each other, but it wasn't his place to correct them. Marduk believed the emperor deeply regretted his behaviour, but when his son rejected any olive branch, no matter how insubstantial, Darius tended to retreat back into the only comforts he could. Belisarius, in turn, was a stubborn mule, refusing to let go of his resentment. It had kept Belisarius going when Nadia died as much as his promise to her to rule well and wisely. Marduk wasn't certain either man would change enough to come to peace with the other. He hoped Selene could act as the bridge between them.

Marduk bowed to Darius.

"I'll take my leave then, Your Majesty."

When Marduk caught up to the prince, the air had chilled. Belisarius paused and looked back at him, his uncertainty plain.

"Am I failing her in truth?"

"Only the next few days will tell, Your Royal Highness."

"No, not 'Your Royal Highness,' Marduk. I am asking you as my friend."

Marduk's eyes widened in surprise. It had been some time since Belisarius had asked anything of him in any capacity outside his role as strategos and advisor. He supposed a matter of the heart was something better suited to discussion among friends.

"She is going to face difficulties now that the nobles know she's both a bastard and unacknowledged, but if anyone has the mettle to face the situation, it's her. Though I don't think you'll find it as difficult to convince her to marry you as you seem to think."

Of course, Marduk had the benefit of knowing through Iliana just how hard the poison mage was studying in order to convince the prince to see her potential. At least Belisarius would have that to look forward to.

"Thank you, Marduk." Belisarius sighed, straightened his posture and collected himself, the princely mask back in place. "Let's get to the bottom of this plot and be done with it."

Belisarius and Marduk sat across the stone table from Grigori Amethyst. The chamber was dim, the bare, windowless stone walls seeming to close in, making the room uncomfortable to linger in. Though it was not the architecture that had him so disturbed. Belisarius repressed a chill as yet another question went unanswered. The lightning mage and former Magister sat across from him, a short man with only the beginnings of grey in his red hair, wry amusement curling his lips. The only sound which had come from him had been the metallic clinking of the chains around his ankles as he adjusted his feet.

Belisarius glared at the silver-tongue mage at his side. She was young in years, but powerfully gifted. She'd been the only one to survive the collective poisoning of the palace's well-guarded interrogators. While they had lived in comfort and seclusion in the palace, they had never been free, and never would be, given the danger they posed. Was she refusing to use her gift? He knew he was keeping both himself and Marduk shielded from her powers with his own gift, but could his proximity be hampering this interrogation? He pulled the field of his magic closer around both himself and the Strategos.

"Why won't he answer?" Belisarius asked of the white-haired girl.

"I don't know," she replied, her voice wavering.

"If you are refusing to interrogate this man-"

"I'm not! I'm trying!" she wailed.

"Push him as hard as you can. He doesn't need to survive, he only needs to give us answers."

The girl let out a frustrated breath before redoubling her efforts. She reached across the table and grabbed the prisoner's head.

"*Who. Taught. You. The. Ritual? Speak!*" she ground out, her body vibrating with the strain.

Grigori's body began to tremble as well, the spasms involuntary, a battle of wills playing out before him. How could Grigori resist the commands of the mage before him? The reason silver-tongued mages had been kept was because no mage, no matter how skilled, wise or strong could repel the compulsion, at least none but a negation mage or one of the Unhearing Knights. Grigori was emphatically not such a man. The situation confounded Belisarius.

"*Answer! The! Question!*" she commanded.

Blood began running from Amethyst's nostrils, his eyes rolling back in his head. The spasm redoubled in intensity. Blood trickled from his ears, and the red-haired mage screamed in agony. The silver-tongue mage released her hold, both physical and magical, before collapsing in her own seat, her breath ragged. Sweat beaded above her pale brown lips, and her hands shook. The former magister's head lay on the table, his breath hissing between clenched teeth, his body limp.

"Someone more powerful compelled him. If I push harder, I'll only kill him." She sighed, weary.

Belisarius nodded to her knight, who bowed. He closed the loop of the magic-suppression collar around her neck and carried her from the room. A wheezy cackle hissed from between Grigori's lips. Belisarius narrowed his eyes. A guard heaved him from his prone position so that the prince could inspect him.

"So, you wish to take your secrets to the grave?"

"Have you enjoyed my bastard, princeling? I had hopes she might kill you in a fit of temper. Imagine my shock!" He coughed up blood when he laughed, yet the smug grin on his face remained.

"Perhaps I shall let her do as she pleases with you. Were you aware that she planted hidden hazards throughout your holdings? One word from me, and your lands become no more than a toxic wasteland. There will be nothing left for anyone to inherit, except death."

That seemed to catch Grigori's attention. As quickly as the fear arose, it was erased, replaced by another smug grin. It must run in the family.

"Your desperation is showing."

"Once you're executed, I will have your personal lands cleared of innocents and your castle ransacked for its wealth. Then I will allow Selene to turn it into a toxic hell-scape as a warning to future traitors. The Amethyst line will be erased when I order the *Damnatio Memoriae* to be performed. Your remaining family will be reduced to nameless vagrants, begging for the tender mercies of the new magister I install in your place."

The grin was gone. Instead, a deep hatred lit a fire in his purple eyes. For men such as the magistri, who prided themselves on their histories, lineages, self-aggrandizing projects and lavish patronages, having every mention of their name and every image of their likeness purged from existence was a punishment more severe than a simple execution. Nothing of the man or his line would remain in the world, and no children or family would ever be allowed to bear their name. There would never be another Magister Amethyst. There would never be another Amethyst anything.

"You and your heir will be executed at sunset tomorrow. Take the time to reflect on the cost of your treason."

Belisarius stood, ready to be rid of this man, this room, Marduk close on his heels. Before they were free of the confines of the dark chamber, Grigori leered, a mad gleam in his eye, and called out.

"And yet if you succeed, my blood will be the blood of future emperors! Long live the prince! Long may he reign!" he mocked.

His next laughing fit ended in wracking coughs. Belisarius refused to face him when he left the dungeon. No matter the taunt, Grigori would be dead, and all memory of him erased. There was no last laugh for a man so condemned.

As he began the long ascent, Belisarius reflected on the failures of the evening. Grigori Amethyst hadn't been their first interrogation, he'd been the last. All the magistri and their heirs had been so compelled. It was a disaster on every front. Not only would he be without confirmation that his uncles and cousins were the masterminds behind the tainted ritual, it also appeared there was a powerful silver-tongue on the loose working for his enemies. He'd been unwise to assume the worst of the dangers had passed now that the traitor magistri were under lock and key. Gods below, what a mess. He'd cut off the head of a snake only to find it had been a hydra all along.

"I'm really not certain how this evening could have gone worse," Belisarius grumbled to Marduk.

"We could have been without a single silver-tongue mage. We should be grateful she was experienced enough to know when a man has been previously compelled."

"And yet we leave empty-handed. The rogue silver-tongue bothers me almost as much as the perversion of the ritual. How could we have missed one all these years?"

"I cannot say, Your Royal Highness. But we do have the Unhearing Knights. Since the deaths of our silver-tongues, they've mostly been training or idle. They should be sent to search for the rogue."

"See that it's done as quickly as possible," Belisarius agreed.

As they passed the boundary between the frigid dungeon's atmosphere and the relentless humidity of the palace above, Belisarius found himself coming face to face with his praetor. Nicephorus was as frazzled as he'd ever seen him. Apparently, his day was about to get much worse.

"Your Royal Highness, your uncles and cousins we thought guilty have been found dead! Their corpses were found in a cave not far from their homes. By the amount of decay, they've been dead almost as long as we've suspected their involvement."

CHAPTER 30

The feeling tightening her chest was not one Selene was accustomed to. Doubt. Insecurity. She'd woken that morning to find that the servants viewed her with derision, and everyone else pretended she was invisible. The only woman who had bothered to speak a word to her had done so with cold fury. Domina Opal had passed her in the halls with a killing glare.

"I should have known you were a liar. The only thing razed to the ground is your credibility. A bastard daughter of a traitor, playing at being a noble. It makes me sick. Emerald really will be the next empress now."

She sought Belisarius, but no one would allow her entry into his rooms, and even the myriad of servants' corridors had guards patrolling them. Iliana and the strategos were nowhere to be found, and her attempts to get even a morsel of information out of his men proved futile. Doubts swirled about in a toxic soup of dread. Selene felt powerless, discarded. Even the librarian, Azar, had disappeared. The last straw was when a gaggle of nobilissimae whispered none too quietly within earshot.

"Poor creature has been wandering the palace looking for anyone who will give her a moment of their time. It's such a sad thing when a woman finds her reputation in tatters."

"She was nothing, then had everything. Now the wheel's turned, and she's been ground beneath it."

Selene turned her gaze on the women. Now that she was no longer a domina or a princess in the eyes of anyone, she didn't have to play nice. Surely, if she stopped short of killing... Selene approached the women, who shut their mouths and looked about with imploring helplessness. Before she got within spitting distance, a stealthy mage grabbed her shoulder. When she glanced back, it was one of the shadow mage spies. The first she'd incapacitated, in fact. Her smile held pure menace.

"Back for round two, Shadow?"

"No. I'm here to escort you to the dungeon."

A sick fear slithered down her spine. Had Belisarius betrayed her? Was she to be punished for pretending to be a noble after all? They wouldn't take her alive! When the shadow mage caught the sight of her bloodlust, he leapt away, his hands up in surrender.

"Amethyst said he won't speak to anyone except you. You're the only one who can help identify the last of the traitors. Will you assist in the investigation?"

Investigation? Didn't the palace keep a whole flock of silver-tongue mages for this very purpose? Suspicious but intrigued, she gave the mage her hand. Though his was gloved, she was in the process of coating her skin in layer upon layer of poison, until it permeated her clothes. Were anyone to lay a hand on her, it'd be the last thing they did. If she were to go to her doom, she planned on taking a great many with her. And if she'd been betrayed, there would be hell to pay.

"It would be my pleasure."

When he took her hand, his grin was a touch savage.

"Hold on tight. I'm told the shadow path can be dizzying."

Selene realised too late he intended to drag her through the shadows to their destination. She tried to flee. If he so chose, he could leave her to wander the darkness forever, never to return to the world as she knew it. Before she could yank her hand from his, he dragged her into a place devoid of direction, her only connection the grip he had on her hand. She tried to scream, but here there was no sound, only the endless void.

The world as she knew it came back to her in a sudden wave of being: weight, direction, time, senses, rightness. Blessed, flickering light illuminated her surroundings as echoes placed her in a cavernous hallway. Another moment, and her eyes focused. They stood on a staircase leading down. The dungeons were below, warded against magical entry or exit. She breathed a sigh of relief, the air cold and musty, just then noticing her claw-like grip on the hand of the shadow mage. Only a slight hint of a grin tugged at the corners of his lips. Selene slapped his gloved hand away.

"Smile all you like, Shadow. Your lovely leather glove is now the most dangerous thing about you."

He gaped at his hand as if it had turned into the head of a snake. He stripped it off using the greatest of care not to touch it with his bare skin, and tossed both gloves away like they were dripping in entrails.

"Are we even now, poison mage?"

"Perhaps."

He made enough of a show of it all that she almost missed him surreptitiously slipping a hand into his cloak to grab something. A knife? A collar? A curse? It was impossible to say, but her instincts screamed danger. Whatever it took, she couldn't let him get behind her.

"First, take me to the silver-tongue mages. They can fill me in before I meet the magister." She played with a poison she conjured on her fingers and gave him a feral smile. "And if they prove troublesome, I have ways of making people talk."

The shadow mage paused, removed his hand from his cloak and swallowed nervously. He nodded, keeping his eyes on her poison.

"This way. There's only one left."

Iliana sat as unobtrusively in the corner of the imposing study as she could without actually disappearing into her seat, absently fiddling with a scroll perched on a rack on the shelf. She'd been asked to attend in case they needed questions answered about potential new weapons, though she suspected a good deal of it was due to Marduk's refusal to let her out of his sight. Her enchantments made her plum pickings for potential enemies.

Though the thought of danger chilled her, she tried to pay attention to the men before her. In a way, it was interesting to watch the prince, praetor and Marduk speaking without carefully considering their words, as they might in the company of others. She could see that, though Marduk and Nicephorus spoke to the prince with respect, they treated him as a friend. There was also a side to Marduk she had expected, but had never seen—his military-minded decisiveness.

"Do we know who killed them?" the prince asked.

"No, Your Royal Highness. But one of the investigators found scorch marks surrounding their bodies. It's possible they were fodder for the ritual," the praetor replied.

"Then we still have a traitor on the loose, just not one we've identi-fied," Belisarius said, his cheek resting on a fist as he frowned.

"Your Royal Highness, is it really alright to have a young woman here?" Nicephorus

hedged. Iliana had not escaped the praetor's notice.

"She was stabbed by her own sister on orders of her father. My fiancée will stay by my side until it's safe," Marduk protested before returning to the topic at hand. "The arrows have been distributed to our archers, and my most trusted soldiers have been assigned to guard the remaining mag-istri. The praetor's spies are keeping their eyes on the remaining members of your family who knew about the ritual. Whoever is ultimately behind this, they are now utterly alone. Even if they covet the power of the ritual, knowing that both an execution and the *Damnatio Memoriae* await the conspirators, the remaining magistri have little reason to offer any support."

The prince seemed to think it all over. Iliana had by now been privy to a fairly detailed explanation of the goings on of the plot and the traitors. Foul magic, taught by a traitor to three magistri, had been the cause of her half-sisters' lifelessness, siphoning off their power and souls. The prince, trying to uncover the players, had used the excuse of a bride show to invite esteemed families throughout the empire to his palace, where he could determine who had been in on the plot. The family members he had suspected of being the traitors had been found dead, having decayed for some time, possibly victims of the ritual themselves. They had been killed almost exactly when his fake engagement had been announced. Oddly, that was the bit that stuck most in her mind.

"May I ask a question?" Iliana ventured.

The prince seemed at the end of his tether, but he waved her on.

"Why did the traitor wait until the announcement of your engagement to kill your family members and take their power?"

The three men stared at her.

"I'm sorry, was that a stupid question?" she asked, cringing from the attention.

"Was the traitor worried you were consolidating your power, or that Grigori had decided to side with you?" Marduk mused.

"If you were truly about to wed the poison mage, the Emperor might step down early or co-rule to give your marriage, and her, legitimacy. Your coronation would happen before your thirtieth year, unlike what had been planned," Nicephorus added.

Emboldened now, Iliana raised her voice again.

"How did the traitor get to your family so quickly? I thought your relatives were in the Ruby Province. Wouldn't the traitor have needed to be in the palace to know about the engagement so quickly after it was announ-"

A scuffle outside the doors cut her off. Marduk placed himself in front of her, nearest the door, slipping a blade from his boot and handing her another. Nicephorus stood between the door and the prince.

"*Let me in now!*"

The clash outside went silent at the young girl's cries. The doors swung open. A girl with white hair, amber eyes and a harassed, terrified look stormed through the opening.

"*You have to listen!*"

Iliana felt the pull of her words, unable to do anything but obey. She sat still, a slave to the overwhelming impulse. The girl's voice had been like that of a dark god. Had she been able, Iliana might have begged to hear more.

"Where is your knight? Your collar?!" Nicephorus asked, nearly hysterical.

"That doesn't matter! If you don't hurry, Selene is going to die!"

Selene lounged across from a young girl with striking amber eyes, pure white hair and light brown skin with an unhealthy pallor. A metal collar around her neck announced her as either a terribly powerful criminal, or a silver-tongue mage. A burly young man with a fighter's stance stood behind her, his eyes watchful. One of the Unhearing Knights, no doubt. Shadow stood near the door in her line of sight, his posture relaxed but officious. She kept careful note of his hands and breathed a little something into the air.

"I've been asked to assist with the investigation. What can you tell me?" Selene asked, hedging. There was plenty she knew, but also plenty she assumed she didn't. The silver-tongue would have been the first to ask questions of her father. If she had failed, then what exactly had Shadow brought Selene down to the dungeons for? She might have come willingly, but that didn't mean she trusted him. Her instincts had been right.

The young mage shot her an aggrieved glare mastered by generations of put-upon adolescents.

"A shitload of nothing. They'd already been compelled not to speak about any important details or names by someone stronger than me. What in the hells is some fancy bitch supposed to change about that?"

Oh! She liked this girl already. And what an interesting development. Shadow began looking cagey. Selene sighed dramatically, pulled herself up off the couch and walked towards her escort.

"It seems she has nothing of import to tell me. Shall we?"

He relaxed once more and nodded. Between one breath and the next she grabbed him by his tunic and pulled his lips down to meet hers. He froze before his eyes rolled back and he collapsed beside her.

"He really should have known better by now, you know?" Selene smiled at the baffled young girl and wary guard. She sat across from the girl once more.

"I'm Selene, by the way, strongest poison mage in Lethe."

"A-Alexandra. Silver-tongue."

"I believe I've been brought here as some sort of trap. You say the magistri can't speak of what they've done or who was in on it with them?"

"Yes. Um, so… is he dead?"

"Him? No. Blacked out from the pain, but still alive. For now."

Alexandra signed the situation to the knight, whose hand never strayed from the hilt of his sword. Smart man. Selene paused to think her situation through. Why bring her to the dungeons if he wasn't planning to imprison her, and if the magistri couldn't say anything anyway? She got up, her hosts tensing in readiness. She rolled her eyes and began searching the robes of the spy. She pulled out a metal collar from a concealed pocket. So was she meant to be captured? Selene peered over at the silver-tongue and her knight. The knight would be a problem. He looked like the type with a stick up his ass. But the silver-tongue? She could be useful.

"How would you like to help me, Alexandra?"

"Sure?"

"First, we'll need to do something about your collar."

"Good luck with that."

"No need for luck when you have poison," Selene smiled.

Alexandra's eyes were already drooping. Her knight's posture had gone lax, his hand slipping off the hilt of his sword. Soon enough, they were both asleep. Selene had been breathing out the sedative since she'd decided she would need the silver-tongue, and the cell was quite small. She waited a few minutes for the poison to settle before she placed a hand on Alexandra's cheek, pulling the poison from her system. The girl awoke with a pained gasp and wide eyes.

"How do I take the collar off?"

"What happened? What did you do to me?"

"I put you to sleep and then woke you up. I needed your knight out of the way. I'm about to walk into a trap, and I'm going to need your help to pull this off. Understand?"

The girl nodded.

"Good. Now, the shadow mage probably intended to collar me at some point. What I want you to do when I wake him up is order him to tell you what his plans were. Once we know that, you go tell the prince. I'm sure you can talk your way there, right?"

"I can, but why would I? Why should I help you?"

Why indeed? What did every hunted creature want?

"Because when I'm empress, you will be freed."

The young girl stared at her, stunned. Shock turned to suspicion.

"I'm also the evil bastard of an evil criminal, so, if you refuse to help, I can make this imprisonment look like a picnic. So, freedom or pain?"

"I'll make you swear to that, that I'll be free."

"If that makes you feel better."

The girl weighed her options.

"All you have to do is touch the stone on the collar, the one at the back. And just so you know, I already had plans to free myself. Daria was going to free me."

Selene spotted the stone attached to the collar, a pale green gem no bigger than her smallest nail. The collar snapped open. Selene removed it from around the girl's neck.

"*Swear you'll set me free when you're empress,*" the girl commanded.

Selene felt as though her brain was subsumed in a thick fog while her ears tingled with delight. She wanted to hear the voice again, the most seductive sound she'd ever heard.

"I so swear," Selene heard herself saying.

In an instant, the need within her vanished as quickly as it had come upon her.

"My gods, it's like you made love to my ears! I feel like I should kiss you or something."

"Please don't." Alexandra's lip curled in disgust.

"You could be the most famous courtesan in the whole of Oblivion! All you'd have to do is order someone to come, and then-"

"Agh! No! Let's just do the questioning thing. Ick!"

Selene couldn't help but laugh. Perhaps Alexandra was a shy creature, even if she did have a foul mouth.

"Fine, fine. Tell Shadow to remain here and not shout when he wakes. We don't want to raise the alarm."

Selene placed her hand on the shadow mage's face and removed her toxin. He gasped when he woke, hyperventilating. Alexandra did as she was told, immobilizing the mage.

"*What was your plan?*" she asked him.

"Collar the poison mage and bring her to her father. They want a hostage to ensure their safe escape."

"Couldn't you just take them all out of here yourself?" Selene asked, puzzled.

Alexandra shrugged and asked the question.

"Only one at a time, and the escape must be public enough to emphasize the prince's ineptitude."

"How did you get through the wards surrounding the dungeon?"

"I cannot say."

"On whose orders are you doing this?"

"I cannot say."

Selene turned to Alexandra who demanded to know the answer once more.

"I cannot say," the mage insisted, blood dribbling from his nose as his body shook.

"It's the same as the others. The compulsion is stronger than mine. So, now what?" Alexandra asked.

Selene considered her options. Belisarius still didn't know the identity of the mastermind behind the whole conspiracy. If she solved this problem for him, he would have to make her empress. It would silence the wagging tongues of the nobles and cement her place in the palace once and for all. There would be no more doubts, no more insecurity over whether or not she belonged. She'd be the hero who foiled the plot of the criminal magistri. She'd also have the chance to kill Magister Sapphire, a fate he richly deserved. Maybe she'd even get her poison into her father.

"If the stone is missing or broken, does the collar work?"

"No, of course not. The stone holds the enchantment."

Selene pried the stone from the collar the shadow mage had brought. This one was coloured lavender. She could feel her grin widen. Removing her earrings, she pried one of the gems loose. It was about the right shape and size. She wedged it in the small depression. Just for added concealment she let down her hair.

"What are you doing?"

"I'm going to walk right into that trap, but with a broken collar. Order the shadow mage to do as he was ordered by his master, but not to do anything to give away that we know of the plan. Once we leave, run to the prince, and tell him to hurry. I'm only about half sure I'll make it out of this alive."

Alexandra gaped at her, gobsmacked. She struggled to find the words.

"Why would you do this? Why not just come with me?"

"Because I promised myself I'd kill Iliana's father. What kind of friend would I be if I let him live?" Selene lied with her winning smile.

Playing hostage was the only way she'd get the information Belli needed, and her only way to be a heroic empress in truth. But Alexandra needed to see her as the one with all the power, else she'd never let her do it. Thankfully, she had the requisite bravado to pull it off. She only hoped it would be enough.

CHAPTER 31

If she weren't in mortal peril, Selene might have snickered. After Shadow had walked her through the unlocked door of their cell and deposited her, she'd observed the magistri grate on each other's nerves. The magistri and their heirs stood around in a large, well-appointed cell in the dungeon, arguing like old women over the last good carrot at the market. Not a one had his collar on, though she wasn't sure why she'd hoped they might. Obviously, they'd been helped by the shadow mage at the least. The only one not engaged in the argument was Dimitri, the little Amethyst pest. The creepy little creature stared at her in her corner like she was going to be a tasty treat for later. She didn't want to tip them off too quickly, but the more she listened, the less certain she was that she would either meet the traitor behind the plan, or hear anything significant. The magistri had been forced to talk around their collective compulsion spell.

"How long must we wait?" whined Dominus Leo Sapphire.

"If we wait any longer, they'll simply take us to the executioner's block," grumbled Magister Sapphire.

"Why does *that* need to be here? It's disgusting." The Diamond Magister waved in Selene's direction, revulsion evident.

"We wait until we don't, gentlemen. Do try not to act like complete cowards," Magister Amethyst replied, caustic. If even the unfeeling magister was beginning to lose his cool, it was time to act. She began releasing her poison into the cavernous room, worried it might be too late. It was several times larger than Alexandra's small cell.

"Why even work with them, Amethyst? Can't you just kill them and take whatever share of the profits they might have reaped?" Selene asked her father in her best exasperated tone.

"May I slap her, Father?" Dimitri asked, jumping at the chance.

"Shut up, you little weasel. We both know without this collar I'd turn you into worm food," Selene said.

"Your progeny is vicious. I'm sure you're proud," the Diamond heir sniffed.

Magister Amethyst gave Selene a calculating glance. She raised her brow.

"She got closer to the prince than we ever could have. It's only a shame she wasn't one of us," Amethyst replied.

"Truly, a tragedy," Selene mocked.

"She serves no purpose, Grigori. She's just extra baggage," Magister Diamond complained.

"Light on brains as well as talent. Why do you put up with him?" Selene asked her father in earnest.

Diamond was exactly the kind of preening fool her father wouldn't usually suffer for long. She could understand why he might put up with the powerful water mage; Sapphire was a cruel bastard and magister of a vast and wealthy province. Of all the magistri here, only Diamond seemed superfluous. His lands were small, and his influence insignificant as the emperor in truth ruled Diamond's province. The light mage magister only held the title because he'd been the traitor to the previous princes who had sparked the Great War, opening the gates to Darius' army at the eleventh hour.

"He has his uses," Amethyst replied, cryptic as ever.

Selene worried she might not catch the master of this conspiracy. If she failed to do that much, would Belisarius toss her aside? Once they left the room, it was going to be impossible to take them all down in one fell swoop. Then again, if the poison she was leaking out into the room didn't work quickly enough, her father would shove a lightning bolt into her eye before he hit the ground. Was Alexandra speaking to the prince yet? Glaring cracks were beginning to present themselves in her master plan, and she wondered if she hadn't just stepped into a dragon's lair. She let bravado cover her nervousness.

"I guess being spineless makes it easy to squeeze through all the cracks in this place."

The Diamond heir had reached his limit. Dominus Philip Diamond slapped her face with his bare hand, leaving her ears ringing and her eyes stinging. Man had some heft in his swing. Selene smiled through the pain. One lowlife down. Magister Amethyst sighed.

"That was foolish, Philip. I told you not to touch her bare skin," Amethyst said.

"She has the collar on," Philip retorted, still full of vinegar.

"That means she can't produce *new* poison. The poison she'd already made before the collar went on is still effective. She might be a bastard, but she's still my blood," Amethyst replied.

"I really like this one. I call it 'Silence is Golden.' Top seller," Selene said.

Horrified, the Diamond dominus wiped his hand on his robe. When next he tried to speak, nothing emerged from his lips, only a harsh breath. Panic suffused his features. The more Philip flailed, the faster the poison raced through his system. His eyes began bulging from his face, his affected hand had swollen to three times its original size, and his lips took on a tinge of blue. The others in the room avoided him like he was plague incarnate. Philip collapsed to his knees, his face distorting into a silent scream as the tortuous final note of the poison did its work. He collapsed on the floor, very, definitively, dead.

"Philip! No! Dear gods, he wasn't supposed to die! Grigori! I demand recompense! I want her dead!" Miroslav Diamond roared.

"Don't! Even dead, she's lethal," Amethyst replied, holding out a cautioning hand. When he looked back at her, she swore she almost saw...admiration? Gods below, her family was deranged.

"You really did do your research, Daddy," Selene sighed.

"Did you truly set traps throughout my estate?" Grigori asked, curious now.

Selene nodded.

"Even after we agreed to our deal?"

"Ha! You were going to kill me sooner or later. I'd have to be as stupid as Philip to believe you'd keep your word."

At that, her father smiled, beaming as if she'd just told his favourite joke.

"She doesn't need her eyesight, Amethyst. Blind is still good enough, isn't it?" Magister Diamond asked, bloodlust in his gaze.

"It might be prudent," Magister Sapphire added, giving her space he hadn't before.

Before they could discuss her potential maiming further, a mage crawled up from the shadow under the table. He, too, wore the uniform of Nicephorus' spies. The praetor was going to have a lot of housecleaning to do when this was over.

"It's time," the shadow mage said.

"Gods, I'll be glad to be out of this dank place," Leo Sapphire sighed gratefully.

"How do you propose we transport her?" Magister Sapphire asked.

"With a long blade at her back, and my son aiming a bolt at her knees," Amethyst answered, ever cautious.

Dominus Leo Sapphire produced a fount of water from his hand which chilled into a sharp-ended pole of ice. He manoeuvred behind Selene, the compelled shadow mage beside him and Magister Diamond in the rear. Dimitri took up his post with his eyes on her. The Sapphire and Amethyst magistri took up the front. Her first poison had failed to affect enough of the room's air, the first gaping hole in her plan. Once they touched the handle of the door, it could spell the end of her gambit. She'd rubbed poison all over it on her way in.

"After you, Aristeo." Magister Amethyst motioned to the door.

Magister Sapphire grabbed the handle with his bare hand and froze.

"What's the matter, Father? Do you hear something?" Leo asked.

"Kill her," Sapphire choked, his voice wet and gurgling. When he turned his head, thick, frothy blood poured from his lips. He collapsed on the ground, shaking violently, red spittle flying.

"You little bitch!" Sapphire's heir heaved his lance back, ready to run her through.

"Stop! We need to escape first, or this is for naught! Selene will go first and act as our shield. Douse her in water. I don't want any more surprises if we need to touch her. Keep your blade at her back. Now, move!"

Magister Amethyst commanded the remaining conspirators like a strategos, his voice whipping them as effectively as his lightning might have. Amethyst father and son took to walking behind her. Damn! She should have begun poisoning the air sooner. Leo Sapphire was all too happy to call forth a cascade, pinning her under the icy deluge. The poisons leached from her clothes and skin. Just before she began choking for breath in the maelstrom, it was over. A shadow mage hauled her up and pushed her forward.

"Actually, I have a better idea," Leo said ominously.

Selene gasped in a breath. It was her last as she was swept up in a tide and tumbled around. When the dizzying motion ended and she dared open her eyes, she was surrounded by a bubble of water. She could hear angry shouting outside of her watery prison and prayed it would end soon. She'd never had to hold her breath this long before. She clawed at the bubble, but vicious currents raced along its borders, keeping her contained. Fucking water mages! She should have just pumped poison into the room the second she'd entered. Selene had gambled and lost.

Suddenly a pocket of air encased her head, and she gasped for breath. They'd left the confines of the cell. Outside her bubble she could see the distorted figures of what could only be the remaining Sapphire sons, their colouring identical to their dead father's. There was another man there who had the colouring of Magister Diamond. In all, four had joined the party. Discounting, of course, all the traitorous shadow mages who'd brought in the reinforcements. Selene was entirely outmatched, outwitted and desperately short of luck.

⟶⟶⟶ ⟵⟵⟵

"The wards protecting their cells in the prison have been undone, allowing entrance to the shadows there. The magistri have had their collars removed. They're waiting and bickering. The poison mage is seated, thus far unharmed, but there is another mage guarding her shadow," the shadow mage replied, bowing deeply.

Belisarius didn't like what he was hearing.

"Why didn't she just poison them already?" Alexandra asked, plaintive and panicked.

The prince held up his hand for silence.

"Will the other spies know you're eavesdropping?"

"Not unless they try to enter or exit from the same shadow I'm hiding in, Your Royal Highness."

"Can you take out the mage hiding in Selene's shadow?"

"Yes, but it will alert the others hiding on the shadow path."

"Continue to monitor them, and alert us if something new happens."

"As you wish."

The shadow mage dissolved into the darkness.

"Why can't we go down and rescue her?" Iliana demanded.

"If we fight in that enclosed space, the magistri could bring the entire dungeon down on our heads, and Selene is likely to die in the crossfire or get dragged into the void," Marduk replied, his voice calm. "We need to draw them out into the open. They want their escape to be public and brazen, so let them have it. If we herd them, we can force a battle in the entrance courtyard, where the archers can get clean shots. They don't know about the arrows."

"Have the archers ready and the healers close at hand. I want all other routes out of the palace inaccessible. Have our earth and barrier mages in the front lines to block their attacks. I want as few casualties as possible," Belisarius commanded.

Marduk bowed, grabbed Iliana by the hand and rushed from the room to carry out his orders. Even before the door to the study closed, Iliana had set in on the strategos about how to rescue Selene. Belisarius wished his only concern could be Selene's safety. He had more than one traitor within his walls, aiding his enemies and undoing palace wards. Most of them could slip into another world altogether to avoid detection. Only the ridiculous showmanship desired by the traitors prevented them all from getting away.

"Your Royal Highness, I want to help." The silver-tongue mage spoke up, twisting the fabric of her dress in her shaking hands.

"How many can you command simultaneously with your voice?"

"I-I don't know."

"How far from your target does your command project effectively?"

"I don't-"

"Does your target have to make eye contact with you first?"

"Um-"

"Have you been trained for combat?"

"No-"

"Then do not ask to help! If you wanted to help, you should have ordered Selene to escape with you in the first place!" Belisarius slammed his fist on his desk.

"But she said-"

"What made you think a poison mage was any match for six elemental mages in their prime with unnaturally strong magic?! You questioned them alongside us! You know how terrifying their powers are!"

"I-I'm sorry," Alexandra replied, tears running down her cheeks. "She said she would be empress, so I just did what she told me."

Belisarius reined in his anger. There was no point to berating a young girl over things which couldn't be changed, especially when one of those things was Selene's recklessness. He could only pray she remained alive, lest her death fog kill them all... lest his heart break irreparably. He breathed deep, forcing a calm he had no business feeling.

"The praetor will need you to determine who we can trust. Nicephorus, summon a few more of your spies, determine their loyalty, and send them to inform the emperor of what has happened. Place him under a protective guard, in this world and the void. There's no telling how many more wards they've tampered with."

"Yes, Your Royal Highness." Nicephorus bowed and turned to the silver-tongue. "Come with me, Alexandra."

He was not alone for long. The shadow mage spy returned.

"The poison mage has killed Magister Aristeo Sapphire and Dominus Phillip Diamond. Dominus Leo Sapphire has trapped her in a water globe prison, and they've met reinforcements: three of Magister Sapphire's sons and the remaining Diamond son. They're about to leave the prison."

"Inform the strategos and then the praetor immediately. I want the route to the entrance courtyard cleared of staff and guests, and the servants' corridors barricaded."

The shadow mage bowed and disappeared.

Belisarius had never felt so sick in his life, his heart galloping in his chest. If she'd killed two of the conspirators, would she survive their wrath long enough to be rescued? The water globe prison was a vicious form of torture, the victim only granted breath when the torturer saw fit to allow it. His hands had begun shaking. Fuck! He needed to act. It was rash and foolhardy, but the thought of sitting in his office made his skin crawl. Belisarius flung open his doors. Two guards stood ready and waiting for his orders.

"Get me my bow and a quiver of arrows from the imperial archers, and do it quickly. I'll be waiting with archers on the bailey of the entrance courtyard." One guard nodded before racing off down the halls. To the other he simply said, "When the shadow mage returns with news, tell him where I've gone."

Chapter 32

Every time Leo Sapphire turned his attention to the soldiers of the imperial army blocking the way, Selene lost her pocket of air. She could only hold her breath and hope, traitorously, that they didn't put up too long of a fight. The first few times, her bubble of air had disappeared mid-breath, choking her as water filled her nose and mouth. When it returned, she was so busy trying to gasp and expel water that she didn't see the pattern to it, until it happened again. Now, whenever she could see the warped outlines of approaching soldiers in their uniforms, terror gripped her and she desperately swallowed air before it was stolen. Mercifully, the conspirators seemed more interested in leaving the palace and causing a scene than killing everyone who tried to stop them.

Leo took up the front, her bubble preceding them like the living shield she was. He created veritable glaciers wherever he saw opponents, freezing them with a flick of his wrist and plugging whatever hallway the army tried to approach from. It was magic on a scale she'd never dreamed possible, and he showed no signs of slowing, no hint that this terrible power of his had a limit. With the power he possessed, it was understandable why he and the magistri had used foul magic on their daughters and sisters. The sheer power was glorious, terrifying and nearly divine. If she'd known what he was capable of, Selene would have run from that dungeon, or failing that, slit her own throat, if only to end the lives of these walking calamities in an instant. She had yet to see what kind of power her father had accrued with his dark bargain, and she wasn't sure she wanted to, either.

Selene hadn't just gambled irresponsibly, she'd thrown her life away like trash, all because she'd wanted a place by Belisarius' side, one with power, prestige and everything else she could get her greedy hands on. She'd craved his respect, and the fearful subservience of everyone else. When she spoke, she had wanted others to heed her. Selene had dreamed of tearing out the wagging tongues of everyone who had ever deemed her worthless, lowly and loathsome, as if she were Darius himself. She really was no better than her father. No; she was worse, because Selene was just as craven and power-mad as he, but she hadn't been smart enough to plan for failure, or wise enough to avoid it.

The traitors would walk out of the palace through the front gates at this rate, living testaments to might making right. What better way to showcase their ungodly powers than to leave the palace in style, with devastation in their wake? What would become of her when they made good on their escape? Would Leo drown her? Of all the ways she could have died over the years, that topped the list as one of the most unpleasant. And if he killed her, what would become of Iliana and Belisarius? Her death fog could kill them all. She'd never hated her magic before, but she'd have agreed to give up her very soul to ensure her death couldn't harm them.

When they finally reached the palace entrance, Selene heard what could only be described as a battle cry. From up on the bailey, indistinct figures popped up, firing a volley of arrows. She mistimed her breath, hastily shutting her mouth and plugging her nose before water poured in. She could see one of the Sapphire sons who had taken up the rear lying on the ground, a veritable pincushion. Another Sapphire son appeared to be a barrier mage, and the rest of the conspirators had been shielded. The remaining arrows slumped harmlessly along the outer edge of the barrier. Her father shouted, and the conspirators tightened their formation. Blessed air returned, and she gasped in relief. The issue with being shielded by a barrier was that nothing could come in, but, conversely, nothing could go out either. For now, that stalemate meant she had precious air.

Belisarius stood atop the bailey at the point furthest from the outer gates. The first volley had hit a single Sapphire son, the one closest to the range of his gift's influence, but not the one currently torturing Selene in the water globe prison. They were following the orders of Magister Amethyst, a brilliant tactician. The surprise offensive had yielded too little, and both parties knew it.

The barrier mage was the most troublesome. Belisarius had been careful to direct his gift like a slithering snake, avoiding the precious enchantments of the arrowheads in his quiver and those of his fellow archers, but he simply didn't have the range or control needed to push his gift outward to the full party of traitors. Would he have to forgo the perfect shot, and take his chances simply trying to shatter the barrier by placing his own enchantment on the arrows?

"What orders for the strategos?" the spy asked from his shadow.

"Block the escape. I want them cornered. Target the shadow mages first. They cannot be allowed to get away. I'll deal with the barrier mage."

"If you are in imminent danger, I will pull you into the shadows, on orders of the emperor."

He disappeared to relay the message. Belisarius needed the eyes of the traitors on the archers, not the ground forces about to flank them.

"Nock! Mark!" Belisarius erased his arrow's enchantment and replaced it with his own as he shouted. "Draw! Loose!"

His arrow hit the barrier early, piercing it and striking the mage in the chest. The barrier held, but only in patches. The mage sank down to his knees, his wide eyes and clenched teeth echoing his grim focus. Belisarius ordered another volley, rewriting the enchantment on his arrow once again. When his arrow flew through the air, it struck his quarry in the neck.

Barrier shattered, Magister Diamond let loose his ritually enhanced gift, flash-blinding most of the archers including Belisarius. He ducked behind the stone railing of the bailey. A deafening roar of thunder and shrieks of agony rang in his ears. The sick scent of burnt hair and charred meat greeted him. When he regained his sight, the archer on his left was nothing more than an exploded corpse.

"Shield yourselves! The arrows are enchanted! Archers die first!" Magister Amethyst called out in a booming battlefield voice.

As he chanced to take stock of the battle, Belisarius saw that both Magister Amethyst and his heir Dimitri were alive, the heir firing precision shots while the father used his lightning like a raging shield, thunder deafening. The Sapphire heir and another Sapphire son still lived, while one more had perished. Magister Diamond, his son and the shadow mages had disappeared. Leo Sapphire launched an all-out offensive against the archers on the walls, the other Sapphire son protecting them with a thin barrier of ice. Leo sent waves crashing along the right wall, sweeping archers from their posts and dashing them on the stone steps below.

The watery prison had been forgotten.

Belisarius sought Selene in the chaos. Smack in the middle of their tightening formation, she lay on the ground near the cooling corpse of a Sapphire son, soaked and taking in the scene with wild eyes. One of her legs had been fastened to the ground with a sheet of ice, pinning her. She yanked an arrow from the nearest body, holding it in her arms as if cradling a child.

"Tighten formation!" Amethyst called out.

A roar sounded from the gate as the imperial troops, headed by Marduk, streamed through hidden doors along the walls and took up position. Marduk wielded an enormous mace and shield.

"Advance!" Marduk bellowed from the gates.

They ploughed headlong into battle, surprising the Amethyst heir and striking him dead with a blow from the strategos' weapon. Magister Amethyst jumped away from the oncoming fray and struck out with lightning. Split second barriers were instantly shattered, only just deflecting lethal bolts. Where they struck the earthen barriers, the uplifted soil became glass. All the rest became fodder.

Belisarius readied an arrow, keeping the original enchantment in place, and fired at the momentarily distracted water mages. He struck the leg of a Sapphire son, alerting Leo to the remaining archers. Before Belisarius could loose another, a monstrous wave struck him, sweeping him along with dizzying force. His back struck stone, and he was mercilessly ground along the bailey. Just before he was swept over the side, two arms reached out and pulled.

The swirling violence of the water was replaced by a world without light or rightness or sound. Terror gripped him, but he kept his gift controlled under his skin. He'd travelled through the shadow path only a few times, and feared what would happen if he negated the powers of the one anchor he had in the endless night of the void. Just as abruptly as he'd entered the darkness, he was back in his own world. A single arrow lay within reach, and his bow was still clutched in his hand, whole and unharmed. He steadied his breath and readied himself to strike. When he dared to look at the scene once more, only Leo Sapphire and Magister Grigori Amethyst remained, fending off the opposing forces with distressing ease. Whatever momentum Marduk had gained with surprise was now gone, leaving the imperial soldiers on the defensive, frozen in glaciers or splattered by lightning. As far as Belisarius could tell, not a single archer remained along the bailey, having been swept over and dashed on the paved stones below. The traitors fought back to back, with Selene's pinned form at the centre. He could feel the thrum of marching soldiers from within the palace, ready to add their immense number to the fray. It might not be enough to turn the tide. Darius had single-handedly turned armies and fortresses to ash during the Great War. Only luck would save them now.

Belisarius watched with horror as Selene gripped the shaft of the arrow in her hand and set her sights on Leo's legs. Turning to face the reinforcements with a smirk, Leo's attention was diverted. In that moment, Belisarius knew he would only get a single shot. As Selene slashed through the tendons of Leo's ankle with her arrow, Belisarius stood and aimed for Leo's head. Leo whipped his head around, holding his hand high, ready to send her to her grave with a wicked blade of ice.

The arrow struck Leo through the skull. He fell to the ground, dead. Selene looked up from her prone position with wide eyes, spotting him. Then Grigori Amethyst grabbed her by her hair and held a deadly bolt aloft, his threat plain.

"If you strike, she will die!"

The fiery sting of Selene's scalp and the ache in her back and neck added to the agony of ice pinning her leg to the stone. It ran from the tips of her toes to just past her knee, preventing her from twisting. Selene lay awkwardly on the ground, her back arched, her weight on her elbows, angling up to prevent her hair being ripped from her head. In this position, she couldn't reach back to touch her father; she couldn't kill him. His bolt of lightning nearly blinded her with its brilliance, tears streaming as it roasted her face.

"You're dead either way," Selene hissed through gritted teeth.

Even with power like his, he couldn't defeat an entire army single-handedly. Eventually, even a battle of attrition would wear him down. If he managed to flee, no one would shelter him, and no ship would take him to safety. The only question was how many people he would take with him before he died. Whatever the number, it probably included her. But if he killed her, her death fog would kill Iliana and Belisarius.

"Yes, I know." His voice was calm. He yanked her head to the side then chuckled softly. "You could have killed us all in the dungeons. Why did you hesitate?"

He'd seen that her collar was a dud then. Her very last trump card was now spoiled.

"Wanted your master."

That earned her another vicious yank.

"Ah!" she screamed.

"I have no master." His vehemence only made her more certain of it.

"Tell that to the one who made you sit on your ass in that cell," she taunted him.

"Your ambition was laudable, but you let it spoil a perfect chance. Now scores of your allies lie dead. Always kill the enemy before you if there is a chance he might escape. Never allow a threat to persist."

"Then why am I alive?"

"Because you were useful. I, too, gambled and lost. But I didn't lose everything."

The magister adjusted his grip on her hair and steered her neck until she was facing the prince squarely. Like a vengeful god standing atop the bailey, his hand up to halt the actions of the imperial army at the gate, Belisarius shook with rage.

"I wanted to know how much he valued you, and the odds of my blood being the blood of future emperors," he spoke in her ear. To the prince, he shouted, "Order your soldiers to retreat, and I will spare her!"

"He won't let you go," Selene growled.

"It's unlikely," he agreed. "But not impossible."

Belisarius grimaced.

"Soldiers, fall back!" Belisarius bellowed, his eyes never leaving hers.

"No!" Selene shouted. "Don't you dare!"

Her father let up on his punishing grip on her hair and sighed.

"Now, I'm certain."

He spoke it so softly that she'd almost missed it beneath the constant rumble of his lightning. Then he leaned in so that only she could hear.

"Do you know what to do when you're sure you can't win? You do everything in your power to prevent someone else from claiming victory. I'll never be the lightning king, so don't you *dare* let that salamander sit on the throne. Swear it, Selene, or I shall kill you in truth and we'll take Nadioch with us to the deepest of hells."

He punctuated his threat with a sharp heel to the small of her back, and a pull on her hair she was certain would snap her neck. She cried out.

"Amethyst!" Belisarius howled from above, his dark eyes full of hatred, white-knuckle grip on the stone of the bailey.

"I swear!" She choked out. The magister dug his heel in hard with a sharp, ruthless motion. A shriek of pain escaped her lips. A deep crack had black swimming around the edges of her vision.

"Gods below, the soldiers have retreated, you bastard!"

"Not far enough!" Amethyst replied smugly.

"Retreat! Now!" The prince called out.

In a quiet, unconcerned voice, the magister spoke to Selene as tears of agony streamed down her cheeks.

"What have you sworn? Say it clearly."

"I swear the salamander won't get the throne!" she hissed. He must be mad. He was going to break her back—he'd already broken a rib! As he placed his lips close to her ear, she envisioned him dead, choking on his own guts, screaming in agony.

"Good girl. He'll underestimate you at his peril. Remember that you and the princeling live because I wished it. Now, give your father a kiss and make my death spectacular."

Never one to look a gift horse in the mouth, she did as he asked. It would be the only order of his she would ever eagerly obey. The bolt of lightning he held disappeared into the ether as he stumbled back, releasing his hold on her hair. Selene fell the short distance to the ground, spent, her breath wheezing. Grim delight lifted the corners of her mouth as the imprint of her lips on his cheek turned black, dark veins forking out. Her farewell kiss. Toxic blood streamed from every orifice, his eyes wide with pain as his mouth contorted in a silent scream. He collapsed onto the stones, dead before he'd hit the ground.

CHAPTER 33

As soon as Magister Amethyst had fallen, Belisarius shouted out an endless stream of orders. Water mages worked to dissolve the ice which had encased soldiers, while healers triaged the wounded. Death and suffering surrounded Selene. The bodies of archers lay hopelessly broken and twisted on the stone paths, jagged scars of upraised earth and blasted mortar littered among the dead. Only gory, smoking parts of the lightning-struck remained identifiable. The lucky ones limped away with burns and gashes or were carried screaming to the nearest healer. Her leg was quickly freed, but given the severity of the situation, she might be waiting some time for a healer.

If she weren't just left there like the fool she was, as she richly deserved.

Selene gingerly rolled over onto her side, sopping wet clothes tangling around her. There wasn't much of her that didn't hurt, but she lived. Perhaps she really was favoured by some perverse coterie of gods, as Iliana was fond of insisting.

"Selene!"

She turned her head, her neck protesting. Belisarius came rushing towards her with a pronounced hitch in his gait, swatting away the hands of a healer who insisted he stand still.

"Your Royal Highness, you've taken a number of blows. Please, allow me to do my job!"

"Her. First," the prince ground out through gritted teeth, eyes narrowed in fury.

"But she-"

"Cannot even stand. If you don't want to be whipped, you will do as I've ordered at once!"

Belisarius knelt down over her, awkward and wincing with pain, eyes haunted as he looked her over. She wanted to reach up to touch him but wasn't sure she could manage it.

"Where does it hurt?" he asked, his voice tight with emotion.

"Most places," she whispered through gritted teeth.

The elderly healer ran his hands over and above her. Once done, he placed his hands over the worst affected areas, evaporating the pain. She'd never had the coin to afford a real healer before. No wonder the healing mages were always so rich. In minutes he'd erased her pain and knitted skin and bone back together. She took a deep, relieved breath, suddenly exhausted. Belisarius took her hand and held it close to his face. He didn't even acknowledge the healer as he was tended to.

"Go help the others," Belisarius ordered.

Selene wanted nothing more than to wrap her arms around him, but the sudden anger in his expression held her back. His grip on her hand turned painful. When he hoisted her into his arms, she feared where he might deposit her. Dark brows slashing low, eyes hard and mouth set in a grim line, he marched from the death and destruction of the ruined courtyard.

The strategos interrupted him mid-stride, only a little worse for wear. Iliana would be relieved.

"Your Royal Highness, the two shadow mages, Magister Miroslav Diamond and his son, Kosta, have fled."

"Do whatever it takes to find them. I want our silver-tongue to personally vet the remaining intelligence apparatus within the palace, as well as any mage with the ability to disappear swiftly. Assign someone to identify and see to the wellbeing of the families of our deceased soldiers. And get those damned wards back up."

"At once, Your Royal Highness," Marduk replied. He turned his gaze to Selene. "Iliana will be overjoyed to know you're safe."

"I expect she'll slap me until I lose feeling in my face," she muttered as gamely as she was able. Truthfully, she had no mirth left within her.

With that, Marduk disappeared into the bedlam. Belisarius strode through the battle-scarred hallways of the palace, a silent and forbidding presence among the panicked cries and calls of soldiers. The palace was in ruins—cracked mosaics, tapestries smoking or torn asunder, shattered potted plants creating a slurry of muck and blood underfoot. Stopped and asked for orders, he was curt and decisive. Just as he reached his private quarters, he was stopped by the emperor.

Darius stood before them, saying nothing before he crushed both in a fierce hug. He kissed their heads, his hands shaking. When he pulled back, he had an ashen pallor and the look of a man confronted by ghosts.

"Thank the gods, you're both safe."

"I need you to take charge of matters for a short time. Do not allow anyone to enter my chambers. Have Marduk and Nicephorus update you with the details."

Darius banished the demons in his eyes, no longer a father, but an emperor.

"I'll give you as much time as I can, but we'll have to make decisions quickly to keep chaos at bay. I'll let you know the situation this evening."

Belisarius nodded. Darius marched down the hallway, making demands of anyone he passed. When the doors to Belisarius' chambers closed, a chill trickled down Selene's spine. She braced herself for what was to come. He set her down on the bed and glared.

"I'm so angry with you I feel like I might start spitting fire. How dare you take such risks! Do you care nothing for your life?!"

"I'm sorry," she apologized, her voice whisper soft.

"Sorry isn't enough, Selene! What were you thinking?"

She couldn't bring herself to tell him the whole of it. She couldn't even look at him as she spoke the shameful words.

"I wanted to be useful. Good enough. I thought I could handle it."

"Thought you—I heard exactly what you told the silver-tongue! You gave yourself the same odds as a coin toss to walk out of that dungeon alive! You let some revenge fantasy cloud every ounce of your limited good judgement! How could you be so reckless?!"

Tears misted her eyes. Would he be done with her when his anger was spent? She knew she would be crushed under the weight of her heartbreak. A tight ache gripped her throat.

"I didn't think-"

"No! You didn't!" he raged.

She flinched. Tears fell in earnest then. She hurt, but at the same time, she knew it was deserved. For the past weeks, she'd allowed herself to believe she was due the respect given to her. Every success had inflated her ego, fuelling a lust for things she'd been a fool to covet. It'd been astoundingly greedy to want this man's devotion, and yet she craved it keenly. Selene wasn't a proper noble; she wasn't even a good woman. She was still that grubby little thief grasping for things she didn't deserve. Not comfort, not love, not him. Belisarius dropped to his knees and held her face in his hands with unexpected tenderness, his thumbs stroking her cheeks, wiping away tears. When she met his eyes, there was fear, primal and raw, tinged with something that threatened to spark a flame of hope.

"Don't you understand? Their lives weren't worth yours! Nothing will ever be worth losing you!" His vehemence was palpable. Her heart stuttered in her chest. "Nothing and no one is worth more to me than you are, you stupid girl." His voice cracked.

"Truly?" she asked. Vulnerable as never before, she needed it to be true, so much that its absence might destroy her. Just as Dihya's death had.

"Yes. So please, never risk yourself like that again. I don't want to imagine a world without you."

Joy bubbled up in her chest. Choking on laughter which turned into a fount of tears, she threw herself at him. Belisarius pulled her into a warm embrace, petting her hair and kissing her head. Between sobs she managed to speak.

"I just wanted you to k-keep me. I thought if I could get them all, you would see I was g-good enough."

When he wiped the tears misting her vision, she could trace the weary circles under his eyes, but also the love and tenderness shining from the depths. She would happily wait a thousand lifetimes to see that look, face a thousand villainous magistri, brave a thousand broken hearts. He kissed her, soft and heartbreakingly tender.

"Selene, I love you. I'm never letting you go."

"I love you, too." She whispered back, heart bursting with warmth for the first time in far too long.

Belisarius' princess consort slept safely in his bed a short corridor away. That was what she was; there was no question anymore in his mind. Selene would be his empress in truth. He was going to need her in the chaotic, dangerous days ahead. If the highs and lows of the day didn't give him premature greys, he'd be shocked. Unfortunately, the day wasn't over yet.

Belisarius sat in his study with his father, Marduk, Nicephorus, and Iliana, who had hoped to see Selene, but was persuaded to wait until she woke. It was one of the few places within the palace that, despite the mess of papers, remained unchanged by the chaos outside it.

"We were lucky the tally of the dead wasn't higher. Having the healers on hand minimized what could have been a one-sided slaughter. What

I don't understand is why Grigori didn't take the chance to escape," Marduk reported.

"I admit that is the one thing which vexes me as well," Nicephorus chimed in.

"Selene said he made her swear to prevent 'the salamander' from taking the throne," Belisarius said.

"Is that an alias?" Iliana asked.

"Likely a pejorative. The magistri were very effectively compelled not to reveal anything regarding the puppet master behind this conspiracy. We haven't been able to locate Miroslav, his son or the two traitor shadow mages yet, which is concerning because the son can teleport," Darius replied.

"Did you locate any other traitors within the bureaucracy?" Belisarius asked his praetor, almost hesitant to know.

"No, but we haven't spoken to everyone yet. Though we can rule out the logothetes and some of the asekretis. As for the spies, hidden security forces, and palace guards, we prioritized them and found no more traitors among their ranks."

"And what of the magistri and their allies in the provinces? Do I need to worry about a second uprising?"

"They're busy jockeying for the chance to cut up the provinces of the traitors. I've managed to hold them off for now, with promises of appointing magistri to the territories in a few days. Until then, I've had the praetor place them under imperial control, the same as we might if a magister died without issue." Darius nodded to Nicephorus.

Belisarius, seeing that those arranged around him were pictures of fatigue, all slumped shoulders, bloodless pallor and listing in their seats, was ready to call an end to the meeting. Any remaining matters could be dealt with in the morning, when they had each had a chance to rest.

"If that is all, I think we should retire for the day."

"Your Royal Highness, there is one matter I would like to discuss. It's not urgent, but it is important," Nicephorus said.

"Please continue." Belisarius waved him on, praying it would be over quickly. He wanted nothing more than to hold Selene close, if for no other reason than to assure himself she still lived. After today, he feared he might never overcome the compulsion.

"If I understand correctly, you will be making Selene your princess consort in truth?"

"Yes, and she is to be addressed and treated henceforth as Princess Consort of Lethe. I know you have personal reservations, but it is time for you to set those aside. She will be your empress in the future, and I expect you to aid her as faithfully as you have me."

To his credit, Nicephorus simply nodded. Whatever personal dislike he might have for Selene, he'd seen fit to put it to bed. The tension in Belisarius' shoulders eased.

"That won't be an issue, Your Royal Highness. I ask because we may need to consider bringing in at least one concubine. From my research into the subject of poison mage fertility, it is nearly impossible for her to give you heirs. Even among poison mage couples, conception is rare, as a poison mage woman can only give birth to poison mage children. I trust you will have discussions with her regarding her duties as empress, and that one of the most vital is to ensure a stable succession, regardless of her personal feelings."

Belisarius had never wanted to punch his praetor before now, and he was struggling to keep a leash on his darker impulses. Already, bile rose in the back of his throat at the thought. Neither his father nor Iliana were quite so circumspect.

"Selene isn't some defective brood mare! How dare you say such vile things!" Iliana looked ready to gut Nicephorus on the spot.

"You overstep, praetor," Darius growled ominously, gripping the arms of his chair as the room heated noticeably.

Unruffled by the animosity directed his way, Nicephorus continued.

"And what happens to whatever hard-won stability we achieve today, and in the days to come, when the empress fails to conceive? Maybe it won't matter for a few years, but what about in the next five, the next fifteen? How long until another member of your extended family, with children of his own, decides he should be adopted to fill the role of heir? Would such an individual contentedly wait to be made emperor? The mastermind has yet to be caught, and could use this to weaken you if they are content to play a less aggressive game. How long until the magistri decide to question your fitness to rule, if you cannot produce an heir to ensure the continuation of peace in Lethe? Exactly how long do you intend to try for children before you are forced to consider adoption? And which family would you adopt from, knowing it would change imperial dynamics and potentially foment unrest amongst rival factions? At the very least, having children with a concubine would help cement your place on the throne, and give the people peace of mind. These are things you must consider."

Belisarius hung his head in his hands. He was torn between wanting to rage at the praetor for this twisted future he envisioned, and asking for a moment to be sick at the thought that Nicephorus might have the right of it. When he queried his praetor, an angry fire in his gut, it was with a restraint he didn't know he possessed.

"And who might you elect to the unenviable position of concubine?"

"How could you even consider this?!" Iliana cried.

Of course, his praetor had a ready reply to a furious rhetorical question. Nicephorus ignored the hateful tone so that he could deliver his answer.

"A noble widow with the rank of illustra who has already proven her ability to bear children. I have one of the asekretis working on a list of names."

"I can see you've given this an inordinate amount of thought. Just how have you managed to see to your other responsibilities, I wonder?"

Nicephorus faced Belisarius' dark temper head on, his resolve unbent.

"It is my duty to see to the well-being of the empire at all times, and in all ways, Your Royal Highness."

"Get. Out," Belisarius hissed.

"As you wish." Nicephorus stood and bowed, leaving a seething mass of fury in his wake.

CHAPTER 34

Selene raced through hallways, imperial red décor blurring together with the force of her tears. Agony drove her faster. Some primal part of her believed, if only she could outrun it, she might escape the pain altogether. When finally she could run no more, she collapsed on hands and knees onto cool grass, lungs heaving, gut roiling. She could slow neither her heart, nor her frantic breaths. There would be a list of women. She would be expected to tolerate the nights he would spend with them. His children would not be her own. The thought of him with other women, after all the tenderness they'd shared just hours before…it made her sick. Sick with wrath. Sick with jealousy. Sick with unbearable sadness. She'd made herself utterly vulnerable to him, and her reward was a hot knife to her heart.

"Selene?"

Selene looked up through blistering tears. Concerned amber eyes gazed down at her. Domina Mina Topaz was dressed in a walking gown and a robe hooked together at the throat. She was alone.

"What are you doing dressed like that, out here, at this hour?" Mina unclasped her robe and settled it around Selene's shoulders, bending down to place a warm hand on her back. "Breathe slowly. Do you want me to call for someone?"

Selene shook her head.

"He-he's going to get a concubine," she sobbed.

Mina's eyes widened in shock and then softened with pity.

"I suppose if you grew up outside a noble household, you wouldn't know to expect such things from a husband."

"I can't accept it! He's supposed to be *mine!*" she shrieked.

"Foolish girl. You fell in love with him, didn't you?" There was nothing but sympathy in her voice.

"I'm such an idiot."

Mina sighed and seated herself beside Selene, settling in as she tucked a stray strand of dark hair behind her ear.

"From my limited experience, one chooses a partner wisely or one falls in love, but rarely do the two coincide."

"But I thought he loved me too. How can he talk about other women?"

"Selene, in my biased opinion, men are disgusting, perfidious animals. It's better to ask yourself if you want to subject yourself to them at all, rather than ask why they do what they do."

Selene finally caught her breath and sat up in the grass. She wasn't the only one who lived believing people were scum. The mantle of her cynicism was an effortless fit, no matter that she thought she'd begun leaving it behind as of late.

"People are scum."

"Precisely," Mina affirmed.

"Where does that leave me?" For the first time in many years, her cynicism failed to ground her. She was lost.

The other woman shrugged.

"I suppose you get to choose what to do now that you know what your future will be as empress. If it were me, I would take charge of the selection. I would find the most hideous woman, with putrid breath, afflicted with warts and boils, probably missing most of her teeth, too. Then I would wish him happy copulating with the creature."

Selene chuckled at Mina's cruel streak, but her momentary mirth was replaced by a hollow ache in her chest. A companionable silence stretched between the two.

"I envy you, you know," Mina told her.

"Why?" Selene asked, baffled.

"As horrible as it feels now, you can still be with the one you love. And if you ultimately decide you cannot live like a noble, you can leave. No family to tie you down, no duty you're expected to fulfil. You can set yourself free, or you can bind yourself to another, but in the end, it will be your choice."

Selene sat in shocked silence. Before she could formulate a reply, she heard a familiar voice call her name.

"Selene!"

Yet instead of solace, it brought only pain.

"I guess that's my cue to leave." Mina stood and brushed grass from her skirts. "Best of luck."

The prince barely noticed Domina Topaz leaving as he rushed to her side.

"What happened? Why are you crying? Has someone hurt you?"

Now that he was before her, acting like she was precious and in need of protection, the knife in her heart twisted. The weak Selene wanted to weep and beg him to remain faithful. The old Selene only wanted to scream, bite and kick. He'd hurt her enough, she decided.

"I don't share." She glared and slapped his concerned hands away. He was baffled as she stood and wiped the remains of tears from her face.

"What are you…" he began before he grimaced. "How much did you hear?"

Selene bristled. The knife twisted anew. That was what he wanted to know? No denial? No reassurances?

"I decided I'd heard enough once I learned about the lists of women."

"That was not my idea. I want nothing to do with it."

"Apparently, what we want has nothing to do with it! Would you really fuck another woman if I can't give you a baby?"

He flinched.

"Selene, no matter what the future holds, I believe we will figure it out together. You're the one I love, only you." He reached out to touch her face. She stepped out of his reach. His expression was hurt, his hand tightening into a fist, his lips thinning as he averted his eyes.

"Was the praetor right about what will happen?"

"Possibly," Belisarius sighed, his eyes haunted.

Bile crept up the back of her throat. Belisarius would do what needed to be done, even if he did care about her. He lived his life as the prince first, and as a man second. She couldn't bear it. She wasn't capable of living like that. All feeling she held for him would be extinguished by resentment and jealousy. She pulled the borrowed cloak closer around herself, a pitiful cloth shield against the pain.

"Find yourself another woman. If I can't have you completely, then I want nothing to do with you."

When she brushed by him on her way back to the palace, he grabbed her wrist and pulled her close, his arms caging her.

"Please, don't go! I love you. I'll do anything to prove it."

Selene fought his hold. How long had she desperately wanted to hear those words? But only hours after first hearing them, now they were salt in her gaping wounds.

"I won't accept it! I won't! I'll kill any woman you take to bed! And you will!" she howled.

"The future isn't set in stone. We could be blessed with children of our own. Please, stay and try with me. Please!"

Selene stopped struggling at the sound of his plaintive tones. He wasn't going to let her go unless she viciously twisted a knife in his heart. So be it.

"*Prince* Belisarius always puts duty before his heart. If I left in my shiny new ship, filled with your gold, would you leave the empire behind to follow me? Would you give up everything to be with me, or would you do your duty and marry a good domina, from a good family, and make little princes and princesses?"

He let go of her. She stepped out of his arms and turned to face him.

"That's not fair," he said.

"Isn't it?"

"I don't get to choose whether or not to be a prince."

"Well, I do get a choice, and I choose to leave."

Selene couldn't believe she'd actually said it. She tried to numb herself against the pain of it, tried to make herself cold to the man in front her, whose heart was breaking before her eyes. He touched his face shakily, surprised his hand was there.

"Oh."

He stumbled back as if physically stunned. She resisted the urge to reach out and hold him. Their pain was necessary now, to spare them both greater pains in future. Better to cut off an infected limb than let it drag you to the grave.

"I... I see," he mumbled.

Before she lost her resolve, Selene turned away and left the prince to his misery.

Belisarius wandered in a daze until he found himself in his father's chambers. The emperor was sitting on his veranda, and seemed surprised to see him enter.

"Father, she..."

The emperor sighed.

"I know. I caught the gist of it from here." He waved to the seat opposite him.

Belisarius fell into it, exhausted and numb.

"Do you know why I fought to be emperor?"

Belisarius couldn't summon his words. He shrugged, his eyes far away.

"It was a simple matter of survival. Nadia and I knew the war would reach us sooner or later, and our kingdom didn't have the defences of the swamps or the resources of the other kingdoms. I wasn't even a king myself, just an unimportant prince, a strategos among many, but we both knew the only way to prevent the war from consuming our lands was to take the fight to them first. The rest is history."

"Why are you telling me this?"

"What do you suppose would've happened if we'd died trying?"

Belisarius blinked owlishly in confusion.

"Do you suppose the sun would've darkened? Would the land have swallowed the rest of the kingdoms whole in retribution?"

Now he scowled.

"Don't be ridiculous."

"Exactly. Someone else would've triumphed eventually, probably the swamp king. Our world would look different, but it would still be here, even if our little family had been wiped from existence. The universe doesn't give a shit if we rule Lethe, or if we're struck dead tomorrow. Life will go on."

"I hope you don't call Magister Emerald 'swamp king' to his face."

His father waved off his concern.

"You know why she's leaving, don't you?"

"I think she made it clear," Belisarius replied darkly.

"Gods below, you damn fool!" He slammed his fist on the table, startling Belisarius. "Then tell her in no uncertain terms there will be no other women, no children of your blood that aren't also hers! Tell her you'll adopt a whole orphanage full of foundlings to satisfy the damn praetor, and then give the man a black eye or two for even suggesting a fucking concubine! I know we raised you to put your duty to the empire first, but I see now we did you wrong. We feared if we raised you like we had the others, you might become another Mercurius, convinced the world was yours, and you could have whatever you wished without consequence. But Belli, neither your mother nor I would ever have wished you to leave your heart behind for this damn rock in the ocean. All we ever wanted for you was to be happy and safe."

"I'm not sure if she'll still have me."

Sympathy softened the lines around his father's red eyes.

"When you die, if you're lucky, some of what you've done will leave an echo, but even that fades with time. Nothing matters more than what you do with your life when you're alive to live it, and nothing will bring you more joy or sorrow than those you choose to spend that life with. If you can't live without her, then do whatever it takes to keep her by your side. Luckily for you, you were born with the resources of an empire to draw on. Though I suspect you already know, she won't be swayed by anything other than having you entirely. And Belli? That's a rare gift, especially for a prince."

Belisarius launched himself from his seat. His father was right. He would mend this rift, would grovel for months, years, however long it took to win her back to his side. What was the use in being royalty if he couldn't carve out a place in this world for her—for them?

"I need to go to her now."

The emperor nodded and smiled.

"I need to tell her that she'll be the only woman, children or no."

"Yes, you do."

Belisarius nearly tripped over himself to get to the door in his haste. Before he left, he turned to see his father's smiling face.

"Thank you."

"Go. Bring that minx back as my daughter-in-law as thanks." He saluted with a small glass of freshly poured liquor.

Belisarius nodded, rushing off to do just that.

Darius sighed, profoundly relieved when Belisarius had left, hell-bent on making things right with Selene. Belisarius was going to need someone strong, ruthless and loyal beside him in the coming days so that he could step down with confidence. Darius sipped his favourite brandy and relaxed in his seat. The chirping of the night insects filled the silence, until the groaning of the servants stairwell interrupted it. Who would dare to enter his room at this hour, without his permission?

When he stood to see the person off, Darius fell to the ground, his body stiff. He engulfed his body in flames, but whatever it was that had poisoned him, it was inside him now. He'd dismissed the guards from his bedroom door, sending them to guard the doors to his outer chambers where the wards for his protection ended. They wouldn't hear him scream. From his position on the floor, he could see the boots of a single person approaching him. They were polished, made of quality dyed leather. Whoever it was belonged to the nobility. He breathed deep and unleashed a stream of fire at the intruder.

Instead of agonized screams, or the scent of singed flesh and leather he'd expected, the intruder chuckled, his shiny boots entirely unharmed by the flames. Only a fire mage had his clothes enchanted to withstand that kind of blaze. The intruder was likely the traitor at the head of this conspiracy.

"Let's see your face then, coward," Darius growled. It galled him to know he would die defenceless rather than in battle. He'd be damned if he died ignorant of the bastard who had threatened his son and his empire.

When the man turned Darius on his side, his eyes widened with horror.

"No."

The man glared down at him with piercing ruby eyes and a smile twisted with menacing glee.

"Yes."

Chapter 35

After Selene had left him in the gardens, she'd retreated to Marduk's apartments, protected by the metals mage. Belisarius demanded entrance to no avail. When Marduk did see fit to let him into the receiving room, he asked him to sit.

"Are you demanding her presence as the prince, or as a man?"

"A man," Belisarius replied.

"May I speak freely, Your Royal Highness?"

"Please," Belisarius sighed.

"She's not going to see you tonight. Even if you order her to, Iliana would probably try to gut you. Given what I've heard, I might be tempted to let her have a go at you. You were raised better than that. Nicephorus is blindly loyal to you and the empire, but he lives in his head so much, I often wonder if he has a heart. I didn't think I needed to worry about that from you, since you damn well knew what it looked like for a man to treasure his wife!"

Belisarius winced. Sometimes he forgot that Marduk had known him since the moment he was born, had watched over him as a brother might. Their relationship had been dictated by their respective roles, but at times like these, he knew that the distance had been a fiction for outsiders. When Marduk spoke, it was to someone he cared about, someone who had deeply disappointed him. It shamed Belisarius to his core for Marduk to see him fail so spectacularly, for the woman he loved to have to seek comfort from others, all because he hadn't been the man she'd needed in her moment of despair.

"I'm going to make this right. She has to know I'll never-"

Marduk held up his hand, stopping him.

"I expect you will, but you can save the explanations for Selene when she's ready to hear them." He smiled ruefully. "Normally, a man first learns to beg for a woman's forgiveness once he's left his boyhood behind. You're a late bloomer, but I expect you'll muddle through just fine. Now, if I allow you to remain any longer, I fear I'll be the one needing to beg for my fiancée's forgiveness."

"I'll see myself out," Belisarius sighed, his ambitions thwarted. Perhaps it would be best if Selene had the night to cool off. He just hoped she didn't want to see him dead the next time he spoke to her.

With weary resignation, he left to sleep alone in his chambers, the scent of her still permeating his sheets. Had it really been just a few hours ago that they'd resolved to be together? And only a few more when he'd been praying for her life? Gods, he'd ruined it in spectacular fashion. Belisarius was adrift, praying he had the chance to prove he could be the kind of man she needed. A tumultuous heart made for disturbed dreams. He woke confused and exhausted to the unusual sound of bells tolling. Within moments he recognised the dissonant clanging. The world tilted on its axis as sick realization churned in his gut. Guards streamed into his room, their shields and weapons at the ready.

"Your Royal Highness, we must move to a more secure location."

He moved through a daze of denial and panic, herded from his rooms through secret tunnels. A mage in the rear sealed them off with curses as he went. Deep underground, he sat in a room enchanted to completely repel magic of any sort. He knew it well. He and Mother had built it, slaving over the enchantments for months. Multiple shafts had been dug to ensure airflow, communication with the outside world achieved by exchanging notes passed up a similarly enchanted shaft operated by pulley. An escape route led to a mountain stronghold known only to a select few.

When the first note arrived, he knew what it would contain. The scrap of paper spelled the end of his life as he knew it.

Emperor Darius Bloodstone has been murdered. The inner palace will be secured before sending word. Do not proceed until the praetor or strategos come to retrieve you.

He clawed back the anguished sobs that threatened to tear from his throat. Belisarius had never been more alone in his life.

Selene, having slept fitfully for a few hours, left the safety of the strategos' apartments to wander the gardens before dawn. Torn between rage and despair, Iliana had done her best to comfort her. Even Marduk had sworn she wouldn't have to deal with the prince until she was ready, offering her the use of a spare room. She supposed she could finally see what Iliana had seen in the man—he was good.

The hour was cool and quiet, a balm on her shattered heart. But everything seemed to remind her of the prince—the stables, the training grounds, the scents of sandalwood and florals that always perfumed his rooms. She needed to leave the continent. Only distance and foreign lands could help erase him from her thoughts.

The cacophonous clanging of bells brought an end to her pity-party. As she hurried back to the strategos' rooms, the imperial army mobilized, marching through halls and banging on doors. Searching the palace grounds, they stationed guards in areas they'd thoroughly vetted. When she tried to speak to one, he told her to seek shelter and remain indoors. Seeing she would get no answers from that quarter, she hurried back to Iliana. In her haste, she ploughed headlong into a person rounding a corner and fell onto her backside. It was the librarian, Azar.

"What's going on?"

He reached down and pulled her up with ease. Had he always been so strong? The leer on his face turned her innards cold. From behind, someone clapped a metal collar around her neck. Poisons were trapped beneath her skin. Dread swallowed her whole. Before she could scream, a sharp pain in her head knocked her out.

A pounding ache woke her.

With no natural light, Selene had no notion how long she'd been unconscious. When she tried to move, she found her wrists and ankles were chained, the metallic scraping alerting her captors to her wakefulness. The walls of her prison were rough-hewn stone, the rock floor beneath chilling her to her bones as her heart skittered and her gut roiled. Azar, Magister Diamond and his son lounged nearby on the only furniture within the cell. A shadow mage stepped out from the darkness. It seemed the wards inside the dungeon had never been repaired.

"The prince has been sequestered somewhere we can't access. The army is still searching the palace. The magistri are being guarded," the shadow mage reported.

"Will you be able to take the women and speak to the magistri before the coronation?" Azar asked.

"I believe so, though Topaz might be troublesome."

"Kosta, take his daughter first, and send one of our asekretis to deliver the message once it's done," Azar directed.

"Yes, Your Royal Highness," Kosta replied before vanishing. A teleportation mage. The shadow mage followed shortly, leaving her with the librarian and Magister Diamond.

Selene didn't understand. Why had the teleportation mage spoken to Azar like he was the prince? Diamond noticed her staring.

"It's awake," Miroslav sneered.

Azar turned to her. Everything from how he'd held himself to the expression on his face was wrong. This was no amiable, bumbling scholar.

Before her stood a nobleman with a regal bearing and cunning in his eyes. His smile made her insides squirm.

"I'd apologize for the rough handling, but I think we both know you wouldn't have come obediently."

Had she hit her head extra hard? Was Azar the traitor all along? Belisarius had said it was definitely a family member, but this man was clearly not related, or the praetor would have known. He chuckled at her confusion.

"Remove the enchantment, Miroslav. It's unnecessary now."

"Yes, Your Royal Highness."

As Magister Diamond removed the earring in Azar's ear, the librarian's entire face rearranged itself before her eyes, his earring disintegrating into dust as Azar grew in height and bulk. Selene had never seen anything like it, never dreamed that what she witnessed was even possible. She gasped. A younger, leaner, crueller Darius stood before her. His smile was predatory, and his bow was all dramatic flourish.

"First Prince Mercurius Bloodstone, true heir to the Empire of Lethe, here to claim what is mine."

"The First Prince is dead." Selene's denial was unconvincing, even to herself.

Mercurius was light on his feet as he approached. He crouched down and lifted her chin.

"You can see for yourself what a lie that is. I've merely been vacationing across the sea with my dear uncle."

Selene swallowed her fear as best she could. His desire for the throne was clear, but why imprison her? If he was as powerful a fire mage as she suspected, he could have turned her to ash in an instant.

"Why chain me up?"

"Isn't it obvious? You have a tendency to find yourself in places that inconvenience me."

"So the big bad fire mage is scared of little me? I'm flattered." Much more of this and her bravado would crumble. He was cold and wicked in a way Amethyst could've only dreamed.

When he laughed, she almost flinched. It was almost like Darius'; rich, deep, but without a hint of true warmth.

"A viper in chains! Just what I'd hoped. I'd already given it some thought, but now I'm certain. You'll make a fine concubine."

Selene's skin crawled. Repulsed, she jerked her head away. When he grabbed her chin again, she spat at him. He slapped her. Hard. Her ears rang. Kosta returned with Mina in tow, shoving her onto the ground beside Selene. She could see that Kosta sported scratches on his face and a split lip. In short order, both Charis Opal and Zoe Emerald appeared in the room, staggering out of the shadows. Mercurius stood before Emerald and bowed, taking her hand and kissing it, transforming into a dapper gentleman.

"I'm pleased to make your acquaintance, Domina Emerald. As you and the other dominae are aware, your fathers have agreed to behave to ensure your safety, and you in turn are expected to wait here obediently, lest something unfortunate befall the magistri."

To her credit, Zoe straightened her spine and stared down her nose at the man before her, her bright green eyes narrowing with distaste.

"And who are you to threaten the Emerald Province?"

She hoped Zoe would fill his lungs with soil.

"Your future emperor, Mercurius Bloodstone."

"I admit, you have some semblance to our late emperor."

"You killed Darius?! I'll kill you, fucking bastard!" Selene launched herself at the man, but Mina held her back.

Mercurius ignored her as Topaz held her hand over Selene's mouth to silence her shrieks.

"Play your cards right, Domina, and you will sit on that throne beside me as my empress. What say you?"

There was only a short pause before Domina Emerald curtsied.

"You have excellent taste, Bloodstone."

"I will come for you when this is done." He kissed her hand again. Before he left, he grabbed Selene's face, all traces of the gallantry snuffed out, and whispered, "I look forward to training you." He turned to Magister Diamond. "Do what you wish, Miroslav, but it must be reversible. Keep watch on her and the dominae. Now that Father is dead and the dust has settled, it's time to make myself known."

Magister Diamond bowed deeply.

"May the forgotten gods see fit to remember you."

With that, Mercurius was pulled into the shadows. Miroslav lost no time advancing on Selene, vengeful fury in his eyes.

"Do you know how bright a light must be to fully blind a man? No? Let's find out together."

CHAPTER 36

"I should be looking for her, not standing here dressed like it's a lavish party."

"I have competent soldiers searching, and the inner palace is secure. She'll be found."

Iliana's gut roiled. She stood next to Marduk in the presence of the magistri, their heirs, Nicephorus and the logothetes under his authority. They'd been hastily assembled once word had been given of Darius' death, gathered to pledge their loyalty in front of witnesses to the new emperor. Belisarius strode into the throne room wearing ceremonial silks in imperial red and the high crown of the emperor, a heavy, ornate piece of gold that, along with the sceptre he held, had been created by melting down the crowns of the former kings and repurposing any precious stones they might have held. Iliana knew what it was to lose beloved parents, so she had some inkling of what he might be feeling behind the cold mask he presented to the court. At least she'd been able to mourn openly. The emperor had been found dead a few hours ago, and yet Belisarius was forced into this spectacle in order to ensure a peaceful, orderly transition of power. It was as cruel as it was necessary.

"We'll search for her the moment this is concluded. Kneel when I do. My oath will count for both of us," Marduk whispered.

Iliana nodded, distracted. Was it just her imagination, or did the magistri appear uneasy? Belisarius sat in the emperor's throne, yet not one of the magistri were jockeying for position as they had the day before, mere moments after the traitors were killed. She was also one of the only women in attendance, something that sat ill with her. Where were the dominae?

"Marduk, do the magistri look... unsettled to you?"

"It's to be expected. They know the emperor didn't die naturally, and that the assassin hasn't been caught."

"I have a terrible feeling."

"Selene will be found safe, I vow it." Marduk's eyes were full of concern and sympathy, squeezing her hand in comfort.

What more was there to say? She couldn't leave the throne room, no matter that her intuition was screaming.

"I will now receive your oaths of loyalty," Belisarius announced. "Will the armies of Lethe pledge their loyalty, or will they forfeit their lives?"

Marduk marched before the podium as Iliana walked behind him. When he knelt, so did she, careful not to falter in her lengthy silk skirts.

"Strategos Marduk and the armies of Lethe pledge their loyalty to the Emperor Belis-"

Cut off by an explosion, all eyes went to the doors. Twice the height of a man, and many times the weight, they were blown off their hinges. The two oak slabs and their iron fittings flew into the room, screeching across the floors, digging troughs in the mosaics, and came to a booming halt before the silk-draped assemblage. Guards surrounded Belisarius in an instant, swords drawn and shields raised.

"Do not make your oaths to that vile usurper! Before you stands the true heir of Lethe, the Empire of Mages. I, First Prince Mercurius Bloodstone, reject your claim to the throne, and demand my rights be recognised!"

Marduk paled. Iliana turned from him to the man claiming to be the long dead First Prince. The resemblance to the late emperor couldn't be denied.

"Gods below," Marduk whispered, horrified.

Iliana had no idea what was going on, but she recognised fear when she saw it. It chilled her to the marrow to see it in the eyes of her fiancé. Luckily, she was wearing a large, flashy metal necklace. She placed her hand on it and dissolved it into a coating on her palm, readying it for whatever purpose she might require. Belisarius' shock was blatant. Was she the only one who saw that the man should be dealt with swiftly? The magistri and their heirs watched in wary silence.

"Your Majesty! Order the guards to arrest him!" Iliana called out to Belisarius.

Before he could react, a stream of fire came barrelling at her. Marduk grabbed her, wrenching Iliana out of the way just in time. The flames singed her skirts.

"Silence, wench!" Mercurius hissed. "Take your animal and leave, before I lose my patience."

"Mercurius Bloodstone died twenty-eight years ago. What vile magic have you cast to appear before us with my father's likeness?!" Belisarius roared.

Mercurius ignored him and turned to the magistri.

"Esteemed magistri, I, too, survived the assassination of my siblings all those years ago. The late Empress Nadia sent me across the sea, in the care of my Uncle Phokas, to protect me from future threats. I was meant to return upon my thirtieth year, but my youngest brother, coveting the throne for himself, conspired to use foul, foreign magics on my uncle and me, making us believe we were naught but exiled nobles, and telling my parents we had died."

"At thirteen?! You must think us all fools!"

Belisarius whispered to a guard at his side, who disappeared into the shadows. Hopefully he was calling for reinforcements. Marduk had regained his composure.

"What kind of magic would let him look like Darius?" Iliana whispered.

"I can only imagine it's some kind of shapeshifter, or the glamour of a fae, but that doesn't explain the flames," he replied, equally quiet.

Unconcerned by Belisarius' outrage, the man continued. "When my beloved mother discovered this trickery, he murdered her, but not before she dispatched a counter-curse mage to save me."

"Lies!" Belisarius shouted. He made to run the man through with his sceptre but Magister Emerald, the closest to the throne, held out his hand.

"We shall hear him out and decide the truth for ourselves, Your Royal Highness."

Something was very wrong indeed. By rights, Belisarius was 'Your Majesty' now that Darius had died. Were the magistri truly entertaining this madness? Belisarius noticed the change as well, his knuckles white as he gripped the sceptre.

"You would have a charlatan on my throne, Emerald?"

The Magister shook his head.

"I beg of you, let him speak."

The interloper continued, emboldened now.

"These past few years, I garnered the support of the former Magistri Sapphire and Amethyst as well as Magister Diamond. But once again, that snake discovered the threat to his lies! He summoned their daughters to Nadioch and cast foul magics on them so that he could accuse their fathers of treason, all while holding their children hostage. Even after he had them thrown into the dungeons and threatened with executions, my late allies refused to die as his pawns, and managed to break out before they were viciously slaughtered. I decided to reveal myself to my father, believing he at least would welcome me with open arms! Emperor Darius had been led to believe that I was dead, and affirmed my claim to the throne just last night. Then that usurper, having learned what my father planned, murdered the emperor! Now we come to the end of this tragedy, and I ask that you pledge your oaths of loyalty to me, your rightful emperor!"

Belisarius looked ready to tackle the man to the ground and start pummelling him.

"How dare you profane the memories of my parents with your falsehoods!"

"Did the man who claims my throne give you any proof that the magistri had used foul magics on their daughters themselves? He has silver-tongues at his disposal, and knowledge of foul magics. How difficult would it have been for him to orchestrate their victimization himself? Was it not convenient that for at least two of my sponsors, he found bastards, one apiece, to testify against their fathers? Can we be certain that the daughters they impersonated are even still alive? Maybe they resisted him too strongly, and paid the ultimate price," Mercurius continued, growing more confident.

"Guards, arrest that imposter! I will not allow these lies to stand!"

Guards hesitantly approached the fire mage, who held up his hands in apparent surrender.

"Do not speak of lies to me, Brother! You stand before men of real power, dignified elemental mages of esteemed bloodlines and good repute! I inherited my father's flames, but you were born an abomination! If you wish to prove me wrong, then go, show them your fire!"

"Collar him!" Belisarius called out.

Mercurius flicked his wrist and held off the guards with an impenetrable wall of flames.

"He cannot produce flames because he is no elemental mage! The man who would be Emperor is none other than a detestable, ignoble, negation mage! He's an unnatural creature who surrounds himself with ferals and menials, because no decent elemental would ever kneel to him if they knew."

Iliana could see the tide of sentiment turning against Belisarius. The guards stopped trying to advance, and the magistri eyed him with suspicion.

"Marduk." Iliana's voice was hysterical with anxiety.

"I know," he replied grimly.

"Despite all these injustices, I am not unjust myself. In view of the forgotten gods and these honoured noblemen of Lethe, I demand the right to contest the throne through ritual combat. No more innocent blood should be shed over this feud, Brother. What say you, magistri? Step forward if you will allow me to prove myself!"

Mage gift aside, how could anyone believe the lies he was spewing? He asked the magistri if the prince had presented any proof, but Mercurius had yet to do more than speak and present himself as the evidence. Surely the magistri would turn their backs on him.

To her horror, each magister stepped forward.

Rage coiled through Belisarius, poisoning his veins and darkening his thoughts. If he lived to see another sunrise, he swore he'd see the end of the elementalist traitors who had demanded this farce proceed according to the whims of a man who should be dead. He'd never imagined that a clever bit of rhetoric, weaving half-truths and lies, would undo his entire claim to the throne and sway men he'd done right by over the years. Belisarius had been well and truly trapped. If he revealed that Mercurius had been the one rampaging through the palace all those years ago, only he and Marduk could back the claim. The lie from all those years ago, that had spared the image of the royal family, had strangled his ability to fend off Mercurius' schemes. Belisarius' ignoble status made him that much less worthy in the eyes of the elementalist magistri. He still couldn't entirely believe the man was who he claimed.

He and Mercurius had been separated, with Magistri Topaz and Opal standing guard at their doors so that neither one got the fight underway before the appointed time. Magister Opal stood in his doorway, nervously running his tanned fingers through jet hair going grey at the temples. Marduk would soon return to him with the sword he would use to slay his supposed brother.

"I deeply regret this situation, Your Royal Highness," Opal ventured.

"If I live, I'll see to it that you do," Belisarius threatened.

"He took my girl to ensure my co-operation. Please, forgive me." Opal bowed low.

The news hit him hard. More traitors and spies, now kidnapping dominae to ensure their fathers' compliance. With only a handful of men, the fake Mercurius had affected a coup. Would the blows never end?

"Whoever he is, he is no emperor."

"It pains me to say this, but he may be. Twenty-eight years ago, the empress begged my brother to transport a young man in secret along with your uncle. He only spoke of it once while deep in his cups, but, until your mother's death, he regularly took shipments from the late empress to transport across the sea to your uncle, where he lived with a younger man."

Belisarius must have gaped at Opal like he'd grown horns. If curved protuberances had sprouted at his temples, it might've been less disorienting. What would Mother have sent across the sea? Something that, until her death, had kept Mercurius from returning? What else but her memory reversal flowers, so potent that even a poison mage found herself returning to the innocence of childhood with a fistful? Gods below, had Mother spared Mercurius' life without father ever discovering the truth? Had Uncle Phokas agreed to the scheme? Once again, Belisarius' world tilted on its axis. It was not magic which gave the traitor his father's likeness. It was Mercurius in truth.

As Belisarius spiralled further into the endless darkness of the Bloodstone family secrets and lies, Marduk returned to his side, a large case in his arms.

"Your Majesty?"

"It's truly Mercurius."

"Yes. Returned from the grave by dark gods, it seems." Marduk scowled, ready to spit. He lowered his voice and leaned in, "Give me the word and I'll rally the soldiers most loyal to me. I'll cut down that elementalist pig myself, and any magister who sides with him, and have their children arrested to ensure the provinces stay in line. The fleets can be redeployed to destroy Topaz and Emerald's harbours. Mercurius is dead, and whoever this ghost is will not take your crown."

"Or maybe he never died at all."

"Your Majesty?"

At that moment, Belisarius knew he might not survive. Even at seventeen, Mercurius had been known as a brilliant fighter, utterly ruthless, and exceptionally intelligent. The man he'd seen had appeared fit and strong. He doubted the intervening years had dulled his brother's instincts. They'd certainly sharpened his political acumen along with his bloodthirst. It would be foolish to assume Mercurius believed himself unprepared to fight, even if he never used a single spark of flame. He knew Belisarius' own gift, and still wished to battle him head on. If Belisarius died, he needed to know the ones he cared about would be safe. He turned to his oldest friend.

"Find Selene and take her and your fiancée across the sea. The ship we made ready for her is still crewed and in the harbour. Take Nicephorus if you can convince him to leave, though I have a feeling he won't be persuaded."

"I will not run like a coward!" Marduk hissed, anger furrowing his brow.

"It's likely my last command, Marduk. If you love me at all, please don't let that monster harm the ones I treasure most."

"If you give up now, then he *will* kill you," Marduk retorted.

"If I fail to make plans in the event of my death, I will repeat my mother's mistake, and doom those I love to suffer. My brother will not look kindly on you or Selene, and I fear what may happen to the empire if Iliana falls into his hands. Will you do this for me? There is no one else I trust."

Belisarius could see Marduk warring with himself. The prince stood resolute. They wouldn't be safe here if he died, and Marduk knew it.

"I will do this last thing for you."

"I'm relieved, thank you. Don't waste another moment, or it may be too late. If I survive, I will send word to you."

"We still don't know where Selene is, Your Majesty. She disappeared while the bells tolled. A few of the guards reported seeing her returning to my apartments, but she never arrived."

"Your Royal Highness?" Opal interjected.

Belisarius and Marduk turned to him, both eyeing him with open hostility.

"If he took her to the same place he took my Charis, she'll be in the dungeons."

CHAPTER 37

Selene did, in fact, discover how bright a light needed to be to rob her of sight. She wasn't proud of it, but she'd hoped her screams would be enough to sate the bloodlust of the magister. Alas, not even seeing her blinded and crawling was enough to satisfy him. He'd taken out a whip and left her back in bloody tatters. Thankfully, his stamina was greatly lacking, and she now found herself bleeding, broken and blind instead of dead. He'd invited the other captors for a drink, waiting outside their cell for Mercurius to call upon them.

"Fuck, I need a healer," Selene whispered in agony.

She hoped one of the other dominae would speak, if only to assure her she wasn't entirely alone in her new world of pitch darkness and pain. She could hear shuffling to her right, and she swung her useless eyes in the direction. A warm hand touched her unharmed cheek.

"I'm so sorry I didn't do anything to stop him," Zoe said, her voice choked with emotion.

"There's nothing you could've done."

"Maybe not. But there's something I can do now."

Warmth replaced the agony that gripped her. Slowly, Selene's world brightened so that she could make out the other dominae in the dim prison cell. Exhaustion dragged her down, but she was free of the pain. All three women's cheeks were wet with tears. Opal was the first to gasp.

"You're a healer?! What the fuck?" Opal swore.

"Not now!" Emerald hissed.

"I'd always assumed you were an elementalist to the core. Now that I know it was an inferiority complex, your actions make a lot more sense," Topaz taunted.

"My mother killed everyone who knew when my nanny discovered the truth, just to ensure my father never found out. If he discovers I am not an earth mage, he'll disown me. And worse. Why do you think I did what I did to be the next empress? If you value your lives, it would be best if you kept this to yourselves." Emerald clenched her jaw.

"Fight later! Get this collar off me before he comes back," Selene hissed.

Zoe touched the stone at the back. The collar snapped open, and Selene tossed it aside, smashing the stone with her chains. Unfortunately, that still left her shackled.

"Damn it!" Selene cursed. "Does anyone have a good idea to get us out of here? I'm pretty sure I could take out the magister if I launch myself at him, but the teleportation mage and the two shadow mages are going to be trouble."

Topaz sighed.

"Well, if we're going to lay all our cards on the table, then I can drag the two shadow mages into the void, far from the shadow path. It's unlikely they'll survive long enough to find a way back. But I can't do that if the light mage dazzles me. He needs to go down first."

"What?" Charis asked, shocked. "But you've never trained!"

Mina's grin was a touch mad.

"You really thought I'd remain the weak girl you rejected? I command the darkness with as much competence as my brothers."

"But why? You were always so afraid..."

Mina gazed at Charis with a wickedness that sent a frisson of fear down Selene's spine. Charis, however, seemed rapt.

"Your griffin spilled all the secrets you confided in him while you thought him a pet. All it took was a few trips through the void to convince him. I know you still love me." Topaz's amber eyes glimmered with delight. "I guess I never let go of my girlish fantasy that I would steal you away on your wedding night. Once I learned that you need me as much as I need you, I knew I'd have taken you from the prince himself if he'd chosen you."

Selene watched as Charis blushed scarlet, ready to throw herself at Mina. Before she could, Emerald cleared her throat, interrupting the two lovers.

"So, what about the teleportation mage?"

Selene thought on it. After one of those mages had attacked Marduk, she'd learned from Iliana that they couldn't teleport with more than one person unless they were really talented, and not at all if they were in significant enough pain.

"I guess we link arms and hope one of us lands a blow? I don't know. Three out of four is going to have to do. Hopefully he's a spineless coward like his father," Selene replied. She feared if they delayed any longer, Mercurius would be able to use their imprisonment against the magistri, and more importantly, Belisarius.

"I can vouch for that," Topaz huffed.

"So, are we ready?" Selene asked, adrenaline pulling her from her lethargy. Three determined sets of eyes met her own. "Then let's commit some murder."

Peering around the corner, Iliana could see a group of five men wearing the colours of Magister Diamond standing guard at the entrance of the dungeons. She twirled back to avoid being seen and whispered to Marduk.

"Five men belonging to Diamond, all armed. I can't be certain, but their swords don't seem to be any better than the regular army's."

"Diamond's men? This should be quick," Marduk grinned.

Iliana watched as he gripped his mace and shield, readying himself. Fear overtook her. What if he got himself killed? Despite her skills, she'd never trained herself for combat. She didn't know if she'd be able to help him in the thick of it.

"Wait! Not yet."

When he gazed down at her, it was with understanding. He leaned down and kissed her.

"You've never seen me in action. I'm not the strategos for nothing."

"At least let me enchant your steel."

"If you can be quick," he allowed.

Iliana felt the great shield he carried and allowed the metal to tell her what it was capable of. Like a conversation with a friend, she pushed her magic into it, making it the best at deflecting blows as she could without undermining its strength. Next, she touched the mace he held, a wicked-looking object made larger than normal to accommodate its giant of an owner. This she enchanted to shatter whatever its owner saw as a threat on contact. She still couldn't believe she was going to send him out there to face enemy steel.

"Don't come out until I call. If anything happens-"

"Go to the praetor, I know."

His grin turned almost cruel.

"Don't watch if you're squeamish."

He raced down the hall at an unbelievable speed for a man his size. The Diamond guards formed ranks immediately. One launched a streamer of fire at Marduk, only to have him duck behind his shield, still advancing, and bash the fire mage with the shield, sending him flying down the hallway. Another slashed with his sword. Marduk parried with a swing of his mace, shattering the sword and the face of the mage wielding it as it arced out. Another of the five fled, leaving just two trying to outflank him. Marduk shielded himself, barely breaking a sweat. One of the men took the offensive, raining blows without pause, pinning Marduk down while the other sent himself flying over the beast mage with a blast of wind. He landed lightly, his sword at the ready to run Marduk through.

Iliana cried out. Marduk tossed his heavy shield at the mage in front while ducking and twirling, landing a vicious, lethal blow to the wind mage's side. The man now at his back tossed the shield aside and leapt at Marduk, sword poised to take off his head. Marduk deflected the blow with his mace and grabbed the man's wrist, crushing it as his momentum shot him forward. The sword dropped from his grip, clattering on the floor. Iliana heard the wet, crunching blow of Marduk's mace as it caved in the last man's head.

"Gods below," Iliana whispered to herself.

Marduk stood calmly amidst the carnage and collected his shield. When he noticed her stare, his expression turned sheepish.

"Sorry. I got a bit carried away, knowing you were watching."

"No wonder everyone gives you a wide berth," she said half in admiration, half in shock. She shook herself from her astonishment at the swift and uncompromising violence. "Alright, I'm less worried now. Let's get Selene."

Marduk smiled, a touch wild, and nodded.

"Stay behind me."

They descended into the dungeons, abandoning the warmth and light of summer for cold darkness broken up by flickering sconces. As they reached the bottom, the voices of others echoed in the darkness. Marduk chanced a quick peek at the speakers.

"She squealed like a sow! Ha!" Miroslav crowed.

"Best get her cleaned up for when His Majesty returns," the shadow mage said.

"I don't need a damned shadow mage son of a whore to tell me what to do! The only one who needs a new robe is sitting right here. I'm the one with poison bitch blood on me," Miroslav said.

"I meant no offense, Your Grace," the shadow mage said.

"Pour me another glass, Kosta."

"Yes, Father."

Iliana saw red. She turned her necklace into a short sword enchanted to cut through anything with ease. She was going to gut the magister and bathe herself in his noble blood. She was going to make a necklace of his bones. She would drink out of a goblet made from his skull. Marduk held her back.

"He. Hurt. Selene," Iliana raged.

"Let me go first. With two shadow mages and a teleportation mage, three of the four can disappear in an instant. We need them to focus on me so that they don't take her somewhere else. Kosta is a teleportation mage, so we need to fight back-to-back," Marduk said.

Iliana nodded. Just as they were about to sneak closer, the boom of a heavy door blasting open heralded a battle cry of vicious shrieks. Selene, bound in chains, was launched bodily from inside the cell, her shackled hands outstretched to take hold of the magister. Iliana and Marduk rushed in, their weapons at the ready. When Selene landed on the magister, they tumbled onto the rough stone floor. He kicked her off and vanished from sight. The dominae Emerald, Opal and Topaz emerged from the cell with Topaz in the lead.

"Diamond got away!" Selene called back. "Get the shadow bastards!"

"My pleasure." Topaz grinned before her entire body transformed into a flickering, inky blackness.

The shadow mages swore and tried to melt into the darkness. Marduk dashed in the brains of one before he'd fully disappeared. As if cut in half, only the top-most portion of his body remained, leaking gore. The other half had disappeared into the void. Topaz's form leapt at the other shadow mage, grabbing him with smoky talons before diving into a shadow as if it were a deep pool.

Iliana rushed to Selene. Her back was coated in blood, her clothes ripped to shreds.

"Iliana?" Selene asked.

"Hold on. I'll get you free," she said.

No normal metal could withstand more than a few enchantments without becoming as brittle as a dry twig. Mind buzzing, she shoved as many enchantments as she could into the chains. When Selene grabbed her in a hug, the chains dissolved into powder.

"We have to stop Mercurius," Selene asserted as she pushed back from their embrace.

"You're too hurt!"

"Help!" Zoe called out.

Iliana whipped her head in Emerald's direction. Zoe stubbornly clutched onto Charis as the teleportation mage tried to rip her from the woman's arms. Marduk charged forward, his mace at the ready. Seeing the beast mage bearing down on him, Kosta released Charis and teleported away. The two dominae collapsed into a heap.

Iliana's nerves were frayed, but she sensed a blade approaching. Eyes darting frantically, she gripped her own blade in hand. She couldn't see it even as she sensed it.

"Iliana, what-"

Iliana heard the whistling of the blade she sensed cutting through the air. She shoved Selene down and raised her own blade up in defence, but too late. Blood spurted from where her wrist once was. Her scream of agony echoed in the gloom.

Selene's heart hollowed out as the gory stump that had once been Iliana's hand spurted blood. Her tortured shriek propelled Selene into action. She reached out to grab the mangled limb below the wound, grasping it as tightly as she could while she pumped the area full of anaesthetic and a powerful sedative. At the same time, Marduk swung his mace at the space behind them. The satisfying sound of bone crunching accompanied the echoes of her friend's tortured cry. The magister reappeared as he fell, mangled. Iliana slumped over.

"Emerald, get over here, now!" Selene barked.

Marduk cradled Iliana in his arms, his weapon forgotten.

"She needs a healer!"

"She *is* a healer!" Selene retorted.

Zoe picked up Iliana's severed hand as her dark complexion turned bloodless. She stumbled over to them and held the hand to Iliana's gushing wound, her own shaking.

"I-I've never done this before."

"Do it now, or she's going to die!"

"What did I miss? Good gods! Her hand!" Mina shouted as she returned and took in the situation.

"Not helping!" Selene screamed back. "Concentrate, Emerald. You're the smartest person I know—you can do this. Marduk, hold the hand in place."

Tears streamed down his blood-stained face, but he did as ordered, his hand steady. Zoe held her hands at the gory junction and breathed deeply, her green eyes haunted but focused. Selene's panic receded as the bone knitted back together, the muscles following, before finally the skin sealed it. Once done, Zoe collapsed on the floor, her breathing ragged. Selene went limp with relief, a strange hysterical joy bubbling up. She took Zoe's face in hers and kissed the healer on the lips.

"Thank you."

"Get off," Zoe groaned, exhausted, as she batted Selene away with a shaky hand.

Mina stood above Magister Diamond. Her form burst into flickering darkness once more.

"Still alive, I see. That's good. Do you know why shadow mages have to stick to the path, light mage?" She leaned over him and gripped his blood-soaked tunic in her talons. "Because there are things in the void, and they hunger."

The Magister made a wet, garbled sound before Mina dragged him into the dark.

"So intense…" Charis whispered as if in a dream.

Mina returned shortly.

"She needs to see a proper healer," Zoe said.

"I'll take her. Come." Marduk spoke to Selene, cradling Iliana in his arms.

"What's happened to Belisarius?" Selene pressed a hand on his blood-spattered tunic.

"He'll be facing Mercurius in ritual combat for the throne. I must see you both safely out of the palace."

"Iliana first."

"I can take three of you through the void to my family's healer. He should be waiting in our apartments," Mina volunteered.

"Take them first." Selene gestured at Zoe, Marduk and Iliana.

Mina nodded.

"Hold on tightly," Mina said. She grabbed onto Marduk and Zoe before they vanished into the void.

"Alright, let's go." Selene grabbed Charis' hand and tugged her to the stairs.

"Go where? Mina will be back soon."

"We need to save Belisarius, and I'm going to need your help."

CHAPTER 38

Belisarius stepped out onto the hard packed sand of the training ground, ceremonial sword in hand, its curved blade reflecting the bright summer sun. He wore nothing more than a pair of trousers tucked into soft-soled leather boots. No defensive clothing or armour was permitted. Combatants were to enter the ring with a blade and their bodies, nothing more. He supposed he should be grateful that he wouldn't be forced to fight his brother's flames. Even if he'd been born one, a fire mage could be scorched if his opponent burned hotter, and Mercurius had devoured many lives with the ritual to burn hottest.

The magistri, their heirs, palace guards and members of the imperial bureaucracies and armies stood at a distance under the shade of stone colonnades that bordered the grounds on two sides. Marduk was nowhere to be seen. It was a relief.

Mercurius marched onto the grounds, brimming with confidence. He had a brawler's build, just as their father had, while Belisarius favoured the leaner build of their mother. He'd sparred with his father in his younger days, but had never once prevailed.

"I've been observing my subjects these past few years," Mercurius told him with a smile.

They kept to the proper forms. Belisarius met Mercurius in the centre of the ring with a few arms lengths between them. They bowed deeply.

"Your taste in right-hand men leaves something to be desired, but your taste in women..." Mercurius goaded.

When they straightened, they held their blades in both hands, rotating them to demonstrate to each other that they carried identical swords. He wished he could have had one of Iliana's enchantments slipped into his steel. If he died and she escaped, Lethe wouldn't know its luck.

Belisarius refused to reply to the obvious taunt. Still facing, they took three steps back.

"When you're dead, I'll make a proper concubine out of the poison mage."

Formalities done, they circled slowly, hoping the other would make a misstep.

"And I'll mount that feral's horns-"

Mercurius rushed in first. He was lightning on his feet, almost as fast as Marduk. Belisarius was pushed back as he tried to protect the distance between them.

"-above my mantel!" Mercurius growled, closing the distance and cutting across Belisarius' temple as he ducked.

Blood poured into Belisarius' eye. The prince used their closeness to grab onto his vile brother's sword hand. Mercurius grinned and snatched Belisarius' own wrist before he could draw his blade across his brother's broader chest. They grappled, wrestling for freedom. Belisarius' heels dug trenches into the hard-packed ground as he was slowly overpowered. Mercurius shoved him aside first, his sword closing the space between them instantly. Belisarius slipped backwards, avoiding a lethal blow, but receiving a shallow gash across his chest all the same.

He recovered as quickly as he could, pain sharpening his focus. He began a single-minded assault, pushing Mercurius into retreat. Though he landed no blows, neither did his brother, and Belisarius never allowed him to get close enough to grapple. The insults stopped as Mercurius was forced to fight with all his concentration. He made to slice across Belisarius' temple again, but this time Belisarius dodged and struck true with his blade, tearing a deep gash in Mercurius' chest.

Mercurius stumbled back, blocking a killing blow with his sword while he flung sand in Belisarius' eyes. Temporarily blinded, Belisarius was struck down with a debilitating slash across his knees. He fell to the ground.

Before his brother could land another blow, Belisarius thrust his sword up, missing Mercurius' gut as his brother leapt back. But he couldn't get back to his feet. It wouldn't be long before he was completely overpowered. Another swing batted his blade away. Mercurius grabbed his sword hand. Belisarius desperately gripped his brother's in defence. Unexpectedly, Mercurius' knee swung up, hitting him squarely in the chest. Belisarius' grip loosened on Mercurius, who tore away.

"Didn't anyone teach you how to play dirty?"

The hilt of his brother's sword came down to brain him.

They'd rushed from the dungeons into the palace above to find a group of mangled bodies at the entrance. Selene towed Charis along with her, desperate to find out where Belisarius was duelling his brother. Charis had told her between gasps that no one would intervene after the duel was begun, and that it wouldn't end until one lay dead. She couldn't believe Belli had been fool enough to agree to it, or to respect the rules of engagement. Honour and rituals were less than worthless if Mercurius won. Darius would never have stood for it. The emperor would have burned the monster to a fucking crisp. Since he was no longer around to do what needed doing, Selene would do it herself.

It wasn't long before they found someone who pointed them in the direction of the training grounds. Once there, they were both out of breath. Selene caught the beginning of the vicious fight, the sounds of clashing steel ringing out above the quiet murmurs of the gathered crowd. They stayed on the outskirts, careful not to be seen. She spotted Nicephorus not far away, apart from the others.

"Stay here. I need to get the praetor."

"What could he possibly do to stop this?"

"Nothing. But we can't let Mercurius win."

Selene dashed to the praetor and yanked him aside.

"Selene? What in the hells-"

"No time! Grab a sword and charge at Mercurius. Keep Belisarius alive long enough for me to take his brother down if you can't."

"I couldn't poss-"

"Do it before we're calling that monster 'emperor!'"

Protocol warred with loyalty in his green eyes before he nodded grimly.

"I don't have much control of my gift."

"I'll take whatever I can get," Selene called back to him as she hurried back to Charis.

"What now?"

It was a good question. She searched the periphery of the training grounds, refusing to be hopelessly drawn in by the fight. If Nicephorus went on the attack and kept Mercurius distracted, she might be able to repeat what they'd done in the cells below. Charis had enough control and strength to launch her effectively using wind, but she ran the risk of becoming the berserker's target, turning herself into fast-moving fodder. But what about striking from above? The roof of the colonnaded walkway would have to do. The risk of getting speared by blade or cooked by flame was real, so she would need to prepare for it.

"Get us up there," Selene ordered, pointing to the roof.

Charis nodded. Concentrating, she whipped up a ball of currents between her hands.

"Brace yourself," Charis muttered through gritted teeth.

A pummelling force shoved her upwards before fading. She scrabbled to grab hold of the smooth, arched roof. It took some doing, but she swung her foot up and got a proper hold. Charis used the same force to propel herself upwards with a great deal more grace and control. At Selene's narrowed eyes, the wind mage blushed.

"It's harder when it's someone else."

"Didn't anyone teach you how to play dirty?"

At that arrogant tone, Selene swung her eyes around in time to see Mercurius bash Belisarius' head in with the hilt of his sword. The prince fell to the ground, unconscious. She bit back a scream. He might not be dead yet. Before Mercurius could swing his sword to take Belisarius' head, Nicephorus entered the ring with a crazed battle cry, longsword in hand. Despite his frenzy, he wielded the blade with consummate skill. He advanced faster than any man had a right to, his steel moving as if it were just another limb on his powerful body. His eyes had gone milky white. Mercurius was forced to retreat from Belisarius' prone form and concentrate wholly on the unexpected assault. Any bloody wound Mercurius inflicted healed in the blink of an eye, the praetor unharmed. The Magistri were protesting loudly about the breach of protocol and the danger the frenzied praetor posed, but the guards held them back.

"Gods below. I've never seen a berserker."

"If he fails to take him down, I want you to launch me at Mercurius with as much speed as you can give me."

"If I do, you'll only get the initial force. Launching you like that will throw me back as well. If he moves around, you'll miss him."

"We'll have to take the chance. Once I make contact, protect Belisarius from whatever fumes or smoke my body produces, because it'll be lethal to breathe. If I die, my body will produce a death fog that will kill everyone. Isolate it with your magic."

A roar of flames interrupted whatever Charis was going to say next. With the prince downed, Mercurius was free to wield his gift as well as his sword. Nicephorus was taking the flames head on, lost to sense and reason.

Selene coated her body in the only toxin she knew to be just as potent when exposed to fire. Even if he left her charred, the smoke would kill him with a single breath. Only her palms were dripping with a different poison. Mercurius landed a devastating blow on the berserker, nearly detaching his hands. Nicephorus' tendons severed, Mercurius knocked the blade from his grip, ending the frenzy which had consumed the praetor.

"Now!"

It was time to end this. A jarring pressure thrust her at the fire mage's back. He caught sight of her at the last moment, his body half turned towards her. Skin touched skin before an excruciating blaze sent her flying. Her last impression was of Mercurius, covered in his own flames, screaming in anguish.

CHAPTER 39

Nicephorus woke. He shot up from a deep and disturbing dream of blood and pain, as he usually did whenever the berserker took over. The young notarios who had been seated by his bedside toppled off his stool and ran from the room before Nicephorus even had a chance to ask for water. He turned his wrists, opening and closing his hands. He should be dead, or at least deeply scarred from the burns he must have suffered, but only a flush of angry pink remained of the horror. It had always seemed monstrously unfair that a gift meant solely for violence and bloodshed should benefit his recovery.

Before he had much time to contemplate his health, the strategos burst into the room. He'd never seen the man so distraught. His curly hair was wild, his beard unruly, his clothes dishevelled, and he smelled as if he hadn't bathed in a few days. It was so alarming, Nicephorus wondered if Belisarius had died.

"Thank the gods you're awake. I've been trying to run the damn place while you recovered. The papers, the endless nit-picking, it never stops, not even for an hour."

"Belisarius, is he-"

"Alive, though it may be a few days yet before he wakes. The blow to his head should've been fatal."

"What of Mercurius?"

"Dead. May he rot in the deepest of hells." Marduk smiled. "His corpse was so toxic we had to entomb it in three metal coffins. Luckily

Domina Opal was at hand to prevent the fumes from killing the rest of us."

"Did...did she make it?"

"Selene? Yes, though she's a little worse for wear. She doesn't have a berserker's innate healing. She's awake now."

Nicephorus got out of bed and put himself to rights as Marduk listed with growing hysteria the mountain of work, bickering, power-grabbing and political gamesmanship that had gone on over the past few days. It was to be expected, and it didn't faze the praetor in the slightest. His mind was already buzzing with what needed to be done, energizing him.

"How much longer before Belisarius is likely to wake?"

"The healers assured me the worst damage is repaired, but that the energy that kind of injury requires to heal is extensive. He's slept for two days so far. They think at least another four or five."

Things could go very wrong in that short period of time, even if he and the strategos stood shoulder to shoulder against the magistri and other nobles. They would need someone to step up in place of Belisarius, even if only temporarily.

"Selene is recovered? Enough to make appearances?"

"She's recovered. As for appearances... well, you'd best see for yourself."

"I will do that. For now, I want you to spread the word."

"What word?"

"That the Empress Selene Traitorsbane is ready to accept the oaths of loyalty from the magistri."

Marduk quizzical expression was broken by a booming laugh. When he'd finished, he wiped tears of mirth from his eyes.

"Leave it to me. Traitorsbane, eh? It's a good name."

Selene had woken up in a plush bed to the fussing of Iliana and an army of servants. She'd been advised that Mercurius was dead, Belisarius was alive but asleep, and even Nicephorus was expected to make a full recovery. However, there was a deep pain in Iliana's eyes. Selene ordered the others to leave them alone.

"What happened?"

"It's my hand…"

It was still attached and her friend could move her fingers, though a scar lingered where it had been severed. Selene frowned.

"I can't… the magic doesn't reach it, and when I touch things, it's like I'm wearing a glove."

"What about the healers? Can't they-"

Selene stopped when tears welled in her friend's eyes. Iliana shook her head.

"They say even the best healer can't guarantee anything when something is being reattached. Same odds as a coin flip that the magic will reconnect when the muscles do."

"Iliana…"

She didn't know the right words to say. She put her arms around the metals mage. Iliana sobbed quietly for a moment before pulling away and wiping her tears.

"I shouldn't complain."

"Shouldn't…that's ridiculous. Complain, cry, scream, do whatever you need to."

"We're both alive, even if a little worse off."

"Do I have wicked battle scars?" She'd always wondered if she would get more respect with a few well-placed marks.

"Not exactly. Do you want to see?"

Selene nodded. When Iliana brought over a hand mirror, Selene looked over the damage. It was a bit shocking. She'd gotten used to how she appeared in mirrors since she'd been kidnapped and forced to practice in front of them. Now the woman who stared at her was a stranger. Her skin was a deep red where the fire had burned her, though her movement wasn't limited. It travelled from her shoulder, up her neck, close to her jaw and up the left side of her skull. Her hair on that side was gone, as was the top third of her ear. She checked under her gown and saw that the same mark travelled down her left side.

"They'll heal you up more over the next few days when you have the energy to handle it, and it'll mostly fade to a light pink before going away. The hair should grow back, but your ear... I don't think there was anything they could do. There was nothing left to attach."

"I don't know, I think I can work with this. It really screams hardened, barbarian warrior queen. Do you think I could get the hairdressers to braid my hair with bones? Can we take some from Mercurius?"

Iliana snorted.

"Not likely."

A knock on the door interrupted them, and the praetor strode in. His own hair had taken quite an extreme restyling, though his burns were nearly healed. The thick blonde mane that remained was a strip of hair running in a straight line from the middle of his forehead down to the nape of his neck.

"We should start a new fashion in barbarian hairstyles," Selene crowed.

"I am afraid I will have to decline, Your Majesty."

Selene flinched at the title. She might have saved Belisarius, but the idea of staying to be his empress, and only one of perhaps several of his women, made her physically ill. Her heart might ache for him, but nothing had really changed.

"Iliana, could you give us a moment?"

"Really?"

"Yes."

Iliana nodded and left the room, her brows pinched with concern. Once they were alone, Selene turned to the praetor, careful to keep emotion out of her voice.

"I'm not the empress. I'm not sticking around to watch Belisarius make brats with other women."

"So you would risk death to save his life, but you refuse to put Lethe to rights while he's incapacitated? I did not take you for a coward."

"Cowardice has nothing to do with it!"

"Then help me help him. I won't insist you remain once he's able, but I will insist you help me hold this unruly land together long enough for it to still be here when he wakes."

"Fine, but I want my ship and the gold ready for when he does."

"I'll see that it's done."

"And don't tell Iliana."

Nicephorus looked surprised to hear her say it.

"She deserves to be happy here, even if I can't be."

"It will be our secret, then."

"So, what do you need me to do?"

"Take oaths of loyalty from the army and bureaucracy as well as the magistri, and decide on who will rule the lands of Diamond, Amethyst and Sapphire. I had a list of possible successors drawn up after we learned of their involvement with the scheme, but His Majesty never had the chance to go over them."

Nicephorus handed her the list. She took it and skimmed over the names. She didn't know anyone, though it was possible she'd met their daughters or sisters over the course of the bride show.

"These names mean nothing to me. What makes any of them good choices?"

"They're wealthy noblemen with experience managing large estates, excellent character references and heirs."

"Wasn't Amethyst able to boast the same damn thing?"

Nicephorus at least had the decency to blush. The more she thought about it, the more she realised only staunch allies of Belisarius should be given the lands, otherwise Iliana might be caught up in another conspiracy. But which of the nobles could she trust to keep things peaceful?

"I have an idea, but you won't like it."

Selene sat on the empress' throne with as stern an expression as she could muster. Her hair had been styled to prominently display her healing wounds and the ragged remains of her left ear. Marduk, Nicephorus and the magistri had all made their oaths without issue. She'd technically won the combat for the throne, after all, and with the army and bureaucracy at her command, there was little any nobleman could do against her. The gruesome end that had befallen Mercurius after she'd hit him with a full dose of mage-corpse poison was enough of a spectacle to impress even the unruly magistri. That done, the men waited for her to dismiss them.

"Before you leave, I would like to inform you that henceforth, the women of Lethe will be able to own and inherit property and titles. As will all those of common birth."

The objections were instantaneous. She couldn't pick out a single voice from the crowd gathered before her. She shot to her feet, bejewelled boots glittering, and pointed the sceptre at the magistri.

"Silence! Had this been in place years ago, it's possible not a single noblewoman would have suffered at the hands of their traitor fathers! Independence, no matter how small, would have allowed them to seek the emperor's aid. Fight me in this, and you will find out just how little patience I have for your wailing!"

The clamour died down to discontented murmurs. It would have to do for now.

"I'm glad that you could be convinced to see reason," Selene went on. She sat back down. "Now, as I'm sure you're all aware, the land of the traitors needs to be partitioned." That caught their undivided attention. When she spoke, it was to a silent room. "Domina Zoe Emerald, step forward."

Zoe approached the dais, but couldn't hide her confusion. She curtsied low and remained so.

"For your service to the empire, I am granting you the title of magistra. You will rule over the lands formerly known as the Sapphire Province, now the Jade Province. Rise, Magistra Jade."

Zoe rose shakily. Magister Emerald's bafflement was short lived. A sly grin took over. He was exceedingly pleased. She knew she'd be able to count on his support for the remainder. His bloodline would now rule two provinces, after all. Zoe would prove to be a staunch ally as well with no need to fear that her mage gift would mean her doom.

"Your Majesty, I'm not worthy," Zoe said haltingly.

"That had best be false modesty, because we both know you're not only capable, but exceedingly worthy. So much so, I expect you to see to the welfare of the traitors' daughters. Though they are no longer dominae, I have granted them each the title illustra, property, and annual stipends, since they were victims themselves."

"I'm honoured you would give me such a task." Zoe smiled.

"Then swear your oath of loyalty to me, Magistra Jade."

Zoe knelt before her and did just that.

"Magistra Zoe Jade swears her loyalty to Empress Selene from this day until my death. I bind myself and my heirs to this oath, else our lives are forfeit."

Once done, she backed away and stood next to her father.

"Domina Charis Opal, step forward."

Charis presented herself nervously and curtsied.

"Though I will not bestow lands upon you, should you wish to claim the right of becoming heir to the Opal Province, know that you have the backing of the emperor and empress."

"I am forever grateful, Your Majesty," Opal replied.

She might not have been able to force the magister to make Charis his heir, but she could get damn close. Nicephorus had assisted her with what to say and what leverage to use. Magister Opal had long bemoaned that his many sons preferred to live their lives chasing after pirates or spending months at sea. Charis had the aptitude, the love of her people, and a very doting father. It might have bucked tradition, but she would leave Belisarius with allies aplenty. Charis backed away to stand next to her beaming father.

"Domina Mina Topaz, step forward."

Mina did so with a slight scowl on her face, no doubt displeased that Charis was now even more likely to need an heir of her own. Even still, she curtsied low.

"For your service to the empire, I grant you the title of magistra, half a million gold coins, and the right to purchase land and properties anywhere in Lethe. Rise, Magistra Obsidian."

Mina's eyes misted with shocked tears. It was as much freedom as Selene could give her; the ability to live her life as freely as she chose, free from her father's control and the expectations of the continental nobles. It also wouldn't hurt to have another magistra on their side.

"I cannot thank you enough, Your Majesty," Mina declared before swearing her loyalty. When she returned to the nobles, she took a place next to Charis.

"Strategos Marduk, Iliana, step forward."

Puzzled expressions greeted her. Some murmuring could be heard from the magistri.

"From now on, there will be no Diamond Province. The lands will be governed by only the most loyal of subjects, and will be known as the Protectorate. As such, I grant you the titles of Illustrus Aegis and Illustra Aegis, with the responsibility to be caretakers of the Protectorate, and of the crown in times when the royal succession is in question. Rise, Illustrus Strategos Marduk Aegis, Illustra Iliana Aegis."

"We are honoured, Your Majesty."

Next was her last piece of business—the Amethyst Province.

"Alexandra, silver-tongue, step forward."

She'd been standing next to Nicephorus with the other bureaucrats, a wary knight by her side. The murmurs grew louder. She no longer wore her collar. The silver-tongue had been working non-stop to oust any other traitors within the palace. She'd been successful in outing several already, and had not used her gift for her own gain or to flee. When she knelt before the throne, she trembled.

"Only one province remains. In my time there, I ensured that should I die or will it, the entirety of Dragomire Keep and its environs would become a toxic wasteland for several decades. Given your service, and the compulsion you placed on me to grant you freedom, I shall give you the title of Magistra Amber and the properties of my traitor father. Know that should you, or any other silver-tongue who decides to call that province home, ever compel someone for personal gain, I will release my poisons without remorse. You may now make your oath of loyalty."

"Magistra Alexandra Amber swears her loyalty to the Empress Selene from this day until my death. I bind myself and my heirs to this oath, else our lives are forfeit," Alexandra replied woodenly.

It wasn't perfect freedom, but it was as much as she could give her.

"You will still be required to work at the palace until a replacement can be found and trained. Speak to the praetor about assigning a manager for the province."

"Thank you, Your Majesty."

When she stood from the throne and dismissed the crowd, she felt lighter. She'd done all that had been asked of her, rewarded all those who'd helped her, and given Iliana and Marduk security and hopefully a little more respect. At least no one had tried to kill her, and only Topaz seemed miffed about not getting more of a reward for himself. Now, there was only one thing left to do.

"Illustra Aegis, follow me."

Once they were safely ensconced in her rooms, Selene sent the servants away and released a breath along with her shoulders. She had one last gift to bestow. There was a box on the veranda's table. Selene waved her over to it.

"I can't believe you just did all that." Iliana spoke first, bewildered as she sank down into her seat.

"I know. I was sure I'd have to kill at least one person." Selene slumped into hers, exhausted.

"You make a good empress."

Selene wanted to curl up under a rock. Every time she heard that title, the hurt in her chest expanded.

"I have something for you."

"Oh?"

Selene pointed to the box and then pushed it towards her friend. Painfully plain, it wasn't particularly big. Iliana opened it. Her blue eyes lit up as she touched a small glittering rock no bigger than a plum with her good hand. Wonder was replaced with the buzz of possibilities whirring through her head.

"This is—I could send enchantments through it instead of my bare hand."

"Exactly! Now *that* I had to poison a few mages over. It can handle as many enchantments as you can pour into it. Might I suggest a gauntlet with claws? I hear 'barbarian queen' is the newest style in the capital."

"Selene..." Iliana's eyes misted with tears.

"What good is being on top if you can't give your friend the best of everything?"

CHAPTER 40

An ill-used leather satchel sat on the bed with the few belongings Selene had seen fit to pack. Her clothes and shoes were plain but made to last. The angry red of the burns had faded to a pale pink and would disappear entirely in a few months. Iliana had fashioned the little gold ear cap she now wore. She'd left her written goodbyes in the praetor's care. Belisarius was expected to wake soon, and she didn't have the courage to see him one last time. She'd done all Nicephorus had asked of her, leaving the empire in good hands and giving Iliana everything she could. She only hoped her friend would forgive her for running away.

"What in the hells is this?!" Iliana screeched as she burst into Selene's rooms. She held a crumpled letter in her hand, blue eyes blazing.

Gods-damned praetor wasn't supposed to have delivered that until after she'd left. Useless cretin.

"I'm not staying."

"You were going to leave without telling me? After everything?!"

"Nothing has changed. The emperor is going to want heirs, and there's fuck-all chance of me being able to do that. I can't stay. I'll just want to murder anyone he chooses as concubine. But *you* can be happy here."

Iliana looked stunned.

"Then I'm coming with you. I'm not leaving you alone."

Tears stung Selene's eyes. It only hardened her resolve. She touched her friend's face.

"You'd really choose me?"

Iliana nodded.

"I love you too, Iliana. Which is why I'm putting you first."

"What do you me…"

Iliana slowly drooped to the floor. Selene guided her onto the plush carpet, snagging a pillow to place beneath her head. She would sleep for several hours, long enough for Selene to get far away.

Belisarius woke with a start, eyes wildly cataloguing his surroundings, dreading the sword about to run him through. A moment later, he realised where he was, touching his head. It was tender, but he was alive. How was he alive?

"Your Majesty, you are safe and whole. The traitors are dead."

"Where is Selene? The strategos? The praetor?" he asked of the servant seated by his bed.

"I shall fetch them for you."

Only a few moments passed before Nicephorus entered the room. Seeing his hair in such a strange style threw him.

"Your Majesty." Nicephorus bowed deeply.

"Tell me what's happened. How am I even alive?"

"Selene ordered me to fight Mercurius before he killed you. I don't personally recall much of what happened after that, but I'm told Selene had Domina Opal launch her at Mercurius, poisoning him to death."

"Is she…" He couldn't get the words out.

"Selene is alive and well. She woke several days ago, and has settled a fair number of issues in your stead, at my behest."

Had she really chosen to stay, even thinking he would be unfaithful to her? He needed to go to her, to tell her she would be the only woman, his one and only love, children or no. He tore out of bed and rushed to grab a robe he could throw on.

"Where is she now?"

Nicephorus' stoicism was replaced with an odd, almost guilty refusal to meet his eyes. It sent a frisson of panic through him.

"She has tasked me with giving you this."

He proffered a sealed scroll. Belisarius tore through the seal and read it, his gut sinking.

Belli,

I fixed your empire. Try not to fuck it up.

Selene

P.S. Your future wife can thank me – I made royal concubines illegal.

"Where is she?" Belisarius ground out as he crumpled the letter in his hand. Nicephorus had allowed her to leave. He'd never gotten the chance to make things right with her. What if he never did? It was a fate he couldn't bear.

"Selene is gone!" Marduk burst into the room. "Iliana was left sleeping on the floor of her room. I've sent the royal guards to search for her."

"A teleportation mage took her to the harbour a few hours ago. She'll be at sea by now," Nicephorus replied.

Belisarius grabbed him by his robe, ready to beat him to a pulp.

"How could you let her leave?! She is your empress!"

"I gave my word I would let her leave once she helped sort out the most pressing issues of the empire. As for her title, she abdicated this morning when she heard you would wake."

He couldn't lose her. Belisarius ran to his closets and rummaged through them, selecting something sturdy. He threw on pants, tunic and a coat.

"Your Majesty? What are you doing? A teleportation mage can't land on a moving object, let alone one he's never been on before."

The praetor was quite correct, but Belisarius had an idea. He grabbed a comfortable pair of leather boots and pulled them on. He turned to Marduk.

"Take me to the griffin."

A knowing look lit his friend's face. He showed Belisarius the way.

"Your Majesty, this isn't the time to be rash! She made her choice!" Nicephorus called after him.

"On the contrary, praetor, it would be foolish if I *didn't* act."

When they barged into the griffin's rooms, they stumbled upon the remnants of a veritable bacchanalia. Nude or nearly nude men and women slept haphazardly across chairs, couches and rugs. Bottles of wine, empty and half-full, decorated every level surface, while glasses were strewn across tables or remained clutched in the hands of sleeping orgy-goers. Belisarius waded through it all and roused Lord Renfreid, shaking him loose from a tangle of limbs.

"Oh! What a pleasure, Your Majesty. Have you come to partake?"

"No. I've come for your immediate assistance. How swiftly can you fly?"

Selene sat listlessly at the stern of her ship, watching as Lethe faded into nothing more than a few indistinct hills in the distance. She'd never been to the sea, but she found she liked the scent. Already the constant swaying and the crashing of the waves soothed her. A few puffy white clouds dotted a serene sky. The captain, a brother to Magister Opal, approached her genially.

"Where would you like to set sail? If we're to go West, we'll need to catch the currents soon."

She blinked up at him, silent for a time, long enough to make the man uncomfortable. Did it matter where she went?

"Somewhere better," she answered.

"Ah. Right," he replied, uncertain.

Her vacant stare drove him off. Not even her mountains of gold sitting prettily in the hull could brighten her dark mood. It was time to stop looking back. No amount of yearning would help her current state. Crossing the deck, she sat at the bow. She'd made her choice, painful though it might be. At least this way, she wouldn't grow to hate herself and everyone around her.

The crew called back and forth to one another, but she paid them no mind, lost in her own thoughts. It wasn't until a shadow passed overhead that she finally looked up. The underside of a griffin in flight greeted her. It soared, turned around and rushed straight at her. Selene ducked. Instead of talons, a body soared over her head and hit the deck rolling. When she dared get up, Renfreid had appeared, buck naked, and Belisarius, dressed like a commoner and battered by the wind, scrambled to his feet and shot Renfreid a dirty look. She narrowed her eyes, her blood boiling.

"What are you doing here?" she demanded.

"Where else would I be?" Belisarius asked with a grin on his face as he approached.

"Sitting on your throne. Choosing a wife," she spat back.

His smile only grew the closer he got. She could strangle him for it.

"I abdicated," he replied calmly.

"You-"

"And I'll have no one but you for my wife."

She stood rooted to the spot, utterly stunned. He must be playing some cruel joke on her.

"Then enjoy your bachelorhood."

He loomed over her, his dark hair a messy halo around his handsome face. He reached out to touch her cheek. Foolishly, she let him.

"It occurs to me that you need the kind of man who will put you first, above all else."

He leaned down until they were nose to nose, their eyes meeting.

"So, I decided I needed to become that man. Please say you'll have me."

"You—what about the empire? I just finished fixing-"

He put a finger to her lips.

"You did, and the empire will still be there even if I'm not. Marduk and Nicephorus have it well in hand." He winked.

The bloody man winked at her?! She gnashed her teeth even as her heart fluttered in her chest. She was losing the battle.

"Didn't you want children?" she asked mulishly.

He shook his head.

"I only want you, Selene. Not the empire, not the throne, not the titles, not children or heirs or anything, *just you*."

And with that, she lost the battle, the war over, her rage and her sorrow defeated. She gazed into the dark sincerity in his eyes. Stubborn man should have said as much before she'd decided to leave.

"You stupid peacock."

Selene kissed him feverishly. Belisarius swept her up in a crushing embrace and kissed her back, fierce and warm and *hers*. His smile was dazzling.

"So, where to, my little poison mage?"

She sighed, only a little irritated.

"Where else? Back to Lethe, obviously. But we're taking the long way back. I'm not sharing you with anyone else for a few days at least." Just because she'd decided to be his empress, didn't mean she wasn't still a greedy thief at heart.

"If that's what Her Majesty desires," Belisarius teased.

Selene smiled.

"It is."

I hope you've enjoyed Selene and Belisarius' story, but the adventure is far from over. Some traitors still walk free, and foreigners from distant lands are about to reach Lethe's shores. Find out what happens when villains of all sorts find their way to the imperial court in the next install-ment of the *Mages of Oblivion* series, *Conspirators' Kingdom!* Get your copy here: https://books2read.com/csk

Craving a steamy epilogue featuring Selene and Belisarius? Sign up to my newsletter to find out how the imperial couple negotiate their new relationship here: https://twolaurelspress.eo.page/jpchy

To find out more about my books and other series I'm working on, check out my website: https://www.elysethomson.com/

Thanks so much for reading, and don't forget to leave a review!

Afterword

From the bottom of my heart, thank you for coming on this journey with me. Poisoned Empire is the book of my heart and I'm delighted to have shared it with you. As you may or may not know, reviews are the lifeblood of any author's career, especially those just starting out. I would be honoured if you could leave a few words about your experience reading my book on Goodreads and whichever store you purchased my book from.

If you're not ready to say goodbye to Selene and Belisarius quite yet, you can get signed up for my newsletter and read the bonus epilogue for *Poisoned Empire!* Other newsletter goodies include my prequel novella, *The Firetongue Heir,* and a bonus epilogue for *Poisoned Empire.*

You can also check out the next book in the *Mages Of Oblivion* series, *Conspirators' Kingdom!* Read on for a sneak peak at the first two chapters.

For links to the bonus epilogue, *The Firetongue Heir, Conspirators' Kingdom,* Goodreads and more, check out the links below! https://link-tr.ee/elysethomson

Book Links

Acknowledgements

No book is made without the love and support of a great many people. Poisoned Empire was no different. I have so many people to thank. Paulina, for being the first to tell me this one was special. Alex, for being my rock through the whole whirlwind journey. My family; Mom, Dad, Sylvia, Ross, Kyle, Garrett and Jen for never doubting me. The book club beta reader ladies Edie, Sharron, Karen, Shelley and Susan for being my cheerleaders. The best writing friends a girl could have (with a group name so lackluster, it doesn't bear repeating) Sophia, Rachel, Asha, Rebecca and Shirley. You kept me sane and gave me a place to belong. My life is richer for having known all of you. And finally, my friends in Pitch'n'Bitch, you always make me smile.

Special thanks to my amazing editor, Rachel Le Mesurier, my talented map maker Alec McKinley and my lovely cover designer, Maria Spada.

About the Author

Elyse Thomson is the pen-name of an author, bookbinder and self-proclaimed hermit residing in Canada's capital. She writes escapist romantic fantasy with daring heroines, magical mayhem, swoon-worthy romance and court intrigue. Having graduated from University of Toronto with a Bachelors in History and Classics, she is delighted to bring her love of all things ancient to her work. When not writing, she's restoring antiquarian books for a select group of clients, playing Dragon Age, or snuggling up with either her husband or her neurotic terrier, Freya.

If you would like to learn more, check out the website and join the newsletter for access to snippets, cover reveals and the exclusive prequel novella, *The Firetongue Heir*.

Also By

Mages of Oblivion Series
The Firetongue Heir
Poisoned Empire
Conspirators' Kingdom
Isles of Corruption

Cycle of Calamity Series
The Starlight Princess
The Oracle of Dusk
The Midnight King
...and more to come.

Book Links